Enthusiastic International Praise for

Fiona McIntosh

"A bold new voice in high fantasy."
Lynn Flewelling, author of *The Hidden Warrior*

"If you are tired of plodding trilogies in which little seems to happen, [her] books are definitely for you."
Robin Hobb

"Fiona McIntosh is a street-smart enchantress . . . [who] knows who her readers are and what they want: thrilling, fast-paced reads."
Sydney Sun Herald (Australia)

"First rate."
Publishers Weekly

"Nothing short of astonishing."
Bookreporter.com

"A good choice."
Library Journal

"Fiona McIntosh keeps getting better and better."
The Advertiser (Australia)

"Fiona McIntosh is a seductress."
Sydney Morning Herald (Australia)

By Fiona McIntosh

The Quickening Trilogy
BRIDGE OF SOULS
BLOOD AND MEMORY
MYRREN'S GIFT

The Percheron Saga
ODALISQUE
EMISSARY
GODDESS

The Valisar Trilogy
ROYAL EXILE
TYRANT'S BLOOD
KING'S WRATH

ROYAL EXILE

BOOK ONE OF THE VALISAR TRILOGY

FIONA McINTOSH

An Imprint of HarperCollins*Publishers*

This book is a work of fiction. The characters, incidents, and dialogue are drawn from the author's imagination and are not to be construed as real. Any resemblance to actual events or persons, living or dead, is entirely coincidental.

This book was originally published in 2008 by Voyager, an Imprint of HarperCollins Australia.

EOS
An Imprint of HarperCollinsPublishers
10 East 53rd Street
New York, New York 10022-5299

Map by Matt Whitney

ISBN 978-0-06-158268-4
www.eosbooks.com

First Eos paperback printing: January 2009

Printed in the U.S.A.

10 9 8 7 6 5 4 3 2

For Will McIntosh, Jack McIntosh, Paige Klimentou
and Jack Caddy . . .
start walking towards your dreams today.

Whatever the dream, no matter how daring or grand,
somebody will eventually achieve it.
It might as well be you.
Bryce Courtenay

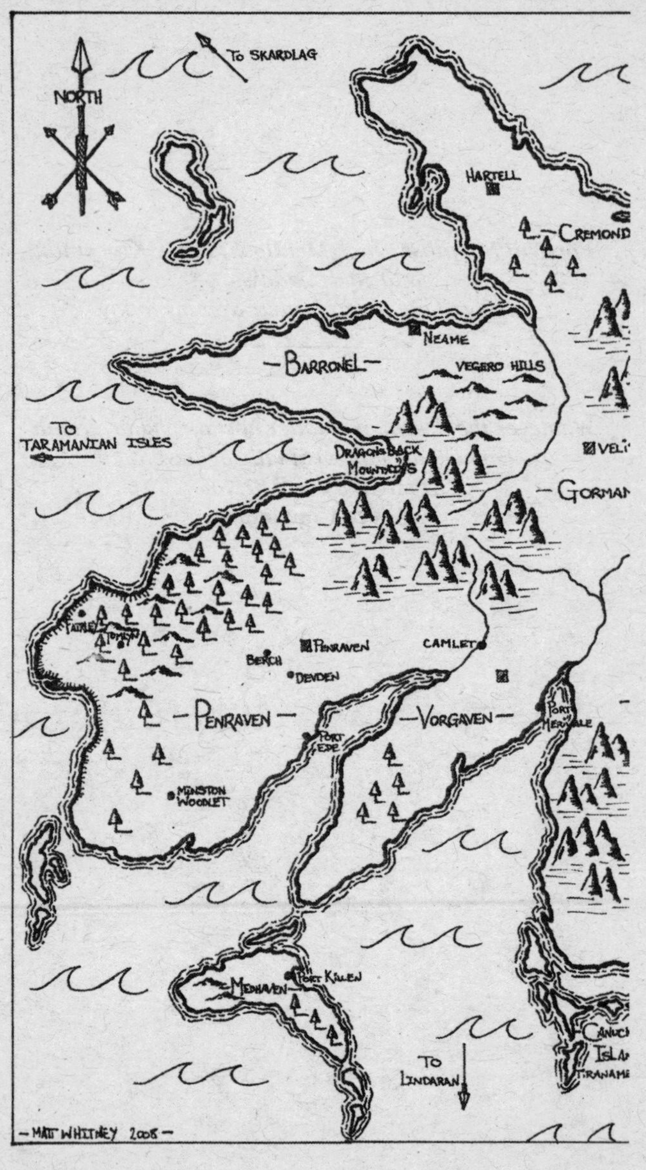

NORTH
TO SKARDLAG
HARTELL
CREMOND
NEAME
BARRONEL
VEGERO HILLS
TO
TARAMANIAN ISLES
DRAGONSBACK
MOUNTAINS
PENRAVEN
BERCH
DEVDEN
CAMLET
PENRAVEN
VORGAVEN
PORT
EPE
PORT
MERVALE
MINSTON
WOODLET
MEDHAVEN
PORT KILLEN
TO
LINDARAN
MATT WHITNEY 2008

THE DENOVA SET
CREMOND
DROSTE
LO'S
TEETH
THE
PLAINS
VELIS
GORMAND
LIKURIAN
STEPPES
DORNEN
DREGON
PORT
TO GALINSEA
TALREN
CANUCK
ISLANDS
TIRANAMEN
LEGEND
CITY
TOWN
MOUNTAINS
FOREST
GRASSLANDS
HILLS
RUGGED
COAST

Acknowledgments

So, where did this idea come from? The seed of story came from The Quickening; King Cailech's threatened cannibalism of his foe was chilling but also precisely the sort of activity I imagine a barbarian ruler might indulge in to ensure his enemies feared him. The notion never left me, quietly festering for years before it bubbled to the surface of my thoughts at the oddest time. I was in Tasmania for Christmas in 2006, busily working on the final volume of Percheron and this odd, very small scene kept nagging at me of a man smirking at a woman as he eats someone she loves. I couldn't get it out of my head and so rather than fight it, I went with it and from this one tiny vignette that took all of five seconds to glimpse in my internal film theater, grew the tale that is sprawling behind this page. With all my stories I have little to go on and no idea where they are headed, but I really enjoyed writing this story, particularly as it does return me to some familiar scenery and an atmosphere reminiscent of The Quickening. My sincere thanks to all of my regular readers and the new ones I've gathered up along the way of this last year, or who may discover me through this story. Thank you for reading *Royal Exile* and I do hope you enjoy this opening volume of Valisar.

There are always people to thank because books don't just write themselves and the author usually has a cheering squad, ready to read and offer support whenever required.

I'd like to thank Ian McIntosh, first reader and ruthless critic, alongside Pip Klimentou, Sonya Caddy and Judy Downs in Australia, as well as Phil Reed and Steve Hubbard in the US for their time and suggestions.

Special and enormous thanks to Sonya Caddy who encouraged me to work with a glossary for the first time (this was Robin Hobb's idea—thanks RH!) and then set to and designed a working model that I soon found invaluable. She has also designed an abridged version for readers. If you see anything in the story that you think needs inclusion in the glossary, email me via my website and we'll fix. And I must acknowledge the lovely work of Matt Whitney with regard to the map of the Set that he has created from the very strange markings I scribbled over a coffee one day. Thank you, Matty. Trent Hayes continues to maintain a brilliant and active website—congratulations, Trent, and my best wishes to all the members at the bulletin board who chat to me daily. My thanks to those who offer ongoing support in my work—especially Bryce Courtenay, Monica McInerney, Lynne Schinella, Jenny Newman, Samela Harris, Gary Havelberg, Sue Hill, Mandy Macky, Margie Arnold and Linda Eldredge. There are many more family and friends, of course, but you know who you are and understand how much I appreciate your support.

This would be incomplete without mentioning my trio of editors around the world from HarperCollins. Thank you Stephanie Smith in Sydney, Kate Nintzel in New York and Emma Coode in London. Most of all, my thanks to the booksellers in these markets who are so enthusiastic about selling fantasy to an increasingly eager audience.

Endless love and thanks to Ian . . . and also to Will and Jack, toiling through their all important Year 12 during the crafting of this novel. Every success, boys . . . xx

Prologue

King Ormond's face was ashen. He wore the sunken, resigned expression of a man who knew he had but hours to live. Nevertheless, sitting on his horse, atop the mound overlooking the battlefield, his anger flared, his jaw grinding as he watched the horde from the plains make light work of his soldiers. His attention was riveted on one man: the enemy's leader, who was easy to pick out in the fray, even from this distance. For while his warriors wore the distinctive colors of their tribe, inked all over their faces and bodies, this man's skin was clean. His features, like his age, were indeterminate from this distance, but he fought with the speed and physical force of a man in his prime. And he led his men from the front, a sign of his bravado and courage.

"Look at the arrogance!" Ormond said, disbelief ringing in his voice. "Are we so pathetic that he doesn't even care to take the precaution of armor? Does he have no fear?"

"Majesty," one of his companions replied wearily. "I believe Loethar is driven by something more complex than a desire for victory."

"General Marth, what could possibly be more desirable than victory when one goes to war?" the king challenged, staring down his offsider.

The general looked momentarily lost for words. He looked away toward the carnage, then back to his king. "Your highness, this man is not interested in simply winning. He is not looking to conscript a new army from the devastation of ours, or even to preserve much of the realm for his own needs. I sense he is only after humiliation for his enemy. He has shown the Set that his pattern is to kill everyone who carries a weapon against him. There is no mercy in his heart."

The king shook his head, despair now haunting his expression. "I can't let this continue. It has gone on long enough. He's been on the rampage for four moons now. Dregon and Vorgaven are conquered and Cremond simply capitulated." He gave a sound of disgust. "The other realms in the Set that have been attacked have fallen no matter what reinforcements have been sent."

Clearly forcing himself to remain calm despite the sounds of death below, the general took a breath. "As I counselled previously, majesty, it is not that he has an inexhaustible supply of fighters but that he has used his men with great cunning and insight. There has been nothing disorganized about his attack on the Set's realms; it has been very strategic and we have not accorded him the respect he deserved. We should have taken him seriously when his men first started appearing. We should have sent our own men to help the Dregons and Vorgavese—"

"For Lo's sake, man! If Penraven didn't why would we? Brennus obviously thought Ranuld could hold Vorgaven."

"We're all neighbors, highness. We are the Set. We should have combined all our resources. Penraven has the largest army, the most well equipped army, the greatest number of weapons—"

"Yes but still he didn't! King Brennus chose not to send his men. Why? Because he trusted Ranuld to keep his end strong against this rabble upstart."

General Marth looked away again, and like his king his gaze was helplessly drawn to the horde's ruthless leader as his sword swung, hacking into one of their men's necks. They saw the spume of blood explode and watched another life be given cheaply to the insatiable ruler of the plains tribes. The general turned back, a fresh look of fury on his face.

"No, majesty. I don't think the Valisar king trusts any of us. Forgive me, I know you consider him a friend, but King Brennus is not coming to anyone's aid. I suspect he has seen the error of his confidence, knows the threat to Penraven is very real. In light of that we are expendable. His priority always has been, always will be, Penraven. He is saving his men for the final confrontation."

King Ormond's gaze narrowed. "He sent men to Dregon, he even—"

Marth shook his head sadly. "A token gesture, highness. We needed to combine our armies to chase this barbarian from our midst. Instead we brazenly allowed him the chance for his early and shocking victory against Dregon and Vorgaven—his audacity to fight not only on two fronts and two borders but to take both cities. His men are not mere rabble, highness. These are warriors . . . trained ones. We should have crushed him the moment he took his first footsteps into the Set."

"We all agreed to wait and see what his intentions were."

"Not *all* of us, highness," General Marth replied and the bitterness in his voice was tempered by sorrow. "We didn't act fast enough. We all left it to each other."

"But who would have thought Cremond would not even offer the slightest resistance? Why? Do they want a tribal thug as their ruler?" Marth shook his head, seemingly unable to offer any light on the Cremond capitulation although it was a longheld belief within the rest of the Set that Cremond, rarely considering itself as close to the other realms, often tended to behave in a contrary fashion. "And then who in his right mind marches across the region, ignoring Barronel, in order to take Vorgaven at the same time as Dregon? None of it makes sense."

"None of it makes sense because that was his intention. Loethar constantly caught us off guard. If we'd acted with speed at the outset we likely would have cut him off before he even established a foothold. Now he's had these four moons to put our backs to the wall, to somehow convince

Penraven—in its own arrogance—to wait and see what happens. Did we really think he was going to say 'thank you' and go home?"

"Brennus and I believed he'd seek terms. Granted, we're both shocked at his victory, but we never anticipated that he'd go after the whole Set."

"I don't know why, majesty. He didn't ask permission to enter it. Why would he give us any opportunity to sit around a parley table with him? He probably can't even speak the language!" Marth hesitated briefly. But what was there to lose in finally speaking his mind? Careful to speak without accusation, he continued. "The Valisars have always considered themselves invincible and I doubt Brennus feels any differently. Don't you see, your highness, that Brennus has allowed us to be the fodder? The rest of the realm has borne the brunt of Loethar's ferocity and yet I think he's deliberately saving the biggest, the best, for last. I don't think it's because he's frightened of Penraven. Quite the contrary. He has been playing games, convincing Brennus that the tribes would run out of interest—another reason why Brennus has hesitated to send the full might of the Penravian army to stand by us. I sense Loethar has deliberately made himself appear to be that yob you called him earlier, when in fact he is a long way from being a dull-headed, thick-skinned ruffian who might tire of the spoils of war and head back to the plains, sated. He has shown himself to be a shrewd adversary and now, my king, he is ready to topple our realm. I admire him."

Ormond sighed deeply and hung his head. "Call the retreat, general."

"No, King Ormond. Our men are going to die anyway. I suspect they would rather die fighting. It is more worthy to fall in the heat of battle and to a noble wound than on one's knees pleading for one's life. That's what the barbarian did in Vorgaven; put people to the sword long after the battle cries had stopped echoing. I think our soldiers should go to Lo yelling their defiance."

The king shook his head gravely. "But you are a general and I am a sovereign. It is our role to think brave and be brave to the last . . . to give our lives for our land. Perhaps some of these men might escape and survive to recount Barronel's bravery to the last. For that hope alone, we should surrender."

"Please, King Ormond. Let us all perish if we must, but let us fight to the last man."

Ormond set his chin grimly. "No. I took an oath when I was crowned that I would not knowingly allow any of my subjects to be killed if I could prevent it. I have to believe some of my people, however few, can be preserved in the chaos of retreat. Let the men run for their lives. But Lo help me, Marth, I will see the blood of the Valisars flour for this betrayal." His voice had become a growl. "Sound the retreat!"

Loethar's teeth seemed to be the only part of him not drenched in the blood of his foe. But he knew that would soon change and while his limbs worked savagely, tirelessly, to deny his enemies another breath, his thoughts focused around drinking the blood of King Ormond of Barronel. For Ormond was all that stood between him and his true goal . . . Penraven.

All the preparation—two anni in the making—had been undertaken for the moment that he was so close to now he could almost taste it. All the relentless training had been worth it—the toughening of his warriors, the breeding of horses, stockpiling of food and water near the main Set border . . . But none of that could compare to his mental preparation. He had grown up on hate, loathing, bitterness, and rage, kept under control, channelled into the groundwork that led to the surprise concerted raid on two realms at the same time.

The overconfidence, the bursting ego of the Valisars demanded that they would never have believed for a moment they were under any serious threat. Not at the outset anyway.

Which is why he'd acted as though he lacked any strategy or battle knowledge, traversing the Set covering unnecessary, almost senseless ground. He made sure his men behaved like the unruly rabble he wanted them to appear, even sending a quarter of them back to the Set's main border, as though they were making a straggly return to their plains, no longer interested in the bloodlust.

And gradually he had streamed them back to the main vanguard, usually under cover of darkness, running alongside wild dogs of the plains that he had had trained since puppies, killing their parents so they knew and trusted only the smell of his men. These dogs made the sharpest of scouts. They knew how to range, how to move silently and how to smell even the vaguest threat of their enemy. Many times they warned the tribes' various leaders to change course, to return to the main army via a different route. They were a large part of why Vorgaven, for instance, had thought it was facing three thousand men, when it was actually confronted by close on five thousand.

Time and again over the four moons Loethar had baffled his enemy, an enemy that was fueled by such self-belief, and worse, such disdain for the horde of the plains, that it had essentially crippled itself.

Now Loethar grimaced as a man fell near his feet, the Barronel soldier's sword slicing into Loethar's leg before the soldier's body fell. Fortunately, Loethar's nimble, intelligent horse moved sideways, allowing the man to fall beneath the advancing warriors and other horses so that the body was quickly trampled until it no longer had a recognizable face. Loethar barely paid attention to the wound on his leg; it hurt but there was no time to consider the pain. His sword kept slashing a path through flesh and bone, moving him ever closer to his prize.

He suspected word had quickly been passed around that the shirtless, armor-less fighter was the one to bring down. But Stracker was always near, his Greens more savage than any of the other tribes.

Loethar saw one soldier's head topple from his neck following one of Stracker's tremendous blows. On the back swing of that same blow, another soldier had his outstretched arm hacked off just above the elbow. The soldier stared at the stump pumping blood and roared his despair, reaching down to pick up his fallen sword with the other hand.

"He's brave, I'll give him that," Loethar called to his man as Stracker rammed his weapon into the soldier's soft belly to finish him off.

"Got to watch out for those sly two-handers, brother," Stracker yelled, slashing another man's throat open with a practiced swing.

"They'll call the retreat soon," Loethar called back, twisting his horse in a full circle, and killing two men in the motion.

"No chance. Barronel plans to fight until every man falls, I reckon."

Loethar managed to wink. "My amazing Trilla, here, for your stallion, says it will happen before you can kill another six of the enemy."

Stracker smiled, his bloodstained face creasing in amusement. "Done! I've always liked that small, feisty horse of yours."

"She's not yours yet, *brother*."

"Oh, but she will be. One!" he called smugly as another Barronel soldier met his end. "Two," he added, slashing across the belly of another.

Stracker had made it to four when he and Loethar heard the unmistakeable sound of the Barronel retreat being sounded across the battlefield.

As Stracker roared his disapproval, Loethar laughed, but he was secretly relieved. He was tired and he knew the blood soaking his body wasn't all his enemy's. He too had taken some punishment. He had fought hard today at the front of the vanguard and the retreating backs of the Barronel force—gravely diminished as it was—was a sweet sight.

"Round them up," he called to his senior tribesmen, trying

to hide the weariness in his voice. "The Greens will join me in taking the surrender from General Marth. Reds and Blues, let them believe we are simply taking stock of their number. All will be killed later."

"And the king?" Stracker asked, drawing alongside, still obviously miffed at losing the bet.

"King Ormond I shall be sharing a drink with later. He will, of course, go to his god before this night is out, but first, Stracker, you owe me that fine horse."

One

"Could he do this?" he wondered, as yet another wail began. He knew he had no choice if the Valisars were to survive.

Two great oak doors, carved with the family coat of arms, separated King Brennus from his wife's groans and shrieks, but despite the sound being muffled, her agonized cries injured him nonetheless. He knew his beautiful and beloved Iselda would never have to forgive him because she would never know of his ruthlessness at what he planned for his own flesh and blood. He looked to his trusted legate and dropped his gaze, shaking his head. They were all servants to the crown—king included—and serve he must by presenting the infant corpse in order to protect the realm.

"It never gets any easier, De Vis," he lamented.

De Vis nodded knowingly; he had lost his own wife soon after childbirth. "I can remember Eril's screams as though they were yesterday." He hurried to add: "Of course, once the queen holds her child, majesty, her pain will disappear."

They were both talking around the real issues—the murder of a newborn and the threat that their kingdom was facing its demise.

Brennus's face drooped even further. "In this you are right, although I fear for all our children, De Vis. My wife brings into this world a new son who may never see his first anni."

"Which is why your plan is inspired, highness. We cannot risk Loethar having access to the power."

"If it is accessible at all in this generation. Leo shows no sign at this stage . . . and Piven . . ." The king trailed off as another agonized shriek cut through their murmurs.

De Vis held his tongue but when silence returned and stretched between them, he said softly: "We can't know for sure. Leo is still young—it may yet come to him—and the next prince may be bristling with it. We can't risk either child falling into the wrong hands. And as for Piven, your highness, he is not of your flesh. We know he hardly possesses his faculties, majesty, let alone any power."

The king's grave face told his legate that Brennus agreed, that his mind was made up. Nevertheless he confirmed it aloud as though needing to justify his terrifying plan. "It is my duty to protect the Valisar inheritance. It cannot be tarnished by those not of the blood. I hope history proves me to be anything but the murderer I will appear if the truth ever outs. Is everything in place?"

"Precisely to your specifications," De Vis answered.

Brennus could see the legate's jaw working. De Vis was feeling the despair of what they were about to do as deeply as he was. "Your boys . . ." the king muttered, his words petering out.

De Vis didn't flinch. "Are completely loyal and will do their duty. You know that."

"Of course I know it, De Vis—they might as well be my own I know them so well—but they are too young for such grim tasks. I ask myself: could you do it? Could I? Can they?"

De Vis's expression remained stoic. "They have to. You have said as much yourself. My sons will not let Penraven down."

Brennus scowled. "Have you said anything yet?"

De Vis shook his head. "Until the moment is upon us, the fewer who know the better. The brief will also be better coming directly from you, majesty."

Brennus winced as another scream came from behind the

door, followed by a low groan that penetrated to the sunlit corridor where he and De Vis talked. He turned from the stone balustrade against which he had been leaning, looking out into the atrium that serviced the private royal apartments. Breathing deeply, he drank in the fragrance of daphne that the queen had personally planted in boxes hanging from the archways and took a long, sorrowful look at the light- drenched gardens below she had tended and made so beautiful. Trying for an heir had taken them on a torrid journey of miscarriages and disappointments. And then Leo had come along and, miraculously, had survived and flourished. But both Brennus and Iselda knew that a single heir was not enough, however, and so they had endured another three heartbreaking deaths in the womb.

It was as though Regor De Vis could read Brennus's thoughts. "Do not fret over Piven, your highness. If the barbarian breaches our walls I doubt he will even glance at your adopted son."

Brennus hoped his legate was right. Brennus was aware that Piven had made it quietly into the world and had remained mostly silent since then. These days odd noises, heartbreaking smiles and endless affection told everyone that Piven heard sound, though he could not communicate in any traditional way.

And now there was a new child who'd managed to somehow cling on to life, his heartbeat strong and fierce like the winged lion his family's history sprang from. There had been so much excitement, so much to look forward to as little as six moons ago. And now everything had changed.

The ill-wind had blown in from the east, where one ambitious, creative warlord had united the rabble that made up the tribes who eked out an existence on the infertile plains. It had been almost laughable when Dregon sent news that it was under attack from the barbarians. It had sounded even more implausible when Vorgaven sent a similar missive.

De Vis could clearly read his mind. "How something we considered a skirmish could come to this is beyond me."

"I trusted everyone to hold their own against a mere tribal warlord!"

"Our trust was a mistake, majesty . . . and so was our confidence in the Set's strength. It should never have come to this. And, worse, we haven't prepared our people. It's only because word is coming through from relatives or traders from the other realms that they know Vorgaven has fallen, Dregon is crushed and cowardly Cremond simply handed over rule without so much as a squeak. I'm sure very few know how dire the situation is in Barronel."

Brennus grimaced. "Ormond might hold."

"Only if we'd gone to his aid days ago, majesty. He will fall and our people will then know the truth as we prepare to fight."

The king looked broken. "They've never believed, not for a second, that Penraven could fall. Food is plentiful, our army well trained and well equipped. Lo strike me, this is a tribal ruffian leading tribal rabble!" But as much as the king wanted to believe otherwise, he knew the situation was dire. He no longer had options. "Summon Gavriel and Corbel," he said sadly.

De Vis nodded, turned on his heel and left the king alone to his dark thoughts. Minutes after his departure, Brennus heard the telltale lusty squall of a newborn. His new son had arrived. Not long later the senior midwife eased quietly from behind the doors. She curtsied low, a whimpering bundle of soft linens in her arms. But when she looked at the king her expression was one of terror, rather than delight.

"I heard his battlecry," the king said, desperately trying to alleviate the tension but failing, frowning at her fear as she tiptoed, almost cringing, toward him with her precious cargo. "Is something wrong with my wife?" he added, a fresh fear coursing through him.

"No, not at all, your highness. The queen is fatigued, of course, but she will be well."

"Good. Let me see this new son of mine then," Brennus said, trying to sound gruff. His heart melted as he looked down at the baby's tiny features, eyelids tightly clamped. The infant yawned and he felt an instant swell of love engulf him. "Hardly strapping but handsome all the same," he said, grinning despite his bleak mood, "with the dark features of the Valisars." He couldn't disguise the pride in his voice.

The midwife's voice was barely above a whisper when she spoke. "Sire, it . . . it is not a boy. You have been blessed with a daughter."

Brennus looked at the woman as though she had suddenly begun speaking gibberish.

She hurried on in her anxious whisper. "She is beautiful but I must warn that she is frail due to her early arrival. A girl, majesty," she muttered with awe. "How long has it been?"

"Show me," Brennus demanded, his jaw grinding to keep his own fears in check. The midwife obliged and he was left with no doubt; he had sired a girl. Wrapping her in the linens again, he looked mournfully at the old, knowing midwife—old enough to have delivered him nearly five decades ago. She knew about the Valisar line and what this arrival meant. *How much worse could their situation get*, he wondered, his mind instantly chaotic.

"I fear she may not survive, majesty."

"I am taking her to the chapel," he said, ignoring the woman's concerns.

Their attention was momentarily diverted by Piven scampering up, his dark curly hair its usual messy mop and his matching dark eyes twinkling with delight at seeing his father. But Piven gave everyone a similar welcome; it was obvious he made no distinction between man or woman, king or courtier. Everyone was a friend, deserving of a beaming, vacant salutation. Brennus affectionately stroked his invalid son's hair.

The midwife tried to protest. "But the queen has hardly seen her. She said—"

"Never mind what the queen instructs." Brennus reached for the baby. "Give her to me. I would hold the first Valisar princess in centuries. She will go straight to the chapel for a blessing in case she passes on. My wife will understand. Tell her I shall be back shortly with our daughter."

Brennus didn't wait for the woman's reply. Cradling his daughter as though she were a flickering flame that could be winked out with the slightest draft, he shielded her beneath his cloak and strode—almost ran—to Penraven's royal chapel, trailed by his laughing, clapping five-year-old boy. Inside he locked the door. His breathing had become labored and shallow, and the fear that had begun as a tingle now throbbed through his body like fire.

The priest came and was promptly banished. Soon after a knock at the door revealed De Vis with his twin sons in tow, looking wide-eyed but resolute. Now tall enough to stand shoulder to shoulder alongside their father like sentries, strikingly similar and yet somehow clearly individual, they bowed deeply to their sovereign, while Piven mimicked the action. Although neither Gavriel nor Corbel knew what was afoot for them, they had obviously been told by their father that each had a special role to perform.

"Bolt it," Brennus ordered as soon as the De Vis family was inside the chapel.

A glance to one son by De Vis saw it done. "Are we alone?" he asked the king as Corbel drew the heavy bolt into place.

"Yes, we're secure."

De Vis saw the king fetch a gurgling bundle from behind one of the pews and then watched his boys' brows crinkle with gentle confusion although they said nothing. He held his breath in an attempt to banish his reluctance to go through with the plan. He could hardly believe this was really happening and that the king and he had agreed to involve the boys. And yet there was no other way, no one else to trust.

"This is my newborn child," Brennus said quietly, unable to hide the catch in his voice.

The legate forced a tight smile although the sentiment behind it was genuine. "Congratulations, majesty." The fact that the baby was among them told him the plan was already in motion. He felt the weight of his own fear at the responsibility that he and the king were about to hand over; it fell like a stone down his throat to settle uncomfortably, painfully, in the pit of his stomach. Could these young men—still youthful enough that their attempts to grow beards and moustaches were a source of amusement—pull off the extraordinary plan that the king and he had hatched over this last moon? From the time at which it had become obvious that the Set could not withstand the force of Loethar's marauding army.

They had to do this. He had to trust that his sons would gather their own courage and understand the import of what was being entrusted to them.

De Vis became aware of the awkward silence clinging to the foursome, broken only by the flapping of a sparrow that had become trapped in the chapel and now flew hopelessly around the ceiling, tapping against the timber and stone, testing for a way out. Piven, nearby, flapped his arms too, his expression vacant, unfocused.

De Vis imagined Brennus felt very much like the sparrow right now—trapped but hoping against hope for a way out of the baby's death. There was none. He rallied his courage, for he was sure Brennus's forlorn expression meant the king's mettle was foundering. "Gavriel, Corbel, King Brennus wishes to tell you something of such grave import that we cannot risk anyone outside of the four of us sharing this plan. No one . . . do you understand?"

Both boys stared at their father and nodded. Piven stepped up into the circle and eyed each, smiling beatifically.

"Have you chosen who takes which responsibility?" Brennus asked, after clearing his throat.

"Gavriel will take Leo, sire. Corbel will . . ." he hesitated, not sure whether his own voice would hold. He too cleared his throat. "He will—"

Brennus rescued him. "Hold her, Corbel. This is a new princess for Penraven and a more dangerous birth I cannot imagine. I loathe passing this terrible responsibility to you but your father believes you are up to it."

"Why is she dangerous, your majesty?" Corbel asked.

"She is the first female to be born into the Valisars for centuries, the only one who might well be strong enough to live. Those that have been born in the past have rarely survived their first hour." Brennus shrugged sorrowfully. "We cannot let her be found by the tyrant Loethar."

De Vis sympathized with his son. He could see that the king's opening gambit was having the right effect in chilling Corbel but he was also aware that Brennus was circling the truth.

In fact he realized the king was distancing himself from it, already addressing Gavriel.

". . . must look after Leo. I cannot leave Penraven without an heir. I fear as eldest and crown prince he must face whatever is ahead—I cannot soften the blow, even though he is still so young."

Gavriel nodded, and his father realized his son understood. "Your daughter does not need to face the tyrant—is this what you mean, your highness . . . that we can soften the blow for her, but not for the prince?"

De Vis felt something in his heart give. The boys would make him proud. He wished, for the thousandth time, that his wife had lived to see them. He pitied that she'd never known how Gavriel led and yet although this made Corbel seem weaker, he was far from it. If anything he was the one who was prepared to take the greatest risks, for all that he rarely shared what he was thinking. Gavriel did the talking for both of them and here again, he'd said aloud for everyone's benefit what the king was finding so hard to say and Corbel refused to ask.

"Yes," Brennus replied to the eldest twin. "We can soften the blow for the princess. She need not face Loethar. I have let the realm down by my willingness to believe in our invincibility. But no one is invincible, boys. Not even the barbarian. He is strong now, fueled by his success—success that I wrongly permitted—but he too will become inflated by his own importance one day, by his own sense of invincibility. I have to leave it to the next generation to know when to bring him down."

"Are we going to lose to Loethar, sire?" Gavriel asked.

"We may," was Brennus's noncommittal answer. "But we can do this much for the princess. Save her his wrath." His voice almost broke upon his last word and he reached to stroke her shock of dark hair, so unlike Leo's and Iselda's coloring.

"And Piven?" Gavriel inquired.

All four glanced at the youngster. "I am trying not to worry about this child," Brennus replied. "He is harmless; anyone can see that. He is also not of our blood," he added, looking down awkwardly. "If anything happens to him he will know little of it and if he survives, nothing will change in his strange internal world. It's as though he is not among us anyway. I am prepared to take the risk that the barbarian will hardly notice him."

The De Vis family nodded in unison, although whether they believed him was hard to tell.

"The queen, er . . ." Gavriel looked from the king to his father.

"Will be none the wiser," De Vis said firmly. "It is enough that most of us will likely die anyway. We can spare her this."

"Die?" Gavriel asked, aghast. "But we can get the king and queen away, taking Leo and the baby across the ocean to—"

"No, Gav. We can't," his father interrupted. "The king will not leave his people—nor should he—and I will not leave his side. We will fight to the last and if we are to fall, we fall together, the queen included. But we cannot risk the royal children."

Brennus took up the thread again, much to De Vis's relief. "Piven is not seen as an heir but he is also no threat. And while I sadly must risk that Leo is found, tortured, abused and ultimately exploited for the tyrant's purposes, I am giving him a fighting chance with you, Gavriel. That said, I won't risk the possibility of my daughter falling into Loethar's hands."

That sentence prompted a ghastly silence, broken finally by Corbel, who looked uncomfortably away from the dark eyes of the baby that stared at him from the crook of his arm. "Tell me what I must do," he asked.

The king sighed, hesitated. De Vis's encouraging hand on his arm helped him to finally say it. "Today, my daughter must die."

Corbel stood alone with the tiny infant, hardly daring to breathe. He wasn't sure she was even breathing, to tell the truth, and for a minute he hoped that she had stopped of her own accord. But her tiny fingers twitched and he knew she clung stubbornly to life.

He made no judgment against the king. He imagined that if he was hurting this much over such a traumatic task, then surely the king was hurting twice as hard to demand it of him. His father must believe him more capable of being able to carry out the grim request than Gavriel and he understood why. His father probably anticipated that he would be able to push his guilt into a deep corner of his mind, perhaps lock it away forever and never think about it, let alone speak of it. Corbel knew he gave this impression of being remote, capable of such hardness, but he was no such thing.

The baby girl, swathed in soft, royal birth linens, shifted gently in his arms. It was time. No amount of soul searching was going to get this job done and the responsibility rested with him alone.

Just do it, he urged himself. *Leave the recrimination for later.* His job was to hand the dead child to Father Briar, who would take her to the king so that he could allow the queen to say goodbye to her. Meanwhile his father would be waiting in the preserves cellar to brief him on where he must flee. Nobody must ever connect him to the dead child. He wanted to say goodbye properly to Gavriel but their sovereign and even their father had not given them time.

He picked up the blanket and said a silent prayer with his face buried in it for a few moments. Easy tears were not something Corbel suffered from but although his body didn't betray him with a physical sign of his grief, he felt it nonetheless as he placed the blanket over the now sleeping, very weak child's face and begged Lo to make this swift. He tried to blank his mind as he pressed on the blanket but thoughts of Gavriel surfaced. How would his brother protect Leo? Would they survive the coming conflict? He might never know; he was being sent away—far away . . . and he didn't know if he would ever return. Accepting this felt impossible and grief began to mix with anger as he sped the child to her death.

Gavriel De Vis had watched his father leave with his brother. There had not been time for he and his brother to share anything more than a look, but that look had said droves about the terrible action that was about to be taken. In that moment in which he and Corbel had learned of the king's plan, Gavriel had despised Brennus for forcing them into this corner. Perhaps Brennus sensed it for as the legate and Corbel left, the king had held him back.

"Gavriel, a word if I may?"

"Of course, highness," he said, curtly.

"I've asked a lot of you today."

"You've asked me simply to keep guard over Leo, which is no trial, majesty. What you've asked of my brother is completely different. Enough to shatter anyone's soul, if you'll forgive my candour, highness." He felt proud of himself for saying as much.

"You understand it could not be done by my hand?"

"I'm not sure I understand it at all, your highness. But I will take care of Leo as my king has asked and because my father demands it."

"I know you will protect him with your life."

"Of course. He is the crown prince."

"There is something else I need to share with you. It is a delicate matter but I can share this information with no one else."

Gavriel's anger gave way to confusion. "Your majesty, whatever you tell me is in confidence."

"I mean *no one*, though, Gavriel. This information is for your ears alone—not your father, not your brother, no one at all. Not even Leo. I am entrusting a great secret to you alone. I would ask you to swear your silence."

Gavriel frowned. "All right, highness. I swear you my silence. Whatever you share remains our secret."

"Not here," the king said. "I shall send for you. Come to my salon. Right now I must away to my good wife. Await my message."

Gavriel bowed, baffled.

The queen's convalescing chamber was attended by various servants and officials who the king had insisted upon. Its atmosphere was frigid, the awkward quiet punctuated only by the sounds of embarrassed shuffles or coughs over the mournful toll of a single bell. The only focus of activity or brightness was Piven, who gently stroked his mother's hair. No one could be sure of the sound, but he was humming tunelessly as he did so.

"And tell me again, Hana, why my newborn child is not at my breast and you cannot find my husband?" Iselda demanded, her face wan from fatigue and worry.

Hana fussed at her queen's coverlets before pressing a warm posset of milk curdled with ginger wine and honey into her mistress's hands. "I've heard the king is on his way, your highness. Now I beg you to drink this without fuss. You need to regain your strength."

In a rare show of anger Iselda hurled the cup across the room, its contents splashing in all directions. Piven sat back in what could only be described as amusement, while Hana flinched in astonishment. The cup shattered against the stone, the liquid soaking into the timber beneath the herbs that were strewn underfoot. Its heat instantly released the sweet smell of lavender mingling with mint and rosemary.

"I shall take nothing, eat nothing, say not another word until my daughter is returned to me. Find her! Do you hear me?" the queen yelled, coughing on the last word as she dissolved into tears. Piven returned to stroking his mother's hair as though nothing had happened.

"As does the entire palace, my love," Brennus said, finally arriving. Hana visibly relaxed at the sight of the tall, dark king whose beard had recently erupted new silver flecks, whose once broad shoulders now appeared to sag, and whose laughter, which had boomed around the walls of Brighthelm, was now only an echo.

"Brennus!" Iselda took his hands as he settled to sit beside her. Piven leapt onto his father's lap. The queen accepted the soft kiss Brennus planted on her cheek, mindful of their audience, and pulled back to search his face. She found her answer in the set of his mouth, the grief in his eyes. She asked all the same. "Where is our daughter? Why the mourning knell?"

"Iselda," Brennus began gently. The hurt in his voice was so raw it hit her like a blow and her eyes spilled, tears coursing down her cheeks and finding a path through the fingers she clamped to her mouth to prevent herself from shrieking her own grief. "Our baby died not long after her birth," Brennus finished. "In my arms."

Iselda shook her head slowly, repeating the word "no" over his soft words.

Brennus wiped away his own tears and over her denials he continued. "No daughter has ever survived. The Valisar line seems to have its own self-defense for the female line— but you already know that, my love." He took her hands, squeezing them, gently kissing them. "She didn't suffer, my darling, I promise. She simply fell asleep as Father Briar blessed her with holy oil. She heard her name spoken and I'm sure she heard me tell her that we loved her with all our hearts."

Iselda's lips moved but no sound came. The death bell tolled mournfully through the difficult silence.

Brennus pressed on. "I knew this might occur and that is why I took her from you, my love. I needed her to be blessed before . . . before . . ." He was unable to finish, his voice crumbling.

"Before the devil stole her soul?" Iselda asked, her voice suddenly hard, her cheeks wet. "Do you really believe that something so small and beautiful and pure would be ignored, cast aside by Lo? Is he really that cruel, this god we pray to and put all our faith in, to not only murder my baby but then refuse her soul passage into heaven?" Her voice had changed into a hissing shriek at his apparent insensitivity. She was very well aware it was unseemly to unravel emotionally in front of the palace servants but she no longer cared. Three children were all Lo had given her to love; of those, one was a grotesque, and now her only daughter was already dead within hours of her birth. Precious Leonel, their hope, was likely as good as dead anyway.

"Perhaps our little girl is the lucky one, taken by Lo peacefully. Where is Leo? Does he know?" she begged, her voice softer now.

The king's red-rimmed eyes closed briefly. "De Vis is with him now but will leave Gavriel with him."

"That's good," she said, relieved, giving a watery smile to Piven. "Leo does love that family as if it's his own," she added absently, before dissolving into quiet weeping.

The king cleared his throat, looking toward the queen's overly attentive aide hovering nearby. Freath was a good man, only slightly older than himself and although not handsome in a traditional sense, there was an enigmatic quality to his dry, reserved manner that was appealing. "I think we're fine here now, Freath. You can organize for us to be left alone."

"Yes, majesty," the man replied. "Er, Father Briar awaits."

The king nodded, waiting for the servants to shuffle out at Freath's murmured orders.

"Why were these people allowed in my chamber? I can understand Physic Maser, but the others?" Iselda asked through her tears as she counted almost eight others being herded out by Freath.

"I must be honest with you, my love. I had no idea how you were going to react. I needed people here for various contingencies. But as always you surprise me with your courage." She watched him hug their vacant little boy close to his chest and inhale the scent of his freshly washed hair. She was glad Piven did not have the mental capacity to understand any of this.

"I don't feel very courageous, Brennus, and I am sure the real pain has not yet hit me. I feel too numb right now."

Brennus nodded in shared pain. "There will be no shame if you prefer not to see her, but I have had our daughter brought up from the chapel. Father Briar is outside."

"He has her?" Iselda asked, tears welling again.

"I thought you might like to hold her, have some private time with her," Brennus said, choking as he spoke. "I'm so sorry, my love. I'm sorry I'm not being strong for you."

"I have always maintained that one of the reasons I have loved you, Brennus, 8th of the Valisars, is because you are capable of such emotion, and are not ashamed to suffer it. I'm surprised you've been so open with it in front of others, just now. But you don't have to be outwardly strong for me, my king." Iselda reached out to stroke his beard. "Just be strong for our people. What's ahead is . . ." She shook her head. "Unthinkable," she finished. Then a hint of her private courage ghosted across her pale face as she stiffened her resolve. "I would like to hold her and kiss her again. Please ask Father Briar to come in."

The king nodded, touched her hand and rose from her bed. "I'll fetch him."

Iselda's heart began an urgent ache for the sister Leo would never have, for the daughter she would never fuss over gowns with, for the little girl Brennus would never know the special joy of being a father to, for the realm that would never have the glamor and excitement of the first living princess in centuries . . . but especially for the future. Because there wasn't one. Without a royal line—and Leo would surely be put to the sword if Loethar found him—Penraven and the prosperous era of the Valisars was destroyed forever.

She watched her husband usher in the priest, and trembled to see him lightly carrying a bundle draped with cream silks. Giving herself entirely over to her grief, Queen Iselda took the tiny corpse of her infant daughter and cradled her tightly against her breast, praying with all her heart that the long dark lashes would flutter open. Her prayer fell on deaf ears. The child's eyes remained determindedly closed; her lips were now blueish in color. Tufts of hair escaped the silken cap, their darkness making her dead daughter's waxy skin look even paler, when only a couple of hours earlier she had been a dark pink with her efforts to be born. Iselda wanted to touch the fairy-like fingers and toes again that had looked so perfect, so tiny, earlier. She was unaware that she was sharing her thoughts aloud.

"We wrapped her up in the silks you'd made," Brennus admitted, then shrugged awkwardly. "It seemed right to do so."

Iselda watched with a broken heart as Piven gently curled the little girl's dark hair around his small fingers and smiled at his mother before he bent and gave the corpse a loud wet kiss on her forehead. His father eased him back onto his lap to give the queen a chance to say her final farewell to her daughter.

Iselda stroked the silken cape she had sewed and then painstakingly embroidered through her confinement the last three moons of her pregnancy. "I unpicked this rosebud so many times," she admitted ruefully. "Just couldn't get it to sit right."

Father Briar stepped forward, bowing again. He glanced at Brennus, who nodded permission. "She was blessed, majesty. She died gently in the arms of our king—a little sigh and she drew her final soft breath. Lo has taken her, accepted her soul with love."

The queen grimaced. "I wish he hadn't, Father. I wish he'd given me even just a few more hours with her. I had barely moments before she was whisked away from me and now she's dead. I can hardly remember how it felt to hold her while she breathed or fix a picture in my mind of how she looked when she was alive."

Father Briar shifted uncomfortably. "Forgive me, highness. Perhaps it is Lo's way."

"You mean our god deliberately steals her memory from my mind to make it easier on me when he steals her soul?" Iselda asked, her expression hardening, lips thinning.

The priest looked between king and queen before awkwardly saying: "Yes, that's a rather nice way to put it, your majesty. I may—if you'll let me repeat that—use it in a sermon sometime."

Brennus blinked and Iselda knew this to be a sign of frustration at the priest's clumsiness. "Thank you, Father," the king said. He turned to her. "Enough?"

She shook her head, not even conscious of her tears. "I could never have enough of her."

"Just remember we have Leo to think about. He must be worried, confused as well. I don't think he needs to see her but he will want to see you, know that you are safe."

She sniffed, unable to tear her gaze away from the child. "You're right. I can only imagine what he's thinking. Bring him to me, Brennus. Let me smell the hair and kiss the pink skin of the living." She sounded resolute and Brennus thanked her with a squeeze to her hand.

"Shall I take her?"

Iselda nodded, too frightened to speak, fearful that treacherous tears and fresh, uncontrollable emotion would threaten her fragile resolve. She bent and kissed the baby's forehead. It felt like marble and her tears, which splashed onto the infant's skin, rolled off, barely leaving a trace. No, there was no warmth, none of the porousness of life present—of that she was sure now and the tiny irrational flicker of hope guttered in her breast and died too. She gave her daughter a final squeeze, hating the stiffness of her tiny body and suddenly grateful to Brennus for having the child swaddled so tightly. She knew now that was his reason for doing so—so she would not have to feel rigor claiming her daughter.

And finally she handed the doll-like infant back to its father. "All this time I haven't asked and you haven't offered," she said sadly.

"What, my love?" he inquired, looking ashamed, she presumed because he genuinely didn't know what she meant.

"Share with me the name you gave our daughter."

He found a sad smile and whispered it for her hearing alone.

"Very beautiful," Iselda admitted. "A choice I certainly approve of. But I would now ask a favor of you, Brennus."

"Anything, my love."

"Send out an edict that no child of Penraven will ever bear that name from this day. It belongs only to her."

He nodded. "It will be done, I promise."

"You'd best ask the funerary to prepare our tombs, including Leo's. I can't imagine we are long for this earth."

"Come now, Iselda. Rally, my queen, for the sake of your son. All is not lost. Loethar will have a tough time breaching our walls."

"How is that supposed to cheer me? Loethar has only to sit us out. Our supplies will dwindle soon enough."

"I promise you this: whatever happens, Leo will escape the tyrant's touch."

"How can you know that? In the same way you knew that the barbarian could never succeed in taking the Set?" It was a low blow but well deserved. He shouldn't have been so arrogant to Loethar. The warlord had called his bluff. She wasn't finished with him yet. "And your other son?"

"The barbarian will not bother himself with the boy." Brennus took her hand.

She shrugged it off. "If you could keep that promise I could go to my death happy. But how can you be so sure?"

Brennus paused. She imagined he was weighing telling the truth against saying something to make her heart beat easier. "I have already taken steps for Leo's escape. He doesn't know it yet, of course, but should Loethar enter the palace, no matter what else occurs, Leo will be protected. In time he will carry the torch of the Valisars against the tyrant. We, my love, are expendable—as is Piven—and I intend to see that Loethar burns all his energies on enjoying my demise, while our healthy son slips his net."

None of it sat easy in her heart, especially the betrayal of Piven. He was an invalid but he could still feel pain and fear. She was weary of grief. "Perhaps her death is for the best then," she said, as he opened the door to leave.

"Why do you say that?" he asked, glancing at the dead girl in his arms.

"Because she would have been a complication to your plan. If she hadn't have died, you might have had to have her killed . . . to be sure she would not be used as Loethar's tool. I would offer Piven the same courtesy if I only had the courage."

Brennus blanched, stared at her with such apology in his painful glance before he left wordlessly that in that heart-stopping moment of his pause Iselda believed she had stumbled upon the real truth of her daughter's demise. As the door closed on her chilling revelation the Queen of Penraven knew she had no further desire to live—the Valisar name and its sinister secret suddenly no longer mattered.

Two

"My sister's dead," Leo said in the bald way that any twelve-year-old might comment.

Gavriel nodded. "I'm sorry for your family . . . for you, majesty."

"I was hoping for a brother—not like Piven, but one like you have."

"Girls are fun too," Gavriel replied, knowing the youngster probably wouldn't catch on fully to his innuendo.

Leo screwed his nose up. "They're not much good at fishing, archery, riding, fighting—"

"Ha! Don't you believe it, majesty," Gavriel said. "They're pretty good at most things and very good at others."

"Like what?"

"Er, well, like looking beautiful, smelling nice . . ."

The boy obviously thought about this for a few moments as Gavriel helped to hoist him up to balance perilously on his shoulders. "Get that one, your majesty," he said, pointing to a particularly fat, ripe-looking pear. The pear landed in Gavriel's outstretched hand. "One more, over there."

As he stretched to reach it, Leo continued, "Smelling good isn't much help in a battle, though, is it?"

Gavriel liked the way Leo's mind worked. He still had that direct, slightly unnerving manner of all children but the crown prince was a thinker and often amused Gavriel and

Corbel with his opinionated insights. He was maturing fast, too. Gavriel was still young enough to recall how quickly one could turn from a youngster disinterested in anything but boyish pursuits into a young man whose every thought seemed to focus around women and enjoying them.

Gavriel could almost yearn for that carefree way of even five anni previous but it was lost to him. And not just because of the toll of years; Loethar was stealing the Set's future, might well steal their lives if he was gauging the mood of his father and the king correctly. The palace was preparing for siege, and the word was already going out that, impossible though it seemed, Barronel's fall was now inevitable. Penraven's people should flee, preferably via the sea, since Loethar had no ships, and no sailing prowess even if he could secure vessels. Penraven's coastline was so vast that anyone who wanted to leave the realm could, finding safety in the Taramanian Isles to the west, or in the eastern kingdom of Galinsea.

But there would be no escape for the De Vis brothers. The sovereign was counting on them to behave as men now; the innocence of childhood was a luxury long behind them.

Leo leapt down from Gavriel's shoulders, ignoring the hand of help. "Eat your pear," Gavriel said, crunching into his. He wondered how he was going to live up to the task asked of him by his king, but was quickly reminded of what had fallen on Corbel's shoulders and shuddered. His brother's task was far more daunting.

"What do you mean?" Leo asked.

"What?"

"You said you wondered how he could kill something so tiny."

Gavriel realized he must have spoken the final thought about his brother aloud. "Nothing. I don't remember."

"You remember everything, Gav. Dates, debts, all sorts of facts."

"Quite. And speaking of debts, you owe me two trents."

"I haven't forgotten. Where's Corbel?"

"Running an errand for our father," Gavriel answered, suddenly unable to swallow his mouthful of pear. He spat it out.

"Worm?"

"No, just suddenly tasted a bit acid."

"Mine's sweet, just like Sarah Flarty's backside," Leo said, then burst into laughter at Gavriel's astonished expression. "Well, you told me so."

Gavriel sucked in a breath at the notion that he'd probably never pinch Sarah's pert bottom again and her promised tumble in the hayloft was likely not to happen, now that he was a full-time babysitter to the crown prince. *Every hour of the day you watch him, you guard him,* his father had impressed after the king had told him what it was that they expected of Gavriel. *He is never to be far from you. And when the time comes you must disappear with him. No farewells, no packing, no notes left behind. He is all that matters. Protect Leo with your life. Raise him.*

Raise him? He wasn't ready to be a father figure. He wasn't even sure he knew how to see to the boy's needs for a full day. He often still felt like a child himself, usually deferring to Corb's cunning. And now his brother was gone.

"Did you see your sister?" Gavriel asked, not meaning to ask something so blunt but needing the image of his brother close. How would they manage without each other?

"Mother doesn't know but father allowed me to see her because I wanted to. She doesn't—didn't—look like me. Did you see her?" Gavriel shook his head, unable to utter the lie. "Well, she had dark hair. Father told me to kiss her but—" he made a sound of disgust—"I didn't want to. She felt stiff, cold."

Gavriel silently praised the emotional armor with which childhood still protected Leo.

"They're burying her in the family crypt. She has her own tombstone being carved. I'll kiss her tombstone perhaps, shall I?"

"Good idea," Gavriel said. "I saw Piven earlier today. I suppose he doesn't know much about it."

The shrug Leo gave was nonetheless rueful. "Piven doesn't know much of anything. Can I ask you something, Gav?"

"Anything. You are the heir to the throne, after all."

Leo grinned. It was an old jest, which the twins used ruthlessly against him. "Is the tyrant going to kill us all?"

Gavriel sighed. "Not you."

"Why not?"

"You have me."

"I know you're the best swordsman we have, but—"

"Of the cohort only," Gavriel qualified, recalling with pride how his father, the best known sword in the land, had marvelled at the result of his concept to train a small group of youngsters into an elite faction. His eldest son's escalating skills were the most impressive of all.

"That's what I mean."

"In that case, best sword, best archer, best rider."

"Ah, but not best climber."

"No, but that's because you're still relatively puny . . . your majesty."

Again Leo smiled. "Well, when I'm your age I'll be a better swordsman, and I'll shoot arrows longer and straighter."

"I'm sure you will," Gavriel said, playing along, glad that he'd sidetracked the prince from the threat of death that loomed over all of them.

"But you do think others will die . . . that the tyrant will win?" Leo continued.

It seemed Gavriel had congratulated himself too soon. "I don't think we'll come out of this without some death, no."

"So my parents and brother will be murdered probably."

Gavriel didn't answer.

"And likely your father because he's legate."

"I—"

"And perhaps all the people of Penraven because they are loyal to the crown."

"Leo."

"It just doesn't seem fair that I should survive, does it?"

Gavriel wanted to say that there was absolutely no guarantee that he would—in fact there was an all too real likelihood that he wouldn't—but that was hardly the encouraging sentiment that his father wanted from him. De Vis had warned him to keep the boy's mindset strong, far away from thoughts of siege or death. So instead Gavriel placated Leo with the obvious. "You are the heir. You are even more important than the king because you are the realm's future. If he died without an heir, that would be disastrous, irresponsible and unforgiveable. But if his heir survives, even if he himself dies, there is hope."

"And hope is a good thing," Leo said, as though finishing Gavriel's sentence.

"It is everything for a kingdom facing such a threat."

"Tell me about Loethar. Everyone ignores me, says I don't need to worry."

"Not your father and certainly not mine," Gavriel replied, surprised.

"No. They're worse. They tell me that Loethar can be beaten and yet their faces say something different. I know they're pretending, shielding me from the truth. I want the truth, Gav. I'm not just a child, I'm the crown prince. I have to know what we face. And I'm twelve now, almost thirteen. That's ancient!"

The prince was correct; he did have a right to the truth. Gavriel wasn't sure he was the appropriate person to deliver it. He swallowed. The reality of the weight of responsibility given to him slotted into place in his mind and made him feel dizzy with fear. He would give Leo the truth as he understood it; the boy needed to know precisely what journey lay ahead of them.

"I'll tell you what I know, what my father has told me."

Leo settled back against a tree. "Start from the beginning of Loethar's life."

Gavriel stretched out his long legs, crossed them at the

ankle and knitted his hands behind his head as he leaned against the tree trunk. He didn't feel relaxed but he needed to give Leo the impression that he was. "Loethar's background is murky. No one really knows who he is but we know he hails from the Likurian Steppes."

"A tribal warlord," Leo muttered with awe.

"If you want to give him a title, that certainly fits, although 'lowlife thug' is my best definition."

"A masterful thug," Leo suggested and at Gavriel's look of disdain, added, "Well, he certainly called the Set's bluff. Why didn't we all just kill him and scatter his mob to their arid lands moons ago?"

"I don't know."

"You do. Stupidity. Obviously each of the kingdoms—and Penraven surely must take the most blame—believed itself invincible simply because he brought a seeming rabble. We didn't respect their determination."

All true. Gavriel sighed silently at Leo's grasp of the situation and continued. "We know of no family and to my knowledge we don't even know why or how this campaign of war began but we assume he dreams of empire. His intention is to cripple the power of the Denova Set, with Penraven the jewel of his new crown."

"Because politically and financially we're the most powerful of all the realms."

"Correct."

"Yes, but why?"

"Lo help me—what is your history teacher doing with you, majesty?"

"He's so boring I don't pay attention. Out here with you it's more fun."

"All right, let's see," Gavriel began. "Penraven, Barronel, Dregon, Gormand, Vorgaven, Cremond and Medhaven make up the Denova Set."

Leo made a sound of exaggerated exasperation. "I know that much."

Gavriel ignored him. "Of the seven, Penraven is the largest, the most powerful and the most wealthy. And Penraven was the first of the realms, so the others tend to look up to the Valisar crown. However, each is its own sovereign state, governing itself. You've seen the seven Kings coming together for the Denova Meet every three years, haven't you?"

"Yes, although I was never allowed to be involved."

"No, well you were ill for the last one I recall and barely six for the one before that, still, I might add, sucking your thumb! The King of Gormand disapproved."

Leo sniggered. "So another is due."

"Yes, it was meant to happen last moon but Loethar's actions have changed everything."

"I still can't believe we didn't take action. And he now controls the other realms."

"Medhaven is hardly a stronghold or much of a prize but my father heard through runners this morning that Barronel was set to fall—probably later today. We have to hope that some renegades somewhere are hatching plans for overthrow in the various kingdoms. It's to those rebels we must look, find them somehow, link up if we can." Gavriel was thinking aloud. No one in authority had said as much but he believed there had to be survivors who were not prepared to succumb to the tyrant's rule.

"And so now he wants to rule Penraven."

"Yes, but . . ." Gavriel stopped himself too late.

"But what?"

"What do you know about your family, majesty?"

Leo spun around to face Gavriel. "That's an odd question."

"Do you know its history?"

Leo began reciting the Kings. "My father is the 8th. Before him, my grandfather, King Darros, and—"

Gavriel interrupted him. "I mean do you know what makes the Valisar Kings so revered . . . and feared?"

The boy shook his head, looked down. "A secret, no doubt."

Gavriel nodded. "You should be learning this from your father, not me."

"But you can give me a hint."

The eldest of the De Vis twins—by just three minutes—felt a stirring, a premonition perhaps. "It's known as the Valisar Enchantment. I've never heard much about it to tell you the truth, but my father told me rumor abounds among the people."

"What is it?" Leo asked, frowning.

"I was told it is a powerful magic that belongs to the Valisar line alone."

Leo's eyes were shining with the intrigue. "So father has it. What is it?"

Gavriel shrugged. "The power of coercion."

The boy frowned, looked at him quizzically. "What does that mean?"

"Well, with it presumably you can bend people to your will."

"Make them do what you want?"

"You could put it like that."

Leo whistled. "Imagine that power!"

Gavriel's mind drifted momentarily. As Leo threw out suggestions of how it might be manipulated to their own ends, he imagined instead what could happen if such power fell into the wrong hands.

". . . and Sarah Flarty could never refuse you." Leo finished, breathless, grinning.

"What?" Gavriel's attention had returned just in time to hear the last few cheeky words.

"Well, you want to kiss her, don't you?"

"I don't think that's any of your business, your majesty. I should never have mentioned her to you," Gavriel replied.

"She's pretty. I like her. You should kiss her anyway and then you can teach me how to because I'd quite like to kiss Duke Grendel's daughter but she thinks I'm dirty."

"Dirty?"

"Says I always smell of horses and mud."

"Young girls can be a bit priggish, Leo. Older ones are more fun," Gavriel added with a wink. "Like that delicious new girl, Genrie."

Leo screwed his nose. "She's hideous!"

"Hardly."

"Old!"

Gavriel shrugged. "Only to you."

"And you . . . ugh!"

"Older women have experience, Leo. Something you can't quite appreciate yet."

"She hates me."

"Ah, here's the truth of it. She doesn't hate you, she's brisk with everyone, very efficient, very . . . desirable. I wouldn't mind her ordering me around—" He stopped, catching himself in time. "Er, where were we?"

Leo didn't seem to mind the abrupt halt and he hadn't forgotten where they'd left their previous topic. "But if the Kings of Valisar have this . . . this power of—"

"Coercion," Gavriel prompted.

Leo nodded. "Why hasn't my father used it to stop the tyrant?"

Gavriel stood, dusted off his trousers and hauled a reluctant crown prince to his feet. "Because your father does not possess this power."

"But I thought you just said—"

"I told you what the Valisar legend says. The reality is that we don't know what it is or who possesses it, how it works, or how to stop it working. Your father told my father that he does not wield any magic that he's aware of, cannot wield anything more dangerous than a sword."

"So it's a lie, then."

"Not necessarily."

"Gav, you're confusing me."

"It's a confusing subject. Come on, majesty, we're late. I promised Morkom I'd have you back to take supper with the queen." He gave the crown prince a gentle push. "We can talk as we walk but keep your voice low—what we discuss is secret."

Leo fell into step alongside his tall keeper. "So if it's not a lie, what is it?"

"No one knows. Your father believes that it is a contrary phenomenon, er . . . by that I mean it's a thing that can appear whenever it chooses. No one knows for sure but I'm told it can skip generations, lie dormant for endless years if it wants."

"How does someone know if they have it?"

"I presume, majesty, they can test it by trying to compel people to do their bidding."

"And my father cannot."

"He denies any ability and I think he would have used it if he did possess such a thing, don't you?"

"Lo sod it! I definitely don't have it. But where does the power come from?"

Gavriel shrugged. "Search me. Born with it, I guess. I learned today that the first Valisar king—Cormoron—who was supposedly bristling with this power—made a blood oath on the Stone of Truth at Lackmarin that he and no other Valisar king would ever be able to use their power against their own."

"Does that mean family?"

"I think it extends to his people."

"Go on, this is good," Leo said, leaping onto a low wall and frowning as he listened, balancing alongside Gavriel.

"When his blood was spilled upon the stone it is said that a serpent appeared and drank the blood. It told Cormoron that his blood oath was accepted and the magic would remain true to the Valisars and their heirs would be impervious to its power."

They'd reached the stairs that led to the royal apartments. Leo touched the carved pattern in the stonework that was a familiar design throughout Brighthelm. "Is that why we have a serpent alongside the winged lion in our heraldry?"

"That is precisely why. It was incorporated by Cormoron

in a proclamation that the serpent would join the winged lion on the family crest."

"Did the serpent say anything else to the first king?"

Gavriel smiled. "I don't know, majesty, I wasn't there," he admitted, ending their conversation.

He saw how Leo, while making his way up to his private rooms, acknowledged various servants who were passing them—one carrying linen, another with an armload of tallow candles, and still another with a basin of water. Even though the crown prince said nothing, he found a smile or a nod to let that person know he noticed them. It was a small gesture and yet its consequences were far rippling. For Leo to have the presence of mind already to look beyond his own world and his own needs, to remember that others made his life so easy, boded well for him as future king . . . if Gavriel could keep him alive that long.

"No one seems scared of Loethar," Leo admitted, echoing Gavriel's thoughts.

"That's because we've never given them reason to be . . . until now. Be assured, majesty, the panic will hit soon enough. I think we've been wrong to ignore the threat but my opinion is worth little."

"Not to me," Leo said and then froze as one of the servants appeared, walking so briskly she was bringing behind her a draft.

"Prince Leo," she said, nodding her head, "Morkom has been looking for you everywhere." Her tone was filled with accusation.

Gavriel saw Leo's eyes narrow. "And he can continue to look, Genrie," the prince said coolly. "He is, after all, a servant. One I appreciate and like very much but a servant all the same . . . just like you."

Genrie bristled and Gavriel found her all the more alluring for her pursed lips and frostiness. The fact was Genrie was efficient, keen at her job, and liked by all the senior people in the palace because she was discreet and pragmatic. But she had an abrupt, at times superior manner that he understood would certainly rub the youthful prince the wrong way. "Er, his majesty is late because of me, Genrie," he chimed in. "Forgive me. He's here now and well aware that he is due for supper shortly with the queen. Who are you having supper with? Perhaps I could—"

"Master De Vis," she began, her tone wintry, "I was expressly sent by the queen to find his majesty and I—"

"And he is found." Leo cut across her words with a sardonic smile. "Thank you."

It was a dismissal and she had no option but to curtsey and move on, but not without throwing a glare at Gavriel.

Gavriel sighed. "Now she'll never let me feel her pert—"

"Ah, the kitchens have sent up some berry liquor," the prince said, ignoring his friend's moans as they entered his suite. "Want some?"

"No, majesty, but you go ahead."

Leo gave him a look of disdain. "Gav, it sounds to me like we're going to be together for a while."

"I should be honest and tell you that I've been instructed by your father and my father not to leave your side. We're as good as glued together from hereon."

That caught the prince's attention. He gawped at Gavriel. "You jest."

Gavriel shook his head. "New rules. You now have a full-time champion."

"What about Piven?"

"He has his nurserymaids. You need a man!" Gavriel said the last with a flourish, flexing the muscles in his upper arm in a light attempt at humor he didn't feel.

The boy gave a low whistle. "In that case can we drop the majesty title? It makes me feel awkward. You and Corb never used to call me that. Your doing it now makes me feel like my father." He tipped water into the small measure of dark syrup he had poured into a goblet.

"In front of others I must show respect, you know that."

Leo drank the contents of the goblet, giving a sound of pleasure as he swallowed the last mouthful. "Fine, but when we're alone I want to be just Leo or dunderhead to you as I've always been." He pushed back the fringe of his sandy-colored hair. "So is that all you know about the Valisar magic?"

Gavriel thought he'd got away too easily on the previous conversation. "I know that it's whispered about as the Valisar Enchantment. Your father told me only today in fact that it's the magic that kills the females of his line. Whether they die in the womb, at birth or beyond it, none has survived more than an hour or so."

"Why? The magic is too powerful for them?"

"Seems so."

"Or perhaps it chooses only the boys to live."

"Yes, more likely."

"My poor sister," Leo mused. "I'd like to have taught her how to shoot a catapult. Piven just can't get it."

"Even if she had survived, Leo, I wonder whether your father could have risked her being found by Loethar."

The boy looked up, surprised. "You mean he's pleased she's dead?"

"No," Gavriel hurried to say. "But I think I sensed that he felt relief that she could not be hurt by the barbarian."

"But why couldn't my father have protected us all if she'd lived?"

Gavriel shrugged. He too wasn't sure about this. "I imagine because a baby is dangerous. It can give you away with a whimper if you're hiding; it needs its mother and the kind of care that if we were on the run we couldn't give. I think your sister's death released your father from having to make that decision," he said, hating the lie as it treacherously left his lips. "I'm calling Morkom for your bath."

"But how is my father going to protect my little brother?"

"I'm not sure. I'm not privy to that," Gavriel replied, utterly sure now that Piven would be ignored and left to Loethar's discretion. No one wanted another child's blood on his hands by killing Piven to save him from the barbarian.

"I shall speak to him about Piven. Where is the king, do you know?"

"I imagine he's at the barracks. Our army is going to be facing the marauders soon. He's probably doing his best to ensure their spirits are high, and their courage."

"What about ours?"

"We'll have to help each other." The words sounded prophetic as he said them. "And I think we have to get used to it."

Loethar licked the blade, enjoying the sensation of the metallic tanginess in his mouth. Blue blood. Regal blood. He could get drunk on it. He looked at Stracker. "Impale him and all the family in the central square. That should reinforce who now controls Barronel and loosen a few tongues as to where any of the Vested may be."

"I presume you want a spectacle made of the rest of the family?"

"Cross them. That always humbles an audience. And don't hasten their deaths. No mercy."

Stracker nodded, glancing at the enormous raven sitting on the back of Loethar's chair.

"I want sorcerers, witches, wizards—call them whatever you will, they're all the same to me," Loethar continued. "But I want to know who the Vested are and where we can find them. Offer rewards, spread fear, use whatever tools necessary but I hunger for my knowledge. I must be fed." He grinned and the malevolence behind his words was heightened by the sight of his bloodstained teeth. He wiped his tongue along them, licking his lips at the residue of taste.

"I shall see to it," Stracker said.

"I plan to be alone tonight," Loethar added, then changed his mind. "Actually, send me up that cowering little princess. And have a barrel of wine brought up with her. Maybe it will help dull the sound of her shrieks."

Both men laughed. Once his Right had departed, the contrived smile froze on Loethar's face. He was close now. Very close. He hoped the Penravians were suffering in their dreams with images of the havoc he was going to loose upon them. He hoped they had heard the stories of what he had unleashed upon the rest of the Set, the terror he had achieved and the torturous pain he had heaped on each realm. Word ran ahead of him, he knew, and he hoped the people of Penraven were listening carefully, for he wanted their king . . . but most of all he wanted what the Valisar royals possessed. He stroked the raven's head and it blinked its pale eyes.

"Almost there now, Vyk," he cooed.

A knock dragged him from his thoughts. "Who is it?" he yelled, convinced it could not yet be his entertainment for the evening.

"It's Valya," came the reply.

"Come!"

Vyk swooped down to stand by the corpse as the door pushed open and a woman stepped through. "Am I interrupting, Loethar? Ah, I see it's all over."

"Would it matter if you were?"

She smiled, slow and familiar, as she crossed the room, not at all fazed by the large bird or its warning caw at her approach. "I thought this too important to wait on. Being this close to Penraven, news travels fast."

"And?"

"One of my spies in the city tells me that a death knell has been sounding for hours. Double shock for the people—you on one side of the walls and a royal death on the other." She laughed.

Loethar's eyes narrowed. "Who? Surely not Brennus."

"No one's ever said the man's a coward. I doubt he'd kill himself to prevent your having the pleasure." She looked down at the dead king at her lover's feet but her expression remained unchanged, unmoved by the sight of the decapitated royal. "But I have to wonder yet again why he didn't try to dissuade you from your path."

"Because he's been too comfortable wearing that all-powerful Valisar crown for too long. He believes in its invincibility. Only now might he be realizing that I plan to teach him that even the Valisars can be toppled."

She gave him a wry glance. "You know the Penravians will flee by ship."

"Yes, I do, because you've already told me that much. It's not the people I care about, Valya. It's the Valisars."

"So all this death and destruction has been about Brennus," she said, baldly.

"It always has been. Him and his offspring and those who support them."

None of the wryness had left her expression. "Just leave Cremond alone."

"I did. I don't break promises. Do we know who's dead in Penraven?" he asked again.

She shook her head. "It could be any of them, but my guess is it's the queen." She turned and spat onto the corpse, surprising Loethar. He wasn't sure whether she was disgusted by the Queen of Penraven or by the King of Barronel, or whether she'd actually intended to hit Vyk. Whichever it was, it was a gesture of genuine viciousness.

"Why would it be the queen? Too frightened of what I might do to her?" he asked.

She ignored his query. "If they've got any sense they've already gone on one of their sumptuous royal schooners."

"He's too proud to flee," Loethar replied.

"I agree. The Valisars are stoic—even those who marry into the family. She would not lose face by taking her life. Don't you see?" She gave a rueful shrug. "I suspect the Valisar courage in the face of certain destruction will inspire their people."

"We'll see how long that inspiration lasts when I have what I seek in my possession. Tell me why you think the queen is dead."

"Childbirth takes many victims," she said, her tone casual, disinterested.

"Childbir—?" he repeated, interrupting himself as the realization dawned. "Why didn't you tell me?" His tone was threatening.

"Sorry, did I fail to mention that the Penraven whore was spawning another brat? She is mother to the heir and also stepmother to a halfwit orphan she took pity upon. Now there is another who probably hasn't survived birth. For you there's only the eldest to worry about. I probably didn't consider it important."

"You surprise me, Valya. I allow you to be my eyes and ears because you're good at it but I expect you to tell me everything you learn. If you don't, your skills are of no use to me, no matter how cunning your mind. I really should punish you," Loethar said, his mind already racing.

"It doesn't change anything," she countered, still sounding confident.

"The news has ramifications."

"Not really. You plan to kill them all anyway, I assume."

"I don't have any plan at this point," he reprimanded, "other than to watch Penraven's famous walls be breached. Beyond that I shall wait and see."

"So, is this our new home?" she asked, trailing her hand across a highly polished marble surface, the top to an elegant piece of furniture that had probably served as the king's private dining table. "I rather like this—what an amazing color it is."

He forced his anger to cool. This was not the moment to lose his temper. "The famed Barronel marble from the deep earth quarries in its Vagero Hills."

"Stunning," she said absently, already moving to study the books in the small library the king had kept on hand in his suite. Vyk followed, hopping behind her.

"Yes, Barronel will be our base for the time being. Make yourself at home, Valya, but not in here," he cautioned.

"Why?" she asked, stopping her slow movement around the bookshelves.

"You are not a king."

"Neither are you," she said lazily, but added, before he could reply, "you are an emperor in the making. You'd better get used to such surrounds and lay your own mark against it. No more caves and tents for you, Loethar."

"And although you are used to the finer things in life, may I suggest that you discover them in another quarter of the palace."

"Where will you be? Perhaps I could—"

He cut her off. "I don't know where I'll be. I may travel to Penraven to get my first glimpse of the Valisar stronghold."

A knock at the door interrupted them. "Come," he said, tiredly, and a burly warrior, his face scarified and colored with inks, entered, dragging a terrified child behind him. The girl was barely more than twelve summertides and was dressed in royal finery but Loethar noticed that her gown was torn, her face stained with tears.

"Stracker said you asked for her, my lord," the man said gruffly in the language of the steppes.

"I have changed my mind. Give her back to the mother."

"Already dead."

Loethar sighed, irritated. "Then send the girl to her god as well. Do it immediately, no pain, make it swift."

"In here?" the man asked, surprised.

The girl began to wail, having caught sight of the headless body that remained of her father.

"No, not here," Loethar said slowly through gritted teeth. "Take her away and arrange for him to be removed as well." The man nodded. "And Vash, speak only in the language of the region now."

"Very good, my lord," he answered in perfect Set, exiting the room, dragging the screaming girl behind.

Valya wore a look of disgust. "Oh, Loethar, were you really planning to amuse yourself with a child? Have you no conscience?"

"About as much as you have," he replied.

She laughed and he heard the false tone she tried to hide. "None, then."

"Precisely. What I actually do and what I want my men to think I do is something entirely different."

"Because if what you're looking for is some companionship of the skin," she began flirtatiously.

He blinked with irritation. "I'm looking to sleep," he said, cutting her off again. "Close the door behind you. Tell no one to disturb me unless it's about who has died among the Valisar royalty. Otherwise I don't anticipate hearing from anyone, including you, for the next six hours."

Loethar didn't wait for her response, but turned and strode away into the former king's bedroom, Vyk swooping behind him.

Three

Corbel rode hard. He knew not just his survival but the survival of many depended on his making his destination. He was riding to a place he had never seen, following directions his father had made him repeat several times over until the legate was sure his son could reach the meeting point.

"Ride for your life, boy," his father had said, his voice gruff from the emotion he was controlling. Corbel had never seen his father cry and it seemed Regor De Vis had had no intention of allowing him to glimpse the depth of his sorrow at farewelling his child. Both knew they would never see each other again. "This will save Gavriel's life as much as your own," De Vis had added. In his father's eyes Corbel had seen the glitter of hope and for that alone he would ride to the curious coastal location and find the man they called Sergius.

"But how will I know him?" he had questioned.

"He will know you," the king had replied.

"And we trust him?"

His father had nodded. "Implicitly."

He had waited. Neither had added anything.

"You know this is madness, don't you?" Corbel had replied, keeping his voice steady. He was not prone to outbursts. He had wished Gavriel had been present to do the ranting.

"And now you must trust us," his father had added, so

reasonably that whatever objection Corbel had wanted to make had remained trapped in his throat.

"Magic?"

Brennus had looked at him sadly. "I envy you, Corbel."

"Really." In his fury—fury that no one but Gavriel might have noted—Corbel had wanted to demand of Brennus whether the king truly envied him the memory of killing a newborn child but his father must have guessed his son's thoughts and had glared at him. "Why don't you use it to escape, your highness?" Corbel had said instead.

The king had sighed. "What a surprise for the bastard warlord that would be. Go, Corbel. Nothing matters more than your safety now. Lo's speed."

"Father—"

"Go, son. We are as clueless to your future as you. But we trust that you will be safe and remember your task. It is something worth committing your life for. One day it might restore Penraven."

Corbel had begun to speak but his father held up his hand. "Not another word, Corb. I have always been proud of you and Gavriel. Make me proud now. Do as your king and your father ask."

Forbidden further protest, Corbel De Vis had bowed. And then Brennus and Regor De Vis had embraced him.

Now Corbel's mind felt liquid, spreading in all directions with nothing to hold it together but his aching skull and the determination to fulfil what had been asked of him, the burden heavy in his heart, its reality terrifying him.

He sped northwest, changing horses at Tomlyn, where a stablemaster was waiting for him, giving Corbel a small sack of food that Corbel ate in snatches without stopping. Once again he changed mounts, this time at Fairley, as instructed, in an identical experience.

Leaving Fairley village behind, Corbel swiftly began to follow the coastline. He rode hard, knowing only that a stone marker would tell him he had arrived. His eyes searched the side of the track, constantly roving ahead for the clue.

Daylight was fast dwindling. He wondered if he'd make it in time. Minutes later, in the distance he saw a man. Slowing the horse, he finally drew alongside the figure.

"Welcome, Corbel. I am told you are burdened with a heavy responsibility."

Breathing hard, Corbel nodded, said nothing.

"Ah, my eyesight is so poor that I see little but I see enough. Come, help me down the track."

"Track?" Corbel repeated.

The man chuckled. "You'll see it when you dismount. It leads to my humble dwelling. It's treacherous only for me; I imagine you'll find the descent relatively easy on your strong, young limbs."

Corbel swung off the horse and saw steps cunningly cut into the cliff face. He could see the hut and hoped they could get there before the wind became any more fierce. The sun was setting in a fierce blaze of pink on the horizon but it was not going to be a still night.

As though he heard his thoughts, Sergius yelled above the roar of the wind, "Storm tonight. Bodes well for what we have to do. I think we'll have some awakening."

"Is that a good thing?"

"Perfect. This sort of magic works best when the elements are stirring, roaring their power."

Corbel wondered if anyone was telling Gavriel about this. Mostly he wondered if he'd ever see his brother again.

"What about my horse?"

The man pointed. "It's going to be too fierce to leave it outside but your father took the precaution of leaving feed and water in that tiny barn—can you see it?" Corbel nodded. "Good, because I can't. It's a blur at that distance. Anyway, tie your horse up in there. Arrangements have been made to collect it."

"Give me a few moments," Corbel said, the wind whistling now around his ears. He guided the horse to the barn and secured her inside with a bag of fresh feed and a pail of sweet water. He hoped she would be collected soon. He wished he could rub her down but there was plenty of fresh hay that she would no doubt enjoy rolling around in anyway. And this was not the time to be fretting over a horse. He secured the door and trotted back to his host. "It's done," he said.

"Let's go," Sergius replied. "How pleasant to have someone to help me make that wretched trek back."

They moved in silence, concentrating on the descent.

"When?" he asked as they finally arrived at the door of the hut.

The man smiled. "Now. Come in; I need you to drink something."

"What?" Corbel asked, following Sergius into the hut.

"No questions, no time. This," Sergius said, reaching for a cup on the scrubbed table, bare but for a few sweet sea daisies in a jug, "will cast away your resistance."

Corbel frowned, looking inside at the contents. The liquid looked harmless and had no discernible smell.

"You must drink it all," Sergius urged.

"Only me?"

The man nodded. "I control my magic but I need you not to fight it. You look strong enough to do just that."

"I don't understand."

"This potion breaks resistance by making you compliant. Without it your body will instinctively fight the magic. We need you to go calmly."

"Where?"

"Into the sea."

"Are you mad?"

"Most people think so," the man replied, smiling kindly. "But that suits me."

"To drown," Corbel said flatly.

"Trust me."

"Trust magic, don't you mean?"

Sergius nodded, his expression filled with sympathy. "That too."

"Where am I going?" Corbel pressed again.

"In a way, you will choose, but whichever way you look at it, it's away from here."

"Sergius?"

"Yes?"

"I'm frightened."

The old man smiled softly, placing his warm, dry hand on Corbel's arm. "Don't be, son. What you are doing is heroic. What I suspect you have already done was extremely courageous, more brave than either your father or the king could have managed—and they are both men of valor. You are doing this for Penraven . . . for the Valisar crown. Drink, Corbel."

Mesmerized by the old man, oddly comforted by his lyrical voice and stirring words, Corbel drained the cup.

And as a bright, sharp awakening lit the night sky, Corbel De Vis walked into the sea, still burdened and filled with sorrow.

Brennus had just finished a rousing speech to his captains. The men had applauded him loudly off the makeshift podium and he could still hear their whistles and cheers. But no matter what he said or however much he had rallied their courage, even they sensed the cause was hopeless. He moved gloomily from the barracks; he had lied to the men and the only one who knew the truth of what was coming next was the man who strode in an angry silence alongside him.

Brennus broke into the awkward atmosphere between them. "There is no point in everyone dying, De Vis."

"Why do only you get to be the astoundingly brave one, your highness?" his legate replied and his sarcasm could not be disguised.

Brennus knew his friend was hurting deeply. Sending Corbel away in the manner they did, with little explanation and no sense of what it might lead to, was taking its toll on De Vis. "This is not about bravery—" he began.

"It is, sire. We are all men of Penraven and we all feel the same way as you do. Why do you think your men proudly cheered for you? They admire your courage, and it provokes their own. We do not cower to any enemy, least of all the barbarian of the steppes."

"He will kill everyone who puts up resistance."

"So we're already positive of failure?" De Vis asked, his tone still sarcastic. "What happened to the mighty Penraven spirit? And, that aside, let us not fool one another, highness. He will kill everyone anyway! We might as well all die feeling heroic, fighting for something we believe in. I have to be honest—with my wife dead, my sons . . ." He couldn't finish.

"What about that beautiful young thing whose hand has been offered. Are you going to ignore her?"

De Vis waved his hand as though the king's comment was meaningless. "Let's just say I have nothing I truly love to live for, other than to serve Valisar. I'm ready to die defending the crown."

"You always have been, Regor." Brennus shook his head angrily. "No, Loethar will not kill my people. I won't permit such pointless savagery."

"He *is* a savage!" De Vis spat, forgetting himself.

Brennus ignored the offense. "Listen to me, Regor. We know what he wants. We shall give it to him without a fight. But the terms are that he spares my people."

"He will not agree to such terms."

"You'll be surprised."

"How can you be so sure, your highness?"

"Trust me. He wants only one thing. And we know he is intelligent. What point is there to razing a city, killing all its inhabitants, when you want to be emperor? He needs people to rule. I'd rather Penravians answered to him until Leo is old enough to know his duty, to take action and avenge my death. This way at least there is hope for the Valisar resurrection."

"You truly believe Leo will claim back the realm?"

"De Vis, don't ask me such a question as though you yourself cannot believe in it! I have to hope. It's all I have left." He shook his head, still very much in a state of disbelief. "I killed a baby!" He didn't admit that he'd had someone else do it and De Vis did not remind him who would truly bear the burden of that murder. "My wife . . ." the king began, his voice leaden with grief.

"She does not know, highness. She will never know. Gavriel will keep the secret."

"And Corbel . . . the murderer? How will he live with himself with an innocent's blood on his hands? How can I? Corbel is as innocent as the child. The guilt is all mine."

De Vis grit his teeth. There was no time now for this indulgent self-recrimination, especially when the child involved was his. The truth was that he did not know how he would come to terms with allowing his son to be given the task and then, in the midst of the young man's fear and loathing, sending him away from everything familiar. "Corbel is gone, your highness. He is old enough to deal with his own demons. He will seek Lo's forgiveness in his own way."

"I've asked too much of your family, De Vis."

"We always have more to give, your highness."

Brennus stopped, took his friend's hand and laid it against his heart. "Let me do this alone, Regor," he pleaded, his voice thick with emotion.

De Vis shook his head sadly. "I cannot, your highness. I took an oath before your father as he lay dying. I intend to remain true to that promise and to my realm. Perhaps you're right. Perhaps it is now time to hand over all hope to our children. But we must make one final sacrifice in order to buy them time, give them that chance to avenge us."

The king finally nodded. "Then organize a parley. Make Loethar an offer he finds irresistible. Surely even the barbarians grow weary of battle."

"I shall send out a messenger."

"No need," Brennus said, smiling sadly in the torchlight. "He will already be here, watching us."

"What makes you say that?"

"He took Barronel. I don't imagine he could be this close to his prize and not search it out as fast as he could."

"Why has he not shown himself then, made demands?"

"Because he's savoring the moment, I imagine. I can feel him out there. He's watching, waiting, enjoying our fear."

"What do you want me to do, highness?"

"Ride out. He'll meet with you. I'll tell you what to say."

De Vis shocked the king by dropping to one knee. "Your majesty, I beg you. Those who chose to flee already have. They've had enough time to reach the coast. Others, well," he shrugged. "They've decided to remain, take their chances, and they already know not to take arms against him. He will not slaughter them. But he cannot take Brighthelm with such ease. If it falls, let it fall with honor, nobly fighting. I shall go and meet with him—if he is to be found outside the city stronghold—but rather than making offers let us listen first to his demand."

Brennus looked pained. "We already know what he wants, man! We can give it to him immediately and avert any further bloodshed."

"Your highness, humor me in this last request. Let me look our attacker in the eye. Let me fully understand what motivates him before I make any offer. If we are to die, let's do so in the full knowledge of his reasoning."

Brennus hesitated. He knew that De Vis's plan was flawed, for it would only prolong the agony of what they faced. It was the vision of Iselda clutching the baby daughter that prompted him to agree. Surrendering slightly later rather than now would give him a few more days with the woman he loved, a few more days to ease his deeply troubled soul . . . a few more days to make his peace with Lo.

"As you wish," he said, sighing softly.

De Vis kissed his king's ring. "Thank you, your majesty."

Four

Del Faren was in love. The object of this love was the daughter of the sculptor Sesaro, who had been commissioned no fewer than three times to produce a likeness in polished stone of King Brennus. Not even into his sixth decade and young for someone already of his stature, Sesaro's soaring career as one of the realm's most popular artisans had already been cut short by fear of war. He had been working on a new fountain, a vast piece that was to grace one of the new squares that the crown had commissioned be built. The city had sprawled way beyond its original boundaries and the central marketplace no longer offered ease of access for people. King Brennus, who prided himself on design, had made a bold decision to re-model the city. He had drawn up his ideas and a city architect had been appointed to oversee the grand project that would yield three main squares. The current central square would function solely as a meeting place for Penravians, while one of the new squares would become the political area of the city, where the realm's dignatories, councillors, and lords would meet for discussion and where formal ceremonies would take place on behalf of the crown. The other new square would be purpose-built for the new covered marketplace. Brennus's recent extended voyage and stay at the city of Percheron—as a guest of Zar Azal—had opened his eyes to the beauty of a bazaar. Although Penraven's market would hardly be filled with the aroma of

Percheron's mysterious spices, Brennus wanted to borrow the concept that people could do their marketing under cover and that permanent shops could be set up for the wealthier merchants. He was intrigued by the cunning use of wind-driven wooden sails in the Percherese bazaar, which brought fresh air through the covered alleyways and drove the stale air back outside. The coolness of its marble impressed him and more than anything his breath had been taken away by the souk's sheer beauty, and the idea that something so functional could still be a piece of art. He wanted to leave a similar legacy to what Azal's great-grandfather, Joreb, had begun, in ensuring that Percheron would be a place of singular beauty for its people as much as the visitor. Brennus hoped that Penraven and its capital of Brighthelm would be talked about as a city of bold beauty and although his city would not sparkle pale and pastel as Percheron did, he had hopes that it would be nonetheless dazzling in its use of the local multi-colored stone.

But all of these plans, including Sesaro's beloved fountain featuring the famous serpent of Valisar, had now been suddenly made irrelevant by the arrival of war. The threat had not arrested the soldier Faren's love for Tashi, however, and he still planned to ask for her hand in marriage, despite her protestations.

"Del, you are very sweet and very handsome but my father will want to give my hand to someone who can afford me the type of life that he wishes for his only daughter," she had explained gently, once again, only the previous evening. "And now with war all but upon us . . ."

"Don't speak of that, my love," Faren had beseeched. "Let us only focus on how much we love each other."

"I cannot deny that I have had feelings for you but we must be sensible. You are a foot soldier."

"An aspiring archer," he corrected.

She had nodded her acknowledgment as she continued. "Nevertheless, if I am to marry a military man my father would agree to nothing less than commander. I hear the legate needs a new wife," she had admitted, laughing coquettishly.

He had known in his heart that Sesaro would not be impressed by a mere archer, but he had remained undaunted, determined that he would win her, come what may. He had grabbed her around the waist and kissed her neck as she had tried to squirm away from his touch. "Bah, surely your father would want you to marry someone who is nineteen, not thirty years older? I will give you strong sons who will continue your father's art and my military career, and daughters as beautiful as their mother to take care of their grandfather in his dotage."

She had smiled at this. He had continued. "I have prospects, Tashi. I can be a major in a few years. Just watch me rise through the ranks with my courage and cunning." He had arched an eyebrow on the last word, laced his voice with a conspiratorial tone to amuse her, and pressed on. "We can have our own farm. I will ensure I'm based here in Brighthelm, we can—"

"Del, you are dreaming. The barbarian is on our doorstep. This is no time to talk of marriage or children, farms or futures. We have to worry about surviving tomorrow. I beg you, stop this."

"I shall speak to your father."

"No!"

"Why?"

"I have told you why. Now, please, you must leave. I have errands to run and you surely have somewhere to be, knowing what our realm faces." And she had pulled herself from his grip, clearly growing tired of the ardent kisses he had been peppering on her sweet-smelling neck.

"Tashi, I love you!" he had called to her retreating back.

And she had turned. "I know, but it's hopeless. You're a boy. My father wants me to marry a man. I cannot see you again."

What Tashi hadn't explained to her besotted young lover was that Sesaro had already promised her to another, and it was only by chance that Faren discovered the truth later in the day. His commander had taken him off his usual duties to help another unit that was working on the battlements. "Your archery skills are put to far better use up on top, Faren," the commander had said. "Tell Commander Jobe that I have sent you. We need keen eyes and steady hands up there."

Faren had leapt at the chance. If he acquitted himself well he could leapfrog perhaps even to captain, and that alone would prove to Tashi's family that he was worth taking note of. Arriving at the battlements, he had presented himself to Jobe, who had nodded his happiness to have another talented archer at his disposal. He had been told to meet the others and to choose a weapon that suited his preferred weight and bow tension.

Faren had been in the process of doing this when he overheard several of the men joking together.

". . . she's a beauty, ripe and ready," one of the men had said.

Another gave a low whistle. "She makes me feel weak whenever I glimpse her running through the market on her errands. The old man's already given his permission, even provided the ring. It was her mother's apparently so the lucky arse doesn't even have to buy that and let's face it he can afford anything he likes with who his friend is."

The first nodded. "I'd give my left nut for a night with her."

This had made the four men laugh and prompted a rush of lewd comments.

"Ssh, here comes the captain."

Faren had noticed a tall man walk up. "And what are you lot up to?"

"Just checking the tensions on the bows, sir."

Faren watched the captain's scowl soften. "Listen, I know this is a rough time for all of us so I don't mean to spoil what little time you have left for normal life. It's all about to change dramatically and I wish it wasn't so, but the legate's aiming to have a parley. We should know by tonight exactly what we're in for."

"Is he marrying her, then, captain, before the parley?" the first soldier had asked, cheekily.

"That's none of your business, Brek. What the legate does is his affair." The captain's mouth twitched at the corners. "But I think I would, war or not!"

This comment appeared to give the men permission to relax and they began to chuckle among themselves about how the "old man" would need to take horse pills to keep his new bride satisfied in the marital bed. The jesting had turned darker, one man commenting that he'd better hurry up and enjoy her delights because Loethar wouldn't spare him once the barbarian arrived.

Faren had only been half listening to the jesting when he heard one of the men mutter the name Sesaro. And then he heard the captain murmur "Tashi" and his attention was more than pricked—it had become riveted. The more he listened, the more his mood had plummeted from intrigued, to alarmed, to dismayed and finally to enraged. They were talking about his prospective wife; it was Tashi to whom they had been making bawdy reference. And if he was to believe their gossip, then Sesaro had promised Tashi to Legate De Vis. It couldn't be true!

"You, Faren! What are you staring at?" The captain shouted, noticing Faren's attention.

"Sir! Er, sorry, I was far away."

"Lo strike me, soldier, how can we rely on you to shoot straight if you aren't even focused on your bow?"

"Sorry, sir."

The captain had sighed. "It's all right, Faren. I think we're all a bit jumpy."

"I couldn't help overhearing, sir."

His superior's expression had turned sour. "Well, we shouldn't be discussing Legate De Vis's personal life."

"Do you mind my asking, though, sir, was this Tashi,

Sesaro's daughter? I know her but she hasn't mentioned anything about a betrothal to me."

"It's not my business to pass on private information, Archer Faren. You know that."

"I do sir, sorry sir, but Tashi is a friend and it might explain why she has seemed distant and worried," Faren had lied. "I thought she was fretting over the war—"

"And I don't doubt she is!" the captain cut in.

"Yes, sir, but I think from what the other men were saying that she's probably upset about the legate."

"And you think you can help, do you, Faren?"

Faren shrugged, his rage burning but tightly disguised. "I can try. We grew up together, you see, so she trusts me."

"There's really nothing you can do, Faren. You misunderstand. The reluctance is not on the part of Sesaro's daughter. Her hand is already given. She is—from what I can gather—the enthusiastic partner to this potential marriage. It's Legate De Vis who hesitates, so unless you have the ear of the legate and can advise him in his love life, I would suggest you get back to tightening that bow and worrying about landing real arrows into the hearts of our enemy rather than make-believe ones into those of lovers."

So it was true. As the captain left him with a friendly squeeze to his arm, Faren had bristled with fury. That was why Tashi had cooled off toward him these past few weeks; she had only been playing with him, teasing him and enjoying his attention, his gifts, his youth. She'd hinted as much earlier today. He had to see her again; hear it from her lips, watch her head hang with shame as she explained herself.

"Sir?"

"You again, Faren?"

"The wax is a bit dry. I think I shall need a fresh pot from the stores."

"You don't need my permission," the captain had said, his tone brisk and slightly annoyed.

"Thank you, sir," Faren said, hurrying toward the stairs.

"Why they send up the dungeon boys I don't know," the

captain murmured under his breath. "I think they get overawed, shooting their bows up this high."

"They'll be the death of us, right, captain?" someone had quipped and everyone who heard it grinned, including Faren. But Faren's had been the grim smile of the executioner.

The day had passed in a strange string of hours for Gavriel, linking weapons practice, a brief ride around the castle park, and kicking around leather stretched over a ball framework of the dried, highly flexible asprey reeds that held an inflated, waxed sheep's bladder. This more frenzied activity had been punctuated by various meals, a visit to the chapel to say a prayer and light another candle for the dead princess and a meeting with the royal tutors who apologized that studies had been cancelled until further notice. All of this was highly unusual for Gavriel, of course, but for the prince much of it was a normal day's proceedings, without the dreaded letters, numbers, and language. After the main meal of their day, which they had shared alone in Leo's chambers, and as dusk gave way to twilight, Gavriel saw to it that the prince cleaned himself up, changed into fresh clothes and was presented neat and tidy to the queen. It had been an hour, probably more, since Gavriel had delivered the boy to the hollow, all-knowing aide known simply as Freath who greeted them at the entrance to Queen Iselda's suite.

"Good evening, majesty," he had said in his slow baritone. He glanced toward Gavriel, his gaze sliding quickly away.

Young though he was, Leo was a perceptive child and missed little. "Hello, Freath. I now have a full-time minder. This is Gavriel De Vis—I think you know his father."

"Indeed, I do," the man had said, not offering a hand. "You may wait outside for Prince Leonel," he said to Gavriel, who sensed the prince wince at the use of his full name.

As far as Gavriel knew, everyone disliked Freath, including Gavriel's father, who was arguably the most generous person he knew. Seemingly ghostlike, the servant had been at the palace for a long time and never seemed to change his intimidating demeanor. Why the queen tolerated him was a mystery but he had been her right hand since Brennus had made Iselda his bride, fifteen years previous.

Leo had been swallowed up into the doorway that Freath now blocked so Gavriel could do little more than snatch a glimpse inside but he smelled the waft of perfume, and spied soft colors and flower arrangements. The door was closed by Genrie as she emerged from the queen's chambers.

"You again," she said.

Gavriel saw no smirk, heard no disdain in her tone, but even so the greeting was hardly friendly. "Yes. Consider me Prince Leo's shadow."

She regarded him, saying nothing and Gavriel felt his throat go dry. She really was very pretty. "Is that what you always aspired to be, Master De Vis? A nurserymaid to Prince Leonel?"

Gavriel adopted one of Corbel's famous expressionless stares, refusing to be baited. "Firstly, he's almost thirteen and needing to mature fast considering the situation we find ourselves in. Secondly, Lo willing he's our next king and the more palace people who treat him as a potential ruler and not a child, the better."

"And you believe that the crown prince will make it to the throne?" Again, she spoke evenly, no derision in her tone at all. And yet somehow it still sounded like a rhetorical question.

He answered it anyway. "I do. One day."

She considered him with interest, a hand on her hip. "And the marauder they call Loethar can—"

"Kiss my arse," Gavriel finished for her. He grinned and was delighted to win a smile from her.

She nodded. "I hope your humor keeps you safe."

"Marry me, Genrie," he teased, moving quickly to stand by her, even daring to circle her waist. "And we can run away from war and—"

"Raise the crown prince together, I suppose?"

Gavriel laughed.

"You're not much older than he is," she said, a trace of condescension in her voice.

"I'm seventeen summertides," he protested, feigning indignation. "More than enough."

"Not for me, Master De Vis," she replied, not unkindly. Untangling herself, she made to move away. "It takes more than bravado to impress this servant," she added.

"Like what? Oh come on, Genrie. May I kiss you—not here, admittedly, although if you insist—"

"I like older men, Master De Vis," she cut him off.

He made a face of disgust. "Like Master Freath, perhaps. Skin like parchment, teeth in decay, that hunched back."

Her amusement vanished. "He's none of those things. I'd hazard that he's barely a few years older than our king."

"I was jesting, Genrie. But don't be fooled by Freath. He strikes me as slippery, and I don't trust him. Be careful."

Genrie's gaze narrowed. "I have no reason to mistrust the queen's aide, Master De Vis."

"Just be warned. Now how about that kiss?"

Genrie flashed a brief smile, which was gone in a blink. Suddenly she was back to her briskly efficient self. "Good day, Master De Vis. In case you were wondering, there are no access points into or out of the queen's chambers other than this one. Prince Leonel is safe."

Gavriel nodded. "For now perhaps," he replied sadly, settling back to wait.

Leo finally emerged from his mother's suite. His once almost white infant hair had darkened to a deep golden and the soft sprinkling of freckles had been lost beneath the browning of the sun. Gavriel felt sorry that the young prince needed to grow up much faster than even a royal normally would if he was to survive.

Leo looked grave; all the former bravado and humor had fled.

"How is she?" Gavriel asked, pushing away from the wall against which he'd been leaning.

"Miserable. Lost, I think."

"Is she coming to your sister's funeral?"

Leo shook his head. "Mother said she died without her help and hardly needs her now. Is that cruel, do you think?"

"No, Leo, that's grief. You'll learn all about this in years to come," Gavriel said, feeling far too wise for his years all of a sudden. But then he'd learned enough about grief through his father, who had never stopped mourning Eril, their mother. He could counsel with genuine wisdom on how grief hardens someone, as it had hardened Regor de Vis. "Come on, I'll take you up to the roof. It might be a while before we can do that again and then you can have some supper."

"Gav, when the time comes that you keep speaking about, what is the plan?"

Gavriel looked around, ensuring they could not be overheard. "We escape through the kitchens and the cellars. My father has worked out our route. We take nothing, Leo, remember that. Just the small sack you've already assembled."

"It's just that when that time comes it probably means my father will be dead." He said it so flatly and it sounded so raw that Gavriel could do little other than to take a breath. Leo continued, unaware of his keeper's discomfort. "And if father is dead that means only one thing."

"What's that?"

"I am king," he replied, his large blue eyes looking up at Gavriel intently.

"Yes, but—"

"And a king does not run from his own palace."

"Leo, you know we cannot risk you," Gavriel said, feeling flustered. He ran his hand through his long hair. "There isn't a good time to discuss what might happen should your father die but you have raised the issue so let's talk about it now."

"Should father die, I would be King of Penraven," the prince reiterated. "That means you will do as I say, rather than the other way around," he added. There was nothing overbearing in what he said even though the words sounded high-handed, and yet Gavriel felt a fresh chill of worry creep through him.

"But while your father is alive we all have to do as *he* says—and he has instructed that no matter what you say or do, I am to get you away from here once the fighting begins."

"But listen, Gav—"

"Leo, if we leave it too late, then they will kill you too. Do you understand this?"

The prince nodded solemnly.

"We cannot risk that the entire Valisar line is ended. You *have* to accept this. I know it's hard and I know you want to be brave and be like your father and stay. I know you don't want to leave your mother either but you are portable, almost invisible. They are not. I will carry you on my back if I have to but I know I can get you away, no one else. This is what everything is about—it's about saving your life, protecting the line."

"And you would give up your life for it?"

"If I have to, yes. That's what honor is about; it's what loyalty is and it's the responsibility that comes with being one of the king's nobles . . ." He could see he was losing the boy's attention with the rhetoric but he was thinking aloud for his own benefit now. He didn't want to die. He certainly didn't want his father to lay down his life so easily. And he definitely didn't feel as brave as Corbel seemed to think he could be. The truth of it was that Gavriel was feeling sad. That was it. It hit him hard and he took a deep breath, only realizing minutes later that the prince was shaking him.

"Sorry, highness."

"Leo," the prince corrected. "What's wrong?"

"Just thinking. Nothing important," Gavriel lied bleakly.

Five

That evening, up on the battlements, standing briefly alongside his father while the prince was kept well out of sight admiring the weapons and talking to some of the soldiers, Gavriel watched with a sense of doom as a rider approached the main gate. He wore the insignia of Barronel but carried no weapon and yelled to the gatekeeper that he was one of the captains from the Barronel Guard. He looked so bedraggled that it was little wonder he drew only jeers from onlookers. But he persisted, until Gavriel heard his father say to one of his own captains that someone should see what he had to say. One of the archers listening nearby, spoke up hesitantly.

"Er, sir?"

"Yes," the legate said brusquely, annoyed by the interruption.

"I think I know that man."

"You do?"

The archer nodded. "I think he is my brother-in-law."

"What?"

"Sir, I, er, I think he's married to my eldest sister. She left to live in Barronel a decade ago. I've only met him twice but I think it's him."

"It's dark, man. How can you be sure?"

"His horse, sir," the archer said. "It's a cantankerous brute. I recognize it by that white flame on its forelock and the splash of white at its right ankle. It was always an odd-looking beast."

"You're sure now?"

The archer shrugged. "I believe it's him."

"Captain, send this man to see what the rider has to say. It will be easier if relatives speak, rather than sending a stranger. Well done, soldier. Your name?"

"Del Faren, Legate De Vis."

De Vis nodded. "I won't forget that name. Take precaution. They're obviously using your relative as a messenger; they must be frightened we'll attack one of their own. Find out what the barbarian wants."

"Sir," the archer said. "Ah, may I give him a note for my sister?"

"You can write?"

The archer nodded. "A little, sir."

"You have one minute to scrawl something and then I want to see you out there and finding out more from him."

The man nodded again, bowed and Gavriel was sure he must have imagined that the archer scowled at the legate as he pushed past.

The expectant hush that had fallen across the city over the past few days had infected the palace as well. Gavriel was sure that even from this height if he listened hard enough he could probably pick up the creaking of the rider's saddle. A lot of people had fled the city but the majority had remained, trusting in their army's strength, the impregnability of Brighthelm and their king's ability to achieve a settlement. Gavriel reckoned many of them believed that Brennus had disguised his magical ability to coerce others but that he would now unleash it to negotiate a peaceful retreat of the barbarians. The De Vis family knew better.

"Taking a long time," the legate muttered to the captain nearby.

"Probably the note, sir," the man answered candidly. "Or he's scared."

"He didn't seem scared when he volunteered."

"He's out, father," Gavriel offered and the conversation was forgotten as everyone leaned over to watch Del Faren approach the rider. The population on the battlements became so still and silent they could just catch the murmur of the two men.

"Not very friendly are they, considering they're family," De Vis commented.

The captain shrugged. "Perhaps his sister has been killed in the fighting."

De Vis ignored the response, turning back instead to see the rider hand Faren a note in return which Faren pocketed.

Gavriel thought the spectacle was done with, and had just raised his hand to the rider who gazed up at them forlornly when a sound whistled out of the nearby woodland. In the blink of an eye the tip of an arrow had punctured straight through the rider's heart and out between his ribcage. As the rider slumped forward, revealing the stub of the arrow's shaft protruding from his back, the horse obediently answered a whistle, turning to canter back into the shadows of the trees.

"Bastards!" De Vis growled. "Get that archer before me, *now*!" he ordered. "In the garret." He turned to his son. "Get the prince and follow me. And someone fetch the king!" Runners took off in various directions.

In the quiet of the garret, De Vis addressed his son and the prince alone. "Your highness. Gavriel. I suspect the moment for your escape approaches. Do you understand, both of you?"

Gavriel glanced at the youngster. "Yes, father. Leo, er, the prince and I have discussed it. I know what is expected of me."

"Don't even look back, son," De Vis replied, his voice suddenly tender. "All our hopes are riding on your shoulders and the courage of Prince Leo."

A man appeared at the door. "Tell him to wait until the king arrives," De Vis called, returning his attention to the pair of youngsters. "All right, then. My prince, your father has been summoned and I'm sorry but this will be your best opportunity to say farewell to him before I ask Gavriel to remove you from here. The secret of your escape will be known only to myself and the king. Your whereabouts I take with me to my grave."

"Don't, father—" Gavriel began but was silenced by a fierce glance from the older man.

"No pretense now. We know what we face. We each have our duty. Don't let our deaths be in vain." He cleared his throat of the emotion that had begun to sound in his voice as the king arrived.

"I heard we've had a rider," Brennus said, striding into the garret and bringing the smell of the queen's perfume in with him. Gavriel inhaled it as though taking in the essence of life. When would he smell something so beautiful again? He glanced at Leo and could imagine the boy thinking much the same and perhaps silently fretting over his mother.

"Your majesty," De Vis, began, "a rider has delivered a note to us."

Gavriel watched Brennus's expression darken.

"Terms, you think?" he asked.

De Vis shook his head. "Where is Faren?"

The archer was almost manhandled in.

"Well, show us, then!" the king ordered, more ferociously than perhaps he intended. Faren flinched.

It was De Vis who snatched the note and read it. "Well, it seems Loethar has perfect command of our written language. Or he had someone write this for him—perhaps the poor sod recently slain. Either way, majesty, he requests that you meet him for a parley."

The king looked surprised. "But this is what we want."

"I can't allow you to take him up on the offer, your highness. I will go in your stead. I agree it's important we meet but we cannot risk you."

Brennus nodded. "Has he said when, where?"

De Vis handed the note to the king. "He is bold. He is happy to meet in front of Brighthelm, in full view of Penraven but obviously out of range of archers."

"Doesn't trust us?" Brennus said, his tone laden with sarcasm.

De Vis gave a grim smile. "Seems not."

"It says here he will meet at the sound of a bell. His, I presume?"

De Vis shrugged. "I'll be ready." He turned to Faren. "You may go."

Once again Gavriel saw the man glare defiantly at his father, although Legate De Vis hardly noticed the archer's expression. "Thank you, sir."

"One more thing."

"Yes, legate."

"How is your sister?"

Faren shrugged, slightly embarrassed. "He wasn't my brother-in-law, sir. The horse wasn't the one I thought it was once I got up close."

"I wouldn't think your brother-in-law would have a horse that answers to the whistle of our enemy."

"No, sir."

"But if it wasn't your family why did you give him the note?"

"He said he would find my sister for me if he could."

"I see. And are you aware the man was shot in the back by our not so gallant enemy?"

"I am, sir, yes. Shocking."

De Vis studied the archer. "I trust nothing incriminating or dangerous was in that note, Faren?"

The archer looked deeply affronted. "Why would I do such a thing?" he demanded, adding "sir" as an afterthought. "He got killed after I'd given it to him, sir. It was too late to worry about it then."

Gavriel couldn't help but mistrust the man. There was something cunning lurking behind that innocent expression, something directed at his father that he couldn't for the life of him work out.

"All right, Faren. Back to your post."

The man bowed to his king, banged his fist against his heart to the legate and departed.

"Something's amiss there, father," Gavriel said, unable to stop himself.

"Yes, I noticed. All the more reason for you to take your leave. Your majesty, I have instructed Gavriel to put the plan into action. The prince and he should leave immediately."

"Yes, yes of course," Brennus agreed.

The Valisar king turned to his son. "Come here, Leo, my boy. We must now say goodbye, you and I."

Gavriel was as unhappy as Leo was to be hurrying down the stone steps away from where all the action was about to take place. The farewell between both pairs of fathers and sons had been stilted as each individual did his best to quell his emotion. Gavriel felt the goodbye as a pain at the back of his throat, as though grief had taken a form and now resided as a diseased lump . . . a cancer.

"Gav, we have to watch what happens," Leo suddenly said, stopping short. "If we leave right now we'll have no idea what has occurred, and therefore what are the best decisions to make once we're on the run."

The prince was right. Gavriel bit his lip as he thought it through. "I was going to give you time to speak with your mother."

"When I hugged her tonight I already felt like I'd said goodbye. She was so sad. I don't want to see her crying like that again . . . unless we can take her with—"

"We can't," Gavriel interrupted. "I'm sorry, Leo."

The prince's lips thinned. "But you agree we need to know what's happening, don't you?"

"Yes. I'm thinking we can see it from the spare watchtower."

"The one with the broken hinge on the door, you mean?"

Gavriel nodded. "No one uses it but we can probably get a

reasonable view of what's happening. We'll also be out of everyone's way."

"Come on!" Leo said, bounding up the rest of the flight of stairs.

They encountered no one of note on their way; a few servants passed, rushing about their business, but they hardly glanced in the boys' direction. Until of course they ran into Genrie.

"Majesty, Master De Vis," the servant said, striding in her usual manner, arms laden with heavy linen. She curtsied to the prince as she stopped.

"Genrie," Gavriel said as they approached. Leo said nothing but Gavriel could all but see smoke erupting from his ears at the delay. "Need help?" he offered.

"I can manage, thank you," she replied. "Where are you hurrying to?" She cast a stern glance toward the prince but she addressed Gavriel. He wished she hadn't done either.

"Actually, none of your business," Leo replied.

"Well, can I let someone know you are in this part of the palace, your majesty?" It was offered sincerely, no hint of curiosity in her voice. Gavriel believed she was genuinely being polite.

"Why?" Leo asked.

She was undeterred by his uncharacteristically brusque manner. "This area is mainly storage. I just thought—"

"Don't think, please, Genrie, not on my behalf anyway," Leo said and Gavriel frowned as the prince moved on. He threw a glance of apology toward Genrie but she appeared unimpressed by his politeness or by the prince's rudeness. She'd already turned her back on him.

Once inside, Gavriel pushed the door closed quietly. "Why are you so determined to be rude to Genrie?"

"I told you. She dislikes me and it's obvious. And that's fine, I don't care. But I don't appreciate her snoopy ways. She's far too interested in my life, always giving me looks of disapproval."

Gavriel sighed and when Leo pointed toward a candle, he

shook his head. "No flame. We'd light up like a beacon from outside and I just know my father will know who it is."

"Mine too," Leo said, conspiratorially. "Have we missed much?"

"Nothing as far as I can tell. If you stand on that old crate, you'll see better," Gavriel said, pointing. "That window will give you a good view."

Leo did as suggested and a silence fell over them both as they spotted Legate De Vis guiding his horse slowly out from beneath the great gates of Brighthelm. He held himself proudly erect and Gavriel noted that his father had shown immense faith in the barbarian leader's request for parley, taking himself unarmed toward the enemy.

Leo seemed to read his thoughts. "Your father is not wearing his sword or any armor," he said, awe in his voice.

"It's a peaceful discussion," Gavriel said, although the callous death of the Barronel rider suggested it was anything but that.

"A peaceful discussion?" The prince scowled. "Before we all start trying to kill each other, that is."

"There's Loethar," Gavriel said, pressing forward, squinting as he saw a shadow move against the line of trees.

"Does he really think he's out of range of our archers?"

"No. He knows he's not. He won't take any chances. They'll talk, that's all."

"I wish I could hear their conversation."

Gavriel nodded silently in the dark of their tower. The torch his father carried threw a bright glow around the parley spot, which was well past the halfway mark between the castle and the woodland. Once again he felt a surge of love for his father's bravery. Loethar moved his horse forward into that circle of light now and Gavriel held his breath, certain that every other person watching—especially the king—did the same.

Initially both men sat seemingly relaxed in their saddles, leaning slightly toward each other. But the language of their bodies quickly changed when the barbarian stiffened. Alarm pulsed through Gavriel as he saw his father open his arms at his side, in a strange gesture that echoed of an attempt to convey innocence. And then, suddenly, the marauder reached behind his back and lifted a mean-looking blade clear of a hidden scabbard. It was a fluid movement, clearly one he had performed countless times previously and Loethar didn't break speed or rhythm as he brought the blade down onto the legate's head with all of his body's force, cleaving a grisly path that ended midway through the soldier's neck.

Gavriel let out a sound of anguish and then his stomach heaved at the momentary glimpse of one side of his father's head falling away before his body slumped unnaturally sideways. The legate's horse started at the unnatural movement, turning a frantic circle before dashing off toward the trees. Gavriel could see little other than what the moon and the torch—now smoldering in the grass—could highlight, but the vague shapes told him that his father had fallen to the ground. The legate's foot was still stuck in the stirrup and although it was bent at an unnatural angle, it clung doggedly and his body was being dragged behind the now panicked horse.

Loethar was yelling from somewhere in the dark. Gavriel could no longer make out his shape but his voice carried through the still, suddenly unnaturally silent night.

"I demanded to see you, Brennus, not your lackey! And now that you have insulted me, not even paid me the due respect, I will slaughter every member of your family and one member from every family who lives in Penraven. Do not let it be said that I am not a magnanimous emperor of the Set for I shall let them choose who dies. But there will be no mercy for the Valisars." He spat, turned his horse and rode for the trees, long before the first archer could refocus sufficiently to unleash a single arrow into the darkness.

Gavriel stood unsteadily, swallowing back the desire to vomit, to scream, to hurt Loethar. Breathing shallowly he gasped, "Leo, we go now."

"Gavriel," an equally shocked prince began.

"Now!" Gavriel yelled into Leo's face and the youngster fled toward the door.

And then they were running.

With the trees to shield them Loethar stood with Stracker at the head of the two units he'd ordered to follow him to Penraven. It had not been his intention to try and take Brighthelm this night but golden opportunities rarely flagged their arrival in advance. And today a particularly precious one presented itself to him via a curious note that had been given to the Barronel prisoner. The Barronel prisoner they had made use of had been swiftly despatched in front of the Penravian audience but the horse had brought his body back and with it a note from a disgruntled soldier called Del Faren. Faren had curiously offered to open the eastern side gate. In return he requested they slaughter Legate De Vis publicly.

"Do you think it's a trick?" Stracker mused, watching lights being extinguished all over Brighthelm as the king ordered its shut down.

Loethar didn't answer immediately, stroking Vyk's large head instead while he considered the situation. He too watched candlelight and torches winking out all over the massive castle, which had been so brightly illuminated for their arrival. A show of power, no doubt. He smiled in the dark. It seemed Brennus had been expecting him but if Valya's information was correct, Brennus and De Vis were blood brothers. The king would not have expected the death of his legate and close friend.

"No," he said finally. "Faren, I suspect, is a traitor."

"Having the head of the army slaughtered is certainly a daring move. He must trust you to be a man of your word."

Loethar shrugged. "De Vis is expendable. It was no hardship to me."

"So you think we can trust this Faren?"

"I trust no one. But I think he will be shocked that we took him at his word and did as he requested in killing De Vis. He'll have little choice now about opening the gate for he knows I can tell the king who betrayed him. I imagine this is a man with a grudge and that desire for revenge has now been answered. A weak man—as he obviously is—will feel compelled to obey the plan, lacking in courage or imagination to do otherwise."

"So we go?"

Loethar nodded. "We only have one chance at this. If we send a scouting party, they may well get in but that won't be enough of us to take the castle." He scratched at his beard, the trinkets of silver that pierced his skin making a soft jangle as he did so. "We all go."

There was no time to pick up anything and Gavriel was grateful that he was already wearing his sword and dagger. As they neared the kitchens, he realized he was running so hard he was almost on top of the prince. As they burst through into the main preparation area, their arrival scattered pots and pans loudly. But instead of seeing Cook Faisal and his team, Gavriel found himself staring at the person he least expected to see in the kitchens.

"Master Freath," he said, stunned.

"Your highness," Freath acknowledged first, before inclining his head ever so briefly at Gavriel. "Master De Vis."

"Why are you here?" Gavriel demanded.

The man looked down his aquiline nose at him. "I wasn't aware I needed your permission."

"Where is everyone?" Gavriel replied, ignoring the reprimand, looking around uncertainly. *Was this a trap too?*

"I imagine you can work that out yourself, Master De Vis. There seems to be quite a show going on out there."

"How dare you, you bastard!"

"Gavriel!" The prince slid away from his champion and stood between the two men. "Be calm," he warned, sounding almost like his father. "Master Freath, where is Cook?"

Freath nodded once politely at the boy's manners. "I have dismissed most of the kitchen staff upon the queen's orders. In fact many staff are dismissed. I think you misunderstood me earlier, Master De Vis. Loethar and his men have already breached Brighthelm. Word has come down from the battlements from King Brennus himself that we have been betrayed by one of our own. Someone opened a side gate, and too many of the barbarian horde breached Brighthelm, I gather, before we realized we had a traitor in our midst."

"Faren," Gavriel murmured.

"I wouldn't know. None but the key staff is required to do anything other than return to their families. We no longer have any stronghold. Our soldiers are now fighting for their lives."

Gavriel felt his insides twist with fear. Brighthelm breached! He thought it would be weeks, possibly months of siege before the Valisar stronghold showed any signs of weakening. And he had held to the hope that Loethar would tire of the endless waiting, that a peace could be negotiated. The vision lingered of his father's shape being dragged behind a horse, his head in halves. "And you, Master Freath? Why do you remain?" Gavriel asked rudely.

Gavriel knew that the Valisar family liked Freath but the manservant worked primarily for the queen and none of the De Vis family came into contact with him much. Gavriel had never fully warmed to the wintry, somehow superior, expression Freath wore most of the time. If he were honest, on the occasions he did come into contact with him, he found the man's acute intellect unnerving.

"I have no family, Master De Vis. The palace is my home, the royals are the people closest to me in the world."

"Indeed. Did the king tell you anything else?"

"That I was to await your arrival and give you a message."

Leo stepped forward. "What is it, Master Freath? Does he wish me to go to my mother?"

"No, your highness. His message was rather cryptic. He wishes you to follow the plan, but not to leave as originally arranged. He believes the marauding barbarian to be far more cunning than we have given him credit for. We already know from his recent action against the legate that he has no honor whatsoever." Gavriel bristled. "Master de Vis, forgive me if I sound insensitive. The fact is your father is dead and nothing can be done to change that. Couple this with the fact that time is of the essence and you have a situation in which my words sound harsh . . . cruel, even."

Gavriel clenched his jaw, unmoved by the hollow apology. "What are the king's instructions for our crown prince, Freath?"

The queen's aide straightened. "He suspects we are already surrounded. You cannot hear it down here but the fighting is fierce. Do not set foot out of Brighthelm."

"Did he tell you what we should do?" Leo asked, aghast.

Freath shook his head, his expression grim. "I'm sorry, your highness," he said, looking only at Leo. "He seemed to think that you alone would know."

Leo turned to Gavriel. "Let's go."

"Where?" Gavriel asked, feeling helpless. He ran a hand through his hair, glowering at Freath. "You'd better return to her highness."

"Oh, I intend to, Master De Vis, now that I've fulfilled this errand. Your highness," he bowed low, "may Lo light your path and keep you safe." At Gavriel he simply nodded as he pushed past them. Gavriel mumbled a curse under his breath at the aide's tall, narrow frame.

"Come on!" Leo urged. "We have to go back into the castle."

"You know if we do that we'll be trapped. There's nowhere to hide indefinitely."

Leo frowned. "There is a way out—it's risky, a bit dangerous, too, but we have no other choice."

It didn't sound very encouraging but Gavriel had nothing else to offer. He ran out after the youngster and behind him heard the main kitchen door smash open.

Gavriel felt a surge of panic break through the stupor he had begun to drift into. "Run!" he growled.

Six

Loethar felt a pulse running through his body that he could liken only to the flashes of awakening that the sky experienced from time to time during a storm. Although he showed little in his expression, he was elated to finally have his prize in front of him: the King of Penraven, 8th of the arrogant, powerful Valisars that had ruled the region and virtually controlled the Set for centuries. He smiled at Vyk, who was awkwardly hopping around the king.

"Hurry up, Loethar," Brennus said testily, as though bored with a game. He ignored the raven that now flew to sit on the barbarian's shoulder.

Loethar certainly admired the man's composure. It was true, he was prolonging this, savoring the moment he'd dreamed about from angry childhood into bitter adulthood. "Forgive my amusement. I expected someone tall and imposing. Instead, here you stand, not so far off my own age I'm guessing, of unimpressive height, with no distinctive features."

Brennus returned the marauder's stare with defiance but also bafflement. "Let's get on with it, shall we?"

"Are you so tired of life, Brennus?"

"I'm tired of you," the king replied and his tone was caustic.

"Yes, I'd noticed. But that's another secret isn't it?"

Brennus sighed, sounding bored. "You have visions of empire and yet you are not honorable enough to lead anything more than the pack of rats you call your people. We think of them as vermin. Don't get too comfortable, barbarian. Someone, somewhere, sometime will deal with you."

"One of your own perhaps?" Loethar asked, enjoying the conversation.

"Who knows? I'd like to think so. I'd like to go to my god imagining a Valisar blade cutting through your head in the same way that you brutalized a good man just an hour ago. A man who did not deserve such an ignoble end."

"Your soulmate's blood is on your hands, Brennus, not mine. If you had not insulted me he would not have had to die in the manner you describe. Your lack of courage killed him." He was amused to watch the king's face redden with rage. It was obvious Brennus did not lack for courage but it was fun to bait him all the same.

"You're too good for beheading, barbarian. The Set will yield someone who will find a way to give you a death that you justly deserve."

"So you keep threatening, Brennus. I will not be quaking in my boots and looking over my shoulder, that's a promise."

"At your own peril, then, barbarian."

Loethar laughed. "You know what I've come for, Brennus."

"A wasted journey. I don't possess what I assume you are referring to."

"The Enchantment is what I chase. With it I shall control the Set without so much as a squeak of trouble from its people. After I've finished with them they will be none the wiser that they ever had separate realms or royals. I will be their ruler, judge, jury and executioner."

"You are delusional, barbarian. I have nothing of what you seek and if I did I would die before I allowed you to use it. Surely if I had any power I would have used it against you already."

"Perhaps I am unreceptive?" Loethar suggested.

Brennus smirked.

"Well, at least you concur that such a power exists."

"If it does I have no knowledge of it. You are chasing an unreachable dream. None of the people of the Set will ever give you loyalty. They will bow to your supremacy, right now, I'm sure of it, but they will hatch plans around you. You are already a dead man. It is simply a matter of time."

The king's threat smacked of truth. Loethar's eyes narrowed. "Bring me the queen." He watched all the bravado that had fueled the king's fighting speech instantly dissipate from Brennus's eyes; although the king said nothing, his expression betrayed him as he warily looked to the doorway of the salon where he had been brought.

Loethar continued conversationally. "This is a magnificent chamber, Brennus. I applaud your realm's artistic skills." The king ignored him, his eyes searching the doorway. "I thought Barronel had enviable style but I'd hazard Penraven has everything a barbarian tyrant could possibly want. I'm going to enjoy making this my seat of power."

He watched Brennus fight to find anything to say and then lose the battle, his shoulders slumping as Iselda was escorted in, her hand tightly holding that of Piven, who was skipping at her side, heedless of the tense atmosphere.

"Iselda," Loethar said, deliberately dropping all formality. "The descriptions of your beauty do not do you credit."

The queen had eyes only for Brennus. She said nothing to Loethar. Vyk's interest had turned to Piven; the bird swooped down to the boy's head, hopping onto his outstretched arm. The boy seemed mesmerized by the great bird.

"And this I imagine is the freak adopted son," Loethar continued.

Iselda's jaw tightened. "Call your filthy vermin off!" she said, flapping at Vyk, who swooped away, landing not far from the child. "This is Piven. He is a simpleton, yes. He is also harmless and deserves none of your attention."

As if on cue, Piven broke from her grip and ran toward Loethar, leaping onto the man's legs. Loethar, taken by surprise, was astonished that he managed to catch the child.

He laughed as he lifted him into his arms. "Now you see, Brennus, if only all your people were cretinous like your son here, we could all be friends." He put Piven down but the boy continued holding his hand, smiling angelically. "I'm going to enjoy killing you in front of him."

Loethar believed it was likely the presence of the innocent child that finally broke the king's spirit. Without warning Brennus lunged toward one of the barbarian's guards and grabbed a dagger. Plunging it into his own neck, he ripped it angrily across his throat, a guttural noise directed at his queen accompanying his final act.

Loethar was upon him in a moment, ignoring the queen's shrieks. Piven, too, moved to the king's side, dipping his fingers into his father's blood as it spurted impressively from the king's neck. The boy grinned vacantly toward his mother and back again at Loethar. Loethar stared down upon the dying king, angry that he had not suspected Brennus was capable of this.

"Your days are already numbered," the king groaned defiantly, his eyes closing as death claimed him.

Loethar roared his anger and ripped his sword from its scabbard. With a howl of fresh ferocity he brought the blade down to sever the king's head from his neck. The queen swooned but she clung nevertheless to one of her enemy minders, clearly determined to remain upright and strong in the face of such barbarity. She did, however, close her eyes as Loethar reached for Brennus's head.

Holding it by the king's wavy, ever so slightly silvered hair, he handed the head to Piven, who couldn't hold it but dragged it over to his mother with a curious look of wonder on his face. Her husband's royal blood streaked the bottom of Iselda's pale gown as Piven tried proudly but failed to lift the head.

Loethar turned to Stracker and murmured, "You know what to do."

Stracker nodded and left the chamber.

Loethar returned his attention to the struggling queen. She was pale and trembling, and seemingly too shocked to weep, but she impressed him all the same with her dignity.

"You'll have a chance to farewell your husband properly, your highness," Loethar said. "I will see you in a few hours. Take the time to compose yourself, change your gown, perhaps."

He watched her take a long slow breath, her eyes still closed. He had imagined she would scream hysterically when he killed her husband before her. But it appeared the queen had gathered all her pain inside while forcing her courage to the fore. He admired that. She was certainly far more beautiful than he'd imagined. Valya would be even more jealous than she already was of the Valisar Queen.

"Take the queen to her apartments," he ordered, "until I call for her." He watched as her husband's headless corpse was unceremoniously dragged away by its feet, no doubt on Stracker's instructions.

"Come, Piven," she said softly, finally opening her eyes, looking only at her child, ignoring the object to which he clung.

"I'll be needing that head, majesty," Loethar said.

"Leave that down now, Piven," she said to her boy, her voice as gentle as a soft summertide breeze. Her kindness reminded Loethar briefly of how he'd often wished his own mother had treated him. For a moment he felt envious of the halfwit.

"Leave the boy, too, your highness." He raised his hand as she swung around, startled. "I will not harm him. He'll be a nice playmate for my raven. They seem to suit one another, don't you think?"

"What do you want with him?" she demanded, glancing down at Piven, who was still clinging to his father's hair. Loethar noticed she had to stop herself from retching as she finally looked upon her husband's remains. He could almost feel sorry for her.

"I like him. He shall be my new pet, alongside Vyk."

"Pet?" she echoed, aghast, her face a mask of despair. "Sooner you kill him, barbarian. He has no concept of his life, in truth. Perhaps he is best dead."

"Fancy a mother saying that," Loethar replied, derision in his voice. "Tsk . . . tsk. Even stepmothers should offer some love."

"He bears the Valisar name. For that you should accord him just a little respect, even if you will not show that same respect to his father or his mother."

"I shall send for you soon, your majesty. I thought that by keeping your son with me it might prompt you to stay obedient. But now that I know you have a heart of stone—that you would wish your own child dead—I can tell you would likely follow your husband's theatrical lead and kill yourself. That would be most disappointing for me. Guards! The lad remains here, chained like the little beast he is now for me. Escort the queen to her rooms. She is to be treated with care and kept under watch at all times. She is not to be left alone—no matter how she begs—for so much as a heartbeat. Take her. Piven?"

The youngster turned and Loethar, pleased that he at least recognized his name, was amused beyond belief when the boy ran to him open-armed.

"Leo, steady!" Gavriel hissed, reaching awkwardly for the prince.

"My father," Leo whispered, his distraught young face ghostly in the dim light of the one low candle they permitted themselves.

Gavriel squeezed the boy's shoulder. "You should never have seen that."

"Now we have both had to watch our fathers die," Leo said, his whisper unable to hide his grief.

There was nothing Gavriel could say to ease the pain. He was still trying to deal with the recurring image of his own father's brutal slaying. He wanted to say that at least King

Brennus had taken his life on his own terms but was afraid his words would sound callous. "What about Piven?" Leo groaned.

Gavriel peeped through the holes bored into the stone. "He looks happy."

"He always looks like that."

"True, but he's safe for now. I think if Loether was going to kill your mother or brother it would already be done." He saw Leo nod, felt a tiny measure of relief. "Let's think about our own situation," he said, hoping to distract his charge.

"What do you think of my hiding spot?" Leo asked, following Gavriel's lead.

Gavriel was sure they'd be whispering like this for days to come. "Inspired. Who knows about this?"

"Only my father."

"So now only you?"

"It's a secret known only to the king and heir, passing down through generations that way."

"So that's why Freath was given such a cryptic message."

Leo nodded. "Father showed it to me when the troubles in the Set began several moons ago. He called it the ingress. It was built into the castle walls by King Cormoron centuries ago."

Gavriel looked around at the narrow corridor in which they found themselves. Leo had had the forethought to grab a lantern as they ran into it via an exquisitely disguised entrance that even someone lifting the tapestry would likely not notice, and had used its flame to light a few tiny candles, that threw a ghostly glow but one still low enough not to attract attention through the peepholes they were now using to spy through. There was not sufficient room for the two of them to stand side by side and Gavriel thanked his stars he didn't suffer Corbel's dislike of enclosed spaces. He touched the cool stone. This hidden walkway had been deliberately designed and built for spying he now realized, exactly as they were, into the king's main salon where presently Loethar presided.

"Cormoran was obviously a man who trusted no one."

"Father used to play in these tiny spaces when he was a boy. His father told him about it when he was much younger than I am. I wish I'd known about it longer. I could have listened to so many conversations."

"Perhaps that's why he didn't mention it earlier," Gavriel whispered, his gaze never leaving Loethar. The barbarian sat quietly in a high-backed chair, watching Piven paint pictures on the floorboards with his father's blood. "Is it limited to just behind this chamber?"

A cunning smile broke across the prince's mouth. "No. There are several access points and all the main public chambers have these hidden chambers in the walls. So do some of the more private ones—my father's salon, my mother's apartments . . ." Gavriel immediately decided Cormoron hadn't trusted his queen. ". . . kitchen. I haven't seen them all. But they're all this tiny and uncomfortable."

Gavriel's attention returned to what Leo was saying. "No complaints," he admonished in a tight whisper. "It has saved not only your life but the Valisar line. There's enough room to lie down, so we can sleep. If we keep the candles low and small, and only lit during daylight hours, we should go unnoticed indefinitely."

"What about food?"

"I'll have to think about that."

"I know how to get into and out of the kitchens. I've stolen birdcakes when Cook's back was turned but this is obviously more risky."

"We'll work something out," Gavriel replied noncommittally.

"Gavriel," the prince said solemnly. "I will never lose that image of father killing himself."

"I know, Leo. Look—"

"No, wait. What I was about to say is that I'm deliberately going to carry that memory. Although few people take me seriously yet, I am a Valisar. That has been drummed into me since I was old enough to pay attention. Whatever I have to do to stay alive and make the barbarian pay for his cowardly deeds, I will do. So I'll find us food and I'll get us out when the time is right. We'll have to learn the movements of their guards first."

Gavriel wanted to cheer for the prince but his throat tightened with emotion at Leo's stirring words and he just nodded, before saying, "We have to take off anything that could make noise, Leo. We'll have to move around these narrow spaces in silence. If you're going to sneeze or cough, you'll have to smother it. We'll need to tiptoe and whisper at all times."

"Lucky we had on our travel coats," Leo added.

And that reminded them both of being on the battlements and what had happened since.

Gavriel deliberately distracted the boy's thoughts again, as well as his own. "We'll have to pick a place to leave our waste. It's not going to smell very nice soon but—"

Leo shook his head. "My great-grandfather thought of that," he whispered. "He and his son built an opening to piss down. It links up with a drophole."

"Ingenious," Gavriel muttered.

"I'll take you later to a spot where we can even sit down to take a shi—"

"Surely not?" Gavriel said, genuinely impressed.

Leo actually grinned. "It's true, I tell you. The kings before us have thought of everything."

"They obviously enjoyed spying on people." Gavriel's attention was grabbed by movement at the side of the room. The man called Stracker was back and the raven, which had been sitting quietly, was suddenly alert on its perch on one of the high-backed chairs. Gavriel nodded at Leo, and put a finger to his lips.

"Back already?" Loethar asked.

"The cook is planning a feast for you tonight . . . if he can stop himself from gagging. He's taken the king's death hard." Stracker laughed.

"Good," Loethar said. "I can still hardly believe I allowed it to happen that way. I should have known better."

"There's someone waiting outside I thought you should meet."

"Who?"

"The name's Freath. Says he thinks he knows where you can find the other son."

Gavriel stiffened behind the wall. "I'm going to kill that bastard," he hissed.

"Lo save us!" Leo murmured as Freath was brought in before Loethar. The aide did not look at all frightened. "But he doesn't know where we are!"

"Are you sure?"

Leo nodded, his mouth set. "I told you—no one else alive knows about the ingress except us two. And Piven, actually—he came exploring with me a couple of times."

"He doesn't count."

They heard Loethar's voice and turned their attention back to the king's salon.

"And you are?"

"The queen's aide. Er, how should I address you, Master Loethar? Forgive me; I'm unsure of the protocol toward overthrowers of kings."

Gavriel watched Loethar's head snap sharply up from papers on Brennus's desk to the man before him. He couldn't see Loethar's face but he imagined the barbarian's eyes had narrowed as he scrutinized the servant, the silence lengthening. Meanwhile Vyk gave the newcomer a onceover, swooping down to hop around him.

"I wish he'd peck his eyes out," Gavriel murmured to Leo.

"You could call me emperor," Loethar finally replied, as though testing the word on his tongue. "Yes, emperor has a nice sound to it, don't you think?"

"Indeed it does, although 'sire' is perhaps easier for your new people to stomach . . . so soon after conquest. I presume all realms now answer to you?"

"You would be right in that presumption."

"Then, as the new head of the Set, perhaps you would call

off your intimidating crow and we can talk about how we can help each other?"

Loethar laughed. Gavriel, appalled by Freath's confidence, almost hoped the barbarian would pull out that mean-looking dagger and drag it across the traitor's throat right now.

"Call me sire, then. And Vyk prefers 'raven.' What makes you think there is a *we*?"

"Well, sire," Freath began, pushing once at the bird with his foot as a warning and then ignoring it, "I have walked among the power brokers for more than two decades. I am an aide to the king and queen of the most influential and powerful of all the realms of the Set. I would urge you not to waste this resource. I have knowledge of a like you can't imagine."

"Such as?"

"Such as who might bend easily to your will."

"And who might not?"

Freath smiled. "It seems we understand each other. There will always be rebels. I can help you with them. For starters, the De Vis boys will almost certainly find a way to rise against you."

"You bastard son of a whore, Freath," Gavriel growled. This was followed by a threat as to what he was going to cut off Freath's body first and where he planned to put that spare bit of flesh. Leo glanced at him, worried.

Stracker laughed. "That is a jest, of course," he said to Freath, his words threatening.

But Freath seemed unimpressed; his expression remained unchanged while Loethar remained motionless.

"I've never been known as a man of comedy, sire. The De Vis family is fiercely loyal to the Valisars. And your somewhat theatrical murder of their father is not something the sons will be easily able to come to terms with, I hazard."

"Tell me about them."

"The boys?"

Loethar nodded.

"They're twins. They look similar but are not identical and they have vastly different personalities. Corbel is the serious one, the younger one, I believe, by just a few minutes, but still waters run extremely deep with that boy. I say 'boy' but he is a man and if my instincts serve me right, he is capable of being single-minded and ruthless."

Gavriel realized Leo had grabbed his arm. He'd had no idea that his own fists were resting white-knuckled against the stone. He forced himself to relax and felt Leo's relief beside him.

Freath continued. "The other boy, Gavriel, is outspoken, has opinions and expresses them. He's more showy than his brother. They're both handsome but one tends to notice Gavriel more. He is an excellent swordsman, I believe, skilled with most weapons, in fact."

"How old are they?"

Freath frowned, thinking.

"A rough estimate will do," Stracker chimed in.

"Actually, I can tell you exactly how old they are. They are turning eighteen in leaf-fall."

"And you believe these De Vis boys should be of concern to me? Are you suggesting I should be fearful of mere nestlings?"

"Not afraid, no. *Aware* perhaps is more appropriate. They will not pay you any homage, sire. They worshipped their father, respected their king and are devoted to each other. Kill one and I suspect you'd kill the other fairly effectively. I doubt very much, considering the way they've been raised and by whom, that they would be frightened to die for what they consider their honor."

"And what is their particular focus of honor?"

"Why, the Valisar king of course."

"King? Did you not spy Brennus's corpse, Freath?" Stracker asked in an acid tone. "There is no Valisar king."

Freath ignored him. Gavriel couldn't help but be impressed by the aide's composure, even as he hated his treachery. "Sire, I do not refer to King Brennus but to his son, King Leonel."

This created a tense silence during which Gavriel felt the hairs on his neck stand on end. Until now all the people in authority had been talking about Leo as the young prince—keep him safe, he's the future, perhaps one day . . . But now, for the first time since the attack on Penraven had turned from threat to reality, Gavriel felt the full weight of responsibility that was resting on his shoulders alone. Leo was no boy prince, a young sapling to be protected simply because he was a Valisar. He was now the sovereign, and while he remained alive, Penraven had its Valisar king.

Leo whispered into the dark. "That's scary to hear."

Gavriel felt a rush of rage crystalize into something hard and unyielding. They would have to kill him to get to Leo.

Loethar's voice broke through the silence. "You call him King Leonel?"

"I don't, sire. But everyone other than myself will behind your back. And as long as he breathes, he is the king—sovereign of this realm, and figurehead to the Set. As long as people keep faith with that they will carry a torch that the Set will rise once again and that you will be vanquished."

Loethar banged his fist on the table. "I could have you gutted before me, throw your entrails onto a fire before you're even dead."

"I know you could, sire. I suspect you won't, though, because as I mentioned earlier I know everyone there is to know in this realm. I am familiar with most of the nobles and dignatories—certainly the royals, if any survive—in the rest of the Set. The transient pleasure of opening my throat would be a shameful waste of the resource . . . sire."

"Brazen, indeed. You impress me, aide."

"Thank you, sire. My previous employers were not so mindful of my use to them . . . or how I could damage them if I chose to."

"I will kill him," Gavriel hissed.

"You'll have to line up behind me," Leo whispered angrily and Gavriel, in spite of his fury, felt a spark of satisfaction at the youngster's threat.

"I shall give you first hack at him," Gavriel muttered back, "but only because you're king," he added before returning his attention to the men they spied on.

Loethar regarded the servant. "And you want me to guarantee your life if I allow you to . . . er, how did you say it . . . share how you can damage the remaining Valisars?"

"My life at the very least, sire. I am suggesting you take me on as your personal aide."

Stracker laughed but there was no mirth in the sound, only menace. Piven chose this moment to reach up from the floor where he had been amusing himself and wipe his hands, sticky from his father's blood, against his white shirt. Clutching Freath's robes, he hauled himself to his feet.

"Ah, Piven, you have been spared, I see," Freath commented, staring at the boy as though he were an insect. "Why is that, I wonder?"

"He amuses me," Loethar said. "I like the idea that once I've dealt with the heir the only remaining Valisar left—although not of the blood—is a lost soul. He can be a symbol of the former Penraven, equally lost."

"Very good, sire," Freath said, finding a tight, brief smile that was gone almost as soon as it arrived. "Shall I make myself useful and have this child cleaned up for you?"

Loethar stretched. Gavriel felt sick. It seemed as though a bargain had somehow been struck during that conversation. He could sense Leo looking at him for explanation but he couldn't speak.

"You may take him and bathe him but put that shirt back on him. I want his father's blood on show for all to see."

"Very ghoulish, sire. Appropriate humbling for watching eyes."

"But first, the daughter." Loethar paused.

Freath filled the pause with a nod. Then added, "Now that

you've seen the corpse shall I inter it into the family tomb?"

"No. Burn it. Then scatter the ashes from the castle battlements. Or, rather, I shall. We'll have her mother present too."

"For the final humiliation?"

"Not quite. I have one left."

"Will you be killing queen Iselda, sire?" Freath asked conversationally.

"I'm not sure. I haven't yet made up my mind."

Gavriel closed his eyes. He wished Leo did not have to share this.

"May I suggest that if you're keeping Piven as a symbol of the downfall of the Valisars—"

"He will be my pet."

"Indeed, sire. I was going to say that perhaps you should keep the queen as your servant. That would be a most degrading role for her."

Gavriel watched Loethar walk around the desk. He could finally see the barbarian's face and it was filled with amusement as he considered Freath's remarkably distasteful idea. The raven was back on his shoulder. If the scene were not so sinister, the pair would look comical.

"Or as your concubine," Stracker added.

Freath said nothing to this, simply blinked in irritation.

"It's just a thought, sire," he said instead to Loethar.

"I shall consider it," Loethar said. "But before you go," he said to Freath, who was bending to take Piven's hand, "I want to know about the eldest son."

"My apologies, of course," Freath said, all politeness.

Gavriel bent down to Leo. "At least your mother remains alive another day."

"What is a concubine?"

"Another word for servant. She takes the night shift, cares for his needs when the day servants are asleep," Gavriel explained carefully, glad it was so dark that Leo could not search his face for the truth he had sidestepped so briskly.

". . . twelve summertides, frail and still very much a

child," Freath was saying. "His head is filled with horses and bladder ball games that he plays badly. Useless with weapons."

In the ingress Gavriel felt astonishment at this comment and knew Leo would be feeling the same.

"But Brennus would surely have been training him for his role."

"Oh, yes, but only in a mild way, sire. Leo is still just a boy. He hardly knows his head from his arse, if you'll pardon my language."

"You don't have to worry over my sensitivities, Freath," Loethar reassured.

The aide nodded. "What I mean is that he's extremely immature—still something of a mummy's boy. We're talking about an indulged brat more than capable of throwing tantrums while incapable of maneuvering a horse or his weapons with any dexterity."

Leo turned and glared at Gavriel. "Lying bastard!" he hissed.

"It seems Freath is out to impress the barbarian. Don't worry about it, Leo. We'll kill him with our bare hands if we must, as soon as we get the chance." Gavriel knew his words were an empty threat but he felt better for having said them.

"So while the De Vis twins are a threat, you are saying the heir to the throne is not."

"No, sire, that's not what I'm saying. The De Vis family is your enemy, and they would have been without your splitting the legate's head in half," Freath warned. "The heir is not a physical threat to you. He wouldn't know how to attack, how to rally a force, how to even plan beyond where to play on a given day. He's still in that childish mindset of the world revolving around his selfish needs, especially his belly."

Loethar looked amused but Gavriel bristled. Freath knew Leo well and he could have been describing a stranger for all his words resembled the prince. "He struggles to make his verbs work, so he is hardly ready to make a realm work for him," Freath continued with utter disdain. "Brennus never expected to lose his throne. The threat from the Steppes was always that—just a threat. It hadn't sunken past the shallowest of consciousness that you might succeed in your desire for empire and that the prince might need to be fully readied in all aspects of sovereignty."

Again Gavriel caught a glance of bewilderment from his new king.

"Your point?" Loethar asked.

"My point, sire, is that you have nothing to fear from Leonel in person. It's what he represents that should trouble you. No one will let go of the fact that the heir exists—if they believe that to be true—because that means the Valisar dynasty is alive."

"I want to know where he is."

"And I believe I can help you. But I do require guarantees, sire."

"So you say. Give me your terms."

"I have heard a rumor that you are gathering all the empowered people from the conquered nations."

For the first time since Freath had arrived Gavriel noticed the barbarian lose his casual stance. Loethar stiffened. "And what's that to you?"

Freath gave a sly shrug. "Well, I can't imagine you'd go to all that trouble and not make use of that collected power."

"And?"

"I want some of it."

Stracker grabbed Freath by his shirtfront, pulling him close to his pockmarked face. "You don't demand anything. You're lucky to have lived this long."

Freath remained undaunted. "Phew, we eat the leaf of the cherrel to keep our breath fresh, Stracker."

Loethar ignored their barbs. "Explain what you mean, Freath, before I allow Stracker to gut you as he so desperately wants."

Freath straightened his clothes, amazing Gavriel with his audacity. He watched the aide take a breath and paste another cunning smile on his face. "Two sorcerers, witches, whatever you care to call them, of my choice and at my behest."

Gavriel watched Loethar's mouth twitch. "What makes you think they exist?"

"Oh, they exist all right, but they are cunning. They will go to extraordinary lengths to disguise their skills but that they exist in the Set . . ." he smiled as he paused, ". . . of this there is no doubt."

Loethar's eyes narrowed. "Do you know who these people are?"

"I may have suspicions, sire, but no, I don't know anyone specifically practicing magic outwardly. There is the usual band of hedgewitches and herbalists, conjurers and magicians. But what I'm talking about are the thaumaturges, the genuine weavers of miracles—phenomena that can't be explained. I'm certain you've already discovered a few. I want a pair."

"And what do you plan to do with them?" Loethar inquired, sitting against the king's desk. His arms were crossed in a deliberately casual pose but Gavriel was sure the barbarian was anything but relaxed.

"They will offer me protection."

"From me, I presume."

"Correct, sire. And from your bad-smelling lackey and your hideous crow."

Stracker scowled but Loethar gave a sharp, tight grin. "I see. And in return you will give me the boy."

"I will try, that is my promise."

"Try?" Loethar's tone was now fueled by disdain.

"He has gone to ground, sire. I have already seen your men searching the palace. I presume they are searching the immediate area and nearby woodland as well. He could not have gone far because I saw him quite recently."

Loethar stood up. "You saw . . . !" he began, breaking off angrily to say: "Where was he?"

"The kitchens."

Gavriel took a step closer to Leo, grinding his jaw as he

put an arm around the new king. It felt like hollow reassurance but it seemed more meaningful than words right now. His mind was racing. Should they attempt an escape now or hold their nerve a short while longer? Freath couldn't possibly know where they were . . . could he?

Leo echoed his thoughts. "He doesn't know anything," he said.

"They took fright at the sound of your men closing in on the palace and ran off. I tried to follow but I'm an old man by comparison, sire. I couldn't keep up."

"They?"

"Pardon, sire?"

Loethar's expression darkened. "You said they—who were the others?"

"Just one other. Gavriel De Vis."

"Are you telling me they ran back into the palace?"

Freath shrugged lightly. "They headed in, but, sire, we have many entrances and doors that lead to other courtyards. They could be anywhere. Though they won't have had time to get far."

"Have you a suggestion of where they may go?"

"I have plenty. But I need a show of good faith, sire."

"I see. Something in writing? A mix of our bloods perhaps, palm to palm?"

"This man knows nothing that I, given a room with a pair of heated pincers, couldn't find out for you," Stracker threw at Loethar. Gavriel gave a humorless smile at finding himself momentarily on side with the barbarian's lackey.

Freath smiled tightly. "No need for torture or indeed any loss of blood. My request is very simple and easy for you to provide. When you have finished with her, I want the queen."

"What?" Loethar roared. His surprise turned into a tumult of laughter. "Iselda?"

Freath kept his face impassive. "She is beautiful. Why not?"

Loethar studied the aide carefully. "No, Freath, this doesn't fit. You're not that displeasing physically, I'll grant you, but I see no passion burning in these eyes of yours—other than for your own safe skin. I don't suspect there is a romantic or even sexual urge in your body. You are lying."

Freath remained unfazed, his voice calm. "You are jumping to conclusions, sire. I said nothing about romance or desire. I simply want her."

"What for?"

"Purely for self-satisfaction. I have served queen Iselda since she came to the palace, sire, and King Brennus even longer. They were the usual arrogant inbreds that seem to take the throne . . ." Leo gasped and Gavriel had to put a hand over the boy's mouth—a hand that was trembling with anger. ". . . services were always taken for granted. Although it's too late to tell Brennus, now it's time for me to share with her all my rage. I come from a distinguished line, sire. I deserved better."

"This is about not being thanked?" Loethar asked, incredulous.

Freath blinked slowly. "Perhaps put petulantly you could describe it that way, sire. I see it as retribution. I am not a man to be toyed with. I deserved better than I got in my years of service. I kept hoping I would be rewarded for my attentiveness, my loyalty, and, above all, my discretion. But each year passed without so much as a glance of appreciation my way."

"You're a servant, for Lo's sake!" Stracker chimed in. "What do you want, a manor in the country?"

"Why not?" Freath demanded, scowling at the man. "The legate was a servant too but De Vis was not only paid handsomely, he was rewarded with horses, land, servants of his own, wealth far more than he'd ever need. And his family line is no finer than mine. He was simply a soldier. I am a man of language, of letters . . . truly, sire, I was the more versatile if you compare me to De Vis. Yet he dies a hero—a wealthy one. If you slew me now, sire, I would die penniless. Pathetic isn't it?"

"Can you kill a man, Freath?"

"If I had to, yes," the aide bristled. "Killing doesn't give you superiority, sire, surely?"

"And have you ever killed anyone, Freath?"

"No, sire."

"It sounds a lot easier than the doing of it, trust me . . . not that I suffer the squeamishness of most."

Freath ignored Loethar's explanation. "If you don't need her for any other purpose, sire, I would have her."

"To humiliate her?"

"To do whatever I please with her. She will become my slave, follow my orders, answer my desires . . . however dry they may appear to others."

"And so for the queen, two Vested and my word, you will help me hunt down Leonel?"

"Yes, sire. And there are so many more ways in which I can help you . . . be assured of that. At no further cost to you than what I've already asked for."

"You intrigue me, Freath."

"So we're agreed. Iselda is a show of goodwill on your part."

"Bugger her senseless for all I care, Freath, although I will be wanting her for tonight myself."

"Of course you do, sire," Freath said, as though they were discussing the shared use of a horse or plow. "In fact I won't lay a finger upon her until you have. Is that fair?"

Loethar nodded. "It is." He looked at Stracker. "How many have we rounded up?"

"In total, about thirty-four who seem genuine in their talents."

"Have them brought here. I'll leave you to pick out the best—and show them to Freath. He can choose from your selection. Order it now." Stracker nodded and left the chamber. Loethar looked at the royal aide again, then grinned. "I need men with your agile mind, Freath. I'm sure I should just slit your throat here and now but there's something about you that tells me I should stay my hand a little longer."

"That's convenient for me, sire."

His words amused Loethar further. "For both of us, I hope. Stracker can be . . ." He searched for the right word.

"Spontaneous?" Freath offered.

Now Loethar smiled genuinely. "Precisely. And on occasion I need someone who can act upon more considered information, someone who thinks through a situation."

"Less of a blunt instrument. I understand. But that doesn't necessarily make me feel safe."

Loethar's smile broadened. Gavriel realized that Freath's cunning made him a perfect match and someone who had, over the last few moments, changed from aide's executioner to new employer. The barbarian called in some of his henchmen.

"This man has access to Queen Iselda. Him alone." He had obviously changed his mind about wanting Iselda for the first night. He turned back to the aide. "You amuse me, Freath. I like your mind, if not you." Freath inclined his head, obviously deciding to take the barbarian's words as a compliment. "As long as you continue to amuse me and keep me informed of everything around this palace and the realm—as I assume you have a well connected spy network—you are safe from my blade."

"In that case, sire, we shall take each other on his word. So, for the young prince, let me suggest you try the secret corridor."

Gavriel felt Leo's mouth open in terror behind his hand.

"Show them!" Loethar ordered Freath, pointing at his men.

Seven

Clovis sat silent and rigid, his fists clenched in his lap, the stone wall hard against his back. His life had been what many might describe as perfect. He was not a rich man—not yet, anyway—but he had been happier than many of the wealthy men he was required to offer his services to. Nor was he poor, not by a long shot. Work was regular and it didn't require him to ruin his back toiling out in the field at the mercy of Lo's moods. He was not old but he was no longer what could be described as a young man; middle years was perhaps the kindest way to term it. But he was hale and he had not yet found gray in his beard or experienced aches in his knees. He had no complaints.

And yet in a heartbeat the world he'd got used to—the routine life he was so comfortable in—had been turned upside down. He'd never loved Leah, not in the way that some people describe love; an angelic chorus didn't strike up in his ear whenever he saw her and his pulse didn't quicken, nor did he feel the rise of passion that he knew he should feel. But Leah was kind, and good. She loved him and he was fond of her. He liked her soothing prattle. She was not beautiful, not even pretty. But she was sunny. She laughed a great deal, especially at his jests, and her big bright smile could light a small room.

Leah had enough love and laughter for both of them fortunately. But what Leah had given to him—where all of his love was given in return—was their daughter, Corin. And whereas he and Leah would describe themselves as plain, Corin was sweet on the eye of all who beheld her. His child had the temperament of an angel and she bound Clovis and Leah, smothering the shortfalls they had as a couple, with her addictively fun personality and stealing Clovis's heart so that he could never leave, even if he wanted to. And the truth is he had never wanted to leave since the day of Corin's birth. For five peaceful, plentiful years Clovis had overlooked the lacklustre nature of his hasty marriage to Leah when she'd discovered her pregnancy, and considered himself a blessed man.

His role as a diviner was in brisk demand and although he charged the everyday folk just a few trents for a quick "impression" as he termed it, the richer people of Vorgaven—of which there were plenty—threw grand parties at which they invited diviners to foretell the future at far greater expense. The wealthiest of all—the shipping families—would invite him to their magnificent homes for personal "tellings."

It had become very fashionable to have a personal diviner on the payroll, someone who would advise on everything from best sailing times to which crew to select. It was a lucrative way to earn a living and recently Clovis had been able to build his small family a dwelling of their own on a tiny parcel of land he'd bought from one of his clients. It looked out to sea toward the Isle of Medhaven and Leah had begun to talk about no longer having to work at the inn. This had pleased Clovis, for he liked the idea that Leah would be at home all the time with Corin, rather than dropping her off at Delly's for a few hours until Clovis could take over child-minding duties.

Corin had been an accident, of course; the result of a dry, hurried copulation one evening in the cellar of The Fat Badger where Leah worked as a barmaid. He had been so drunk he was cross-eyed and honestly believed that he'd had it off with Alys Kenric, who wasn't unlike Leah in coloring, except much prettier. He had been celebrating a particularly rich haul from a wealthy merchant from Cremond who had revisited with a heavy purse to thank Clovis for his advice in buying black tourmaline from a small mine on Medhaven. The merchant had thought him mad at the time but Clovis realized the man had nevertheless taken his advice and purchased a substantial amount of quality stones. Who could have known—other than Clovis perhaps—that the second son of the Vorgaven royals, Danre, would choose for a bride the daughter of a very senior noble in Cremond. Or that this bride would have a fascination with black silk and black jewels. The merchant made a handsome profit from his tourmalines and had been anxious to thank the diviner from Vorgaven. Clovis had lived to quietly rue the day of that purse landing in his lap, because he certainly had held no ideas about marriage or even falling in love. But Leah had become pregnant and Clovis was pressured by her folk to do the right thing and Corin was the reward for his sacrifice.

But now Corin was dead.

Her small pretty head had been hacked from her trembling shoulders when the barbarians had come for him. And Leah, screaming with disbelief and horror as her daughter's head had rolled beneath a chair in their new home, had been viciously stabbed, mainly to stop her noise, the marauder had explained.

"She was ugly anyway. What was in your head?" the attacker had added. His name was Stracker, Clovis had learned. With not even a chance to comfort his dying wife or cradle his dead child, Clovis had been hauled off in a state of shock, none the wiser about what these men had wanted from him.

He knew now, though, as other men, women and even some children had arrived to join him, all bearing the same stunned, suspicious expression, all having lost loved ones in the rout. The leader of the marauders, the barbarian Loethar, wanted to round up all those who were empowered.

So now Clovis sat with a motley crowd of dismayed and disturbed people, some crying, most staring blankly. They were presently accommodated—although that was a loose term—in a barn on the border of Barronel and Penraven. Clovis had been one of the most recent arrivals as prisoner and had only had to march for six days to Barronel from the day he was captured; others had been captive for weeks. Some even for several moons. Kirin, a younger man, half Clovis's age, was an old hand at being Loethar's prisoner. He had been taken from Cremond and was a fount of knowledge as to what he'd seen on the march.

Kirin slumped down next to him now. As usual he tried to buoy his friend's spirits. "We're being moved again."

"Where to now?" Clovis inquired half-heartedly.

"Into Penraven apparently."

"So the mighty Valisars have submitted to the barbarian, too."

"It's no surprise. Penraven should never have waited to send troops. But we've had this discussion before. I would guess that, unlike our realms, it's had sufficient warning so its people could take precautions, flee to safer lands."

"We had so little warning in Vorgaven."

"And in Cremond our royals seemingly couldn't wait to give up their throne. How humiliating for their people."

"Ah well, it could be viewed a number of ways. At least their people didn't suffer. If I lived in Cremond, my Corin would be alive."

Kirin sensibly did not respond to this comment. "Loethar has sworn only to kill those who bear arms against him. It's a pity his henchman and those Green warriors haven't heard those orders clearly enough. If it were left to them there'd be no people remaining to rule."

"He certainly seemed to enjoy making my family suffer," Clovis replied, his voice choked. He rallied, cleared his throat. "And Loethar's called for us to be brought to Penraven?"

"So it seems. They're marching us to Brighthelm—the main palace and fortress—within the hour. It may only take half a day's walk."

"I'm not sure I care," Clovis replied, hanging his head between his knees as the vision of Corin's arms reaching up to him just before her death threatened to undo him once again.

"Rally your spirit, Clovis," Kirin urged.

"Why? I have nothing to live for."

"Nothing worth dying for here, either. Wait until there is something you value enough to give your life for. That's not him," Kirin said, pointing at their barbarian guard. "Or him," he added, pointing at another.

"They're just going to use us. Why don't we just kill each other here and now?"

"I won't give him anything of me, Clovis, least of all my blood. If just for the memory of my slain parents, I'm going to defy him and live."

"Brave talk," Clovis said, uncharitably.

Kirin made a clicking sound with his tongue. "So you'd let the person who slaughtered Corin in cold blood have your life as well . . . before you even began to think of revenge?"

"It's easier that way."

"But it's not courageous. And you make light of her life if you don't fight back on her behalf."

"My talents don't stretch to killing."

"There are many ways to skin a cat. Revenge doesn't always require bloodletting."

"So what's your plan?" Clovis asked, finally raising his head and looking at his young friend.

"I'm going to lie. You should too."

Clovis frowned at Kirin. "Well, that's *very* daring. I'm sure that should bring the entire barbarian nation down."

Kirin smiled, unperturbed by the sarcasm. "Listen to me. Let's make a pact that we lie about our skills. I know that you are a master diviner because you told me. Do they know that?"

Clovis shook his head. "They haven't asked."

"So they've discovered your skills how?"

He shrugged. "Word of mouth, I suppose."

"So second, third, possibly fourth hand news to some barbarian guard who told someone else and you were picked up."

"Possibly."

"Not possibly. More than likely, given the circumstances of the war being waged on our realms. Nobody had a list of the empowered that I remember."

"And so?"

"And so they believe you are empowered but they probably don't know how or to what extent. If you told them that you grew donkey ears at each full moon they'd probably believe it if you were convincing enough."

"And kill me for being a useless twot after all."

"Well, at least then you'll have died defying them." Kirin grinned sadly and Clovis felt his spirits lift ever so slightly. "Listen, all you have to do is downplay your skills. Don't tell them what you're really capable of if they don't already know."

"You speak as though from practice! And if they do know?"

It was Kirin's turn to shrug. "Then dilute it. Lie through your skills. Bend the truth at every opportunity."

"Do you know I don't even know what it is you can do."

Kirin hesitated.

"The truth," Clovis urged. "We must trust each other, if not anyone else."

The young man nodded. "It's hard to describe. I can see inside people."

"Inside?"

"If they're sick I sense what's wrong," the younger man said cautiously.

"There's more, I think?" Clovis prompted.

Kirin sighed. "Their minds. I can, well . . . enter them sometimes. It's not easy if they're closed to me. Some people have the ability to shut themselves off. It's easier if I can touch them, and at the very least I need to be looking at them. It's called prying."

Clovis was stunned into silence. "I've only heard that term once. I was told it is impossible," he finally said.

Kirin shrugged.

"I don't believe you," Clovis dismissed.

"I wouldn't believe me either."

"People's minds can't be read or eavesdropped upon," Clovis pressed. "Impossible, I say."

"Then why have a term for it? Actually you're wrong in your description. Thoughts are like explosions in the mind. I see them ignite, spark into color. Everyone's different, of course."

"You're telling the truth?"

"I have no reason to lie to you. Prying exists but it is very rare. I've never encountered anyone else who possesses such a power but I'm sure they exist, no doubt hiding it as I do. I'm originally from Cremond and my parents took me to a sage. She lived on the very tip of the coast—a wild and unforgiving place it was, too." He saw Clovis frowning in consternation. "Well, anyway, she confirmed that I had the skill to pry. I was only ten summertides then but she gave my parents a chilling warning that my power would be the death of me if I didn't guard it. She cautioned me that I must keep this power a secret from all and avoid using it ever. I took her warning to heart. We ended up starting a new life in Dregon and so my secret was safe. No one knows the truth but my parents, the sage—who is in all likelihood dead—and now you. The sage said there was more I could do with my abilities but she never explained what, exactly." Kirin shrugged. "I was never curious enough to ask."

"Surely?"

"No, I swear it. And the woman told me I'd work it out one day."

Clovis was genuinely taken aback. He had often caught himself feeling smug about his ability to look into the future, to see things that had the possibility of occurring. It was not precise and it was fraught with the danger of giving the wrong guidance but he always proceeded with caution and could honestly say he'd never advised anyone so wrongly that it could come back and bite him. In fact it was his judiciousness and subsequent success through that cautious approach that had earned him his solid reputation as a genuine practitioner. He had heard of prying, obviously, but thought it was akin to the Valisar Enchantment—something people spoke about and yet had never seen any solid proof of. He was sure it had been a Set myth! Perhaps charlatans claimed they had the prying ability but even now, despite the earnestness of Kirin's words, he doubted it truly existed. Looking inside people just seemed too far-fetched. If he were honest, too, he would admit that it offended his own sense of worth to think that this young man thought he possessed a talent that made Clovis's fortune telling seem like a circus act!

Kirin must have taken his silence to be apprehension. "I don't relish this talent but I have been blessed with it by Lo. There's more to it, though."

"Even more?"

Kirin grimaced, ignoring the wry comment. "Do you pay a price for your skill?"

Clovis glanced at him quizzically. "The other way around," he said, smirking. "People pay me."

"I didn't mean that. You see if I use my magic simply to do parlor tricks, the effort is minimal. But if I draw upon my true power—prying—I think I lose a bit of myself."

"What?" Clovis asked, his face clouded with confusion.

"I can't explain it. Sometimes I can lose time even after a simple 'trickle.' Once when I was younger and brash about my talent, using it unwisely, I became very sick."

"So you can just enter someone's mind, know what they're thinking?"

"I have no idea any more. I really don't make use of it. I haven't . . ." Kirin gave a soft gesture of helplessness. "Not in fifteen years or more have I used my full power. It frightened me, as I explained, and still does. I'm scared it will send me mad. The last time I used it without any care I didn't even know my own name afterward. That sort of repercussion is a great deterrent."

Again Clovis looked at him with incredulity.

"It's true," Kirin continued. "I had to re-learn my name, I didn't recognize friends. I was young and I think because I was still growing my body seemed to work out how to heal but the sage warned me that it could not repair itself indefinitely."

"So you haven't used your full power since you were ten?"

Kirin nodded. "I use only part of it. I made a promise to the seer, to my parents, to myself. I've had no need to make full use of it. Call me odd but I'm just not curious by nature. And now that I'm older and can see how sinister it is, I have no desire to make full use of it. It's been so long I probably can't even remember how to use it." He gave a soft deprecating chuckle, and then his face darkened. "No, that's not true. I can never forget how to use it. But I have no need for it. I can resist it. It doesn't call to me and sometimes I can forget that it's even there."

"So, what, this other stuff you do is a different sort of magic?"

"I have simply learned how to borrow from the real source. It's as though I have a secondary link to it—a far less dangerous one—that allows me to siphon off some of the power. It doesn't hurt me too much this way and when I was younger I earned a living with the gypsies—you know, telling people how many fingers they had up when I had my back to them, or which card they'd touched on the table." He laughed mirthlessly. "It wasn't a career but it was a living. More recently I've settled down in Cremond at the Academy of Learning."

Clovis was impressed. The Academy at Cremond was effectively the seat of learning for the whole Set. All the talented young scholars ultimately passed through the doors of the Academy on their way to being physics, astronomers, poets, artists, mathematicians. "You're a teacher?"

Kirin shook his head. "No, but I helped students to discover what they would be good at learning. Some came in believing themselves to be excellent at arithmetic and I could tell after not very long in their company that they might be more suited to astronomy, or another may have wanted to pursue literature and yet I could tell very quickly that he has the hands and the mind to be a great physician. Often just talking to them will reveal much of this but a trickle of my magic is always especially helpful." Kirin sighed. "I liked my job. It was well paid and solid. I loved the quiet of the Academy and the joy of being around learned people. It seems even using just a shred of my power has incriminated me with the barbarians."

"I'm intrigued. You said everyone is different?"

"Yes, of course."

"So some people are very open to your power."

"Mmm yes, from what I can recall some are transparent, others can be murky . . . silent, as I said."

"Do those people not think?" Clovis asked, stretching.

Kirin put his head to one side as he considered the question. "They think, but their thoughts are buried deeper. As an adult now I think I can understand that they may wish to hide things from themselves. They may also be adept at shielding their thoughts."

"But why shield private thoughts?"

Again Kirin shrugged. "Some people are very private. They don't want their facial expressions to reflect what's on their mind, so they teach themselves how to separate the two. I could take cues from both, of course and with the right questioning to someone who is not suspicious, I feel sure I would know what is prevalent in his mind. And then there are others still who are genuinely blank, maybe through age or illness. But I would be able to sense that instantly."

"Does the work at the Academy ever get you into trouble?"

"I'm very careful. My employers simply believe I am a skilled scout. And Clovis, as I've warned, very few people know what I can really do. I'm sure you've gathered that it's not something I am especially proud of—no one likes an eavesdropper."

"Unless they can use you for something they need to hear, of course," Clovis qualified.

"That's right, and that's the time when it would feel most wrong, somehow shameful. But after what's been happening, perhaps I can put it to some good use at last."

Clovis shook his head. "So you're going to bring down the barbarian all on your own with your hidden talent, eh?"

"I'm not delusional," Kirin admonished, his tone suggesting that his companion's constant disdain was wearing thin. "But I don't intend to help him ruin the Set either. I don't want to die. And neither should you; you have more to gain by taking revenge. I'm going to be clever about this, that's all."

Clovis turned to fully face his new friend now. He scratched his beard. "Tell me."

A sly grin stole across Kirin's face for a moment, before he looked quickly around, banishing it. He spoke softly. "They're not keeping us alive out of charity. My guess is that the marauders want to make use of us as you rightly assume—why else would they be gathering all the Vested? If Loethar was scared of magic, he'd be killing us. Why keep us alive? Why march us across the Set, adding more to our number as we move around the conquered realms? He has a plan for us. We can work against it from within."

"Spy, you mean?"

Kirin stood, wiping his dusty hands on his trousers. "Of a fashion."

Clovis joined him, stretching his legs. "For whom? Who's left to spy on behalf of, to fight for?"

"We'll find someone. Ourselves if we have to. But we cannot capitulate, especially those of us who do possess magic.

The fact is we're off to Penraven, the seat of power for the entire Set. It's the right place to be for any sort of uprising."

"Uprising?" Clovis hissed. "Your mind is definitely damaged. You sure you haven't been prying lately?"

Kirin scowled at him. "Do you want my friendship or not?"

Clovis felt abashed, ashamed that he was behaving so uncharitably to a fellow who had done plenty in these last few days to keep his spirits up and keep him eating. "Forgive me."

Kirin sighed. "As far as our enemies are concerned, you should claim to tell the future . . . badly, is that fair?" Clovis nodded. "And I, well, I simply do parlor tricks that are one part low-level magic and nine parts misdirection. All right?"

Clovis nodded. For the first time since he'd lost his family, he felt as though there was a reason to be breathing. Kirin was right—it felt good to fight back, even if it was only with words right now. He spat on his hand and extended it. "To an uprising."

Kirin followed suit, spitting on his hand before clasping it to Clovis's, grabbing for the chain with his other hand to stop the noise. "To secrets," he murmured. "Come, let's see if there's any stray food around to fill empty but newly courageous bellies."

Clovis fell into step alongside him, the chains around their feet clanking as the irons rubbed mercilessly at their ankles.

Eight

There was nowhere to run and Gavriel's mind was racing. He didn't know his way around these dark, narrow concealed corridors and he was afraid that they would be trapped by their own ingenuity. Something inside him, however, snapped back to a more primitive place, turning the hot fear from Freath's betrayal into a cooler fury where his inner voice said: *Come and find me, Loethar. I won't give myself to you.*

And so they waited, tense and alert for the first sounds of the intruders' arrival. Gavriel held Leo tightly by his side and held his breath while doggedly keeping the barbarian in view through the cunningly placed peepholes. Loethar paced as the raven watched him silently from the top of the stone mantelpiece. In Gavriel's heart a faint hope began to flare. Surely they would be upon them by now? But no one had come, not even the sound of boots running along these secret passages.

Suddenly the door to the royal chamber burst open and Stracker returned triumphantly, dragging Freath by his robe. "Nothing!" he spat. "As I presumed, empty promises!"

Gavriel couldn't believe it. He watched Loethar's gaze slide from Stracker to Freath. "Well?"

Freath shrugged himself free of the Right's grip, and again very deliberately pulled his clothes straight. "They are not there," he said, looking unperturbed.

"Where exactly did you think they were, Freath?"

"There is a small, very well concealed corridor from the cellars that leads to a secret chamber. It was a place I knew your men were unlikely to find quickly or at all, but the De Vis boy would certainly know about it." He shrugged once more. "It was worth a try."

"Shall I kill him now?" Stracker asked.

Loethar studied Freath, who—to his credit, Gavriel noticed—did not flinch beneath the barbarian's dark gaze. "No," he said finally. "We wouldn't have known about the secret corridor had he not told us and I agree, it would have been a logical place to run to." Gavriel watched Stracker's face flicker with disappointment and although Freath tried to disguise it, Gavriel saw the betrayer softly swallow his relief.

Loethar turned back to the royal aide. "Are there any other secret chambers or places that you know about within the palace?"

Freath shook his head. "Not secret, no. There are plenty of hiding spots and I'll be happy to hunt those all down with a couple of your guards if you wish, sire?"

Gavriel felt Leo's body relax beneath his hand. The boy looked up and in the very dim light Gavriel could see the prince's eyes glittering with triumph. "I knew he didn't know. He knows nothing," he whispered, venom in his words. "Now I have another enemy."

Gavriel nodded, unprepared for the ferocity of the youngster's tone. He looked back into the king's chamber.

"Are you really going to trust him?" Stracker was asking, surprised.

Loethar nodded. "Why not? He's a fawning parasite with no loyalties. So long as he's useful to me he does not trouble me." The leader tipped his head slightly to one side, regarding Freath. "And who knows what information he may yet share with us." Freath gave a gracious nod but said nothing. "In the morning when the prisoners arrive, let him have his choice, as promised."

Gavriel could see that Stracker struggled to keep his anger in check.

Loethar continued in his curiously quiet but nonetheless intense manner. "Is my dinner ready?"

"Close, I imagine," Stracker replied.

"If it is, have the queen sent down to join me. Good evening, Freath. Enjoy your sleep. I'm afraid Stracker will want to post a guard but you are free to come and go around the palace, providing you do not mind a shadow for the time being."

"As you wish, sire. Thank you."

Freath was led away, Stracker stomping ahead.

Gavriel finally let go of Leo. For the first time since arriving in the ingress he felt relatively safe, almost calm. It was now clear that no one knew they were here and it was unlikely they would be discovered by anything but their own stupidity. If they remained alert and smart about everything they did over the coming days, perhaps an escape plan could be hatched.

Loethar was glad to see the back of Stracker, whose penchant for violence simmered only barely below the surface of his skin. So far it hadn't mattered; Stracker had been a boon, his naked savagery impressing the barbarian horde, inspiring it at times. But now that the realms were under their control, it was time for consolidation. The Set needed a chance to take stock of its own weak circumstances, to realize that there were no kings running their individual realms any longer, that there was now only one ruler . . . him. He had no plans for ruination but the people of the Denova Set must understand that their livelihoods and security depended entirely upon acceptance.

He stroked Vyk's head as he spoke his thoughts aloud. It was only with Vyk that he could ever be entirely honest, fully himself. "They'll be frightened, suspicious, angry at first. I don't doubt there will even be thoughts of rebellion in small pockets but we'll search them out and stamp on them as soon as they flicker into life."

The raven blinked and turned its head slightly as though listening carefully.

"And ultimately they'll learn to do it my way—the way it should always have been, eh, Vyk?" The bird shivered slightly, flashing the almost metallic black-blue of its feathers. "Bloodshed was the only way." Loethar looked around. "We had to teach them the ultimate lesson . . . the truth behind the lies."

Gavriel was yawning, only half listening to Loethar's soft words. He glanced at Leo, noting that the boy's eyelids were already heavy and he suspected the youngster would drift away in the next few minutes, for which he was grateful. They had both seen enough blood and chaos, both felt enough hurt and experienced enough violence in the day gone to last a lifetime. He hoped Lo would spare Leo bad dreams this night and simply allow the boy his rest. And he, too, needed a quiet mind, free from the brutal images and his spiralling despair, to anchor him into some clear thought. Plans had to be made. He'd ignored the barbarian for the last few minutes but his attention was arrested from his own thoughts by Loethar's last comment to the raven. How odd that this man felt so close to a dumb bird . . . even a dog found a way to communicate with its master but no raven was ever going to share any emotional attachment or give anything back. Perhaps that was the point, Gavriel decided. Loethar was surrounded by people keen to please. The raven might as well have been a stone wall for all it gave back, but it was a living creature . . . maybe that was all the barbarian needed for company, a silent companion that asked for nothing.

Gavriel frowned as he watched Loethar take the bird to the window, allowing it to launch itself from the palace. He heard the barbarian tell it not to get lost and then chuckle to himself.

What had he meant about the truth behind the lies? Gavriel

yawned silently again as he watched the lean man pour himself a goblet of wine and sigh after he swallowed the first sip. This was the first time he'd really focused on the leader's appearance rather than his actions. For someone who was chief of the marauders he was not especially imposing. Yes, he was tall, but he didn't seem to capitalize on his height by drawing attention to himself. Where Stracker displayed his rippling muscles, Loethar was doing a good job of hiding them—if they even existed—on a narrow, almost hollow-looking frame. Gavriel wondered what it was about Loethar that impressed his people, impressed the men of his land enough to go to war against the Set. Loethar didn't possess the instantly seductive charm of Brennus. He bore none of the distinctive tatua that Gavriel had heard were common to the barbarian army. His black hair was lank and flowing freely; his beard was long, unkempt, and covered most of his face. He jangled as he moved due to all the silver rings and jewellery that hung from his ears, lips, and nose. He didn't speak with a booming voice; he didn't say much at all, in fact, and he certainly revealed as little about himself as possible . . . except perhaps to the wretched raven.

But there was an intensity to the man, Gavriel had to admit. Something genuinely charismatic about him when he spoke in that restrained manner of his, and together with that uncompromising stare, he was compelling. He certainly seemed to have Stracker under control—but why? Stracker was almost twice Loethar's build and could easily, Gavriel imagined, pound the man into a blob with his bare fists. What influence did Loethar have over these primitive people?

He glanced once again at Loethar, now slumped in a high-backed chair, his goblet empty and tipped aside in his lap, and watched the usurper scratch at his horrible beard. The quiet scene was disturbed by a knock at the door, followed by Stracker's entrance with the queen.

Gavriel saw a glance pass between the two men. "Where is the boy?" Loethar asked as he stood.

"On his way down," Stracker answered. "He has been

washed and tidied . . . and yes, his bloodied shirt is back on his body."

Iselda winced. "What do you want me for?"

"I thought you might care to take supper with me. You must be hungry."

She looked at him, astonished. "No, I think my belly is the last thing on my mind." She gasped when Piven arrived, carried by Freath. "Why is he . . . ?" She didn't finish.

But Freath guessed her question all the same. With a glance toward the barbarian leader he addressed his former queen. "Iselda, your son now belongs to Loethar. Pet Piven is his new title. He is to permanently wear the shirt that bears the blood of his father as a constant reminder."

"Of what?" Iselda whispered, horror spreading across her beautiful, pale face.

Freath looked to Loethar.

"Of whatever the blood reminds him in his locked mind, madam," Loethar replied. "But for me it will be a reminder that all that is left of the Valisar line is this pathetic, mad, bloodstained child."

Iselda's lips trembled but to her credit and to Gavriel's everlasting pride, she held her head high, refusing the tears that threatened. "You suit your name, you know that? I don't know what it means in your primitive culture but in our sophisticated one, the name Loethar—though so ancient as to be almost dead—means betrayer or evil one."

"Ah," Loethar said. A glimmer of a smile flashed. "That's where I must correct you, Iselda. It means no such thing. Your bastardization has tarnished what was once a very proud name of your people. In its original form of Lowther, it actually means 'true.' But over the centuries it was lost, changed, and somehow got itself corrupted to Loethar. Because of the old word 'loe' people believe it means to betray. But it doesn't mean betrayer, Iselda. Even in the more modern form it means—"

"I didn't come here for a history lesson, barbarian," the queen sneered. "In any language it would mean the lowest of life to me." She deliberately looked away from him to her aide. "Freath, you've had Piven in your care obviously?"

"I bathed him," Freath answered and Gavriel noticed the aide no longer used her title.

"And you did not drown my helpless son? You did not save him from this . . . this animal?" she hurled at him.

"No," he answered, seemingly unaffected by her emotional tirade. "Why would I?"

"Freath!" she gasped again. "For my sake, of course! And to save him any pain or humiliation at the marauder's hands."

Her aide simply sneered and let the child's hand go. Piven looked at his mother serenely but walked across to Loethar and smiled.

"You see, he even likes me. Perhaps because I don't weep or shriek as you do, madam," Loethar said softly. "Or perhaps because he knows that with me he has a chance at life, whereas left to his surviving parent, she would strangle him in a moment."

"What kind of beast lives inside you?" Iselda said to Loethar, her voice turning deep, almost animal-like in its growl.

"An angry one, Iselda. Now quieten yourself. I despise noise, especially from a woman, and if you make any more I shall take it out on my new pet here," Loethar replied, tapping Piven on the shoulder.

"I believe you," she said, eyeing him with such loathing that Gavriel held his breath, begging her inwardly not to do anything rash.

"Good. You are very beautiful when you are calm."

She looked away from him, clearly determined not to give him any reason to hurt her child.

"I have a surprise for you, Iselda."

"Another one," she said, disdain dripping from her voice. "I hate surprises."

"Well, I'm not sure this one is much to your taste either but taste it you will. Here, come sit opposite me. Stracker, have the table set in the manner a queen would appreciate."

Servants were allowed to come in—Genrie approached

with a very young serving girl Gavriel recognized. He couldn't recall her name but he noticed that her face was tear-stained and she was shivering. Genrie deliberately noticed no one it seemed, other than the former queen, throwing her soft glances of concern. Iselda was ignoring everyone but Piven, who sat on the floor with Vyk, newly arrived through the open window at almost the same time the servants had entered. The raven had climbed onto Piven's wrist; the boy made no sound as he stared gravely at the large black bird.

Gavriel's attention was caught again by Genrie, who shooshed the other girl away, as her shaking hands were a detriment to setting up goblets and wine decanters. Genrie, by contrast, looked composed. He knew she was one of Freath's favorites—perhaps that was why she had leapt to his defense when Gavriel made fun of him—but now he wondered if her defensiveness meant she was also his accomplice. Genrie was rather young for her senior position in the palace, and setting tables was far below her but she went about her task with her usual crisp efficiency.

When it was done she had the audacity to curtsey to the queen. "Your majesty," she said. "I know you won't enjoy the meal but I urge you—"

"Stop!" Loethar said, his voice quiet but angry. "You, girl. What is your name?"

"I am called Genrie," she replied, looking at him unabashed and unable to hide the defiance in her eyes. Gavriel felt inspired by her courage, even though he feared for her safety. She must be able to see the fresh bloodstains on the rug, not far from where she stood, and imagine from whom they came.

"Apart from addressing someone you do not have permission to talk to, do you always ignore your ruler?"

"No, sir. I have never ignored him. Nor would I if he were in this room with us now."

"Magnificent," Gavriel breathed, even as he realized that this might be the last moment he saw Genrie alive.

A chilled silence had descended upon the room. Gavriel could see Iselda pleading with Genrie through her stare not to inflame the situation any further.

"How old are you?" Loethar demanded.

"Old enough to hate you. Old enough to die for it."

Loethar stared at her, transfixed. Gavriel was sure most would have begun to tremble—or at least fidget—beneath such intense scrutiny. Finally he spoke. "And do you want to die?"

"No, sir. I want to live long enough to see *you* die."

Loethar surprised Gavriel by laughing, and although it was soft, there was a rueful tone in it. "Perhaps you will, Genrie."

"For what you've done to our king, you can be sure that people will queue to be your murderer, me among them."

Gavriel, amazed by her pluck, watched Loethar nod thoughtfully before saying, "I'm sure that's true."

"But it does not seem to frighten you," she sneered.

"That is also true. Now, Genrie, I've tolerated your indiscretion because I can appreciate this is an upsetting time. I need you to leave quietly now and take your weeping companion with you."

"You haven't seen what Tilly has seen. She has every right to weep." Genrie threw another concerned glance toward Iselda.

"Nevertheless, get her noise out of here or I'll ask Master Stracker to take care of it. He tends not to be terribly gentle. I'd recommend that you don't anger him."

"I have no fear. You control him like the dog on a leash that he is."

"That feistiness is attractive, Genrie, and I'm going to permit you to live despite your disrespect—for now—but beware it doesn't become your undoing."

The servant ignored Loethar. "Queen Iselda, whatever happens in the next few minutes, just remember, we are all loyal to the Valisars and no matter what this barbarian says to you—or shows you—"

"Get her out," Loethar said wearily and Genrie was instantly set upon by Stracker, who enjoyed twisting her arm painfully as he pushed her toward the door. She finally—and sensibly—remained quiet, although Gavriel wished he could cheer loudly so she knew someone appreciated her pluck. The queen who was the recipient of all that courageous encouragement just stared at Genrie departing seemingly unresponsive.

"Ready to eat, Iselda?"

"I'm not hungry," she snarled. "What did that girl mean?"

"Ah, so you were paying attention."

"Explain it."

"I'm not inclined to. Although I can show you, perhaps." Gavriel heard cunning in the barbarian's tone, and with it came a fresh wave of anxiety that froze him like ice. Fear coursed through his veins and he glanced down at Leo, taking in the slightly open mouth, regular rise and fall of the chest, and limbs scattered haphazardly. The boy was asleep; good.

". . . I don't like games," Gavriel heard Iselda reply.

"Oh this is no game, Iselda. I am deadly serious. And whether or not you're hungry I expect you to remain at my table until I have finished."

"As you wish. You're in charge," she said dismissively. Gavriel couldn't blame her; he felt sure that taking this approach of complete disdain was the only defense left to the queen. He reminded himself it was only a matter of hours really since she had delivered a baby. And that baby was already dead to her, she had no idea where her eldest son was, but he was as good as dead the moment he was located. And Piven might as well have been dead for all the comfort he offered. Her king—everything the realm revolved around—was also dead and, horrifically, by his own hand. It would be eating away inside her that Brennus would be remembered for taking his own life. It didn't sound so heroic and yet Gavriel would attest that preventing Loethar from that final gleeful blow was the most heroic of all acts. Perhaps with this scornful approach, Iselda was rather hoping Loethar would tire of her and have her killed or kill her himself.

Iselda seated herself as required. She ignored Loethar's gesture for some wine. "Freath, am I to understand that you are in cahoots with this usurper?"

"Are you still so ignorant, Iselda, that you believe I would be on your side?" the aide replied.

At this the former queen leaned back sharply, as if struck. Her voice was filled with shock when she finally spoke. "You betrayed us?"

"He's not that courageous, my lady," Loethar offered, setting down the decanter and reaching for his goblet. "He is an opportunist. He has seen who rules the realm now—the Set, in fact—and has thrown in his lot with me."

"Freath!" she exclaimed. "What have they offered that you could turn on us?"

Freath smiled grimly. "They have given me you, Iselda. You are my prize."

"Me?" she stammered, her voice tiny, disbelieving. "I don't understand."

"Oh come now, highness, don't be coy," Freath cajoled. "You've looked in the mirror often enough. But more importantly, you have used me as a slave when I was glad to be your servant. You ignored me when I would have been happy just to have a passing smile of thanks from you. I have served you since you arrived at the palace as a young bride. I protected you from the detractors who said you were the wrong choice for Brennus and I made sure of your strict care for all your confinements. I have been a loyal, diligent guardian . . . far more than a simple servant. But I do believe you wouldn't even recall my first name, not that it was ever spoken between us." His final words came out like a hiss.

"I . . . I . . ." Iselda stared at him, frowning, confusion clearly battling with her private thoughts.

"Go on, try and remember it," he jeered.

Iselda settled her features to banish the puzzlement and instead nodded as her composure returned. "You're right. I don't know it. Nor do I care to ever have it register in my mind again, let alone pass my lips. You are treacherous slime, lower than the dirt that clings to Piven's boots. You're not worthy of my breath so I shall not waste any more of it on you."

"Excellent," Loethar said. "I'm glad that's settled. Freath, you may leave us. After tonight I shall have Iselda sent to your chambers."

Gavriel felt the bile rise to his throat. He forced it back down as Loethar continued.

"The Vested will be here by daybreak. You have the choice of two. Make it quick or I'll renege on our offer. You're not that important to me, Freath. I'm simply allowing that you may be useful."

"I can be very useful, sire, if you'll give me a chance."

Iselda sneered, muttered something beneath her breath.

"Leave us," Loethar commanded. "Stracker? Have my meal brought in. Then you too may join the men."

Stracker nodded at Freath to follow him out. A few moments of tense silence followed during which Gavriel realized he was holding his breath. The door opened and he strained to see one of the large food wagons being dragged in by a near hysterical Tilly. She was shaking so hard she was struggling to put one foot in front of the other.

"Oh, save us," Loethar muttered. "Where is the other girl? Where is Genrie?"

"Refused to serve, now sporting a broken face for her trouble," Stracker's voice answered from the doorway. Gavriel felt his blood boil. Poor Genrie.

Gavriel didn't hear Loethar's reply because Tilly, in her hysteria and her clumsiness, had knocked over the huge silver dome that was covering a salver on the wheeled wagon. Gavriel recognized the tall dome as being one of the coverings they used for presenting the roasted swan or stuffed upright otter that was so popular for the royal feasts. The dome was sent clattering across the flagstones, making a terrible ruckus and Gavriel instantly looked down toward Leo, disappointed to see the child sitting up and rubbing his eyes.

"What's going on, Gav?"

"Nothing, go back to sleep," Gavriel murmured, but to no avail. Leo was already yawning himself awake and stretching.

"Let me see."

"There's nothing to see, except—" And that's when Iselda began to groan as though in the deepest of pain.

Gavriel looked back, unable to stop Leo, who he knew was now taking in the terrible scene with the same sense of horror and despair. Placed in the middle of the platter was the torso of King Brennus, roasted, his skin blistered and sizzling. His head was badly sunken into his shoulders, and his crown was placed lopsided on the cooked head, the eyes drooping while the mouth gaped, juices oozing from the bubbled, roasted tongue. Gavriel felt his stomach lurch. He dry retched, covering the sound as best he could.

"It would have taken too long to roast him whole, so I had him cut in half," Loethar said conversationally above the din of Iselda's keening.

Piven arrived at the table with what appeared to be a vague look of curiosity on his face. He was barely tall enough for his eyes to draw level but he tipped his head to one side, absorbing the image before him. As usual he uttered nothing, and his face had already returned to its usual expressionless appearance.

"Why?" Iselda managed to growl through her sobs.

"Well, if you must know, my lady, it is my intention to consume your husband. Now as odd as that sounds, it has merit. You see, contrary to what history tells us, I believe all Valisars possess special enchantment—some more than others, I'll grant you."

"You are deluded!" Iselda stammered. "Brennus had no

powers." And then she gave herself entirely over to her grief, weeping, bent double as though in physical pain. Gavriel noticed that her breathing soon became shallow and rapid as her gaze turned suddenly unfocused.

"Well, just in case," Loethar said quietly, "I think I'll start with his heart, unless of course you feel that it belongs to you?" There was absolutely no mirth in his words and Gavriel did not know whether he meant it in jest or was genuinely asking her permission. He would never know, for as the barbarian king began carving away the cooked flesh of the royal, Gavriel gagged, running around the corner to bring up the stinging, acid liquid that burned his throat.

But one person kept rigidly watching the shocking scene. Leo held his position, eyes wide, mouth agape, his expression hard to read as Gavriel returned, wiping his mouth.

"Leo," he whispered, shaking with distress for the boy.

"Today I make a soul promise," Leo uttered and his voice was so torn with savagery that no whisper could hide it. "But I will only carry it out when I am a man, old enough and strong enough to stand shoulder to shoulder with the barbarian who eats the flesh of my father. Until then I am a shadow, I am invisible to him. He shall never know my identity until the day I look him in the eye and tell it to him before I kill him. Witness my soul promise, Gavriel."

Gavriel was so taken aback he couldn't even stop Leo's blade. In a blink the boy was pushing it into Gavriel's hand.

Gavriel shook his head, horrified. Again Leo didn't hesitate. With his friend's hand still closed around the hilt he grabbed the blade, opened his shirt and dragged the blade across his chest, slicing open his own flesh, blood blooming instantly in its wake. Leo winced but he did not cry out. Gavriel opened his mouth in a silent groan, staring at the young blood on his hand, all over the knife.

The soul promise was the weightiest oath anyone could make. It required a living witness to perform the cut, achieve a deep wound across the chest to signify the scarring of the soul. Now Gavriel and Leo were bound in blood, through the most savage of oaths.

"I am a king in exile," Leo muttered, uncaring of the blood that ran freely down his chest. "And he will feel my wrath."

Nine

Kirin nudged Clovis. "Look. What do you think's going on up there?"

Clovis gazed upward toward the battlements as a tiny bowl of what looked to be dust was upended. The dust caught the soft late summertide breeze and was borne away.

"I don't know. You're the one who can get into people's heads," he grumbled.

"Ssh!" Kirin cautioned. "And you're the one who sees things."

"I see nothing other than a woman who could be the queen."

"What?" Kirin squinted as he concentrated. "You've seen her?"

"Only from a distance and in paintings."

"No, I don't think so. That woman looks like she's feeble-minded. Look at how her mouth hangs open."

"I can't see as well as you, Kirin. Your eyes are younger."

"Well, what I can tell you is that Loethar's on the rooftop and Stracker's next to him. Promise me you'll steer clear of him."

"As if I have a choice," Clovis commented absently. He'd never told Kirin that it was Stracker who slaughtered his family. Although Kirin seemed excited by their loose plan to work against the barbarian king, Clovis was tired from the enforced walk to Penraven, and anxious about what awaited them here.

They were being herded through the vast main gates of Penraven, where in a moment of whimsy perhaps, Cormoron—the original great king of the Valisar dynasty—had installed an impressive bell in one of the huge pillars and a shadow timepiece in the other. It was famous throughout the Set and attracted a lot of travellers. Clovis noticed that there were in fact four of these great dials in the massive pillar to the left and he quickly realized this meant that anyone, inside or outside of the palace, could know the exact time of day. What a marvellous piece of ingenuity. It intrigued him that something so simple as light and shadow could inform people of something so complex as the hours of the day. He didn't have time to appreciate the ornate, richly-colored artwork that adorned the face of the timepiece that pointed east, welcoming people to the city, although he'd heard much about its beauty and the brief glance he was afforded told him it was magnificent. He reminded himself to check on the opposing face which he'd heard was made of the stunning, creamy white marble from quarries to the northeast of exotic Percheron. The marble dial had been a gift from Percheron to Penraven on the occasion of the marriage of one of its princesses to King Brennus.

As Clovis passed underneath the gates he looked back to see that it was no lie—the marble was painted with special black inks flecked with gold dust. He had just a moment to take in that the timepiece split the day into the four tides—the working day—and he wondered if he would soon hear the great bell boom noontide, for the sun was surely at its apex and the shadow timepiece told him so when he glanced back over his shoulder.

It was as if the man in the belltower heard his thoughts for at that precise moment the noontide bell was struck and a deep gonging sound rang out over the first courtyard, although Clovis was sure it would be heard throughout the complex that Brighthelm looked to be. *Perhaps the man in the tower reads minds*, he thought, and smiled mirthlessly.

* * *

On the battlements, Loethar shook out the last of the dust from the bowl; watched as the wind dispersed it.

"Another Valisar heir gone," he said, his tone satisfied. He looked down at Piven at his side and wondered if he should kill the halfwit too. And yet in just such a short time he'd grown rather fond of his shadow. The boy, strange and lost though he was, seemed to like Loethar. Freath had told him that Piven liked everyone because everyone was good to him. No one upset him—he was too hard to reach anyway—and the only time the child showed any emotion was in response to heat or cold, pain or hunger.

"And even that he seems to grow out of," Freath had admitted. "These days you wouldn't know if Piven was hungry unless you heard his belly grind. And pain no longer seems to register as it used to."

The child was harmless and although he was aligned to the Valisars he was not blood and Loethar felt sure this orphan could be used to his own ends. Humiliation was a very strong weapon and to be seen befriending one of the precious—and easily the most vulnerable—members of the family, especially turning him into a dumb pet, might help reinforce his power over the people.

"What is your intention for the Set?" Freath had asked him only that morning.

He'd decided to be honest. "I have heard of a great tyrant from the far northwest many centuries back who overthrew a particularly powerful king. To help reinforce his image and to make his conquered peoples feel more kindly toward him he had opted to rule with as little oppression as possible, throwing festivals, building infirmaries, and encouraging the scholars and thinkers to come forward with their ideas. It was a far subtler means of manipulation. Erecting statues of him surrounded by children, or riding a dolphin, or walking with popular gods, had a far keener effect on the psyche of the people than aggression could ever have achieved."

Freath had nodded. "I think you refer to Thorasius."

"That's him." Loethar continued. "Suddenly the tyrant became benefactor, and within two decades he was a father of the nation."

"And you have learned from this," Freath finished for him.

"I have no quarrel with the people of the Set, only its rulers, and especially its leading family, the Valisar dynasty."

Freath had made some inane remark but Loethar knew his candour had given the bitter aide pause for thought.

His mind came back to the present and he looked at Iselda, whom he noticed was quickly becoming a mere echo of the defiant woman he'd met. Pity. She'd impressed him with that disdain but seeing her husband's roasted carcass had punched the final fight out of her. The burning of her daughter's corpse, which she insisted on witnessing, and the loosing of the infant's ashes just moments ago might have been the final nails in the coffin. He took in her absent gaze, her silence—not even tears any more—and the total lack of any interest in anything around her. Perhaps it was all over for Iselda. This woman's death—if it occurred—would especially please Valya, he was sure, if not himself.

"We are done here," he said to Stracker, who nodded.

"The Vested have arrived," his Right said.

"Remember what I said," Loethar said, a hard gaze at the man, who glanced briefly at Freath and nodded.

Stracker departed and Loethar looked toward Freath. He shrugged. "She's all yours, now. Enjoy yourself."

"Thank you, sire. Come, Iselda. I have long awaited this chance to be alone with you on very equal terms."

"Leave Piven with me," Loethar said, when he noticed Freath glance at the boy. "His new leash should be ready today."

"As you wish, sire," Freath said, bowing. "Do you need me for anything further?"

"Not right now, Freath. Go have some fun with the queen. Although it will be like lying with the dead."

Freath's lips pulled back over his small teeth. "It matters

not to me, sire. Call me whenever you require me to attend you," he said, before guiding the near catatonic woman from the top of the palace.

Alone at last. Loethar sighed. He was sure Valya would arrive soon and perhaps his mother might deign to enter Penraven. He hoped not, although he suspected a pride of mountain lions wouldn't keep Negev from her chance to finally gloat over Iselda, or her corpse.

Stracker was waiting for them, and Clovis found him once again far more imposing at this closer distance; he no longer needed Kirin's warning to give this man a wide berth. Even unarmed, the man was a mountain. Even with his fury of his family's blood on this man's hands, Clovis didn't think he'd survive a duel against him.

He stole a glance at him now, though, because he felt relatively secure while the barbarian's attention was fully riveted on the middle-aged man currently doing his utmost to impress his captor. Clovis looked at Kirin, who pursed his lips. They were both thinking the same thing. This man—Clovis couldn't remember his name—was apparently able to make things disappear and he was selling his skill with great gusto.

"I saw him once," Kirin mumbled in the queue. "He was nothing more than a charlatan in a travelling show."

"Well, if they believe him, he'll be Loethar's Left before he knows it!" Clovis said sourly.

"That's my point," Kirin whispered. "He has no idea that in his grandiose efforts he's probably signing his own death warrant. They'll discover he's a small time conjuror and probably slash his throat for wasting everyone's time."

Clovis shivered, even though death had sounded so attractive only the previous day. "So we stick to our plan."

"Yes," Kirin said, his tone firm. "Don't deviate. I promise you it will save us but more importantly, it will give us a chance to help whatever rebellion force ever gets the courage to fight back."

"What makes you think your apparent lack of magic means they won't slash your throat this instant for being of no use to them at all?"

"Well, Clovis, this is where we musn't fully undersell our talent," Kirin urged, slightly more acid in his usual optimistic tone. "It's a fine balance, I agree. Ah, he's been put into that group. I wonder what that grouping means?"

Clovis shrugged. So far that group contained the fellow who claimed to make things disappear, a woman who apparently could understand the "mind of the sea," another woman who was a healer—always handy, Clovis thought—a youth who claimed to control weather, a girl who used animal intestines to divine the future and a man who could talk to trees. He looked away, no longer interested. "I don't know, Kirin," he said, his voice heavy with weariness.

"Don't let us down now that we've come this far."

Clovis shuffled another few paces further, trying to ignore Kirin's pulling his shirt to hurry him along. Finally it was his turn to face Stracker. He glanced at Kirin, but his friend's expression was suddenly and deliberately blank. Perhaps he was trying to suggest they act as though they did not know one another.

"Name?" the guard asked, well and truly bored it seemed.

Clovis was impressed that all the barbarians of rank spoke Set. "Er, I am Clovis of Vorgaven."

"Ah." Stracker took over, making a mark near what must have been a name against a list. "We are told you read the future."

Clovis felt this throat close. He gave a nod and after a nervous glance sideways at Kirin, added, "Er, well, that is what people want to believe. Who am I to turn down a chance for a living?"

Stracker looked up from his list, surprised, and then frowned at Clovis. He flicked the parchment. "Are you telling me this is a lie?"

Clovis shrugged, feeling himself beginning to perspire beneath the man's hard look. He wanted to take the man by the throat and squeeze hard but wondered whether his hands would even fit around the bull-like neck. He knew Kirin was willing him to convince the barbarian but Stracker looked capable of immediate violence, as though he wouldn't even wait for Clovis to form his argument. The dark green ink and its designs rippled over the ropey muscles and veins of the barbarian's thick arms and shifted on his face as his puzzlement turned to a snarl. Clovis swallowed. "Forgive me. I am not lying but I also don't want to make any grand claims. It is true that I see things now and then. But they are unpredictable readings. I actually tend to be a good observer of people and those instincts combined with the little sentient skills I do possess seem to impress the wealthy community in which I used to live."

"I see," Stracker said, his eyes narrowing. "So you admit to some magic?"

"I don't want to mislead anyone," Clovis reiterated, "but if it prevents an untimely death, then yes, it would not be a lie to admit to some sentient skill," he lied.

"Stand over there," Stracker said, pointing to a lonely corner of the guardhouse.

"But no one else is there," Clovis observed bleakly. He'd ruined it for himself.

"How clever of you. Yes, I can see that you have sound observation skills, Master Clovis," Stracker said acidly. "Move!"

Clovis did so reluctantly and with the help of a shove from one of the guards. He let his mind go blank as he turned his attention to Kirin, who was pushed forward.

"Name?" the same bored guard asked in the same weary manner.

"Kirin. I'm from the Academy at Cremond."

"A teacher," Stracker snarled, striking off the name when he found it.

"No, not at all. I don't know how best to describe my role other than someone who interviews students and divines their best study paths."

"Divines?"

Kirin nodded. "That's how it was described."

"It is magical?"

"Low level. We call it 'trickling,'" Kirin said. Clovis was astounded by the younger man's composure and ability to lie with such confidence under this sort of scrutiny. Kirin's voice wasn't even shaking, whereas Clovis was still sweating from Stracker's brief, angry attention. Kirin looked calm, almost jaunty.

"Tell me what trickling means," Stracker growled.

"Well, although I don't have a lot of power within me I can direct whatever I have toward someone and learn about . . . how can I put this? . . . um, his mood, you could say."

Stracker frowned. "Mood?"

"Disposition. Is that a word you understand?"

Now Stracker's expression darkened, his eyes hooded. "Be careful, teacher. I have the power to spill your blood right now."

"Oh, I know that, sir," Kirin said smoothly, censuring all cockiness. "My respect," he added, bowing. "I meant no insult—I was just trying to find a word that was meaningful to both of us. My talent is unusual and I must say pretty useless in most situations, other than at the university. With its help I can place people into their right study area."

"Any useful application at all that you can impress me with, teacher?"

Kirin puffed his cheeks, blew out the breath quickly. "Well, I suppose I can pick what might be the right tasks suited to people so they work efficiently; I can sense hidden talents, I can even get a good idea of whether a new marriage will be strong or weakened through discord. You see, quite odd and possibly pointless but there are practical benefits." Kirin smiled easily.

Stracker considered him. "Why aren't you scared like everyone else?"

"Another of my abilities is to hide my emotion, sir. I am terrified of you but I realize there is very little I can do should you decide to hurt me, torture me, injure me, kill me. I am, sir, as squashable, you could say, as an ant is to a mountain lion."

Stracker gave a dark grin. "Mountain lion, eh?"

"You look as intimidating," Kirin admitted.

"Over there, teacher, with the other useless one."

Kirin nodded and moved to join Clovis.

"Well that makes two of us for the executioner's blade," Clovis said.

"Don't be too hasty," Kirin replied.

The majority who had made the journey were interrogated and were put into a third group that was herded off almost immediately. Clovis felt instantly alarmed when he heard the guard leading them away discussing which accommodations they were to be given; it seemed those people had impressed and their lives would be extended. His own group's motley number had swelled to include a woman who apparently could talk with animals, another woman who was a healer—again, handy—a water diviner, a youth who claimed to dream the future, a girl about the same age who used blood to divine the future, a wizened man who could make things grow, a silent girl wrapped in a headscarf, and finally a youngster who could dislocate all his joints and fit into a small wine barrel.

"Hardly magical," one of the Vested standing with them commented.

"Well, you try it," the young contortionist replied. "It's a unique skill. Almost as impressive as your ability to know which plants will yield good harvest." The youngster was right, Clovis decided; each of them had talents that were unique but, to all intents, relatively useless. He hoped Kirin had made a wise choice in leading them down this path.

Another group, of which there were at least twenty, maybe more, were left standing opposite his small clan. They looked nervously around, probably muttering the same anxieties as his group, Clovis assumed.

Stracker sent the last person over to the other group, a

young lad probably eleven summertides. "They're all lying or of no aid to us. Kill them," he announced casually, then added, "except the boy. Send him to my chambers."

Collectively the larger group quailed. Some of the women began to scream; others who had clearly tried to protect family members through lies gathered their weeping children around them. One man stepped forward to protest and Clovis had to suck back a cry of shock when he saw Stracker slash his blade across the man's face. The wound opened, spilling blood in a torrent before Stracker gutted the man in front of the horrified onlookers.

"Shut up!" he roared above the dying man's guttural noises. "I had intended to go easy on you so don't make this any more complicated for yourselves. Go quietly. You have no choice. You have tried to pretend you have skills, or your claim to sentient skills are of no use to us. Either way, we do not need you."

"Turn us loose," a woman begged, clutching the arm of a man next to her. "We can't hurt anyone."

Stracker smiled. "But you have insulted me. Did you think we from the Steppes are such imbeciles as to be taken in by your pathetic attempts to present yourselves as empowered?" He paced before them. "Each of you," he said, "offered yourselves to us." He pointed behind him. "The group over there, and the group that have gone, were all named by others as having powers that can't be explained. You are all irrelevant but you have sold yourselves as important. You took the risk, you gave it a good go, but you have failed. I have no use for you and I certainly don't want to feed your hungry bellies."

"Please," voices begged him.

Clovis was trying desperately not to look up from the ground where his gaze had been firmly directed but he glanced up helplessly and saw the fatally wounded man keel over, saw the desperate expressions on the doomed faces, and was reminded that this was how Leah and Corin must have sounded, pleading for their lives from the same brute. He gagged. Though he didn't want to vomit, he couldn't help himself retching and he raced to bend over in a corner, losing the pathetic bread and thin gruel they'd been given this morning.

The squeals intensified as the guards corralled the group into another courtyard and Clovis blocked his ears, unable to bear listening to their cries. He felt a steadying hand on his back.

"Be calm." It was a woman's voice. Clovis wiped his mouth on his sleeve and looked up. "You can do nothing but pray for a speedy despatch for them."

"How can you be so heartless?"

"Heartless? My husband of nine years is with them," she said, giving him a hard, unblinking look. "I can't save him. I can't even say goodbye to him. Do you think screaming, clawing at him, begging that animal will change anything?" Clovis shook his head dumbly as he straightened, glancing briefly at Kirin, who was staying well out of this exchange. "So I'm using every ounce of my body to force myself to stay calm, as you must. We will only fight back if we keep our minds clear and on one goal only."

Clovis closed his eyes. Another rebel!

"I am Reuth," she said. "And I will have my revenge." She looked up and he saw her convey a message with her eyes as the last of the group was finally shuffled away. He could see the deep sorrow in one man's face; he had to be the husband.

Clovis turned back to the woman. "I'm sorry, please forgive me. I too lost my wife and child to the same brute. My wounds are still too raw. Are you the one with visions?"

She nodded and he saw her eyes were wet. Clovis couldn't imagine what it was costing her to be so brave, knowing the man she loved was about to be slaughtered. He should console her, he thought, but he did nothing, said nothing, and she continued, "Not that they believe me and it's a very contrary skill. It chooses when and where, how and why. But it may save my life. We must stay alive, as best we can."

"I'm not as brave as you," he said.

Kirin joined them. "Then we'll all be brave for each other." Everyone else could hear their discussion and murmured agreement although every face looked as pale and traumatized as the other.

Fresh screams began outside. Reuth visibly tensed and reached for someone, anyone. It was Kirin who hugged her, pressing her face close to his chest to stifle any sobs. Clovis felt sick for being unable to offer any comfort to this courageous woman.

"What will he do to the boy?" someone asked.

"He will use him to feed his perverted sexual appetite," Kirin replied. "At least until he gets too bored with the boy."

"How do you know?" Reuth asked, wincing at the shrieks.

Kirin shrugged hastily. "I have to get out of here," he said, not answering her.

"It will stop soon," Reuth said to him quietly. "And then we will know what they plan for us. Let us say a prayer for them."

Obediently, everyone joined hands, though each kept his prayers private.

"It is over now," Kirin finally said ominously, and Clovis began to believe in his friend's abilities for the cries stopped upon his last word.

Stracker strode in, sheathing his sword. "What are you lot talking about?" Then he grinned maliciously. "As if I couldn't guess." Everyone straightened.

It was Kirin who spoke. Clovis had to wonder from where the young man drew his confidence. "We were wondering what you had in mind for us, sir."

"Come with me and you shall find out," Stracker replied. "Single line, hands on each other's shoulders."

Clovis shuffled behind Kirin. He could feel Reuth's hands on his shoulders and could smell the blood in the air as they headed to their fate.

Ten

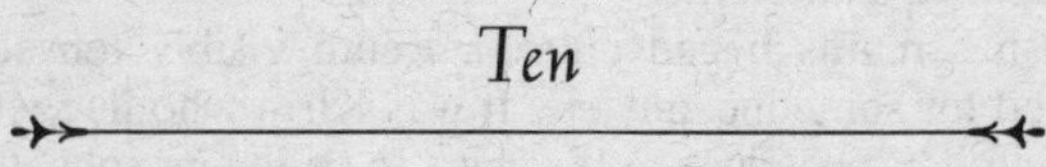

Gavriel had no choice but to risk it. Leo needed food. On cue, his own hunger pangs gave a low grind, reminding him that the situation was urgent.

How clever, he thought, as he dragged his hand softly against the various areas of the wall that were false. To all intents it looked like any other thick stone slab but the false panels' cunning design allowed voices to be heard clearly and spy holes to be drilled with ease.

At first he'd thought there were only a couple but Leo had shown him that many areas of the wall facing into the king's salon were indeed fake, giving them this ability to eavesdrop.

Leo was currently distracted, drawing up a rough map for Gavriel to show him the network of corridors as Leo understood them. The chalked maze that had taken shape on the wall astounded Gavriel, despite its amateurish scrawl.

"This many?" he said, impressed by just how many corridors there were.

"These are the ones I know, the ones father allowed me to play in now and then."

"Your mother doesn't know about them?"

Leo shook his head. "I told you, Valisar fathers and sons only. Piven came in with me a few times but . . ." The king shrugged.

"I know," Gavriel said, feeling an intense sympathy for

the boy. He knew what it was like to have a brother to play with. Gavriel looked up at the drawing. "This is impressive, Leo."

"Father insisted I memorize my way around this region of the ingress. I really don't know the rest at all or even how extensive it is."

"So he was teaching you?" Gavriel suddenly understood the convenient chalk.

"Yes, we'd come in here, the three of us, and father would get me to walk through the ingress with him. Then he'd test me, getting me to scribble on the walls. He'd rub it off though so that I could memorize my way. He was planning to take me much further when . . ."

Gavriel saw the young king's face darken.

"Yes, well, he'd be so proud of you now," Gavriel quickly said. "Because it's doing just what it was intended for."

"It was intended as a means of spying," Leo said.

"I don't doubt it but I'll stake my life on the fact that Cormoron built it as a final secret means of escape."

"I'm hungry, Gav. I'm feeling sick I'm so empty."

"Right, that was what I was going to suggest I do next," Gavriel said brightly.

"I'll show you," Leo said, immediately putting down his chalk and wiping his hands on his clothes.

"No, Leo. That's too dangerous now. You are now king and my father and your father—Lo keep their souls—made me your keeper."

"My champion," Leo corrected.

"That's right. I am your protector and guardian."

"They picked the right twin, then, because you are the better fighter, aren't you?"

Gavriel smiled. "Not sure Corb would agree with you there but I do. He was never good enough to best me and I know it galled him, although he didn't say much."

"Where is Corbel, anyway?"

This was the question Gavriel had been dreading. "Er, I'm not sure. He was sent on a task before the barbarians arrived.

Hopefully he's had the good sense to get away completely." Returning to the matter at hand, he said firmly, "Right, food. I'm going to follow your map to the kitchen and Leo, you've got to be prepared to eat whatever I find. You can't be fussy and it could be raw."

"Not raw meat?"

"Probably not meat at all. I'm hoping to find some bread, perhaps some cheese."

"That's fine. Get some milk if you can. Hopefully someone's remembered to milk the cows. Oh and—"

"Don't even mention honeycakes," Gavriel warned, winning a grin from the king.

"I suspect after last night's dish, no one will want to use the oven again," Leo said and Gavriel thought him brave to even mention it. He knew he should say something about the former king but was lost for appropriate words.

"If I see them and can balance them, they're yours, I promise," he said instead. "So, down this corridor, past four openings, then the one on the right, turn left . . ." Gavriel screwed up his face, thinking hard, before saying, "left again?"

"Right," Leo corrected with a sigh. "Don't get lost. Here, shall I give you the string that father used to teach me with? It's somewhere back here where he left the chalk and other things."

"No, I need to remember and I've got it straight now. Past four, right, left, right."

Leo nodded. "How long before I should be worried?"

"Don't worry at all. I have no idea how long it's going to take, especially if I have to wait for someone to turn his back or leave the kitchen."

"Let me at least come part of the way with you," Leo begged.

"No. This way if anything goes wrong, you have a chance to get out. If you hear voices, Leo, run. Make your way around the ingress as you know how and go to the opening you've spoken about. Take whatever chances you have to but get out of here if the ingress is discovered. All right?" Leo nodded. "No, you have to promise me aloud."

"I promise."

"Right. Keep an eye on Loethar. I have no idea what the time of day is but I reckon it's got to be close to dawn, if not already, and he's bound to make an appearance. Listen to what he says to the damn bird. He talks to it as if it's going to talk back!"

"I think he talks to Vyk because he's not going to answer back," Leo said, frowning. "Perhaps the raven is the only creature he truly trusts."

"I'll be back soon," Gavriel, said, shaking his head at Leo's fanciful thought. "Talking to a bird," he muttered with disdain as he loped off.

It was almost dawn and Clovis found himself standing in what looked to be an unused yet simply furnished chamber alongside his companions. Understandably there was tension in the room and specifically a sudden wariness about each other. He stole a glance at Kirin, who was ignoring everyone, staring out of a tiny window, and then looked toward Reuth, who sat quietly on the floor, her arms wrapped about her knees. In fact even the few whisperings had ceased and all were immersed in their own thoughts, a grim silence hovering around each.

Apart from Kirin, about whom no one knew anything anyway, Clovis was sure that all of them were only mildly Vested. The truly Vested of the land didn't often admit to it. Seeking fame and fortune from sentient power seemed to be the realm of the mildly afflicted only. He smiled ruefully as he acknowledged that he fitted this description adequately.

The door suddenly creaked open, disturbing his thoughts. People stood warily, unsure of what was going to happen. Clovis melted back to join Kirin at the window.

"Here goes nothing," he whispered, immediately nervous.

Kirin looked bored. "Stay calm, stay true. You become instantly more interesting by being silent, unruffled. Watch the others' anxious expressions and keen desire to please. It can work against them in this situation."

"What are you, some sort of oracle?"

For some reason—perhaps it was their internal distress—they both found Clovis's comment amusing and actually laughed quietly with each other.

"You two! At the back. Yes, you jokers." Stracker's voice interrupted their humor. They straightened their expressions. "What's so funny?"

"Nothing much at all," Kirin answered, "but I've found keeping a sense of humor—even about impending death—is probably wise when you don't have any control."

"And so you're laughing at me?"

"Not you," Kirin added. "Just our own wretched bad luck to be in the wrong place at the wrong time."

"And to be Set people, rather than from the Steppes," Clovis added, desperately trying to mimic Kirin's manner.

He wasn't sure he'd managed it but he did notice that the stranger who had arrived behind Stracker twitched what might have been a suppressed smile.

Stracker glared at them both, then turned to the stranger. "All yours, for what they're worth. Take your time, they aren't going anywhere fast."

The stranger nodded. "In here?"

"Where else?"

"Interview them in front of each other?"

"Keeps them honest," Stracker said, grinning maliciously. "Anyone gives you lip or trouble, have the guard take them out. They'll have their throats slit immediately—Vested or otherwise. Do you all understand?" he asked, suddenly taking them all in with a fresh scowl.

People nodded or mumbled their assent.

Stracker pushed a scroll of parchment into the stranger's hand. "Here, you'll need this," he said, before striding out.

The man who'd been left behind turned to face them all, slightly bemused.

"Well, it seems we're to be in each other's company for a short while. Let's see what it says here." He walked over to a table where a single chair had been placed. No one had dared sit but the man did so now. "Er, everyone is welcome to make himself as comfortable as he can. Let's begin with the two 'jokers' at the back, shall we?"

Kirin pulled a wry expression as Clovis glanced his way.

"Us, sir?" Clovis asked.

"Yes," the man said, evenly. "Over here, perhaps, so that we don't have to talk across everyone else."

They joined him at the table, standing before him.

"Names?"

Kirin put his hand against his chest. "I'm Kirin," he said. "From Cremond."

"Clovis," his companion replied.

"Are you relatives?" the man asked, consulting his paperwork.

They shook their heads, sharing a quizzical look.

"Oh, it's just that you seemed friendly enough with each other."

"Would it help if we were related?" Kirin asked.

The man grimaced. "I'm afraid not. Master Clovis, it says here that you have an ability in telling fortunes . . . is that right?"

Clovis nodded. "I used to live in Vorgaven and I mainly worked for the wealthy seafaring traders. I could give them an insight into buying/selling, weather patterns, what to invest in, that sort of thing."

"And how accurate were you in your predictions, Master Clovis?" the man asked, eyeing him directly.

"No one complained," Clovis replied, deliberately vague. He felt Kirin's body weight shift next to him. Kirin wanted him to underplay his talent.

"Are you a rich man?"

"No, sir."

"Do you own your own dwelling?"

"I do, er, did, yes."

"Where exactly?"

"Do you know Vorgaven?" Clovis asked.

"Indeed."

"Our house was on a small piece of land on the peninsula that looks out to Medhaven."

"That's old Jed's land isn't it?"

Clovis was impressed. Roxburgh was one of the more powerful of the sailing merchant dynasties and no one called old Master Roxburgh by his first name. "Yes, I was able to secure a small holding on it."

"Then you are not poor, Master Clovis."

"I didn't say I was. You asked if I am wealthy, which I am not."

The stranger smiled. "It seems to me that your predictions, however ordinary you think them, obviously pleased enough of the right people. You'll do."

"Do what?"

"Just wait over there, Master Clovis," the man said. "Now you . . . what is it you do?" he asked Kirin, effectively dismissing Clovis, who had no choice but to shuffle away, his clanking chains noisy in the thick silence.

"I am from the Academy at Cremond."

"And you are a teacher?"

"No. I've explained this all before."

"Then take a moment to explain to me, Master Kirin. It seems your life might depend upon it."

Kirin quickly summarized his position at the Academy.

"I see. At the Academy did you know Scholar Shuler? He was part of the administration so I'm sure you would have run across him."

Kirin looked worried as he thought deeply. Clovis could see that his friend was uncomfortable and he begged Lo inwardly to bring this man, Shuler, and his face to mind. He felt sick when Kirin shook his head. "I'm sorry, sir, but I have no recollection of this person."

"Good, because he doesn't exist," the man said smoothly. "I was simply testing you. A desperate person agrees to anything." He twitched another attempt at a smile, failing again. "So, you can sense aspects of people—is that a fair way of putting it?"

Kirin nodded.

"Can you sense what they may do next?"

Clovis believed this was a trick question. The stranger was leading Kirin somewhere and he was sure Kirin was damned either way he answered.

"Master Kirin?" the man prompted.

"Er, sometimes I can get a feel for what they believe their alternatives are, and I can on occasion guide them in making a decision. Of course, this is not a precise skill, sir. How I interpret something is likely to be very different to how you might, for instance. It's all very subjective."

Now the man did smile, genuinely. "You're a slippery character, Master Kirin. Intelligent too. You do want to survive this . . . well, shall we say trial?"

"Why don't we say that? It's such a convenient word to hide behind, with the nice suggestion that there's anything fair or even remotely objective about this interview."

The stranger sat back and regarded Kirin with a hard stare. Clovis was sure if a pin dropped you could hear it anywhere in the room, such was the intense, heavy silence that surrounded his friend's remark.

"You're a brave man, Master Kirin," the stranger finally said softly.

"I am young, I have only really just begun living the life I want. I have a mild talent for essentially what amounts to little more than being a good judge of character, perhaps being able to get to the truth of someone. That's all. I am tired of trying to use it to barter for my life. So if it's as worthless as I feel it is, let's stop this charade. If I'm to be killed, let's get it over with. I'm sure far better people with more meaningful lives have already gone to Lo on your leader's whim, although why a man of the Set would join these barbarians for any other reason than pure cowardice, I can't think of one."

Clovis gasped, along with the others in the room.

"You may move over to stand with your friend, Master Kirin," the man said firmly. "Next, Jervyn of Medhaven, where are you?"

Kirin retreated, glaring at the stranger, who ignored him, Clovis noted.

"What the hell are you doing?" he growled under his breath as Kirin arrived to stand alongside him.

Kirin turned his back to the stranger and winked at Clovis. "We've got nothing to lose. Trust me, my friend." Then he staggered, clutching for the wall.

"What's wrong?" Clovis asked, grabbing at Kirin's arm.

"Nothing. Tired, I suppose."

"Tired? You've got a dozen years on me!"

"I meant tired of all this artifice."

"Well, it was your idea," Clovis reminded him. "Now you've got him fired up and probably in a mean mood."

"I don't think so," Kirin murmured. He took a deep breath and stood straight again. "I think he liked us."

Clovis sneered but he noticed Reuth had been called. For some reason he held his breath. The conversation went much the same way as all the others. The man interviewed all of the people slowly, deliberately, never raising his voice or threatening. He simply listened, prompted and made a few notes.

Finally he sighed and looked up from his desk. "Master Kirin? Come here, would you? You too, Reuth."

Clovis frowned, nodded at Kirin who looked a bit pale, he had to admit. Perhaps the young man's bravado was failing him?

"Yes?" Kirin said, moving once again before the interrogator.

"I'm going to give you a second opportunity to fight for life."

"I told you, I'm not interested in bargaining for my life any longer."

"Not yours, Master Kirin. His," the man said, pointing at Clovis. "Tell me what I want to know and I will save his life. Continue treating me with contempt and I shall have him brutally tortured and killed in front of you. Now, come stand here beside me, please."

Kirin moved slowly, a look of disbelief on his wan face. He glanced toward Clovis who could do nothing but stare back.

"Good," the man said. "Now perhaps you've already met and spoken with Reuth Maegren."

"Briefly and for the first time today," Kirin said.

"That's fine. It matters not. Reuth tells me she has visions but like you and your companion, she chooses not to make much more of her talent. If anything she is reticent about it. Do you understand what I mean when I say reticent?"

"Yes, curiously enough for this peasant, he does understand," Kirin said in a cutting tone.

"Careful, Master Kirin. I want you to use your skills—the ones you think so little of—and tell me if she lies."

Kirin looked at him, aghast. "I can't—"

"I'd like you to try, Master Kirin. Remember, your friend's life depends on your candour. Do your best and you'll save him a lot of pain."

"May I know your name?" Kirin asked.

"Certainly. It's Freath."

"I'll remember that."

"For when you kill me, do you mean?"

"There's no violence in me, so I doubt your death will be by my hand."

"Shall we get on?"

Clovis could see Kirin's jaw grind. Moments later Kirin opened his eyes. "The woman does not lie. She has visions. They are reliable but they are infrequent. There, satisfied? Whether I'm right or wrong is up to you now to decide but I've done as you've asked. I trust Master Clovis is safe?"

"For the time being," Freath said. But as Kirin moved away, he stopped him again. "Not so fast, Master Kirin. Your friend is safe at this moment because of what you told me about this woman. But now I wish you to give me similar insight into everyone gathered. I presume you'd happily lie about Master Clovis so we'll leave him out of it. Let's begin with . . . Jervyn of Medhaven."

Kirin hung his head. Clovis understood now that his friend was indeed torn between two evils. He didn't want to display his skills but at the same time lives were in the balance, especially his and he realized as new as their friendship was, Kirin would not easily let Clovis suffer.

"Jervyn has no ability to divine using water, the man who claims to make things disappear is a conjuror at best, the woman who can understand animals is simply very good with them—she has no magic. The healer woman is very talented at what she does. The girl who reads blood is simply ghoulish but the boy who dreams the future possibly has an untapped skill. Old Torren can make things grow—he has limited but unique power . . ." On Kirin went, as though reciting from a list in his head, damning some and saving others. All the while he seemed to shrink. By the end of it he looked haggard.

"Master Kirin, are you unwell?"

"Yes," he replied.

"Make room for him to lie down," Freath ordered. By now the chamber had quietly split itself into two groups: those Kirin had denounced and those he had supported. It was only those from this latter group who moved to help. The others, rather understandably, Clovis realized, would have happily let him drop dead. Freath called for a guard and ordered that Kirin be seen to. Shortly after they carried his friend away, Stracker returned to the chamber.

"Well, Freath, how have you fared?"

"I have chosen."

"Good. Give me the names."

"What will happen to the rest of these folk?"

"Never you mind," Stracker said, though his smile was malicious.

"But I do mind. I wish to speak with your leader."

Stracker laughed aloud. "No."

"Then you will risk his wrath. He will want to know what I have discovered."

"Stop worrying, Freath. They're all safe, because they all have talents. Choose the pair you want."

"They are all safe?" Freath confirmed.

"I give you my word. Now hurry, please. I have to report to Loethar."

Freath began. "Everyone over here is of no use to me. The people over here possess unique skills that your leader should know about, especially the middle-aged woman. The older one is a talented healer, which I'm sure will be handy for you, and the youngster has valuable insights through dreams. The old man uses a magic of his own to make things grow—again a rare talent, one you should make good use of."

"And the jokers?"

"They're my choice, Stracker. Masters Clovis and Kirin are mine."

"I passed the younger one on my way in. He looks half dead. Are you sure you want him?"

"I'm sure. Now let me go check on him."

Stracker stepped back, sneering as Freath passed by. As soon as Freath had gone, the barbarian called his guards.

"Take this lot away," he said, pointing to those Kirin had named as untalented. "You know what to do."

Men and women from that group instantly began to cry out, screaming for mercy. Clovis pulled Reuth, Torren, the youth, the silent young woman, the old man and the older woman back toward the window.

"You lot wait here. Don't try anything foolish," Stracker warned and was gone before they'd even had a chance to finish mumbling their agreement.

* * *

Gavriel was nearing the kitchen and although the walls were impenetrable here, he found himself tiptoeing. Fear and anticipation were combining to put him on edge. He was very aware that Leo would be counting the minutes as well and the longer he was away the more anxious the king would become. This was the first time in two days he was no longer within touching distance of his charge and that was making him additionally nervous. His father's words rang ominously in his mind: "*Do not* leave him for so much as a second. You and he must all but inhale the same breath of air," De Vis had ordered before he'd squeezed his son's shoulder and gestured to his twin to follow him. Gavriel had not been privy to Corbel's journey or where he would go after he had killed the baby. Though Gavriel knew Corbel could not, would not have ever denied his father anything, this murder of an innocent was cruel to ask of anyone.

Gavriel's stomach complained loudly of its emptiness and he banished thoughts of his family. The sound seemed to echo around the tiny alley of the ingress that he was now crawling along as the roof of the secret tunnel dropped low. He could see the glints of shiny pots and pans in the distance through a grille, which he'd reached on his belly. He had to admit he'd never noticed the cunning opening so high in the kitchens. But then the kitchens themselves were a vast complex of chambers and everyone who entered had their mind on food, eyes always drawn to the endless array of pies, breads, stews, roasts, custards and tarts that seemed to continuously be coming from the ovens and cooking areas.

He looked out now into the kitchen and was relieved to find it deserted, though it seemed so unnatural. Cook always had someone on duty to stir the pot of porridge or prepare vegetables for the next day, keep the ovens stoked. The kitchens never slept but this dawn—he thought he could hear the first stirrings of the larks outside—it was silent and lonely. No doubt a reflection of the whole palace. Still, desertion suited his needs.

The sky was beginning to lighten, throwing some murky

but nonetheless welcome illumination into the cavernous chamber through the high windows. He squinted into the dimness, scanning quickly for any easy way to get to food. He hoped he wasn't going to have to climb down and make a dash for the larder. Any stale bread, overripe fruit, perhaps even soup left to allow its fat to separate would do.

But there was nothing left out. Nothing! "Lo's wrath!" Gavriel cursed, knowing he had no choice now but to put himself into the vulnerable situation of having to come out into the open of the kitchen, make his way across the entire chamber to the pantry and cold larder and then steal back with whatever food he could loot and carry and, more importantly, climb back up through the small hole with. Lucky his father had insisted he and Corbel stay so lean. They used to joke that their father deliberately starved them to make real men of them. The truth was the legate simply maintained that a trim man was a healthy one; a lean man could run faster, ride easier, and last longer in any sort of stamina contest.

Gavriel slipped his fingers through the grate to see about unhooking it. Just then he heard a light humming sound—a woman's voice. He pulled his hands back as if burned.

Lo's balls! he swore silently. It would have been a catastrophe if he'd been caught hanging out of the opening. He watched the woman move around the kitchen and realized she was Genrie. Her hair was not pinned up today. It made her look younger, less stern, and the wavy auburn tresses shone as the light hit them. It mattered not that her face was bruised from Stracker's battering; she was still delicious to him. Lost in her activity, she began to hum softly and Gavriel found her voice suddenly sweet and comforting. She awkwardly set about pulling out a haunch of cold meat from storage, then a round of cheese from the larder. She sniffed a pail of milk from the cool room for freshness and poured some into a small covered flask spilling only a little. After she set some oats on to cook in a pot over the embers, she brought out a pouch of nuts along with some apples. Gavriel imagined she was up before the birds to either break her own fast or she had been asked to prepare something for one of the barbarians. Either way she didn't look practiced and he could understand why. This was not her domain. Cook would be furious to see the haphazard manner in which everything was being pulled out and left to clutter the freshly scrubbed working table. There was no order to what she was doing—which was odd because Genrie seemed so very tidy and controlled.

He flinched when she called out. "Tatie . . . are you there? Lo save me, is anyone up this morning?"

There was no reply. He watched Genrie give an exaggerated huff of disgust before she flounced off, muttering aloud, "Well, I'll just have to drag the ale barrel up myself though why they'd need that at this time is beyond me." She disappeared down a corridor leading from the kitchen toward the main palace cellar.

Gavriel couldn't believe his luck. Without waiting a moment longer, he unhooked the grate and lightly lowered himself to the ground. Hurrying to the food scattered over the bench, he hacked off some of the ham, pushing it into his pocket carelessly. He'd have to think about using a shirt to carry food another time. He stuffed apples into the other pocket with a couple of handfuls of nuts and seeds. Slicing off some cheese and bread, he threw those hunks into his shirt to scratch against his skin. He knew Leo wouldn't care. Paupers can't be fussy, Gavriel heard one of his tutor's favorite adages in his mind, although his tutor certainly hadn't meant for it to be applied to the King of Penraven. In his panic the notion nearly made him laugh aloud. He looked over his shoulder; there was no sign of Genrie, but it wouldn't be long before she or someone else would turn up. As a last thought, he grabbed the flask of milk. She would be furious but he hoped she would forget about it, put it down to someone lazy passing through the kitchens and grabbing whatever was around. She'd never suspect it was the missing duo—she probably wasn't even privy to their disappearance and the subsequent search underway. And even if she was, Gavriel reasoned as he hoisted himself back up to the grate's opening, the ring on the flask's lid dangling delicately from his clenched teeth, she hated Loethar and surely would not share her suspicions.

He heard her humming again down the corridor and winced at the soft clank the milk flask made as he accidentally put it down too hard in his rush to get onto the safe side of the grate. But she obviously didn't hear it. With his heart pounding from the close call he slid the plate back across the opening just before Genrie returned, wiping dusty hands on her apron. He had been careful not to take much. Only the cannister of milk could be instantly noticed as missing. But Genrie did not seem to notice anything amiss and Gavriel was able to let out his breath slowly. Finally, when he was sure his heart had slowed enough for him to steal backward on his belly, he blew Genrie a soft, silent kiss.

"Pretty but dim," he said, intensely grateful that she had not lived up to the sharp intelligence he had always presumed she possessed. "Pity."

And he was gone, relieved and also a tiny bit smug that he and Leo might survive another day—this time with full bellies.

Eleven

Kirin blinked. He had no idea where he was.

"There you are," a kind voice said. "You had us worried." Nausea suddenly rose in Kirin's throat and he found he couldn't respond.

"Don't speak," the man said. "Take your time. I can answer some questions I'm sure you have. You're still at Brighthelm Palace and you've been brought to the infirmary. I'm Father Briar and I belong to Brighthelm's church, which is essentially Penraven's spiritual home. I also look after the private chapel in which the royals worship. You've been here for just over four hours. I imagine you're thirsty, so I'm going to try and help you sit up and sip from this cup of water."

Kirin felt an arm slip beneath his shoulders, smelled peppermint tea on the man's breath.

"Help me if you can, Master Kirin," the priest said gently.

Kirin didn't want to move. He liked the soft voice and all of its reassurance but he was sure moving meant throwing up. He knew this feeling, had hoped he'd never experience it again. As expected, as Father Briar hauled him up, Kirin retched.

"Oops, here we go," the clergyman said, getting a bowl in front of Kirin just in time. "Go ahead, don't be embarrassed. I'm a man of Lo but I also think I'm a frustrated physician." Kirin could hear the smile in the man's voice.

"Water," he croaked and the man immediately reached for the cup.

It was cool and sweet. Kirin felt his body relax. He wouldn't be retching again—a small blessing. "Thank you," he managed to say, before leaning back helplessly onto the pillows.

"Let me go clean this up," the clergyman said and Kirin was suddenly alone. It was not unpleasant. He could hear birds twittering outside somewhere and the air inside was moving gently so he assumed a window was nearby. The light in the room was bright—it must be midday or so, if he'd been unconscious for the time the priest mentioned. With the gentle sounds around him he could almost believe that he had dreamed the invasion of the barbarian horde but the surprise that he was no longer dressed and the arrival of the stranger called Freath told him he was not in any dream.

"Awake? Good. We must talk."

Kirin checked he was fully covered by the sheet. "Where are the others?" he croaked, finding his scowl. He cast an eye around for his clothes and especially his boots.

"Dead, probably. Our new masters have, in their wisdom, chosen to kill the few empowered people who likely could have been of help in whatever cause they chose them for."

Kirin felt the shock of this news ripple through him as though a bolt of thunder was passing via his body. He couldn't speak for a moment.

"All dead?" he finally uttered, his numb lips hardly moving.

Freath shifted uncomfortably. "No. Your friend Master Clovis is safe, as well as the woman Reuth. I rather hoped the old man, older woman and the boy might survive."

In equal measure and with similar force as the numbness, relief now flooded Kirin. "Clovis is safe?" he repeated.

"You and he now work for me."

Kirin wasn't sure he understood but he pressed on, his voice finding its timbre and volume at last. "And what is it exactly that Clovis and I are supposed to do?" he said, risking sitting up. Giving a groan, he put a hand to his head. "Where are my things? Can you see my boots?"

"Is it wise to sit up?"

"It will pass," Kirin said gruffly. "My stuff?"

"We'll find it. What is wrong with you—do we know yet?"

"I know."

"Are you going to enlighten me?"

"No."

"Why?"

"I despise you."

Freath took a seat next to the bed. "I know."

Kirin stood and turned away, in a deliberate snub. "You and your savage employer have let talented people go to their death."

"Were they really talented?"

"Did it matter?"

"To me it did."

"Why?" Kirin said, rounding on Freath.

"I needed to know that I had genuinely skilled practitioners of magic. Now I do."

"What makes you so sure?"

"I'm sure, Master Kirin," Freath replied calmly.

"And they were all talented in their own way," Kirin added, his voice becoming more ragged. "Anyone who can make plants grow in spite of disease or poor rains is a wizard. Anyone who can heal using only touch and herbs is surely a living marvel. Even the mere conjuror possessed the skill of being a magician. Surely these people were innocent enough to be saved! Loethar's already conquered the Set—he's got nothing to lose by letting people live, letting people try and get on now."

"Does he not?" Freath asked, dropping his piercing blue stare as the priest re-emerged.

"Ah, you're up, Master Kirin. Do you feel a little steadier?"

"Er yes, thank you, Father . . . ?"

"Briar," the man repeated.

"That's right." Kirin shook his head slightly, embarrassed.

"Thank you, Father Briar. Er, where are my boots . . . my clothes?"

"Perhaps Master Kirin could remain here a little longer, Master Freath?"

"I think not. He looks fine."

"He's hardly hale, Master Freath," the priest protested.

"No, but I think it's best if he comes along with me now. Otherwise we all risk Emperor Loethar's wrath."

"Emperor?" Kirin growled even though Freath's grave expression did not change.

"It's the title he accords himself."

"And you, you treacherous bastard, go along with it to save your own neck."

Father Briar frowned, clearly uncomfortable, as Freath straightened and stood. "I saved yours too and that of your friend. You should be grateful to me. Now I shall not ask you politely again. Please follow me."

Kirin looked at the priest, who gave a sad, sympathetic smile. "Lo keep you safe, Master Kirin. I'll fetch your things."

"I'll just be outside," Freath said. "It's a lovely morning."

Kirin ignored him. The priest returned with his clothes. "Would you like some help getting dressed?"

"No, I can manage. Er, who undressed me?"

"I did. I took the liberty of having one of your socks darned." He shrugged, smiled sadly. "A small kindness among all the fear and bloodshed goes a long way, I'm sure."

Kirin felt dizzy again. "I'm sure," he muttered.

"Master Kirin, do you—"

"I'll be all right. Just give me a few moments to dress. I'll do it slowly." He forced a brighter tone. "Take lots of deep breaths."

"If you're sure?"

"I am. Thank you for everything."

The priest nodded. "Be well, Master Kirin. I'll leave you to Master Freath."

Kirin dressed slowly, gingerly. He did begin to feel slightly better and finally pulled on his boots, his most precious belongings. He'd spent almost a moon's wages on having them crafted by Cremond's cobbler to the nobles, and he felt reassured to have them back on his feet. He stepped out of the infirmary and into the sunlit morning where Freath awaited him. The aide was right. It was a day to lift anyone's spirits. The fragrance of roses was on the air, not a cloud could be seen, joyous birdsong combined with the sound of bees buzzing excitedly around the wild darrasha bushes that grew in a haphazard fashion around these outbuildings.

"It's criminal that a day could dawn so bright when the world itself is so very dark," Kirin said, for the first time feeling the complete helplessness of their situation. Of all the Vested, he'd been the one that kept everyone's spirits up, had determined to personally stay strong and optimistic. And now almost all of those innocent people had been slaughtered. He hated Loethar for that but he hated Freath, a man of the Set, so much more. "It feels as though there is no reason to breathe," he added, the despair that he had kept at bay since Loethar had first entered the Set spilling over.

"You're alive, Master Kirin," Freath said. "I hope I don't need to remind you again."

"For whatever good that will do me," Kirin muttered.

Gavriel's and Leo's mouths were stuffed full of ham and bread. *Amazing what feeding a starved belly can do for the spirit*, Gavriel thought. Leo was grinning, chewing hungrily.

Gavriel swallowed. "Mmm, even the plainest food tastes like a feast when you're hungry, doesn't it?"

Leo nodded enthusiastically. He took a gulp from the milk flask but still couldn't speak for his full mouth.

Gavriel pushed the last of his bread and cheese into his mouth and wiped his hands on his trousers. "Right!" he said, giving a soft belch that amused Leo. "It's time to make some plans," he continued.

Leo had finally swallowed his last mouthful too. He mimicked Gavriel with a quick but suppressed burp and a final swig of the milk. "It's time to go," he said.

"Pardon?" Gavriel had not expected this reaction. If anything he had thought Leo would be frightened about leaving the security of his home and the ingress.

Leo shrugged. "We can't stay here much longer. You got lucky with the food, Gav, but what about later this evening when we're hungry again, or tomorrow morning when we're cranky because of it or tomorrow night when we feel starved? It may be impossible to get food again."

"Water's our real problem," Gavriel added gloomily. "I guess King Cormoron didn't plan such a hasty retreat into the ingress, or he would have made provision."

Leo shrugged. "He probably believed he would stock it with necessities if he ever needed to use it to hide from enemies. Anyway, we have to leave. My father is dead, my mother looks like she's given up, Piven is lost. There's nothing to stay for."

"We can learn everything that Loethar's up to."

"But why? We're helpless here. It's not like we can do anything with that knowledge."

Gavriel nodded. "You're right." But he had no plan.

"Gav, I've been thinking."

"Dangerous," Gavriel joked.

Leo grinned sadly. "I was thinking about what it is to be Penraven's king."

Gavriel sighed. "Leo, you're suddenly so much more. From what we've heard, seen and can work out, all of the Set Kings have fallen. In every other realm's palace so have the families. Everyone is either dead or incarcerated. It might be that you are the only heir who is currently alive . . . but more importantly, the only one who is potentially free."

Leo frowned. "The thing is, no one who should know is aware I'm alive, are they?"

Gav shook his head.

"So even being free is useless to the Set unless . . . well, unless I declare that I'm alive."

"And we won't be doing that! It's not safe yet," Gavriel replied, taking a high-handed tone.

"No, but don't you see, I might as well be dead along with my father and sister, or lost like Piven and mother, if I don't fulfill my destiny. Just keeping me alive isn't enough."

"Destiny?"

"Father talked about it all the time."

"Did he?"

Leo nodded. "He would always try to see me before I had to go to bed and there'd always be some little jest or mention between us of the day when I would be king."

"All fathers do that, Leo, especially royal ones," Gavriel comforted. "He would not want you risking death now."

"That's where you're wrong, Gav. I think that's exactly what my father would want from me. To him the Valisar dynasty was everything. He would have risked everything, including the lives of our family and his people, if he thought there was a slim chance that I might escape Loethar's arrival. And I think that's just what's happened. He knew the barbarian was coming. He probably never thought Loethar would succeed but just in case he'd gone to great lengths to teach me about the ingress, to start including me in conversations about the running of the realm."

"You never mentioned that to Corb and myself."

Leo gave a sheepish shrug. "I was not supposed to. He probably never thought it would come to it either but I do know he would expect me to risk my own life for the realm, for the Valisar crown."

"He protected you—that's why we're in this tiny corridor! And I've sworn to keep you safe. We cannot do anything yet." Gavriel felt as though they were standing on opposite sides of a fence.

"He protected me so that the crown always had its Valisar king—no other reason. I'm not saying he didn't love me, or any of us. I'm simply saying duty was first with father. The crown was everything." Leo kicked at the wall, suddenly looking angry at his admission.

"What are you saying, Leo? I'm losing track of why we're arguing."

"We're not arguing. I want Loethar to suffer for his sins. I want him humiliated and his barbarian horde devastated and banished from all lands in the Set."

"All right," Gavriel said slowly, unnerved by the sudden passion that was sizzling off the youngster. "What are you proposing here?"

"We have to make use of our one advantage. Hiding here was necessary so we could plan. But now we have to be daring. We must get out and allow anyone who is willing to make use of me."

"That's very brave, Leo. It—"

"It's what's expected of me, I imagine."

Gavriel stared at his new king and felt a wave of pride rush through him. Leo was young but he was right. Penraven would need its surviving heir to be the catalyst for rebellion. "You're talking about fighting back, Leo. But I doubt anyone there is feeling terribly rebellious just now. The realm—all of the Set, I imagine—is bleeding, reeling from the onslaught of the barbarian horde."

"I disagree," Leo said, almost loftily. "I think now is when our people will be feeling the most outrage. I know I do, you do. If we leave it too long they might get used to the new ways. We have to tell them how our king died, how our people have been slaughtered mercilessly. We must let them know that the Valisar crown has survived, that they must rally to the Valisar heir . . . king!"

Gavriel paused, impressed by Leo's fighting talk. "Who do we tell? How do we do it?"

"As I said, I've been thinking. I was with both our fathers when they were discussing a renegade. They called him a highwayman but from what I could tell of their conversation, his thieving had become more serious. He was regularly robbing from the crown. And they said he was well organized. I presume that means he had friends."

"And you think this is the man who could start a revolution against the Set's enemy?"

Leo looked abashed. "Well, to be honest, I was simply thinking that someone like this highwayman might have a reason to support the old ways, especially if I promised him freedom from prosecution for his past."

Gavriel stared at the king. "You have thought this through, haven't you?"

"Well, you were gone a long time finding food."

"I couldn't have been. It was too easy—I didn't even have to sneak into the pantry. I told you, witless Genrie made it all easy."

"Witless? I think she notices too much. She's really curt and obviously hates me simply because I happened to be born royal. Be careful of her."

"Oh, she's not that bad."

"She all but scowls every time she sees me."

"She's ambitious."

"And so that gives her a right to sneer at someone who couldn't help being born a royal?"

"Spoken like a true king, your highness," Gavriel said.

"Well, I don't like her."

"You should. If not for her we wouldn't have been fed today."

"You obviously like her, Gav, but we shouldn't trust her."

"She is the only one, save your father, who stood up to Loethar. You should see the beating she's taken for speaking up. I can't help but think she's to be admired."

"She treats everyone as she did Loethar. She's always argumentative; that's her contrary manner. Everyone but Freath feels the bite of her tongue. She seemed to get on well with him, of course. Nasty birds of a feather flock together!"

"Don't be cynical—it doesn't suit you. He's her superior."

"So am I!"

Gavriel knew he couldn't win this one. Switching tactics, he asked, "Anyway, are you talking of the highway man from the north?"

Leo shrugged. "He was only just becoming a real problem for the crown. His name is Faris . . . Kilt Faris."

"Ah, that's right!"

"It's an option, I suppose, and one we'll have to consider when we're ready to make a move."

"It's time for us to leave now."

"We can't just—"

"We can. I told you. I know a way out."

Gavriel took a slow breath. So much was riding on his decisions now. It was all very well for Leo to suddenly feel kingly and twenty feet tall, and instantly courageous now that they'd eluded Loethar with such cunning. But Gavriel knew that the new king's life and thus the future of Penraven and in turn the Set, depended on his every move.

"I know we can't remain here indefinitely. Just give me another day, Leo," he said calmly. "I need to think things through."

"One more day? Fine. Then we go. Come on, I'll show you how."

Leo pushed past him and Gavriel had no choice but to follow.

Kirin stood in the hallway, being introduced by Freath to an extremely pretty but unnervingly serious, brisk woman called Genrie. He was just saying his hello's when Stracker interrupted the introduction.

"He wants to see you," Stracker snarled with no care for the others standing by.

"Of course," Freath replied, looking briefly toward the woman.

"Your chosen has recovered, has he?" the barbarian replied, his sneer lifting the tatua around his face into a ghastly pantomime of sharp shapes.

"A slight fever, that's all. He'll be fine."

Kirin didn't contradict Freath. He didn't care which of the enemy lied to which, or why.

Stracker smiled in his devious way. "Feeling a bit vulnerable, are you, Freath? Better make sure you get all that magic up and firing around you."

Freath said nothing but Kirin choked back a gasp of understanding. So he and Clovis were to be shields of some sort? He wanted to laugh aloud. They weren't warriors who could throw up some sort of magical barrier around people. What was in these people's heads? They'd been interviewed enough times for their captors to know they were akin to seers, nothing more. He wished he could risk a pry but just the thought of it brought a fresh wave of nausea so he ignored the temptation.

Freath was suddenly pushing him toward the woman. "Genrie will take you from here to rejoin your friend. I shall see you soon enough, I imagine."

Again Kirin said nothing in reply. Instead he summoned his best look of disdain for Freath and in turn directed it at the woman who now gripped his upper arm and pulled him away as Stracker led Freath in the other direction.

"What happened to your face?"

"I annoyed someone."

"That bastard Freath, I suppose."

She glared sideways at him. "Don't make assumptions."

"Where are we going?"

"Freath told you," came the curt reply.

"He explained nothing, though."

"Then neither will I."

Kirin sighed. "What is a young, lovely-looking woman like you still doing here?"

"I worked for the queen, Master Kirin. I wouldn't abandon the royal family."

"What family?" he sneered. "As I understand it they're all dead or daft."

Genrie bristled but said nothing and kept marching him onward.

Kirin tried again, apology in his tone. “Help me and my friend Clovis get away, Genrie . . . if you care about the Set. Come with us, in fact!”

She stopped, looking at him as though he were insane. “What do you mean?”

“People like us should be helping each other escape.”

“Please don’t ask such a thing of me again. If you do, I will tell Master Freath.”

“But, Genrie, surely you can’t—”

“Master Kirin, please don’t presume to know me or my motivations. If you were in my shoes you might know the dangerous path I tread. Now, please, let me show you to where Master Freath ordered. He is in charge and I don’t disobey his orders.”

Kirin’s heart sank.

“This is your idea of a joke, I presume?” Gavriel said, feeling dizzy as he poked his head out.

Leo looked back at him quizzically. “No. Why?”

Gavriel’s dizziness turned instantly into fear. “I . . . er . . . this is the only way out that you know of?”

Leo shook his head in bemused wonder. “Oh, wait a minute, I’ll just list all the choices we have,” he offered.

“All right, all right, no need for contempt.”

“Well, Gav, what do you expect under the circumstances? I’m offering us a way out.”

“Not a very happy one,” Gavriel replied, grimacing at the rising nausea.

“The only one. I’m tired of cringing in the ingress, Gav.”

“We’re not cringing!”

“We’ve got to risk escape. We’ve been lucky so far but it can’t last.”

“And so your answer is to climb down from the highest point of Brighthelm?” It was Gavriel’s turn to be acerbic. “This is not called *the gods* for nothing, Leo.”

The young king stared back at him and couldn’t quite mask the disdain in his gaze. “Not climb down, no. That would be suicide, if not from a fall, then from all the enemy arrows that would strike us on the way."

Gavriel blew out his cheeks with relief. "Good. But there is no other way."

Leo pointed.

"I see a tree," Gavriel said. "So what?"

"That is where we climb down."

Gavriel stared at the king as though he had lost his wits. "How, pray tell, my king, are we going to get from here," he said, his finger stabbing the stonework of the tiny opening they'd clambered through, "over to there? Or is that a minor ruffle in your amazing plan that we still have to smoothe out?"

Leo actually grinned, infuriating him.

Loethar had expected the visit, but he hadn't anticipated that it would be so soon. But he shouldn't have been surprised when Stracker woke him just after dawn and told him of the impending visitors. Now he was back in the salon. Vyk was glaring balefully upon them.

"Why does that wretched bird always have to be around?" the older of the two visitors lamented. It was a rhetorical question, spoken purely in complaint.

Loethar yawned. "I warned you not to come until I sent for you."

"I was bored."

"More like you couldn't wait to gloat."

"That may be. But this is my rightful place. What are we waiting for, by the way?"

There was a soft knock at the door and then it opened.

"Him," Loethar said. "Come in, Freath. Ah, Piven too. Good." Stracker arrived after the child, who took no notice of the present company. Instead he scampered up to stroke Vyk, who looked unimpressed by the attention.

"Stracker said you asked for me, sire?" Freath bowed before turning and also bowing graciously to Loethar's company.

"I did. Freath, this is my mother, Negev. But she has a title.

She is known as Dara, which I suppose could be very roughly translated to mean king's mother in your language."

Freath bowed low. "It is an honor to meet and serve you, Dara Negev," he said in his most polite Set.

The woman did not hide her sneer as she tipped her head to one side, studying Freath before replying. "Is it? I'm sure you'd be more honored serving your queen."

His response was careful. "I have no queen, my lady. She is as lost as her child, who you see here."

Negev smiled, not even looking at Piven. "Slippery," she commented instead, throwing a glance toward her son.

Loethar did not miss her message. "And this is Valya," he said carefully, glancing at the woman.

Again Freath nodded, having already bowed to her. "I'm sorry Penraven gives you a wretched salutation but let me be the first to offer a warm welcome."

Valya stared at him with distaste. "He's a traitor, is he, Loethar . . . has he swapped his allegiance?"

"Apparently," Loethar answered, amused, but eyeing Freath with a steely look.

"No, madam, there was nothing to swap," Freath said, obviously deciding to speak up for himself. She arched an eyebrow in query at him. "I was never loyal to the Valisar clan. I was simply its lowly paid servant."

At this Loethar laughed. His mother and Valya took his lead, appearing equally amused. Freath's expression remained somber, unchanged. "Is Iselda not giving you what you want in the bedroom, Freath?"

Both women turned surprised expressions to Loethar.

"You gave him the queen?" Valya asked, aghast.

"I gave him a broken, ordinary woman, stripped of her former title, in return for his services. A small price to pay for a man who knows everything there is to know about the Valisars and this realm. He was as close to Brennus and Iselda as Stracker is to me."

"But Stracker should be. He is your brother, Loethar," Negev admonished.

"Half-brother, mother," Loethar corrected, looking at Freath.

The servant showed no outward sign of surprise at this news. Instead he moved briskly to the banal. "Can I organize some refreshments for your guests, sire?"

Loethar sighed although he tried to cover it by turning away. "I take it you've come to stay, mother?"

"Darling Loethar. You are amusing," Negev replied with undisguised condescension. "I'm home, my son. This is my rightful place now."

"As I thought," he said stiffly, looking at Freath again. "Give my mother the queen's old suite of rooms."

Again not so much as a flicker in the man's expression told him Freath was in any way alarmed by this order. "Very good, sire. Just give me an hour to have everything removed."

"No, leave it," Negev said. "It will amuse me to rifle through her things."

Freath nodded at the woman. "As you wish, Dara Negev. Is there anything specific I can have sent up for you?"

"I'll need a servant, of course," she said, a slight tone of irritation in her voice.

"Of course. You shall have Genrie."

"The defiant girl?" Loethar asked.

"The very one, sire."

"Well suited. You'll like her, mother." Loethar found himself glancing toward Freath and enjoying a shared conspiratorial look. The feisty maid and the overbearing Dara would make an explosive pair. "I'm sure you can find a comfortable chamber for Valya?"

"Loethar, I'll be happy to share yours," Valya chimed in.

He was both relieved and grateful when Freath without a blink of hesitation answered for him.

"Er, my lady, do let me have a beautiful suite made up for you. You deserve your privacy and I will organize someone to wait on you."

Loethar leapt in to reinforce the point. "Thank you, Freath. I think Valya would enjoy being pampered a little, wouldn't you?"

Eyeing them both, Valya replied, "Yes, of course."

"Good," Freath said, coming as close to a smile as the man obviously could. Loethar's gaze narrowed. Freath was proving more than helpful. He was sharp; he already understood plenty, which was impressive, considering he'd hardly had more than a collected hour or more in Loethar's company. He couldn't forget that the man was a traitor but he'd already decided that Freath would live, no matter how much Stracker wanted him gutted. Refocusing on what Freath had been saying, he noted that the aide was casting quiet glances his way, as though he knew Loethar's thoughts had been wandering. ". . . draw and heat some water for a bath for you," he was offering Valya.

"I, er . . ." She hesitated, looking at Negev, who simply shrugged her bony shoulders.

"You should, Valya. Can you remember the last time you enjoyed a hot soak?" Loethar asked. She shook her head. "Then enjoy yourself. This is what they call the spoils of war. It doesn't always mean riches. Sometimes it simply means the peace and leisure to enjoy life's pleasures."

"At someone else's expense," Freath finished.

Negev's eyes turned hard but Loethar saw the jest behind the dry words and tone and laughed. "Exactly. Go, Valya, be pampered. Mother, I shall see you later, I'm sure. Why don't you . . ." He paused, unsure of what to suggest.

"Make myself at home?" she asked.

He let out a sigh. "Yes."

"I intend to. And when will we meet Iselda? She's all there is left, I gather, having heard of Brennus's demise. Pity."

"Er, well, no, there is Piven, here."

"I was wondering when you might explain the boy's presence among us."

"Is something wrong with him?" Valya inquired. She

looked as though she could smell something bad. No maternal instincts simmering there, Loethar noted.

"Freath knows more about him, if you care to listen to him."

Both women glanced Freath's way and the aide took up the thread of conversation easily. "Of course, sire. Piven is the middle child of the Valisar royals. He is adopted and, as you can probably tell, not of sound mind."

"He's a halfwit," Loethar stated.

Freath acquiesced with a tight expression that Loethar assumed was an attempt at a smile. "The only heir is Leonel and he has gone missing, although I'm sure your son will hunt him down soon enough, madam," Freath assured, a small nod toward Loethar. "Piven's half-sister was born a weakling just a day ago and she died, predictably, within hours of her birth."

"Her ashes were cast to the winds," Loethar added.

"Was Iselda present?" Negev asked, and there was an ugly eagerness to her tone.

"She was. I insisted upon it," Loethar replied.

"Excellent," Negev breathed. "I hope she suffered."

"She still is, madam," Freath answered. "She has become catatonic."

Negev frowned.

Loethar explained, knowing his mother would expect him to. "She has withdrawn entirely, I gather, and is now as unable to communicate with the outside world as her invalid son."

"Why is he still alive? A simple drowning in a bucket should do it."

"He is alive, mother, because I permit it."

"Why? Look at the imbecile! What use is he?"

"I have my reasons. And it's his very idiocy that makes him harmless as much as interesting."

Valya touched his arm. "He is attached to the Valisar, Loethar. That should be cause for his death."

"When I need your counsel on running a realm, Valya, I

will ask for it. The child lives until I decide differently. Besides, watch this. Piven!"

"How clever, he knows his name," Dara Negev commented quietly to Valya. Loethar heard her acid remark nonetheless as Piven turned from Vyk and ran toward Loethar, beaming. Loethar lifted him easily with one arm and Piven threw his arms around the man's neck.

The two silent watchers grimaced at the sight.

"I have never enjoyed such blind adoration," Loethar quipped, setting down Piven.

"Have you not?" he heard Valya mutter under her breath but he chose to ignore it.

Leo, recently returned from the roof, rolled away from the peepholes. "I can't take any more of this."

"Stay calm," Gavriel soothed, despite his own anger. "We mustn't lose our heads now."

"I'm not going to stand by and watch them hurt Piven."

"Leo, listen!" Gavriel said, grabbing for the king's arm. "Loethar said he has no intention of doing so—"

"Were we watching the same scene? He didn't say anything of the kind. All the barbarian said was that Piven would live for as long as he permitted him to. He could order my brother's death tomorrow if he tires of him. Any why wouldn't he? Piven's affection and smiles can interest a stranger for only so long before his vacant ways become irritating."

Gavriel turned away, angry. "It's that wretched Freath. Look at the way he keeps burrowing his way deeper into the good books of the enemy. I can't believe we had such a snake in our midst all these years. He's making it so easy for them."

"He's a traitor. And that Genrie is right there alongside him in treachery."

Gavriel growled his despair. "All right, all right, Leo. We go. But we don't just leap off a roof in broad daylight. We need a plan. We also can't take Piven. I have to say that, in case you're hatching some audacious notion about rescuing your brother."

"No, I realize I can't get to him but so far it looks as though he has the barbarian's indulgence." He gave a rueful shrug. "Typical Piven. Everyone loves him, even our enemies."

Gavriel said no more about the invalid boy. "We need to assemble some things and we need some food to get us by. Yes, I know what you're going to say," he said, lifting his hand to prevent Leo's leaping in. "Rabbits will sustain us but I don't know when we'll be in one place long enough to lay traps and catch them. If we're on foot we need food we can eat on the run. At least enough for a couple of days."

Leo groaned. "Not back to the kitchen."

"We have to. Let me do this my way, I beg you. I know you're anxious to be gone. I am too after watching those hideous women's arrival and that sodding Freath sucking up to everyone." He didn't say that he had an awful sense of doom on behalf of Queen Iselda, but Leo's thoughts were apparently following his own.

"I want to see my mother before I go," the king said.

"You mean talk—" Gavriel began, his tone filled with disapproval.

"No, I mean simply to see her once more."

"It will upset you."

"Yes, it will. But you must understand, my father raised me to be king and taught me not to tolerate fools, or cowards. I have no control over my mother's situation—or Piven's. Father wouldn't want me bleating over my family's fate. He would want me to spend my time exacting revenge over it. Has it occurred to you that he knew we would be watching when he killed himself?"

Gavriel nodded. He felt as though Leo was maturing at triple the normal rate of someone his age. "I imagine he had to accept there was a good chance but went ahead anyway, no matter how much it might upset you."

"Upset me?" Leo gave a mirthless grunt. "He wanted me

to see it, Gav! That's why he did it! That's why he made it so gory." Gavriel frowned as Leo continued. "There are moments when I feel I can never forgive him for doing that to my mother, to me . . . even to Piven. But my head tells me it was a show, specifically for my benefit. He wanted me to feel sickened and enraged. He was deliberately pushing me into making a soul promise to exact revenge."

Gavriel suddenly knew Leo was right. He knew the former king well enough to know that was exactly how Brennus's mind worked. His father had told him often enough that the king would always, always put the throne first. "I hate him for doing that to you, Leo."

Suddenly, and despite all his brave talk, the young king crumpled, finally weeping. Gavriel could do nothing except hug the boy, mourning an entire family lost within the space of a day. He would see Leo sit the Valisar throne one day, he swore silently. Even if it took him his entire life, to his final breath.

Finally the trembling stilled. The boy king pulled himself away with an embarrassed sniff and what seemed to be a new resolve.

"You will never see me shed tears again over anything or anyone," Leo whispered and the threat was spoken in such quiet rage it chilled Gavriel, who could say nothing in response. But he didn't need to; the king was already moving. "Get the bow we discussed. We need nothing else except our cloaks—food be damned. We go farewell my mother."

Twelve

Freath had stealthily moved up the stairs, well in front of the two women, just in time to intercept Genrie. He knew he had only moments. "I didn't want to ask earlier in front of the Vested. Did it happen?" he murmured.

She nodded once and he saw the bruises on her beautiful face had darkened to purple. "Exactly as you said it would," she replied, self-consciously touching the spot where his gaze rested.

"Don't be too brave, Genrie. I couldn't bear—" But time ran out on him. "And see to it that fresh linens are provided immediately," he ordered as Valya rounded the staircase.

"Who is this?" Valya demanded.

"Madam, this is Genrie. She will attend to Dara Negev personally and will also supervise your attendance. Genrie will organize a maid for your hour-to-hour needs. I hope that will suit you."

"Do you beat your servants?" she sneered, glancing at Genrie's bruised face.

"I don't, no. Your friend Stracker does."

"Freath? Is that your name?"

"Yes, madam."

"I couldn't give a hog's arse about you servants but I want you to be sure that Stracker is no friend of mine. Is that nice and clear for you?"

"Perfectly," Freath replied and could tell his composure irritated her.

"Good. You girl!"

"Yes, mistress?" Genrie asked.

"Call me that again and I'll order your tongue cut out. You may address me as Lady at all times. Only speak when spoken to and do not raise your eyes to me like that, you slut."

Freath noticed Genrie bite back a gasp. "Apologies, my lady," she murmured, eyes appropriately downcast.

"It's nice to see you making friends already, Valya," Negev said, her tone so dry it made Freath want to cough.

Valya immediately changed approach. "These Penravian peasants need to understand who they're dealing with," she said, in an injured voice.

Freath winced privately.

"And now they do, thanks to you," the older woman commented, turning away. "Show me my suite, Master Freath. It is of no consequence if Iselda is still there. I shall take immense pleasure in having her thrown out."

He said nothing, simply nodding. Looking at the younger woman he said deferentially, "Genrie will show you to your chamber, my lady. Please let us know if there is anything at all we can do for you."

She didn't acknowledge him, but simply turned on her heel. "Show me!" she said, scowling at Genrie, then throwing a glance over her shoulder at the older woman. "I am going for a ride, Negev. I need to clear my head of its anger."

"I think that's a very good idea. Don't get lost," Negev replied. Somehow Freath wasn't sure Loethar's mother was being sincere.

"This way," he said. "The former queen's chambers are in another wing."

"Good. I find Valya quite tiring."

With his back turned to the older lady, Freath could raise his eyebrows slightly at her admission. "She is probably feeling odd and unwelcome."

"That's because she is odd, Freath, and she is most unwelcome. She is as much a foreigner to me as you are."

"I see."

"Do you?"

"I think so. I shall be careful to minimize your contact with her if you wish, Dara. Just guide me in what it is you desire."

She had drawn alongside him and was staring at him. "Oh, you are good, aren't you, Freath? And there I was simply putting you down for a crawling coward. Slippery really doesn't sum you up well enough, does it?"

"I'm not sure I understand."

She chuckled. "Yes, you do, Freath. I can see why my son likes you. Very strange. My son doesn't let anyone close—his closest companion is that wretched bird. Not even I take precedence."

"Oh, come now, Dara, I'm sure—"

"I speak the truth. My son is a very lone individual, Freath. For him to allow you to live is extraordinary enough but to allow you into his inner sanctum has me puzzled. He obviously sees in you what I do."

"Which is?"

"A far more complex mind than you'd like us to believe. You want us to see only the obsequious servant. But I know rat cunning lurks behind that expressionless façade."

"Really, Dara Negev, I think you are getting me wrong. I am truly no more than a formerly wronged servant getting his due. I have been completely honest in my desires. But I will give my loyalties to your son, if he'll allow it."

"Well, incredibly, I think he already has, considering what he has permitted you so far. Beware of my other son, though, Master Freath. He lacks Loethar's finesse and subtlety."

"I plan to stay well out of his way, Dara."

She laughed again. "Wise words."

"This is the entrance to the former queen's suite." Freath motioned to the double doors at which they had arrived.

"Lead the way, Freath," she said and he heard the hunger in her voice once again.

"Just give me two moments, Dara." At her look of surprised enquiry, he hurried to add, "Indulge me, madam."

She nodded, a look of disdain on her lined face, her lips pinched into a scowl. "As you see fit. I shall sit here. Do not test my patience, Freath."

Clovis and Kirin were still none the wiser as to their purpose. They were currently being held under guard in a small chamber with only a small window, more for air than for seeing much through.

"Where are we?" Kirin murmured again.

"I told you I don't know. I was bundled up here after you'd collapsed and I was so worried, I didn't really pay attention."

"And they told you nothing about Reuth? Nothing at all, no clue to her whereabouts?"

"No, I tell you," Clovis replied, irate. "I thought she was behind me. I thought they all were. But we were separated. I ended up alone here with that creepy Freath fellow."

"What did he say . . . exactly?"

Clovis sighed. "He said I was to wait here and not to make a noise and not to draw attention to myself. And if I listened to him I would be safe."

"That's all?"

"Well, he said he was going to find you and discover what had happened. So what happened?"

Kirin leaned back against the wall and crossed his arms. "I pried."

Clovis's mouth opened but nothing came out. Kirin waited, and finally the bigger man asked the inevitable question. "Who?"

"Who do you think?"

"Stracker?"

Kirin nodded wearily.

"And?"

"I couldn't do it for very long. I actually only glimpsed within him because it's dangerous. As I told you all, he likes men, preferably boys. Killing brings him pleasure, so he usually combines both preferences."

"I fear for that boy he took," Clovis said, shaking his head.

"You should."

"What else?" Clovis asked hurriedly.

"I felt his darkness. The man is evil, angry, cruel. I couldn't dwell in his mind—as I say, it was dangerous. But then when Freath got me to look into the minds of the others, it pushed me over the edge."

"It made you sick."

Kirin pushed away from the wall, frustrated. "It's not just my health, Clovis. If that's all it was I'd risk it. To pry properly and to make it yield meaningful information I must have quiet. I need to be sitting still in a dim, peaceful situation with no interruptions. It's usually best if I have a bed nearby and pail at the side!" he said, giving a mirthless smile, "because I need both immediately after even the shortest pry."

"And for long ones?"

Kirin shrugged. "I've not tried since childhood. I have no idea of the extent of the injuries should I attempt it. The only reason I did it today was because I was frightened for all of us. I can't be completely sure because I haven't done it for so long, but I think the person I'm prying into can feel my presence."

Clovis was taken aback. "Truly?"

Kirin shrugged. "If I had the courage to feel sick again I'd test it on you but I seem to recall that someone who is well attuned to the spiritual is more likely to feel me prying."

"You're losing me."

"The act of prying connects two people. It leaves a trackable trace for a short time for anyone Vested, unless I can snap the link fast enough. I haven't had enough practice to know what that time span is or whether it differs from person to person. That's why I pried into Stracker for only a moment or two."

"But we still don't know what he wanted!" Clovis said, not disguising his own frustration.

"No. But I do know he wasn't being honest. We were picked for different reasons. The first group was useful to Stracker and he's sent them somewhere, who knows where or why. The third group was destroyed for being pretenders or generally useless. Us in the middle? Well, he is using us for subtle purposes but I don't know what. It has something to do with Freath but I . . ." He trailed off, feeling angry, dejected.

"It's all right, Kirin. We're alive," Clovis calmed.

"Coming from you that's meaningful. I thought you wanted to die."

Clovis closed his eyes for a moment, before wandering across the small chamber to try and catch a gust of air from the small space serving as a window. "I thought so too," he said, breathing out loudly. "Until death beckoned. Then I realized how frightened I was. And someone who welcomes death isn't scared of it. I heard those people screaming and I knew I wanted my life to go on."

"Who could blame you?" Kirin said softly. "If we're going to remain alive we have to fight. We can't just become barbarian puppets or we make a mockery of your family, of the royals who've lost their lives right around the Set, and of all the innocents whose lives have been snatched."

Clovis was nodding. "I agree. I'll fight with you in the subtle way you suggest."

For the first time it seemed that Kirin had something to smile about.

Gavriel had followed Leo for a long way in silence. Now he gave a low whistle and the king turned in query.

"Do you know where you're going?"

"No, I'm just mindlessly strolling, Gav."

Gavriel's expression turned droll. "I'm much bigger than you, Leo. King or not, I can punch you senseless, and no one will ever know."

"Except you won't. You and Corb were always an empty threat."

Gavriel ignored the taunt. "So we're close, are we?"

"Mother's suite is just up ahead—that small flight of stairs will bring us behind it."

"I can't believe your father allowed you here."

"He didn't."

"But you know it so well."

Leo smiled sadly. "I always wanted more time with her. Once I was Piven's age, father felt it was time for me to 'leave my mother's skirts' as he put it. I followed his wishes with gusto but sometimes I've looked at Piven playing five sticks or 'stalk the donkey' with mother and . . ." He shrugged.

"What?" Gavriel asked gently.

"I felt jealous," Leo confided. "And the really silly part is they're not even playing the games properly. Piven just moves the pieces around randomly but I see how mother loves to watch him playing and how much pleasure he brings her, even though he's so unreachable. I imagine she would have felt like that about me when I was younger. My best days with mother took place when I wasn't really aware of it. I can't imagine how she's coping."

"We all cope in our own way, Leo," Gavriel said. "You are withstanding all this sorrow in the best way you can and her way is to withdraw within herself. Like Piven, in a way."

"Yes," Leo said, "but I would see her once more and say goodbye in my own way . . . even if she doesn't know I'm there or that I'm farewelling her."

"It doesn't have to be for keeps."

Leo looked up at him, their tiny candle flame casting an eerie glow onto his darkly golden hair and Gavriel saw an old man's expression in the young king's face. "I think we both know that it is. I am here to say goodbye to my mother because I know I'm never going to see her again. He's already forced her to lose herself and I imagine her death at his hand, or by someone close to him, is not long away. I don't want to be around to watch both my parents die." Then he looked ashamed. "Gav, I'm sorry. I realize I'm not the only one suffering."

"I'll save my grieving until I'm reunited with Corbel."

"When we get out of here, the first thing we must do is find him."

Gavriel smiled. "That may not be possible."

"Why not?"

"Because I have absolutely no idea where he was sent. Only our two fathers knew and they have died with the secret."

"Why a secret?"

"Ask me that another time, Leo."

The king frowned and, as if grasping that the subject was too tender to press Gavriel further on, he simply nodded. "Let's go," he murmured and Gavriel gratefully fell into step. "By the way, we can't hear anything in mother's room. We can only watch."

"Why?"

Leo stopped. "We're here," he whispered. "I don't know, probably because even old Cormoron must have felt it was vulgar to eavesdrop on the queen. This suite has always been the royal apartments for the king's women."

Gavriel nodded. They found a series of peepholes, but no thin walls so they couldn't hear anything through the thick stone. Set in the wall was a small old timber box that looked like it had been there a while.

Gavriel put his face close to the wall, blinked to focus properly through the small openings and immediately saw Queen Iselda standing and staring blankly through her tall open windows. He tried to imagine what her view would be from this part of the palace and decided it would be very beautiful, overlooking the royal private gardens and the northwestern tip of the Deloran—the great forest that stretched south, tapering to a straggly thicket by a town called Minston Woodlet. Between the gardens and the forest Gavriel imagined Iselda could see across to the jagged, ruggedly beautiful coastline.

"Mother loves the view from that window," Leo whispered.

"I was just imagining how lovely the scene that she's looking out upon must be. Makes me want to see it, too."

"Someone's here," Leo murmured.

Gavriel flicked his gaze to the door and felt his breath catch. Freath had just entered the queen's chambers.

Thirteen

Freath knew he had only a minute or two. The queen was standing at the window, her back to him. He hoped she was lucid. Her grief and confusion had plunged her into such a state of silence and loss that most hours he could not reach her.

"My queen, forgive me, but the crone of the Steppes comes. It was all I could do to keep her outside for but a minute more." He held his breath, only releasing it when he heard her beautiful, sad voice respond.

"It is over, loyal Freath. You have done all you can. Let her and her son do what they will. There is no reason for me to take another breath."

"But, your majesty, think of Piven and—"

"Piven is already lost. And from what you say he is a novelty for the barbarian. Perhaps that will save my little boy's life." Her voice carried away thinly into the soft wind outside.

"But there is Leo to live for, highness," Freath pressed, mindful of the seconds he had left.

"Are you sure? Give me proof."

"I grow weary, Freath," called an ominous voice from behind the door.

"Just making her presentable for you, Dara Negev. A moment more," he begged, quickly turning back to Iselda. "I have no proof, your majesty," he whispered across the room. "All I can say is that I believe he lives."

"Why?"

"Genrie said that food she left out in the kitchen disappeared."

"Is he alone?" she asked fearfully.

"I feel sure Gavriel De Vis is still with him. Prepare yourself, majesty, she comes. Lose yourself if you must and say nothing. Pretend you hear nothing for I know she will take pleasure in punishing you."

The Queen of Penraven turned and gave Freath a heartbreaking smile that arrived and left within a blink of an eye. "She can no longer hurt me. I don't want to live, Freath. Do whatever you must do to preserve Leo. Don't let me be used against him." Then she turned away.

Freath opened the door to be confronted by a slit-eyed Dara, the line of her mouth equally thin. "I'm sorry, Dara Negev. She is lost to us this hour—as she is most hours—but I have made her presentable for you. Please come in."

Negev pushed past, strutting in, looking every bit like the fantailed farla hen with her bright array of colored skirts peculiar to the people of the Steppes.

"Ah, Iselda, we meet at last," she said, ignoring the royal title and any protocol. She laughed. "I'm sure Valya is actually looking forward to meeting you more than I but I am pleased to look upon the common slut that this kingdom once called its queen. And from Galinsea, no less. Pah! And they call us barbarians!"

Although Freath hid the wince he felt at the cruel words, he noticed his queen did not react at all to the baiting. She didn't even turn from the opening through which she stared out mournfully across the Penravian vista. He moved to stand behind her.

"As demented as her son!" Negev spat.

The words of bait seemed to snap Iselda into the present and back into her normally dignified disposition. Finally straightening her shoulders, she turned to focus on the barbarian woman. "Perhaps, but from what I hear there still remains a Valisar heir at large. I believe he will one day return as a man to cut you and your barbarian spawn into pieces and serve you to the palace dogs . . . for that is all that you are worth, you hag. Go back to your beggared life while you still can." She glanced at Freath, pointing angrily at him and he realized what she planned to do, what she demanded of him. "I hope you burn in Lo's pits for your treachery. Do your worst, traitor, for you can no longer hurt us. May King Leonel deliver your death in most hideous fashion," she said in a dark voice he never thought he'd hear from his beloved Queen Iselda. "I will not be used by the usurper for his cause or for his amusement." That was his cue. Freath closed his eyes for a fraction of a second, forcing back the sob that wanted to escape his throat, before he grabbed the back of the queen's garments and, letting out a roar of anger, lifted her easily onto the ledge of the window and flung her out. She screamed lustily as she fell—no doubt for everyone else's benefit, for her courage was never in question. He leaned against the wall near the opening, pretending to watch her hit the ground, but surreptitiously closing his eyes. *Let her die immediately*, he beseeched Lo.

Behind him he heard a gasp and he took a long, steadying breath while he pasted a look of disdain into his expression and turned back to face Negev. He even found the wherewithal to brush his hands as though the job were well done. "Good riddance to bad rubbish, Dara." He could hardly believe his savagely sardonic tone, nor his composure. It wouldn't last. He needed to get out of this chamber as quickly as he could. "My apologies if my actions startled you but I'm sure you agree she had outlived her use to any of us? She was turning into a harridan in her lucid moments and your son was right: she was a mere lump of flesh otherwise and absolutely no fun at all." Before Negev could form a response, he pressed on, in the same uncaring tone, even finding a bitter smile. "I, for one, could not put up with another moment of that bellyaching and cursing. Excuse me, please. I'll make sure someone cleans up the mess of what's left of her."

Dara Negev still seemed to be catching her breath. "My son will not approve of this!" she hissed as he passed her.

It took all of his courage to pause and face her again. "Well, with all due respect, Dara, she was mine to do with as I pleased," he sneered. "That was our arrangement—and I have chosen to end her pathetic life. I think I'd decided as much earlier this morning after I raped her to the sound of her hideous, idiotic babbling. I suppose we should be grateful that at least she made sense just now—it would have been a bit of a letdown to have killed her when she wasn't aware of what was happening, don't you think?" He banished the vision that kept swirling through his mind of the queen sprawled on the gravel, her lifeblood leaking beneath her. "Maybe something you said gave her a moment of clarity." He gave a soft mirthless chuckle.

"What did she mean about her son?" Negev demanded, gathering her wits again.

He had begun approaching the door again and had to get out now. "I can't imagine, Dara Negev. She probably still believes he's going to make it to his thirteenth anni. I doubt it, don't you?" He pulled open the door, praying this was the last parry he'd have to make.

"My son must be told. Go about your business, Freath, but let my son know what has occurred first."

"Yes, Dara, as you wish." Freath managed to bow and was surprised to find he could still ask, "Shall I escort you—"

"No!" she growled, as he had hoped she would. "I must let Valya know."

Freath fled the chamber, hoping he could continue to mask his grief and wondering if he would ever—could ever—come to terms with his part in Iselda's death. As he walked, almost trotting with his desire to begone from the queen's apartments, he made himself appreciate that the Valisars were brave to the last and silently reminded himself that he needed to show the same resilience and courage. Stopping on a flight of lonely stairs, he made himself take some steadying breaths. As he leaned back against the cool stone he felt a welcome composure gradually settling over him. Now only the two sons remained—one mad and useless to their case, while the other was still far too young to have such responsibility heaped upon his small shoulders. He wondered where in the castle Leo and Gavriel were at this moment.

Genrie had heard the commotion outside, and had looked down out of one of the windows to see with horror the remains of Queen Iselda. She pulled back, filled with despair, almost unable to believe that her queen had jumped to her death. The woman called Valya had already gone for her ride, hurling insults within orders over her shoulder that a bath should be readied for her return. Genrie knew she needed to find Freath and quickly before any sneering member of Loethar's people told the queen's aide. She went looking and finally found him leaning against the wall halfway down a stairwell.

"Master Freath, the queen, she's—"

"I know," he interrupted softly. "I did it."

Of all the responses Genrie could have anticipated, this would not have been among them. She stared at the man she admired more than any other. Loved, even. She hadn't admitted her true feelings to herself until this minute but the fear, the atrocities and intensity of the last couple of days had brought all sorts of things to the surface, making her behave recklessly. The pain at her cheek was testimony to that.

"You . . . ?" She couldn't finish her sentence. "Why?"

His beautiful blue eyes wouldn't look at her. "They would have killed her. She wanted her death to count, to achieve something. She forced my hand."

"What was the point?" Genrie asked, horrified that Freath could sound so calm.

"The point was to protect my disguise. As long as they believe I am a traitor, I have the opportunity to work from the inside to help our new king. Iselda did this for Leonel, no one else."

She stared at him, lost for words, using the time instead to gaze at the features she found so strangely handsome. Was it only her who found him charismatic and irresistible? Master Freath was so distant, so measured that most of the other servants found him unapproachable, hard to judge. She didn't though. To her, Freath was wise, safe.

Freath pushed away from the wall, rubbing his head wearily, and now she could see how ashen he looked, how suddenly hollow and broken. "Genrie, I think we must get you away from here. It's going to get even more ugly."

"What will they do to you?" She hurried down the stairs to join him, now gravely worried for him.

He shrugged. It was an unusual gesture; Freath was always so in control, so sure. "If not for Leonel, I'm not sure I'd care. Have you got somewhere to go if I could get you out?"

How could he know how much those words hurt her, for she had never shown him, never given him any inkling of her feelings? Hesitantly, somewhat frightened by the intensity of the moment, she leaned toward the man and kissed him gently, not lingering, afraid of a rebuff. It would be polite but it would be firm. She pulled away, awaiting his reaction.

Freath cleared his throat. "Well, that wasn't the reply I was expecting." His voice was gruff.

"I'm sorry, Master Freath, I—"

He surprised her by pulling her back toward him, looking deeply into her face. "My name is Herric. Just moments ago I had never felt so adrift. You kissed me and I've never felt so anchored. Please, Genrie, do that again."

He kissed her back this time and tears threatened to squeeze from her closed eyes.

Freath shook his head when they finally parted. "Did it show?" She looked back at him quizzically. "I tried so hard to hide how I've felt about you these last two anni."

His words made her catch her breath. "No, you hid it very well, Master Freath." He smiled briefly at her formality.

"I'm sorry about that, Genrie. I'm forty-four anni. I gave up on romance a long time ago. And although I've been captivated by you since the moment you started, I didn't for a moment imagine you could ever return my feelings."

"For someone so brave that is a cowardly admission."

He smiled more easily now. She'd never seen such softness in his face. "Where you are concerned, yes." He kissed her tenderly again before his expression darkened. "And now I have more reason to fear for you. I want you to leave. It is getting too dangerous, this fine tightrope we are both walking."

"I agreed to follow your lead before they stormed the palace. Nothing has changed."

"But you are taking the greater risk. I have some protection through Loethar's favor. Now the queen's courageous death has added to my disguise. You are too vulnerable."

"I'm not leaving you, certainly not now. Don't ask me again. I love you, Master Freath. I'm staying come what may."

He touched her face gently. "I can't believe you're saying that. I'm probably going to have to ask you to repeat it sometime later when I've convinced myself I dreamed this."

She hugged him tightly. "I love you. Remember that always. Now where are you meant to be?"

"With him." She nodded. "But tell me quickly about Leonel," he added, his voice dropping.

"I arose just prior to dawn, laid out the food as you asked—everything I could find that was easy for them to grab. Then I yelled out for help so that they'd know there was no one else around and made a big show of going down to the cellar. I gave them ample time and as you predicted some of the food had been taken when I returned. I'd left a flask of milk but I wish I'd thought to leave water in the same fashion—they must be thirsty."

"That poor boy. He's lost everything, and now to be in exile in his own palace."

"How can he survive?"

"The same way we must. Using his wits. He has the advantage of being hidden, plus he has Gavriel De Vis with him. Under the circumstances, we couldn't have asked for a finer champion. King Brennus chose well."

"De Vis is just a young man," Genrie said.

"Leonel trusts him, and that short age gap will keep them close. If you knew Regor De Vis as well as I did, you'd know the breeding is there—we can all trust his sons. Gavriel would lay down his life for Leonel, or for Penraven, for that matter. We can't ask for more."

"De Vis asked me to kiss him just a day or two ago," Genrie said playfully.

"You've only kissed me twice and already you're trying to make me jealous," Freath sighed. "He's youthful. I would expect nothing less than his wanting to kiss every beautiful woman he comes across."

"Beautiful, eh?"

"And brave. Stay brave, my Genrie. No heroics, please promise me."

"I promise," she said and kissed him farewell. "Go. The two witches will be looking for me too, I imagine."

Freath reluctantly let Genrie go and hurried away down toward Loethar's salon. He had refused to tell her how the king and De Vis would be watching or where from in the kitchens and fortunately she was astute enough not to press him. He blessed his luck that he'd had those few moments with King Brennus before the royal was dragged before Loethar. Captive and already guessing his fate, Brennus had refused Freath's words of sympathy, telling him instead of the existence of the ingress. Freath realized that his ear was not a desperate option either. He knew the king had absolute faith in him. He must not lose his nerve now. Newly determined, he continued his descent toward the salon where he would find Loethar. He was not looking forward to seeing the queen's smashed corpse but as he knocked on the barbarian's door, he hoped with all his heart that Leo would never learn the method of his mother's death.

In the ingress a terrible silence lay between its two occupants. Gavriel had attempted to say something into the shock of the void but Leo had raised his hand and uttered a single word, "Don't!"

Gavriel waited anxiously, watching the young king's chest heave as he battled to wrestle back a hurricane of emotion. The luminous glow of the candle revealed the dryness of the royal's mouth as Leo licked his lips nervously, his forehead creased into a vertical line at its middle, as he concentrated hard on breathing steadily, no doubt talking himself back from the precipice of despair that Gavriel was sure he teetered on. He himself was still in shock over what they'd witnessed and now he knew they had to leave immediately. There would be no time for food, no time for any supplies. What they already had and what they could pick up on the run through the secret corridors up to the roof was all they would have. He imagined the feel of the fresh air on his face; that might help Leo remain steady. He tried not to think about what came beyond that. Surely to lower themselves from this height was close to suicide. *Why not suicide?* Gavriel wondered. *Everyone's doing it*, he thought bitterly, echoing the sort of dark humor that Corbel would appreciate. But Corb wasn't here to help him. Blood was pounding through his veins, urging him to take the king and flee. Again his mind helplessly returned to Leo's audacious idea to lower each other down on a rope.

"We slide down it, of course!" he'd said, incredulous that Gavriel had had to ask. "We move silently from the palace to beyond the castle gates."

"How do we anchor it precisely?"

"Petty detail!" the new king had replied, giving an irritated shrug. "We have everything we need. Father stocked the ingress with weapons, ropes, cloaks, candles—all sorts of supplies, just in case. You know he checked them annually, had the weapons oiled, sharpened?"

"No, I didn't," Gavriel had replied, somewhat petulantly. How could he!

Leo's plan was the stuff of boys' daydreams. Gavriel knew there was a good chance they would fall to their deaths, or at best suffer nasty injuries.

More splattered bodies to be cleaned up, he heard Corbel's somber drone in his mind.

The king's voice was wintry when it came, interrupting Gavriel's bleak thoughts. "Piven's fate is in the lap of Lo now but I must survive if I am to see Loethar and Freath answer for their sins. If I do nothing else with this life, I will claim their last breaths; my face will be the last they see."

Gavriel could only nod. He knew the king needed this fury in order to survive. Perhaps—dare he even think this?—the deaths of the king and the queen were the very triggers needed to turn Leo from crown prince into King Leonel. The boy standing before him now was certainly no child but a genuine King of Penraven and instinctively Gavriel knelt.

"King Leonel, as my father did to your father, I pledge myself wholly to your service and to your protection. I will follow you wherever you go, I will lay down my life for you." The words were rote but he had never meant anything more deeply in his life and to prove it he snatched the knife from his belt and without hesitation slashed open his palm. Leo remained silent, listening gravely, watching somberly, as Gavriel offered up the most primitive of the Valisar blood covenants, first performed on King Cormoron by his brother. Dipping the fingers of his uninjured hand into the blood pooling in his palm, Gavriel reached up and smeared his blood onto the face of the king.

"I offer you my blood covenant, King Leonel."

Clearly moved, Leo nodded. "And though we have no witnesses except ourselves, let it be known that I accept your pledge and from this day you will be called Legate Gavriel De Vis." Mirroring Gavriel's actions, Leo took the blade, opened his own palm and painted the resulting blood onto Gavriel's cheeks and forehead. New king and new legate solemnly clasped bleeding hands together. "The Blood Covenant of the 9th is sealed," Leo pronounced.

Fourteen

Loethar was not sure what to make of this latest and rather incredible development. Iselda had needed to be dealt with and he was privately relieved the matter was already taken care of but it was nevertheless a bold move by a mere servant.

His mother was still ranting. *Why do women always harp on about something that cannot be changed and always when a matter should be left alone!*

"But, Loethar, could we not have made more use of the royal wretch? Imagine the punishing effect it could have had on the people. This traitorous servant to the Valisars has usurped your authority, surely?"

"I have spoken with Freath. I did agree that Iselda was his property to do with as he pleased," Loethar answered. "If I didn't want him to ill-treat her, I should have made that more clear." He shrugged. "As it was, I gave him no instructions regarding Iselda."

Stracker arrived and, without waiting for permission to enter the discussion, announced, "She's being scraped off the cobbles now." His amusement was evident.

Loethar didn't share it. "There you are, mother. She's gone to her god now. Nothing more to be done about it."

"And still you allow this man into your bosom."

"Bosom?" Loethar turned on Negev. "Where? Where is he that he is so close to me, so deeply involved in my thoughts and actions? I'll tell you where he is, mother. He's piling the remains of the woman he just murdered into a slops bucket. Hardly the work of my right hand man, wouldn't you say?"

She refused to answer him, turning instead to her other son. "Is this true?"

Stracker nodded, then laughed. "He horrified onlookers by refusing the wych elder chest as a coffin. He insisted that she was not worth the cost and instead tossed her remains into a couple of crates. I'm beginning to like your servant, brother."

"Are you satisfied?" Loethar growled.

Negev didn't look chagrined but had the good sense to finally leave the subject be, instead turning to her next axe for grinding. "Well, now that you ask, no. I have helped you get to this point—both of us have," she said, touching Stracker on his broad chest.

"And?" Loethar said, keen to get this out of the way now. It had been building for months.

"Well, son, we have given you more than simply a throne."

"You didn't give it to me, mother. I took it. And my half-brother has certainly played his part and your cunning mind has also played its role, but please never flatter yourselves that you handed me any of the Set thrones on any platters."

"Forgive me, Loethar, that was wrongly spoken. What I meant," she soothed, "was that we're here now. You are on the throne. You are the emperor already, if I'm not mistaken. So what is the next step?"

"We arrived only two days ago. We have since slaughtered any number of important people, including the Valisar king and queen. What else would you have me do in this time span, dear mother?" His last two words were spoken so acidly, Negev took a small step back, a movement that was not lost on him.

Her reply, nevertheless, lost none of its bite. "I want to understand your intentions, Loethar."

"I see. So crushing the last of the great family dynasties of the Set is not enough?"

"Except you haven't!" she levelled angrily at him.

He glared at her. She still believed he needed her counsel,

and it was true that she'd been a formidable woman alongside his warrior father—equally brave, far more conniving and ambitious. Even in old age, she was a force that he had to reckon with. In his quietest, most private moments, he often dreamed of ending her angry, bitter life. A blanket over her face, a poison, a stray arrow. But think it though he did, he could never follow through. It was not a matter of courage—he had that in droves. It was a simple promise given to his dying father that he would forgive his mother her overbearing ways and protect her until she took her final breath. He'd sworn he would as the older man took his own last breath and if there was one person he would keep faith with in life, it was his tribal father.

"You haven't!" she repeated and he despised her in that instant.

"What do you mean?"

"The crown prince is alive. You admit it yourself. And that Valisar whore got to rub my face in her dirt, reminding me that Prince Leonel lives, that he will emerge to slaughter you, slaughter all of us!" Her voice had built shrilly as she spoke until she was near yelling.

Stracker broke the tension, laughing as her voice broke on the last word. "He could only be about this tall!" he cut in, his incredulity at her howling claim obvious. "I could snap the life out of him with one hand, even if he were capable of lifting a sword with any menace."

Negev visibly calmed herself, her nostrils pinched as she inhaled a steadying breath. "Stracker, dear, you're my flesh . . . my blood runs thick through your veins. But you should never believe that you are more imaginative than I. I am well aware of the boy's age and I can guess at his height—I did raise two sons of my own. This is not about strength or fighting capability. This boy is no longer a prince."

Stracker frowned at her and Loethar sighed inwardly. His half-brother was not dumb—not by a long shot—but he could be obtuse when his arrogance overrode everything.

"You haven't grasped it, have you, son?" Negev cajoled. "Look to your brother. He will enlighten you."

Stracker glared at Loethar, who regarded him with a small measure of sympathy. He, too, had been on the receiving end of their mother's sharp tongue all of his life. "As soon as Brennus breathed his last, his heir became king. Our mother is simply making the point that the boy is now King Leonel in spite of his youth, and as long as he remains alive, he becomes a symbol of hope for Penraven."

Negev couldn't contain herself a moment longer. "He is a symbol of freedom, a rallying point, a hook upon which to hang an entire region's hope! Faith is an incredibly powerful force, especially among those who have been crushed. As long as King Leonel is at large, the people of the Set will endure. As long as the stories of his survival race like a plains fire out of control from realm to realm, his stature and his presence will grow, whether he's this tall or this tall!" she said, mimicking a child's height and then a man's with her hand. "And as long as he continues to grow, any rebellious element within the people will have their fiery dreams of vengeance stoked."

"He's a child!" Stracker hurled back at them, incredulous. "You're scared of a child?"

"Only what he represents," Loethar said patiently. "Leonel the boy is, at this moment, irrelevant. It's the fact that he lives that matters. The blood of the Valisars pumps strong through him for he is the rightful heir. Did Iselda give any indication that she knew where he was?"

Negev shook her head. "No. But she believed him alive, revelled in the knowledge. She must have known something."

Loethar's expression darkened. "She could have just said that out of maliciousness." He shook his head, thinking of the dour manservant's actions. "I still can't believe Freath was so brutal. He seems so very conservative and contained."

"Well, believe me, he enjoyed it. It surprised me too," his

mother grudgingly admitted. "The look on his face. Animal-like fury." She shook her head. "It doesn't solve the issue, Loethar," she added pointedly.

"No," he said, noncommittally.

"So, we hunt him down. Destroy him," Stracker said. "Send me. I'm done here."

Loethar nodded to himself in thought, cast a glance absently at Vyk, who was as still as a statue. He looked back at Stracker and his mother.

"May I?" Negev asked. He nodded. "I think you should take your brother up on his offer. Let him get together a group. Keep it small. You'll move more easily around the realm that way," she said, turning to her eldest son. "He's had a couple of days on us and perhaps he's getting help. He is only young so he'll be scared, no matter how courageous he is. He also won't be as resourceful as you or Loethar. Try and think as you did when you were his age, Stracker. At twelve summertides your belly's needs overrode everything—trust me on this. He'll stop often to eat, not thinking so carefully about cover of darkness. He'll take risks when he's famished—perhaps try and steal food from remote homes or from other people's traps. Put the word out. Put a reward up. Make it generous. Someone with a grudge against the royal family might just speak up. I would urge—"

"Stop, mother," Loethar said wearily. He rubbed at his eyes. "There is a far more simple solution, one I believe will not only win the entire Set's attention but will satisfy my half-brother's lust for bloodletting."

Stracker grinned with sinister anticipation. "I can't wait to hear it."

Negev, clearly unhappy at being interrupted but unable to wipe her curiosity entirely from her expression, looked to him expectantly.

"There are times to win hearts and other times to impress one's control. Stracker, get your Greens on the march. Surround the realm. And then you may kill every male child aged between eleven and thirteen summertides. If there's one skill Penraven possesses, it's excellent records. The Valisars are notorious down the ages for it and, according to Valya, one particular aspect they loved was the census. Ask Freath to help—in fact I'll tell him to. He'll know where to find the books that will give you names, locations and ages. Make it swift and brutal. No torture, Stracker. Behead each publicly; leave the families nothing but the headless bodies to bury. You will make it known that every one of these boys is being slaughtered because the prince—and you must never call him king, Stracker—is a coward. Put up notices for those who can read, send out criers for the majority who can't. It is summertide now. They have until the first leaves begin to fall before the next wave of killing begins. We will be merciless if the prince is not given to us. Are you confident the armies are quelled?"

Stracker nodded. "Totally, in all realms. All weapons have already been confiscated, all senior members are dead. There will be no opposition. They're still trying to clear their dead!"

"Good. Then begin with the army sons just to make sure they understand that it is our rule now. You will move in one rolling cull, starting in Penraven and moving into the other realms until the prince is found. Once that is done, the numbers of boys in the prince's age range will be all but annihilated. Those remaining will stick out like a pimple on the nose and can be dealt with swiftly. Stracker, remember that people are extremely resourceful. Once word gets out of the slaughter, they will do everything to protect their children. Some boys will be turned into girls overnight; others will be sent off into remote areas, certainly to the coast to find any seaworthy vessel. They will wear false beards or will miraculously age. Our men need to be vigilant, so lead by example. We cannot expect you to catch all in your net but those who remain will have to go to ground and then we can begin to hunt him more methodically with a lot less chance for him to disappear into the cities or villages posing as some peasant."

Stracker nodded. "I get you."

"Heed me. Don't waste time making these boys suffer. We're using shock tactics. We need this to be a hard, fast strike to do away with as many potential King Leonels as possible. The less you play, the more vicious it will feel. You must put the fear of the barbarians into these people once again, so that they have no dreams of rebellion to cling to."

Negev was frowning. "But the prince could simply hide."

"Yes he could," Loethar replied. "But he will need to be awfully patient and at his age he probably won't be. Not unless he receives a lot of help from others. And that's how we will catch him. If others are involved, the secret is shared. And we all know what happens once a secret is shared. Tongues will wag. Information can be bought."

"You want me to put a price on his head?" Stracker asked.

"No. Money only goes so far when it comes to betrayals of this nature. I am talking about a blood price. The killing of the Set's young males will be the first warning, will set the scene, shall we say. After that, we will threaten to kill every male child over the age of eleven and under the age of eighteen summertides if Leonel is not yielded by the thaw. The people will already be mourning a lost son and the thought of losing another will very quickly loosen tongues. Believe me, someone somewhere will have knowledge of something—a chance sighting, a whispered rumor here, an overheard conversation there. The moment Leonel declares who he is to one other person, we have a chance of catching him."

Stracker exploded into delighted laughter. "Never let it be said that your mind wasn't capable of great evil, Loethar."

His mother's eyebrows arched and she looked suitably admonished. "Inspired. A way to completely terrify the population as well as make the boy feel utterly conspicuous simply by remaining alive. Those with family will yield the boy without hesitation if it means their precious sons will survive."

"Exactly," Loethar said, satisfied. He turned away to

scratch Vyk's head. "Incidentally," he added, "if the prince is found, the killing stops. It's important we keep faith. I want the people to feel the ruthlessness when called for, but also the fairness of my rule if they obey."

"You see, Stracker, this is why Loethar is emperor, and you are not."

Negev's eldest son didn't seem offended by the insult. "So long as he keeps giving me tasks like this, he can remain emperor."

Loethar paused at his half-brother's words but almost immediately returned his attention to the raven. The wording of Stracker's reply was revealing, he thought.

His mother interrupted his quiet moment. "And what will you do, Loethar, in the meantime?"

He sighed, turned back to face them. "I'm not sure. I'm half tempted to take a lone and very unannounced ride around this realm, possibly the Set."

"What? But that would take months, at least!"

He shrugged. "This is my empire. And there is not much to do in these early days of settling the realms down—the Set will probably run itself easily without me, with you supervising."

At this her expression became smug. "Please take that endlessly grinning creature with you. He is too strange for my tastes."

Loethar pulled on the leash and Piven turned his grin on his new master, then strained toward Vyk.

"Perhaps I will."

"And Valya?"

"Where is Valya?"

"Riding," Stracker answered.

"I have no idea what to do about Valya. Marry her, I suppose—it may shut her up."

Fifteen

As the barbarians were plotting his death, the king and his legate were running.

"Do you know your way?" Gavriel asked, worried.

"I'm taking us to where the weapons are stored. There aren't many but there's a selection. We can grab the bow, rope, arrows, swords—enough for two people certainly," Leo said quietly over his shoulder.

"Wait, Leo. I need to say something."

The king turned. "You can't talk me out of it. I know what you're going to say."

"It's a flawed plan, your majesty."

"It's all we have. I don't intend to spend another night in this forsaken ingress. I suppose you want me to watch Piven die next?"

Gavriel knew the youngster didn't mean to hurt him but his words stung all the same. "Then you have me all wrong."

"Gav, I—"

"No, you must listen to me. You are king. But you are not in charge here. I admire your courage but we are not going to make a suicidal attempt to—"

Leo's expression adopted a new set of shadows as his face darkened. "Maybe you are not going to make that attempt but I intend to, with or without you, and you can live with the knowledge that you were too cowardly."

Gavriel refused to rise to the bait. "Leo, I swear if I have to sit on you or tie you up, you are not going to climb down from the rooftops. I'm sorry to be so blunt about this but your father and your mother have died to keep you alive and—" He stopped, his attention momentarily caught. "Have we been down this part of the ingress before?" he suddenly asked, frowning and reaching for the candle that Leo was swinging rather angrily, its flame flickering dangerously.

"No. I have brought you down a new corridor to get to the weapons."

"Give me the candle," Gavriel asked.

Leo did so sulkily. "You'll have to tie me up, then."

"With the deepest respect, shut up, your majesty," Gavriel replied as he swung the light toward the wall, squinting as he bent to look. "What's this?"

The king turned and reluctantly bent to look as well. His head twisted on a slight angle as he considered it, their disagreement forgotten for a moment. "I've never seen that before."

"Whose drawing is it?"

Leo shook his head. "It must be father's but it doesn't look like his markings."

"It doesn't look aged enough to be Cormoron's, or even from recent history. And why is it drawn so low on the wall?"

Leo shrugged. He rubbed at the markings. "The chalk is reasonably fresh, definitely not Cormoron's or any of our ancestors. Father preferred charcoal. And I never used yellow chalk like this. I always had white chalk from the Garun cliffs."

"Yes, that's what I thought. So you don't recognize even what it signifies?"

Leo blew out a breath. "Well, let me see." He bent closer, scrutinizing the drawing. "Actually it's very good, very clear. Here," he pointed, "is where we've spent most of our time."

"Your father's salon," Gavriel said, to be sure.

"Correct. And here," he traced a line with his finger, "is a branch of the ingress I don't know but we can find easily enough if we commit this pathway," he traced it again, "to memory."

"But what is it a map of?" Gavriel said, waving his hand across the clearly marked channels. "It doesn't look like the ingress any more."

"No, you're right."

"Can we take a look down that pathway?"

The king gave him a long hard look of unbridled exasperation.

"I know. But you'd agree it appears authentic, whatever it is."

Leo nodded. "It looks very genuine. But look at these signs. I don't know what they mean."

Gavriel squinted. "Those blobs?"

"Yes. I count four of them."

"Let's go find out. How long do you imagine it would take us to get to this point once we've grabbed some weapons?" Gavriel asked, his finger resting on what looked to be the ochre blob closest to the king's salon.

Leo pulled a face of uncertainty. "I honestly can't tell you. I can't imagine this map is drawn to any sort of scale. None of them are. They are meant to be simply a directional guide."

"Then we must commit it to memory. How about if we try this and if we fail then we work out a way to go off the roof tonight."

"De Vis, I'm going off the roof tonight come what may."

"We'll see. Indulge my curiosity for now."

Leo sighed. "Follow me."

Freath stared at the two men, still ashen from his most recent task. Beside him stood Genrie.

"Why are we here?" Kirin asked, looking around nervously.

"The chapel is the most private place I could find at short

notice. Father Briar has offered to keep watch," Freath replied.

"What for?" Clovis asked, worried.

"For anyone loyal to Loethar," Freath answered softly.

At his words both Vested balked. They regarded him with fresh suspicion and each looked reluctant to say anything.

"You've met Genrie. She is loyal to us," Freath continued.

"Us?"

"Those who would see King Leonel on Penraven's throne."

"What?" Clovis roared. "Wait, this isn't making sense. Kirin, it's a trick."

"It will make sense if you'll keep your voice down. In fact, stop talking," Genrie said, irritated. "Just listen to what Master Freath has to say."

"You're loyal to the Valisars?" Kirin asked, obviously stunned.

Freath nodded. "We're all there is. No one else—save Father Briar—can be trusted. And I mean no one but Genrie and myself."

"But you . . ." Clovis began, frowning. His voice trailed off as he glanced between the two palace servants.

"I had to," Freath said quietly. "It was the only way."

"To what?" Kirin demanded.

Freath straightened. "To infiltrate our enemy. King Brennus demanded it of me; the queen refused my offers to help her escape before the barbarian took her captive. I was given very strict orders by the king to give the impression that I was a traitor."

"You've been lying?" Clovis said, aghast.

Genrie sighed. "Well, that took a while for the trent to drop. We've both been lying, Master Clovis."

"But all those people who died?" Clovis continued.

"Could not be helped," Freath said, genuinely disturbed. "I tried to save those I could."

"Such as whom?" Clovis sneered. "All I saw were innocents being carted off to be murdered."

"Whatever you think, Master Freath is walking an incredibly dangerous path and no one is safe, least of all him," Genrie said sharply.

Clovis opened his mouth to reply but Freath held up his hand. "Master Clovis, believe me when I say that I have many lives on my conscience—Lo forgive me for her majesty's death—but I need to explain—"

"Wait!" Kirin demanded. "What do you mean? The queen is dead?"

Genrie nodded miserably and Freath sighed audibly. "Not long ago."

"How?" Kirin asked.

"I killed her," Freath replied, his voice raw with anguish. "There was no choice—I had to in order to save her any further degradation at the hands of the barbarians. She made me become her executioner in order to preserve the fragile shield I currently have."

"She asked you to kill her so that it looked right?" Kirin repeated, incredulous.

"Queen Iselda wanted to die, Master Kirin. But she wanted her death to aid our cause." Freath felt the weight of his grief settle around his shoulders once again.

"Listen to me, both of you," Genrie snapped. "Our queen bought us security in a single courageous act . . . and don't for one moment think it didn't take an equal amount of courage for Master Freath to hurl her from the window of her apartment!"

"Hardly equal," Freath muttered sorrowfully. "The bravery was all hers. I threw her to her death feeling only fear."

Clovis spun away to bang his fist against the wall. "I don't believe he's lying," Kirin said. "Although I have barely touched him."

"Did you—?" Freath asked, horrified.

"I used barely a dribble," Kirin grumbled, a mixture of distress and anger mingling in his voice. "If I pry I can tell a lot more about you than you'd perhaps want. I sense, however, from the trickle, that you are being straight with us.

Although a good liar can elude me if I don't use my full power."

Freath's brow creased to form a single angry vertical line just above the bridge of his nose. "You didn't need to level your magic against me, Master Kirin. I give you my word I will always be straight with you."

"That is as may be," Clovis said, indignation spicing his tone, "but you have given us nothing with which to trust you. So far we have only seen you be a puppet for the barbarian."

"Open that door, Master Clovis," Freath said gruffly.

"Why?"

"Just do as I say."

Kirin moved more quickly, wrenching back the small oak door to reveal a huddle of people in the tiny adjoining chamber. "Clovis!" a familiar voice called.

"Reuth! You're all alive," Clovis breathed.

"The few of us that Master Freath could save," she said, smiling tentatively at the former royal aide. "Thank you again."

Freath gave a small shake of his head. "I didn't do enough," he muttered and he turned away, ignoring Genrie's reassuring touch on his arm.

"Where's the girl? The blood diviner?" Kirin asked, frowning.

"We lost her," the boy said. "The soldiers wanted her. He offered her," he said, scowling.

Kirin glanced at Freath who nodded, eyes closed momentarily in prayer for the girl's memory. "I had to let them have her in order to save this many. I'm sorry. None of my choices have been without their cost. They think all of you have perished."

"Why, though?" Kirin demanded.

"Stracker believed his men dealt with everyone here but I told one of the senior men I'd take care of it, offering them the girl as a plaything. He didn't even hesitate and I'm taking the chance that he won't even mention to his brute of a superior that he left the killing to me. They're burning bodies tonight and I'll just say I threw all of you into the pit if asked."

Everyone fell momentarily quiet. Finally, Kirin spoke into the awkward silence. "Perhaps we should all introduce ourselves?"

"Good idea," Freath agreed. "Everyone's been sworn to silence in that cupboard until now."

"I'm Tolt," the boy said, looking around. "I dreamed some of this—not quite the same—but it had many similarities. If I had more experience at it, I'd probably have been able to interpret it."

"Hello, Tolt," Kirin said, smiling gently. "And you?" he said, pointing to a woman.

"I'm Eyla," she replied softly, nervously. "I do my best as a healer."

Kirin gave her an encouraging glance. He looked at the old man next to her. "Ah, you are the one who can help things to grow."

The man nodded self-consciously. "Torren is my name."

"I'm Kes," a young man said. "I can change the shape of my body."

"The contortionist," Freath muttered. "Is that magic?"

The boy grinned. "I'll say."

Everyone found a sad smile at his confidence. "You are the woman who can talk to animals, if I'm not mistaken?" Kirin continued.

She shrugged. "I understand our creatures. They seem to understand me," she answered cryptically. "I am called Hedray."

Kirin turned to a willowy young woman with her face partially covered by a shawl, her head wrapped severely in a scarf. "What is your power?" Kirin asked gently.

The woman remained silent.

"She hasn't said anything to anyone," Tolt explained.

Kirin reached for her hand but she pulled hers back, afraid. "I won't hurt you," he assured. "We are here because we trust each other and we will have to look after one another. All of these people are your friends. I am your friend. I am Kirin and I can see things in people. Over here," he said, pointing, "is Clovis. Clovis can see things too but not about people so much as events—how situations may turn out."

The girl looked up at them all through large, soft gray eyes. "I am Perl," she finally said, allowing her gaze to travel briefly around before resting on Kirin. "I don't wish to say any more."

Kirin nodded. "In your own time, Perl."

"And I am Reuth," the final Vested spoke up. "I suffer visions of foreboding. I never know the details, only that something bad is going to happen. It is a contrary gift, revealing itself in strange ways that I can't really explain. But it is accurate."

Freath frowned. "Have we also lost the boy who reads runes?"

Everyone frowned, trying to remember him.

"You're right," Clovis admitted. "He was in the holding place when we were first grouped. I don't remember his coming to the chamber when Master Freath interviewed us." The others seemed to agree, shrugging and nodding.

"And this is Genrie," Freath said. "Without her none of you would be alive. She is my eyes and my ears whenever I cannot see or listen. She is loyal to the crown, loyal to all Penravians—as am I. Our king and queen are both dead, as is the legate." He ignored their gasps, knowing he could not spare them the shock. "The newborn princess is dead, and already cremated, while the youngest prince, Piven, is in the custody of Loethar. We have no idea what the barbarian's plans are for him. But—"

"Is Piven the deformed one?" Tolt asked.

"Not deformed. He is simple, that is all. He is a very special child and much beloved," Freath admonished gently.

"Is he completely trapped by his condition?" Reuth asked. "Perhaps we could use him."

Freath shook his head. "He is entirely imprisoned. He will be no help to us. He has become the barbarian's plaything." At everyone's immediate distress, Freath held up a hand. "Not in a sexual sense. At present the emperor—as he plans to be known—finds the child intriguing. We believe the eldest child is alive." A murmur greeted his words. "And he is what this is all about: preserving Leonel's life, working toward putting him on the throne."

"Us?" Tolt asked, looking around at the others, pointing at them. "Him . . . and her, you mean?" he jibed, stabbing a finger toward Hedray. "Me? I don't even know how to hold a dagger, let alone throw one."

"No one's talking about weapons here, young Tolt. We are talking about something infinitely more subtle. Each of you has practical skills. Some in addition possess magic; perhaps one or two of you have untapped potential. Whatever the specific case, you are Vested and you are alive. It is your duty to make those skills and powers available to the crown. Unless you're happy with the barbarian and how he runs a realm, by all means, take your chances with him."

"Master Freath," Reuth began, "I gladly pledge myself to your cause—you don't even have to ask for my loyalty, to tell the truth, but I do understand Tolt's confusion. What can our odd little group possibly achieve?"

Freath shook his head. "I don't know, Reuth. I've never organized a rebellion before." Though the words were honest enough, his tone was dry. "We must do our best, as best we can."

It was Clovis who asked the most pertinent question. "What now, Master Freath? You cannot hide these people indefinitely."

"No, I can't. Father Briar and Genrie are going to find a way to get you all out—one by one if we have to and over several days, depending on how closely we are watched. I mustn't be seen here again other than in duties for Loethar. He does not trust me so please no one make an error and betray me. Hopefully you all will be gone, save Kirin and Clovis, over the next few days."

"But to where?" Reuth persisted. "Where can each of us hide or be safe?"

"Scatter," Freath advised. "Get away from here. Hide your skills entirely. Do not be tempted to earn money from your talents because it is my guess you will be hunted down by Loethar's people. We have a mark—a tiny blue moon crescent. Ink it onto your skin. Choose a place that is mostly hidden—between the fingers, behind an ear. Somewhere you can bear for a needle to mark your skin and that you can hide from everyday glances, but, that you can also readily show if you need to prove your loyalty."

Silence greeted his speech. Freath cleared his throat. "I realize there is nothing to stop your simply disappearing, blending in with the rest of the survivors and knuckling down to life under barabarian rule. Nothing, that is, other than the memory of how innocents were slaughtered just a few feet from where you cowered. Nothing, perhaps, other than knowing that your king killed himself in front of the barbarian to prevent Loethar being able to humiliate Penraven further with a public death. Or that the legate whom we have revered for a score of years had his head cleaved in half by the cowardly barbarian during what was supposed to be a parley for peace. Or even that your queen bravely sacrificed her life so that I could keep my cover of traitor and save all of you. There is nothing more I can think of to say to persuade you other than the reminder that somewhere not far away runs a lad, just twelve, who is now king. As long as Leonel remains alive and out of the barbarian's reach, he is the reigning royal of Penraven. And as long as we have a Valisar king alive, we have something worth fighting for."

"How do you know he lives?" Kirin asked.

Freath glanced briefly toward Genrie. "I know. You will have to trust me on this."

"You've seen him?" Clovis persisted.

"I saw him escaping the warriors. I know that Loethar is furious that he has not yet been found."

Father Briar suddenly entered the chamber, a look of urgency on his face. "There's movement outside. You four should get out of here," he said to Freath, glancing at Kirin, Clovis and Genrie. "The rest, back into the crawlspace. I will get fresh water to you later."

Everyone groaned softly.

Freath straightened. "Our time has run out. We will not speak together again like this. Genrie will give you needles and ink for those who wish to take the mark. She will also give each of you a homing pigeon. When you are settled and feel safe, no matter whether you are in the realm or beyond, let your pigeon go. It will find us and tell us where you are. You will hear from us. It may take months, possibly years, but stay strong, stay loyal to the crown. Help us by seeking out other Vested. They will have deeply hidden their talents but some will have escaped the barbarians. Find them, conscript them. Good luck, everyone. Come, Kirin, Clovis. Remember, as far as the barbarians are concerned you are now my servants and you need to act accordingly."

The pair nodded and followed him. To Genrie Freath cast a backward glance. "Be careful," he whispered and she nodded, her gaze flicking to Kirin but darkening at his enquiring expression.

The king's salon was deserted as they passed through the part of the ingress that had been home to them these last few days. Leo didn't even spare the peepholes a moment of his time, leaving it to Gavriel to steal a glance before hurrying after the retreating back of the king.

Within minutes they were in a part of the ingress they'd not yet explored, although Leo seemed to know his way with confidence. Suddenly he stopped, muttering to himself.

"What's happening?" Gavriel asked.

Leo's eyes were screwed closed. "I'm just double checking whether I was supposed to take the second or third turning."

Gavriel said nothing, hoping the silence would help Leo concentrate on his mental map. He looked around furtively, his eyes picking up by chance another of the distinctive yellow markings. "Leo, look!" he said urgently, holding their candle closer.

"Lo save us! An arrow."

"Someone wants us to go this way," Gavriel said, pointing down a very slim corridor.

"I knew we had to turn right. I just wanted to be sure we were in the correct part of the ingress."

"I guess this confirms it." Gavriel moved closer to the opening, wondering if his shoulders would even fit through.

"It can't be a trick, can it?"

Gavriel scoffed. "How? No one else knows of the passages save the Kings and heirs."

"This ochre chalk worries me."

"Me too but you'll just have to imagine it's white like yours or the charcoal of your father. We have no choice."

"But who could have drawn it here if not father or myself?"

"One of your predecessors. Why not King Darros?"

Leo laughed lightly. "My grandfather was a huge man. He couldn't have fitted here. Even so, father told me Darros always used the gray chalk of the Chalcene quarries and my great-grandfather, before you ask, used the pale blue paste made from crushing the sheeca shell from our beaches. The chalk is too fresh for any Valisars further back."

"Leo, we must trust it. Perhaps your father did this and used a fresh color specifically to guide us here."

"Why wouldn't he have told me?" Leo persisted.

"I don't know," Gavriel answered, wrestling to keep his tone patient. "I actually don't care, either. You assure me no one but us know so we must trust it. We are going down here and we're going to follow the ochre arrows if we find more."

Leo nodded unhappily and stepped into the small opening. Gavriel followed, feeling instantly twice as claustrophobic as he'd felt in the main corridor. "This is horrible," he grumbled, eyes peeled for any further clues in the ochre chalk.

"It should be a short tunnel if my memory of the map serves me. It will open up and we'll have the choice of two paths. We go left."

They moved forward in silence. Gavriel had long ago given up trying to work out where they were in relation to the palace layout. As Leo had promised, they came to a choice of paths. Without pausing, the king turned them left.

Gavriel realized they'd stepped up their progress to a trot, both in a hurry now to reach their destination. He calculated they'd been on the move for what must translate to five hundred strides or half a span. They were a long way from the queen's apartments.

A few minutes later the path, which had been steadily narrowing, reached a blind end.

"Lo's wrath!" Leo spewed. "I knew it! I knew this was a waste of our time." He swung around angrily, glaring at Gavriel and throwing down the tiny sack that contained their meager supplies.

Gavriel felt his heart sink.

"The blobs meant dead ends, that's all," Leo raged, sliding down the rough wall to sit. "Now we have to go all the way back."

Gavriel joined him on the floor. "Eat the bread and what's left of the cheese, Leo. You must be hungry." He needed to think. Out of habit he passed the light of the candle flame all around him. It was Leo who gasped and suddenly looked up.

"Unbelievable!" he muttered.

Gavriel followed the king's gaze. Above him was a small opening. "Tell me you can see another arrow behind me," he said, dryly.

Leo nodded, still amazed.

"Ha!" Gavriel leapt to his feet. "And up we go," he said, his hand touching the chalked marking. "Come on, I'll give you a leg up." He carefully lifted Leo into the hole.

"I can't see anything," the king called. "It's too dark. Sounds big, though."

"Here, take the candle and our supplies," Gavriel said, standing on tiptoe. "And move, I'm coming." He jumped and gripped the opening, using his feet to push off the wall and up higher through the hole. When he was halfway through the hole he stopped, arrested by what he was staring at.

"Strike me!" he murmured.

"A cave? How can that be?" Leo asked, incredulous.

Gavriel pulled himself clear of the hole and stood up carefully. The ceiling was low. He shook his head with wonder. "What is this? Where are we?"

"Is that birdsong?"

Gavriel listened. It was distant but Leo was not mistaken. "I think you're right. Let's go."

They picked their way through the hollow area they'd found themselves in and walked toward the noise.

"So the ochre blob on the map meant the opening through the ceiling of the ingress," Leo said.

"I don't think we were in the ingress. The stone of the wall changed texture slightly. I think by the time we met that blind ending, we were already beyond the palace walls."

"What are you saying?"

"I think the ochre blobs on the map denoted ways of getting into and out of the palace. Secret entrances," Gavriel said, unable to hide the excitement in his voice. "I think that's why we hear birdsong, your majesty. I reckon we're going to come out close to the woods!"

Leo swung around, a disbelieving look on his face. As he turned back around Gavriel felt a soft gust of air ruffle his hair. He and Leo began to laugh. It was true. Freedom beckoned.

Sixteen

Valya was fuming. She hated Dara Negev and her constant condescension. It was obvious that the old hag hated her, which was fine; the feeling was mutual. However, they both loved Loethar. But what was infuriating her so much was that whenever Loethar's mother was around him—or even in his thoughts—her lover became remote. And she hated that more than she despised Negev. Stracker, meanwhile, made her feel ill to be around and she was glad they had so little to say to each other and even less to do with one another.

For all that she loved Loethar, Valya was increasingly realizing that she barely knew what went on in his mind. All through the battles he had been so focused. He cut a decisive yet patient pathway through to Penraven, never faltering in his desire to conquer the Valisars. The other realms of the Set had simply been the obstacles . . . the annoying fat he had to cut away to get to the true heartbeat of the Set. And yet she knew deep down that Penraven's wealth was not Loethar's motivation; its power had certainly been a driving need, but not his ultimate passion. Nor had the desire to call himself emperor—or anything he pleased, for that matter—given him the impetus to wage war. She had never learned what lay at the base of his motives. Whereas she and Negev—even Stracker—were far more open in their motivations.

Just weeks before, Loethar's lovemaking had been ferocious and voracious and he had come to her often, so often in fact, that she had begun to consider herself a potential wife. She'd love that title—it would give her the status she craved over Negev. Most importantly she'd be Empress to the Set. Just like Loethar, she had craved Penraven's downfall the most. In fact—

"Rider coming!" her companion said, interrupting her private thoughts.

She pulled up her horse, a fine roan. "What is it?" she hissed. "I do so wish I could ride alone!"

"Loethar's orders," the man said in the same bored tone.

"But why? Why must I have an escort?"

The man looked at her with a vague expression that spoke of tedium. His face bore the distinctive tatua that was distracting enough to hide what his eyes were saying. His tatua was green; one of Stracker's men, then. "Ask him."

She gave a sound of exasperation and waited angrily while the rider approached—a Blue this time, the Mear tribe. She didn't wait for him to address Stracker's man first. "Why do you seek me?" she demanded.

The new arrival nodded to both of them. "I have been asked to bring you back to the castle," he said, directly to her.

The petty win pleased her. Every smattering of attention she could win for herself was important. "Why?"

The younger man had ridden fast. He was breathing hard. "Queen Iselda is dead."

"What?"

"She was flung from the top floor of the castle by the servant."

"What servant?" she demanded, shocked. "Not Freath?"

The man shrugged. "I think that's his name." He grinned at his fellow warrior. "She was splattered all over the courtyard, gray matter oozing from her broken skull."

"What happened?" Valya suddenly regretted her ride.

Now she'd have to learn from others why Iselda had suffered this final humiliation. She wondered if Loethar felt cheated of killing her himself. But then he'd already given her to the colorless and dour manservant for his own pleasures; presumably Loethar had no interest in Iselda. This was good. She'd be damned if she was going to share Loethar with any woman now that she was so close. "Well, hurry up. What do we know?"

"Nothing." The Blue glanced at the Green.

"Don't look at him! He wasn't there either, you fool."

"Do not insult us," the Green warned. "He is young and I might be your escort for today but given the choice, neither of us would choose to wait on you. As our leader's woman we will tolerate you, but do not treat us as though you have any law over us."

Bravely spoken for a mere foot soldier, Valya thought. She knew it didn't help her cause to make any more enemies; she was already such an outsider, relying entirely on Loethar's charity for the small deference his men paid her. "Forgive me," she conceded, digging deep for the right tone of humility and switching into the language of the Steppes. "I have been under some strain recently. We all have. I worry for Loethar."

"Don't," the Green said. "He is very capable. If he weren't, he would not be our leader."

"Of course," she said, as politely as her fury would permit. "I had hoped to ride a bit longer, though."

The Blue shook his head. "I was told to fetch you with urgency."

She nodded, her anger barely disguised now. "Lead the way."

They were surprised to find themselves emerging from a curiously angled cave mouth that required each to help the other climb out. As they drew closer they realized there were several openings above them, from which the soft breeze and the birdsong were filtering through. The entrance itself was relatively small and very well disguised by hanging branches and overgrowing mosses.

Gavriel hauled himself out before reaching down to drag the king from the opening. "We did it, Leo! We're out!" he said, grinning triumphantly.

Leo nodded ruefully. "You were right to make me listen, Gav. The idea to leave from the rooftops—"

"Was the only option at the time," Gavriel assured. "It's all right, Leo. I'm just a coward. I don't care for heights."

The youngster grinned. "We'll have to work on that. Where to now?" he asked.

Gavriel didn't hesitate. "We need the cover that the forest gives us. It's broad daylight. We cannot risk being seen."

"We can make it to the forest in moments if we run hard."

"Yes, this copse offers only scarce coverage—it's really just some bushes, isn't it?"

"Probably grown deliberately to cover the entrance."

"You're right," Gavriel said. "I wonder why your father never told you about it."

"Because we always believed the kitchens were the way out. You're sure this isn't a trap, aren't you, Gav?"

Gavriel put a hand on the king's shoulder. "Still worried about the ochre chalk, eh?" The boy nodded. "Don't be."

Leo shook his head. "So you're not suspicious?"

"No. Utterly relieved. Now let's get out of here."

"Where are we going?"

"No idea, your majesty. But my plan is to put as much distance between us and Brighthelm as we can. We'll keep heading north and then think about where to go once we feel a bit safer."

"I'm ready. After you, Legate De Vis!"

The two warriors had already entered the first courtyard but Valya had been straggling and was now twenty, maybe almost thirty strides behind the pair. She didn't care much for this gloomy castle, much preferring Graystone, her family's hall in Droste.

The scenery of Droste was more lush, with softer hues and rounder lines. Penraven appeared jagged, more elemental, with its sea nearby and rocky cliffs. Although the forest she had just begun to explore was certainly dense and rich with sounds and colors. It could grow on her—would have to, in fact, if she would be forced to make this home. And even Penraven would be better than the garforsaken Steppes—those treeless plains that Loethar called home. She would rather die than live there, on land too dry to support a forest and yet not dry enough to be a desert. *But it might as well be!* she said to herself uncharitably as she thought of the tented villages in which the tribes lived. The tribesmen, without boundless water with which to wash regularly, smelled of the horses they raised. Loethar didn't fit in there, really. And yet he also stood very much on the outside of the people like herself. She was more in tune with the people of the Set than he could ever be.

She heard a familiar cawing sound and looked back over her shoulder to see Vyk lifting from a window of the small suite of rooms in the castle in which Loethar had chosen to live. His suite was far away from her chambers. So far, in fact, that it didn't seem likely she would feel the warmth of his skin any time soon. She sighed to herself as she watched Vyk glide away toward the woods; the bird had more attention from its master than she did these days. She followed its flight, wistfully thinking about how she might dissolve the current standoff that had seemed to erupt between them, when her attention was caught by a flash of movement.

She halted her horse and squinted into the distance. Males. One taller; both, she thought, seemed young and were running hard. Poachers? Did it matter?

"You!" she called out to the Green, instantly embarrassed that she had not bothered to learn his name.

The Green turned slowly, his dark gaze showing its usual disinterest, bordering on disdain.

"I just saw something." *Stupid!* she told herself—her words were stupid. "Men!" she corrected.

"Men?"

"Well, youths, perhaps. I'm not sure."

"Why is that worth mentioning?"

"They were running."

"Boys tend to do that," the Green said sourly.

"They looked stealthy."

His mouth shaped itself into a smirk. "Stealthy?"

She pointed, exasperated. "They ran into the woods. It was furtive, I tell you."

"And?"

"Don't you want to check and see what they are doing?"

He shook his head slowly. "Why?"

Valya vented her frustration with a groan. "Because who knows what they're up to. They could be the enemy."

"We are in enemy territory. It is highly likely you saw locals but I doubt they can trouble us if they are merely two boys."

"Not just boys. Oh, I can't be sure," she tried to correct again. "Young. One tall. Running. Furtive."

"Were they carrying weapons?"

She shook her head. "I didn't see. A sword, perhaps. Possibly a bow. I couldn't see properly and I just got a glimpse of them."

"A single sword—perhaps a bow—against the might of the tribes that have already crushed their realm?" The Green paused, shook his head. "I doubt we need to panic."

She flinched at his sarcasm even though he had kept his tone even. "We should tell Loethar."

"You think it's worth alerting the leader of the entire barbarian tribes—the new Emperor of the Set—about two running people?"

"I do," she persisted.

"Then you can tell him."

Valya made a sound of exasperation. "At least send people to check. I can show—"

"Our chieftain has ordered us to bring you before him. That is my duty. Do not force me to carry you."

She stared at the man in frustration, his tatua looking all the more sinister for the snarl in his expression. Valya momentarily considered ignoring him and ordering anyone who would listen to her to chase down the two fellows but something in the way he climbed down from his horse told her he meant every word. He would chase her instead and drag her—probably by her hair and screaming—back into the castle. And that would not do. Her status among these men was fragile enough and dependent entirely upon Loethar's indulgence. This warrior would relish the chance to belittle her on the premise of following orders . . . and then all the Greens and no doubt the Blues and Reds would privately celebrate that the Droste whore had been cowed. She would not give him that satisfaction.

"As you wish," she said, briskly clicking at her horse to continue. "I shall mention it to Loethar."

He simply gave her a sly smile and turned his great back on her. Valya fumed. She would make him pay for these last few moments.

After running full pelt for as long as their lungs would permit, they'd stopped, bent over and sucking in air. Gavriel felt as though they'd been crashing through the woodland for an eternity.

Leo recovered more quickly than he did. "We've made some good ground," the king said, breathing hard.

"I worry they've seen us," Gavriel gasped.

The king replied with a confident shake of his head. "We'd hear horses if they had."

"We have to keep moving," Gavriel said, straightening but feeling his chest protest.

"Where to?"

Gavriel shrugged. "Let's follow the line of the woods—the Deloran Forest thickens as it goes north. Where is the rebel you spoke of?"

Leo shrugged. "No idea. North is all I know. I wasn't paying enough attention."

"Well, we can't fret on that now. We have to get you away—as far away from Loethar as possible. Come on."

"Look!" Leo suddenly said.

"What?" Gavriel frowned, looking up to where the king pointed. "Oh, sod it!"

"He can't hurt us."

"Look how he watches us. He's so sinister."

"He looks like a raven, Gav."

"I think he's evil."

"You and everyone else. Why are ravens hated so? I'm told they're extremely intelligent."

"That's the problem. Corbel said you can teach them to speak."

Leo's eyes sparkled. "Perhaps Loethar's taught this one."

Gavriel shook his head. "No, we've spied on him enough that we'd have heard the bird say something if that were the case. But I think its silence is just as horrible, especially combined with that sly look. Don't you think it always appears to be thinking . . . calculating?"

Leo gave a mirthless laugh. "It's strange that it's found us specifically and when we least want to—" He stopped abruptly as Gavriel whipped around.

"Run, Leo! Don't you see? This is no coincidence. He will mark our position! Maybe he has been trained. Maybe he *is* able to follow us." Gavriel took off, making sure Leo followed him deeper into the woods. "This way," he hissed over his shoulder. "We mustn't lose direction."

"You don't really believe—"

"Save your breath. Just run," Gavriel snarled, looking up, trying to see the raven. He couldn't sight him but he suddenly didn't trust that the bird wasn't a spy of sorts.

They ran until they both fell to the undergrowth, exhausted.

"I feel sick," Leo gasped. "I've never run that far ever."

Gavriel's words came out ragged. "I know. I shouldn't have frightened you. I'm sorry. We're fine now."

"Is he here?"

"No," Gavriel said, sliding back to sit against a great trunk of a tree, his breathing finally becoming shallower, easier. "I spooked us both. I shouldn't have—"

He broke off as Vyk swooped down, landing heavily in front of them.

Leo scrabbled backward, bumping into Gavriel, who hauled him behind his own body, up against the tree.

"Gavriel—" Leo muttered but he didn't finish his thought. His wide, fearful eyes said enough.

"Be calm," Gavriel said, staring at the bird, who was eyeing them with a sinister appraisal. It hopped closer and both boys flinched. "It's a bird, that's all. It cannot hurt us," Gavriel soothed, as much for his own benefit as Leo's.

"You could shoot it," Leo said.

"Of course I can," Gavriel said, surprised he hadn't thought of that action first. "We'll soon see who owns the forest," he added, angrily reaching for one of the few arrows they'd been able to bring. Nocking it into position on the bow, he took aim, amazed the bird had not so much as blinked. Vyk turned its head slightly, watching him intently.

"Wait, stop!" Leo hissed.

"I've got such a clean shot," Gavriel murmured angrily, his gaze never straying from the pale eyes that stared straight back at him.

"It's not scared of us, Gav."

"I don't give a flying—"

"No, wait! You said it was very intelligent. A smart creature would run for its life right now, wouldn't it? Especially a bird! It would fly at the first hint of danger."

"Lo save me, what's your point, Leo?" Gavriel said, exhaling loudly.

"Don't kill it."

Gavriel lowered the bow. "You were so scared of the raven only a minute ago. And now you want me to spare its life?"

"*You* scared me, not the raven. You were the one who said he was sinister, that he's leading Loethar to us. But he's not doing anything now, is he? And he's on the ground, so who can see him but us?"

"All right, good point," Gavriel had to grant. He ran a hand through his unruly hair. "What now?"

"Nothing," the king shrugged.

"Nothing? The raven has clearly followed us!"

"I know, but let him be. Let's just get on our way."

"Why? This evil bastard belongs to Loethar. I want to kill everything that belongs to the barbarian who slew my father, effectively murdered both your parents and is the reason my brother is gone, you and I are running for our lives, and our realm is crippled. Do you want me to go on?"

Leo said nothing. He continued to stare at Vyk, who hadn't so much as ruffled a glossy feather.

"Tell me, Leo, please. Give me one good reason why I shouldn't blast this creature to its maker and strike a blow for Penraven."

The king looked embarrassed when he finally dragged his eyes from Vyk. "I don't really know, Gav, but Piven likes him."

"Piv—?" Gavriel stopped himself saying anything further but knew his expression must be one of disgust laced with disbelief.

"I have you," Leo attempted to explain. "My brother has no one familiar, save the treacherous Freath or that nasty Genrie."

Gavriel sighed. "Piven doesn't need anyone familiar. Each day everyone's a stranger to him, even those he has known for his entire life. It doesn't make any difference to him, you know that."

"Yes, I know," the king said, sorrowfully, "but he always recognized Vyk, don't you think? He always ran up to the raven; even though the barbarian keeps him on a leash now, he is always straining to be close to Vyk."

Gavriel looked back at the raven, who hopped a few steps to the side and wiped its big black beak on the ground. He sighed. "And you think there's a friendship there?" he asked.

"No, I know Piven can't form a friendship really, but unlike us he's not scared of Vyk. He recognizes him. It's something, isn't it? A bond?"

Gavriel didn't know what to say. He exhaled, blowing out his cheeks. "I suppose both of them are silent and damned creatures. Perhaps that binds them in some strange way."

Leo's eyes sparkled. "That's right! Perhaps Vyk comforts Piven somehow—in a way we don't understand. He certainly amuses him."

"Everything amuses Piven," Gavriel muttered, not unkindly.

"We can't kill the bird. Let's just go."

"But why did it follow us all this way?"

"I don't know . . . food perhaps?"

"It eats flesh, Leo, not stale bread and mouldy cheese."

"I have no idea why it's here! But I don't want you to kill it. Let's just go." Leo got up, brushing the leaves from his backside.

Gavriel stood. He jutted his chin out. "That way, come on."

They trudged off, Leo behind Gavriel. The king looked over his shoulder. "It's coming with us."

"Well, I hope he likes a long walk on those very short legs," Gavriel said uncharitably, refusing to look at their new companion.

Valya had not been invited into Loethar's personal rooms before. She had been told to await his arrival and, secretly pleased that Loethar was not tapping his feet impatiently for her, took the time to calm herself and to take in her surrounds.

It was a beautiful chamber with a series of large double doors opening onto various balconies through which she could view the sea. She realized it had a similar outlook to that of Iselda's former rooms but this was more remote, tucked away in a corner of the castle and not on such a high level as Iselda's apartments.

The room had definitely belonged to a man. A man with good taste, it seemed, from the sparse but finely made furniture. She made a soft clucking sound with her tongue. Weaven timber was scarce—there was almost none left in the Set. Whoever owned these rooms must have travelled into Skardlag to buy the raw wood. Her father had craved anything made of the honey colored timber shot through with golden striata. He owned only one small piece—a bowl—but he'd treasured it as though it were wrought from solid gold. She'd never understood his fascination, although she could appreciate its beauty now that she looked at the larger, more solid pieces which seemed to possess an internal glow.

Apart from the furniture there was little drapery in the main room. There was, however, a beautiful bronze sculpture of a horse and various paintings hanging around the walls. Again the artworks were few, like the furniture, but they were of similar exceptional quality, the likes of which she hadn't seen in many years, since leaving the Set in fact. She looked toward what must be the bedchamber, wondering if any more fine pieces were behind that door.

Her musings were interrupted by that very door opening.

Valya gasped. "Why?"

"Always hated it," Loethar replied, rubbing his now clean-shaven face.

"I've never seen you without your beard. I hope you don't mind my mentioning how much younger its loss makes you?" He gave an awkward twitch of a smile as he approached, moving toward the tray of wine and glasses that had been set up. Valya was privately amazed. Gone was that unruly mask he had obviously hidden behind, banished were the strange piercings that had once borne rings and jewels. Before her stood a handsome man, his dark features much easier to see, now that he'd washed and combed his hair into a neat pigtail. The fresh garments he wore—he must have found them in these chambers—accentuated his lean limbs and broad shoulders, making him appear even taller than he was. "You were never one of them," she said, drinking in all the detail as her gaze roved over this new Loethar. She could smell the scent of soap, the fragrance of herbs that had aired the clothes he now wore.

"Why do you say that?" he asked, and sounded genuinely interested, his dark eyes sparkling.

"Pour me a wine, and I shall tell you."

He smiled and she felt her heart leap. Perhaps the strange detachment he'd been suffering of late had disappeared with the unkempt beard. That smile was what she loved most about him; it was hard to win, and all the more precious because he gave it so reluctantly.

"To you, my lady," he said, arriving to stand before her, hair wet, eyes shining with what she suspected was some special knowledge. He held out an elegant pewter goblet. "It is very good."

She took the goblet, ensuring her fingers touched his hand—just lightly enough to send a message of affection. "Thank you. This is an unexpected treat—and I don't mean the wine."

He had the grace to look slightly sheepish. Another good sign. She raised her glass. "Sarac, Loethar!" she said, wishing him fine health in the Steppes language.

"To new beginnings," he replied before drinking.

"All right. Do you mind my saying that you look very . . . er, handsome today?"

His brow crinkled. "Why would I mind such a compliment?"

Valya sipped before she spoke, then regarded him carefully, her head cocked to one side. "I am wary around you. I no longer know what is the right thing to say."

He scoffed gently. "Say only the truth. That is all I ever want to hear."

She nodded, sipping again. "Whose clothes do you wear?"

"Freath tells me they belonged to Regor De Vis. It seems

we were of a similar size. I shall have my own made soon enough."

"This style suits you," she said, careful to see how Loethar would react before fully committing herself.

"This is how I mean to dress from now on. If I am to be emperor of the region, I must fit in."

"Getting rid of all the metal hooked into your face is sensible too, as is your new astonishing neatness." He said nothing but he didn't seem angered by her comment and she took that as encouragement. "So, it is not your intention to change the conquered people into—"

"No," he said, firmly. "They are Set. They remain that way. Any changes I implement will be gradual and subtle."

"Wise," she said, sipping again. "I'm amazed. You look like you've always belonged here." She walked around him, admiring how well the garments were cut, and how closely they fitted his body. "The legate was important to the king."

"They were closer than brothers."

"He had family, did you know?"

"Yes. A wife, dead, and two sons from that union."

"Where are they?"

"We don't know. It's important that we find them."

"Are they a problem?"

"I suspect at seventeen summertides they will be. I was."

She smiled at his quip. "I can't imagine your mother ever felt out of her depth with you."

"No, but then she wasn't a mother in the way you might anticipate mothers should be. We've never really talked at length about your family, Valya, have we?"

It was obvious he didn't want to discuss his own folk. "Other than hating them, you mean?" she said, sweetly. "I'm sure I've told you enough."

He looked amused. "Well, you had good reason. It was not your fault they had no sons."

Valya sighed. "I guess not, although my parents certainly made me regret I was not born a boy every day of my pathetic existence."

He held her gaze and she was sure—just for a moment—that he shared her pain. She didn't fully understand his state of mind with all these new changes but she also didn't want this new tenderness to be spoiled, so she kept her bitterness at bay, fighting down the anger that seemed to accompany any mention of her family.

"I don't understand why the engagement to Brennus didn't make you rise in their estimation."

"Oh, it did, but not in the way I'd have hoped. All father could see was a great strategic alliance. All mother could see was wealth."

"And you?"

"Escape, Loethar. You know that's what I've always wanted."

"Not power, then?"

She laughed. "I didn't say that. I won't lie—you know me too well—of course I want power. But perhaps not for the reasons you think."

"For what reasons, then?"

She frowned at him, confused. "What is this all about?"

He shrugged, looking injured. "Haven't you always complained that I never linger long enough to talk with you? Aren't you enjoying our 'conversation'—over a goblet of wine, no less, and without interruption?"

"Yes, but I'm baffled by the topic. I've told you much of this before."

"Perhaps I want to hear it again. Perhaps I want to be sure about you, Valya."

Her frown deepened. She wanted to ask why but again she censured herself. It would be better, in this moment, to simply enjoy the attention she had craved for so long. "All right. I like the idea of power for the freedom it would give me. The escape from the claustrophic sense that with every breath I take I let my parents down. Especially since the breakdown of the troth."

"Did they blame you for that?"

"Of course. I think I still hear my father's disdain each

day I wake. He said: 'See, even foreigners are preferable to you.' "

He nodded. "She was from Galinsea, as I understand it."

"A Romean princess, no less."

"How did they meet?"

She shrugged. "From what I could glean, old King Darros of Penraven took Prince Brennus to pay respects at the funeral of the Emperor Luc. Galinsea and Percheron were such powerful trading regions that the Set couldn't ignore the important event and Darros represented all of the Set rulers." She sighed. "The short of it is that Brennus met the young Iselda, one of the daughters of the Romean prince and . . ." She looked up, smiling bitterly. "My betrothal was forgotten."

"She is very beautiful," he said.

"Beautiful? Not any more," Valya replied, her tone more savage than she had meant it. "But, Loethar, did you not recognize a kindred spirit between you and Brennus?"

She saw him blanch.

"And what's that supposed to mean?"

Valya gave a small shrug. "Brennus was as ruthless as you are! Never think for a moment that the love he was purported to show for his family ever threatened his decision-making regarding the realm of Penraven." She saw Loethar's eyes narrow and enjoyed the knowledge that she was telling him things he hadn't previously known. Well, he had only ever had to ask. She was not so enamoured by their relationship to fail to realize it was a convenient one for him. Her knowledge of the Set, and the customs of this region this far west, not to mention her own lineage, were critical factors in his tolerance of her. "The man was a tyrant in his own way." She turned to gaze out one of the windows. "I have no doubt he loved Iselda but he also claimed to love me. He made plight troth to my parents. Droste would have been a very handy alliance for the Set, but not nearly so sparkling as the alliance forged with Galinsea and ultimately Percheron through his marriage to Iselda. Even though she was a lesser princess, a mere second or third cousin to Emperor Luc—whereas I was first born, the direct heir to our throne!"

"Would your father have permitted you to rule?"

Valya shrugged. "I sometimes think he'd rather have poisoned me than permit me the throne. Even now, I am sure he's working to see his nephew take the crown."

"Not while I live, Valya," Loethar promised. His words sent a thrill through her. "But how was Iselda more appropriate for Brennus?"

"Iselda came directly from King Falza's line. She was of his blood, and that carried tremendous status. The Set trades through Percheron—I'm sure you know that?" He nodded. "Well, that match allowed Brennus to forge those vital links to the east. And the beauty you speak of was simply the diamond dust on the top of an already sparkling betrothal." She balled her fists. "How could Droste compete with that?" she spat.

He didn't reply immediately and Valya held her tongue. Her bitterness had ruined the pleasant atmosphere, she was sure. She heard him pour more wine but only turned when he surprised her with a light touch on her arm. She hadn't even realized he had moved silently next to her.

Loethar handed her her goblet, its contents refreshed. "Here, it's had a chance to breathe now. It tastes even better." She took the cup. "You know, Valya," he continued, drawing closer still until their shoulders touched. "Everything about life is perception." She looked at him quizzically but he was staring out to the sea, not looking at her. "What one man casts aside as unnecessary could be the very thing that another man has been searching for."

She frowned. "I understand the sentiment, but what are you saying?"

"Yes, let's not speak in couched terms. Let me be plain. Droste may not have been such a gain for Brennus if at the time he felt secure with all the realms of the Set working in such alignment. But I would like to see Droste as part of the Set—a new member. It is more strategic than Brennus gave it credit for. Droste is the source of the great river that feeds this region; its mountains are very important to us as much of Lo's Teeth is unexplored—we have no idea what riches are to be found in the foothills alone. Droste has music and art and though Cremond is the seat of learning for the Set, perhaps Droste can become its cultural center point?" Valya's eyes had widened. She could barely believe what she was hearing; was more than a year of maneuvering and cunning finally going to pay off?

Slowly letting her breath out, she repeated carefully, "What are you saying?" She put her goblet down on a small weaven table nearby. Her fingers were suddenly trembling.

He smiled almost self-consciously and cleared his throat. "I'm saying that I consider Droste to be far more valuable than Brennus did. I think we should make the union of Droste and the Set official."

She stared at him, and knew she was blinking with nervousness as well as excitement. "Marriage?"

He looked down momentarily, then fixed her with his dark gaze. "Yes. Marry me, Valya."

It took her a moment to make sure she had heard him absolutely clearly. Then she squealed and threw her arms around his neck. It was girlish, perhaps even childish, and everything she knew he would detest but she was beside herself with happiness. "Loethar! Yes! Of course!"

He held her away from him. "Good. Thank you."

But she wanted to feel his arms around her again. "Oh, please hold me close. Mean it, Loethar. Tell me you love me."

He encircled her with his arms obligingly. "I think this will be good for both of us."

She pulled her face from where she'd buried it in his neck and stared into his face, suddenly unreadable again. "It doesn't matter whether you can express your feelings. I can and I need to tell you that I love you."

"I know you do." He looked embarrassed.

"You frighten me sometimes."

"Do I?"

She nodded.

"There is no reason for you to fear me, Valya. But don't try and understand me. I need you to just accept me."

"I will," she said, knowing in her heart she was lying to both of them.

"And be loyal. Continue to be my eyes and ears."

"My loyalty to you will never be in question. But I beg you not to shut me out. To be of real use to you, I need to know what you are thinking."

"I shall try."

"Does your mother know that you were planning to propose?"

"No. We shall tell her of our engagement together."

"She won't be pleased."

"Why do you say that?"

"Dara Negev hates me, as I suspect she would hate any woman who won your affections."

"You have her wrong, Valya. My mother hates anyone who might sway me from my cause."

"If that were the case she should welcome me with open arms."

"She is a tough woman to please, I'll grant you. But you'll win her over."

"Protect me, Loethar. Let her know that you hold me in high regard. I need your support."

"You are to be my wife. You will be empress, Valya. I should imagine that is enough support for you to wield against both your mother and mine."

She felt a surge of fierce delight at the very notion of seeing both her parents at the wedding. "Kiss me," she urged.

He leaned toward her and she parted her lips to welcome him, to bind this moment in the tender and loving intimacy of a deep kiss, but he did not dwell. If anything the caress of his lips felt cursory, dry, and she felt her joy dented still further to see him wipe his mouth surreptitiously as he turned away.

"I will set arrangements in motion," he said. "Thank you,

Valya. I will contact your parents to ensure they are aware of this development. They must at least be curious as to your whereabouts?"

She diverted her pain into her scornful tone. "The king and Queen of Droste have probably not given my disappearance much mourning. They would have had a sense of good riddance, if anything. It solves the problem of who takes the crown."

"Well, not any more. Now you bring the empire to their doorstep. If they really are how you describe them, the royal couple will fall over themselves to be dutiful parents to you and allies with me."

She nodded. "That's exactly what will happen, Loethar. You don't even know them and still you have their measure."

"I don't need to know them. I have observed enough of people's nature to understand those like your family."

"And what about your own family?"

He turned back to face her. "I didn't choose them," he said evasively.

"No, but you do control them."

"To a point."

"Loethar," she began, her voice now streaked with disdain, "do you honestly believe Stracker wouldn't still be arm wrestling in tents and helping mares give birth if not for you?"

He remained irritatingly calm. "Stracker would be the first to admit that I am the son born with the brains, he with the brawn. He likes it that way."

She shook her head. "No one would even pick you for brothers. How could you two sons come from the same man's seed?"

"Who said we did?"

Valya froze. She'd said it as a meaningless insult, nothing more. In a rare awkward moment, she found herself open-mouthed and staring. Then, embarrassed, she began to stammer. "I . . . I really didn't mean. What I mean is I . . . well, I'm—"

"It's all right, Valya. I'm baiting you."

She wasn't sure he had been. "Warn me the next time you plan to make a jest, my beloved, for I can never be sure with that serious countenance of yours."

He nodded. "I must practice a happy face, you think?"

She smiled now and placed her hand on his chest, glad for the excuse to touch him. "Well, now that you're emperor you must certainly make yourself accessible to your new people. A smile, especially one as charming as yours, can only help your cause."

"I will remember that. I'll have to try not to smile when I impale their young king in Penraven's grand city square."

Valya shuddered inwardly. For all his tenderness of just moments earlier, he was still a conqueror before all else. She had taught herself—Lo knew she'd had enough practice—how to behave in the ruthless manner that would impress him. But he frightened her all the same. He was uncannily able to keep everyone off balance; his mind seemed to work at a different speed and with a strange and sinister grace that allowed him to see things quickly, differently. He was always one step ahead of most others.

"And I always think Stracker's the bloodthirsty brother. He has nothing on his elder," she said, affectionately in a contrived light jest.

"I am not the elder brother," he said calmly, ignoring Valya's obvious shock.

"I . . . I don't understand."

"Stracker is older than me."

"But—"

"This is how our father wished it," he added, his tone final.

She nodded, unsure of what to say, finally murmuring, "I'm glad." Deftly switching topics, she asked, "No news then on Leonel?"

"No." His expression turned sour. "It galls me to think the boy was in the palace when we took it. He had to have had help escaping."

"What sort of help?"

He shook his head, irritated. "Freath mentioned something about seeing him with one of the De Vis sons just prior to our taking the castle and . . ." He stopped, shrugging.

"What is it?"

"No, nothing."

"Tell me," she said, placing her hand on his muscled arm, relishing the chance to touch him again.

He gave an expression of reluctant acquiescence. "I had given strict instructions that the palace and all exits be guarded . . . every possible entry or departure point was manned. We stormed the castle in a concerted effort that would have left no one any time to make an escape. I know not one of those royals ever really believed they were under threat of death; parley was at the top of their list, not escape. And we know the prince was here when we took Brighthelm—Freath saw him. He had nowhere to go. Nowhere to hide! Every last crevice has been searched. I don't know how he has escaped our clutches."

"You said he was with one of the De Vis sons. What does he look like?"

Loethar shook his head. "Freath says he is tall and strong-looking. A man, albeit young."

She nodded. "So there's only two of them?"

"Just two, both young. They should have been easy to entrap." He walked away, stretching, obviously finished with the conversation.

"Loethar," she whispered, staring at his back as he stretched, his spine giving a satisfying crack. She felt the blood drain from her face.

"What is it?" he said, turning. "What's wrong? Are you sick?"

She shook her head, thinking it through, running the scene back in her mind. How long had it been? Nearly two hours perhaps. She snapped her attention back to Loethar's face, now so close she could kiss him again, could see the soft shadow of where his beard had hung from for so long.

"Talk to me!" he demanded.

"I'm sorry. Forgive me. It's just that . . . I think we just saw them," she said, her voice tiny, frightened.

Loethar gripped her shoulders and she watched his face change from quizzical, slightly baffled, to controlled rage. It happened in the blink of an eye and once again Valya was reminded that this was no ordinary man she was attaching herself to. His hands dug into her upper arms and her fingertips went numb in the space of moments. "What did you say?" he whispered.

He had heard, she knew it, but he just couldn't believe it. Still she went through the motions and explained. "I was out riding," she began, nodding, making sure he was hearing her.

Exasperation flickered in his stare. "I do recall. I sent a runner to fetch you."

"Loethar, you're hurting me," she murmured.

He let her go. "And?"

Valya rubbed one arm and then the other as she continued. "I had one of your men with me as escort, as you've insisted. A Green. Another rode up, a Blue, and said you wanted to see me. We were riding back, were almost into the bailey when I happened to look around and I saw your horrible raven leaving the palace. It must have been from this room," she said, looking around.

"It was. Go on," he said, his stare impaling her, voice hard.

"Well, I followed Vyk's flight and as he flew into the forest line I thought I saw two figures." She watched his jaw grind as his lips thinned. "I was too far away to see clearly but they were running. One was taller than the other. I guessed both to be youngish men."

"And you—"

"I did! I argued with the escort warrior. I insisted we do something about it. I described the pair. I said they looked furtive; I said they were running." She huffed. "The Green treated me with disdain, I have to tell you. He talked to me as though I were a pig farmer's whore and did nothing, didn't even look in the direction I was pointing. He even threatened me; he told me the men only tolerate me because of you." Her gaze flicked away from his unnerving stare. "I kept telling him it was worth looking into and all he said was that his duty was to bring me to you because I'd been summoned. I demanded that you be alerted. He all but said he'd drag me before you if I didn't comply and follow him."

"I see," Loethar said, his fury barely controlled. "And this happened right before I saw you?"

She shrugged helplessly. "Well, no. We argued over it for a brief time. And then I had to travel from just outside the bailey to this chamber."

"Too long," he growled. "Who were these men of mine?"

"I don't know their names."

"Could you recognize them again?"

"Of course."

He grabbed her and there was nothing gentle about it. "Come with me," he snarled.

Seventeen

Kirin and Clovis looked around. Their accommodations were sparse but airy and light. Herbs in jars around the room lent a fresh fragrance to what was clearly a long unused chamber.

"All right?" Freath inquired, pushing open a window and allowing a soft breeze to blow in.

Kirin thought he was jesting but realized the former aide to the now dead queen spoke in earnest. "I'm surprised we have this much," he admitted.

Clovis nodded, looking pensive. "What a strange day this has been."

"And each will get stranger, I'm sure," Freath said. "I'm glad you are friends and can look out for each other. Now I must leave. If you are sent for, don't dally. If I speak to you cruelly, ask odd deeds of you, or even strike you, you're welcome to scowl but do as you're bid. Behave reluctantly but don't overdo it; I may not be able to protect you. The barbarian will be suspicious if you don't resent my lordship over you but it will seem equally questionable if you disobey me and I don't impose harsh punishment. Feel free to be very frightened." He sighed, then warned, as he opened the door to leave, "We walk a fine line now, my friends."

"Freath, wait," Kirin implored. "I'm still not sure why we've been chosen like this."

Freath closed the door again. "I must be brief. I asked Loethar for two of the Vested for my own purposes. I used the excuse that it was to ensure my protection, and of course he agreed because he thinks I am a coward as well as a traitor. I also think he readily agreed knowing that he would see to it that Stracker offered me a choice of only those they believed were not truly possessed of any high magic."

"I see," Kirin said, glancing at Clovis, knowingly. "They thought they were granting you false security."

"Just so," Freath replied.

"So how can we be of any use to you?"

"Come now, Master Kirin. I think we both know that you have set out to disguise your true talents. I knew any Vested worth his salt wouldn't admit to possessing real power. Those who made big noise of their abilities I knew were destined for a poor end—for even Stracker is not completely stupid. He was clever enough to siphon off those who seemed genuinely talented, leaving behind a few vaguely empowered individuals from whom I was permitted to choose. I saw straight away that both of you were hiding something and I took the risk that it was your powers that you were underselling." He shrugged. "And I was obviously right. I saw how sick you became after engaging in what I assume was prying into Stracker. Is this so?" Kirin nodded. "We have no time to talk now but I will need to learn the extent of your abilities. Master Clovis, the same goes for you. As far as Loethar is concerned I have demanded you as my protectors in exchange for whatever I can tell them about the Valisars." He held a hand up as they both began to speak. "Of course I intend to tell them nothing of any use. Just as they intend that I have very little protection."

Clovis wore a baffled expression. "But, Master Freath, how are we supposed to offer you protection when we can't even protect ourselves? I am a diviner but although Kirin can pry, neither of us can offer you safety against injury."

"I realize that. Hopefully it no longer matters—hopefully

I have proven myself to Loethar with my act of barbarism against the queen. I do not want your talents to protect me. I need your talents for what I seek."

Kirin held out his hands. "I really don't get how—"

"Your skills will help me to find an aegis," Freath interrupted.

Clovis shook his head in dismay. Kirin responded for both of them. "But surely you know that most people don't believe such a person even exists?"

"Do you?" Freath asked pointedly.

"I . . . I've never really thought about it."

Clovis sighed. "I've always thought aeges were simply myth, to tell the truth."

Freath flicked at a bit of lint on his dark clothes. "Well, I have to believe such a person does live. The history books say King Cormoron had an aegis. It is written that for every Valisar king, there is one."

"Surely that's just legend?" Clovis said, bemused.

"I've never even heard rumor of someone being able to champion with magic," Kirin said.

Freath shrugged. "Until very recently I sneered at the suggestion that prying existed."

Kirin stared at Freath. "You didn't know?"

The older man shook his head. "I have read a lot and listened a great deal to people cleverer than myself. But until I met you I had never met a Vested. Only now do I realize they are everyday people, living everyday lives . . . and probably half the time wishing they were not special." Kirin looked down as Freath's words struck a chord. "But neither of you can be considered ordinary, no matter how everyday your lives are. You do possess powers and you must now use them for the good of your realm. I beg you. Put all your skills to use. If such a person as an aegis lives, I want to know his name. And this is not for my sake but for my king, whenever we can find him."

"Freath, even if such a person does exist—he could be anywhere."

The aide's expression was rueful. "Do you think I don't know that?"

Kirin shook his head. "It's pointless, surely?"

"No! I think he does exist. I'll tell you why. When we first got wind that the barbarians were encroaching into Set lands Brennus began to put certain steps into place. I cannot tell you what those were." He raised a hand to silence Kirin. "Trust me, please. One of the duties he gave me was to read all the ancient texts to find out everything I could about the phenomenon of the aegis. Interestingly, it was well documented. I discovered two in Valisar history, although most of us only know about the most famous—the one bonded to Cormoron. The other, more obscure aegis was hunted and supposedly bonded to a wealthy merchant during the reign of the 4th Valisar king. But we have only sketchy details of that one. I suspect it's not true."

Kirin, exasperated, was glad when Clovis responded for both of them. "So if we have two that we know of in eight kings or however many centuries—nearly five, perhaps?" At Freath's nod, he continued, "What makes you think one exists now?"

"There are signs," Freath replied.

"What signs?" Kirin demanded. "I know a bit about magic, Freath. I've read plenty too and I've never heard about signs that herald an aegis."

"That's because after the aegis was bonded by the merchant, the Valisars deliberately set out to destroy all information about them. The merchant was cagey about his protection anyway, so that worked in the Valisars' favor. He didn't want anyone to know that the little girl he bonded to him was anything more than a servant."

"So it was easy to cover all trace of the aegis and how the magic works, you mean?" Clovis asked.

"Precisely so. No other Valisar king has needed that sort of protection. The Set has lived in peace since Cormoron's times."

"So various aeges have come and gone," Clovis remarked.

"Most will have lived and died without anyone knowing, without even the aegis really grasping his potential."

"I think you're clutching at straws, Freath."

"Straws of hope *are* all we have to cling to, Master Kirin. I mean to discover the aegis originally born for Leonel. The fact is, Loethar has already done most of the hard work. Everyone who is Vested, anyone who was even whispered about as having a talent, is being held somewhere in and around this palace."

"Or dead," Clovis added sourly.

"Indeed," Freath replied. "All I'm asking is that you try. If an aegis exists, you two can probably seek that person more effectively than anyone else I can think of. Plus, you can do so without suspicion." They both nodded unhappily. "Kirin, don't make yourself too sick, though. We need you alert. Wander around the palace, see what you can learn. Now I must go. I have left a length of fabric in that drawer over there," he said, pointing. "Wear it around your arm at all times. It will permit you certain freedoms as it marks you as my servant. Be careful."

"Wait!" Kirin urged. "You said there were signs the aegis would display?"

"Ah yes, although they are subtle. He will be marked by Lo. Something about him will be different, although it's different each time and we never know what it may be. Cormoron's aegis was said to have never grown hair anywhere on his body. The merchant's child was mutarl—"

"What's that?" Clovis asked, frowning.

"A Penraven expression," Kirin explained. "White haired, pale skinned, strange eyes, poor sight."

"Ah, we call this pearled."

"Aeges also tend to be restless souls. Until they are trammelled, they tend to wander, though they remain isolated." Freath gave them both a final glance of encouragement and then the door closed and he was gone.

Clovis sighed. "An aegis?" he repeated.

"He's dreaming," Kirin replied. "Confusing his myths with history."

"We must stay optimistic. If we exist, who is to say an aegis is simply folklore?"

"Do you know what is said to be involved in binding an aegis?" Kirin asked. Clovis shook his head. "You have to trammel them. And to trammel an aegis requires you to bind them with a powerful magic that you draw from them alone.

"You have to consume part of him," Kirin continued, turning away in disgust. "Their spirit is then bound to you. Their magic protects you."

"Consume. You mean *eat* them?" Clovis asked, in a tone of disbelief.

"Yes, eat. So that part of their body is now part of yours and they are helplessly bound, by their very creation, to your needs. It's hideous. There have been tales of suspected aeges having fingers and toes hacked off, even whole limbs, in order to be roasted and eaten. Most of the time the hunters are wrong and innocent people die. An aegis will hide himself to the utmost of his ability."

"Because he doesn't want to be consumed," Clovis finished.

"That, too, but mainly because his skills are only good on behalf of others. It's only once he's been trammelled that his true powers are potent. Then he can protect both himself and the person who bound him. Until then, he's as helpless as you or I."

"That's a good thing, though, isn't it? I mean, to come into one's powers?"

"No, think about it. You're living your normal life, perhaps not happily ignorant of what you possess but certainly not required to use it—not even capable of using it, in fact. Along comes any old stranger, who recognizes your inherent power and trammels you. Suddenly you're under their complete control." As Clovis frowned, Kirin added, "Oh, didn't I mention the trammelling binds you so closely to this stranger that you follow him against your own inclination? You no longer possess a mind of your own. You cannot leave your binder, or lie to him, or do anything to harm him. When he walks, sleeps, eats, so do you. To be too far from him makes your very bones ache. To be separated for any length of time threatens your sanity, although your powers do not wane. You share his sufferings but not his joys. The aegis gives without cease but cannot take. It is not a gift; it is a curse from the gods."

"I had no idea. And how do you recognize someone cursed in this way?"

Kirin smiled without a skerrick of warmth. "You don't. Any aegis will go to any length to hide his potential power—though, as Freath said, they are supposed to be marked somehow. I suspect many are marked in such subtle ways that they live their lives unnoticed. But clever Freath knows our skills can look beneath the skin. He knows if anyone can find an aegis we can, no matter how hard he may try to mask what he possesses."

"Cunning," Clovis agreed.

"Well, I'll do it for the Set. If Penraven's young king is all that is left of our royal families, we must fight for him."

Clovis handed Kirin one of the lengths of fabric. "We'd better heed Freath's warning with these. Here, let me tie it on you." Once the cloth was secured, Kirin tied the other around Clovis's arm. "It's probably wise I try some divining first," Clovis added.

"I was hoping you'd say that," Kirin said, relieved.

"Where do we begin?"

"We need to find the first group, or at least learn where they've been sent."

"And let's keep away from that Stracker," Clovis added.

They found Stracker eating in the barracks that had once housed the Penraven army.

"Brother!" he exclaimed, unable to hide his surprise,

"welcome, join us—not that you look like us any more!" There was a question in his voice, his expression.

"Not now," Loethar said, walking to a more private corner. Stracker followed. "I need you to assemble the Blues and Greens that were on duty this morning," he said.

"Why?" His brother stared at him.

"It's important," Loethar growled. "Do you know who accompanied Valya this morning on her ride?"

"No, but it's easy enough to find out. What's happened?"

"She thinks she might have seen the Valisar and De Vis escaping."

Stracker's eyes widened. "What?"

"You heard me," Loethar said in shared disgust. "She asked the men to investigate but according to her they refused."

"How long ago?"

"More than two hours now."

"Is she sure?"

"That it was them?" At Stracker's nod, Loethar said irritated, "No, of course she's not sure. But the two people she saw running into the woods fitted the description of the two we seek. I can't believe they might have slipped our net."

"How could they, Loethar? There is no entrance or departure point we haven't got guarded day and night. We rotate the guards every hour. They couldn't slip past us."

"Just bring them in," Loethar said, wearily. "Let's hear their side."

Stracker turned to bark orders and before long men were noisily assembling in the courtyard outside.

Loethar walked to where he'd left Valya. She looked good in her riding garb, he noted. She had taken to wearing Set clothes when they'd first arrived into the region; gone were the highly colorful skirts that the Steppes women favored. Although, in truth, even though she'd done her best to fit in, her bright golden hair and pale skin had always identified her as an outsider. Now she draped herself in finer fabrics of richer, more elegant colors that she'd obviously looted along the way of their various conquests. He noted that her riding skirt was too big for her and the jacket a touch small for her heavy breasts but she carried it all magnificently on her statuesque body. He couldn't deny the lust Valya fired in him. He knew that she loved him but he couldn't feel the same way. It wasn't even her fault, really; he had carried so much hatred for so long that he didn't think he had room for love. He could not imagine love ever entering his consciousness, as long as he continued to hate the Valisars, until every last one of them was destroyed.

"Come, Valya, I want you to find the two men in question."

"Must I?" she asked, looking self-conscious.

"For me," he replied.

She moved, took his hand and allowed herself to be guided before the assembled men.

"These aren't all the Blues and Greens, only those who were on duty earlier," Stracker said.

Loethar nodded. "Is anyone still on duty who was on this morning?" He ignored the surprised stares from the men at his new appearance.

"No. We rotate them too often," Stracker replied.

"Good. Valya, if you please."

She picked out the messenger easily enough. "Him," she said, pointing. "He was the Blue runner who brought the message that I was to be brought before you."

Loethar nodded at Stracker, who motioned to the young man. "Come here, Farn."

The man approached, looking appropriately wary.

"And the other?" Loethar asked her.

"Green. I don't see him," she said, her eyes narrowing as she scanned the rows of men.

"Walk among them," Loethar urged.

"No need," Stracker said, his head dipping over to the far end of the further line where a man moved toward them. "Him."

"I was the escort," the Green bellowed. "There is no need to seek me. I come of my own choice." He knelt before Loethar. The Blue followed suit.

"These two?" Loethar asked Valya once again.

"Yes. Him especially," she nodded at the Green. "He treated me with disdain."

"What is your name, warrior?"

"I am Belush."

"And, Belush, I am given to understand that despite the lady's urging, you ignored her requests to follow the people she saw slipping into the woods."

"That's true. I had strict orders to get her to you. We follow orders. We did not wish to let you down."

Loethar nodded. He could not fault the man's logic. "Did you not think it would be prudent to ask anyone else to check into the strangers?"

Belush didn't answer immediately. Finally he nodded. "I should have. But the woman treated me with such contempt, my lord, I was angry at her attitude."

"I see. Do you know who she is, Belush?"

"She is the Princess of Droste, as I understand it."

"Then you already know she is of royal blood and should be accorded some respect. Did you also know, Belush, that the Princess of Droste is soon to be not only the Empress of the Set but also the queen of the Steppes?"

At this news a murmuring went up among the gathered men. Belush hesitated. "I did not, my lord."

"You, Farn. Did you not consider the lady's request at least worthy of follow up?" Loethar demanded.

"I was simply following my orders, emperor. It's been drummed into us never to deviate from an order," the younger man stammered.

Loethar drew his sword and a tight silence bound the gathered men. "I applaud that you think in this manner, Farn, but, you see I gave very strict orders that the King of Penraven was to be found at any cost. Those were everyone's orders. And you dismissed that edict in favor of a simple command to fetch the Princess Valya. All you would have had to do was mention her concern to your superior and something could have been done about it. Now their trail is already hours cold."

"I had no idea, my lord," Farn bleated. "I wasn't thinking."

Privately, Loethar hoped Farn never knew it was coming. And the way his eyelids curiously fluttered a few times once his head rolled to a stop by Valya's boot, he assumed that the young warrior was taken by surprise. Loethar watched the Blue's body slump forward, knowing the Mears now had a grudge against Valya. He would have to watch that. To her credit she was stoic in ignoring how her clothes were spattered with the Blue's blood but he did notice her nudge Farn's heavy head away, no doubt trying to avoid the way his eyes stared with accusation at her from near her boots.

Belush had not moved position, not so much as flinched. Loethar admired his courage because the Green would know he was next.

"Anything you want to say, Belush?"

"Only an apology on behalf of the Drevin tribe for letting you down, my lord. My pride got in the way of good sense."

"Your pettiness has allowed the Valisar boy to escape our clutches."

Belush said nothing, but he hung his head in shame. Loethar waited. Wondered what Valya might say or do. He was sure he had her measure. Nevertheless, even though she did not, could not know it, he had privately handed her control. In the space of a breathless moment he watched Valya take in Stracker's disgust that a good man was about to die and he assumed that she accepted she was being blamed. If he could feel it, then she must surely feel the fresh hate emanating from the men and directed at her . . . she could, if she was quick and her pride could be set aside for a second, earn their respect but it would take a magnanimous gesture. He would not offer it or it would make a mockery of the Blue warrior's death and would compromise him. He watched his knuckles whiten around the hilt of the blade just before he raised it. He gave it another second's pause at the top of its arc before he reluctantly began its descent.

"Stop!" Valya cried.

"What is it?" he deliberately growled, hiding his relief.

"I want him," Valya said.

"For what?"

"To humiliate. Make him my servant. Let him run after my every bid, my every call. He can run my errands and run my baths." She tinkled a laugh at her own jest. "Why lose a good warrior when you can teach him the lesson you want over and over again by giving him to me?"

"Kill me, my lord," Belush urged.

Loethar's gaze narrowed as he looked from Belush's now raised and pleading eyes to Valya's hard look.

"Make him obey me, the object of his disdain," Valya urged. "I shall teach him not to dismiss me and you can make use of his fighting skills whenever you need. I don't believe you need more bloodshed to make your point. We're better off sending out trackers right now than wasting another moment." She glanced briefly at the men. "This would please me, Loethar. Perhaps we can teach Belush some respect," she added.

Loethar stepped back and lowered his sword. "As you wish, Valya. Belush, you now belong to her. You will obey her every command. I know you don't value your own life but I promise you that I will kill a member of your tribe each time you disobey the soon-to-be empress's orders."

"Yes, my lord," Belush answered. Loethar could hear the forlornness in his voice.

"From now on Valya is to be known as Princess Valya. When we marry she is to be empress. Do you hear?"

As the men assented—Stracker included—Valya glanced at Loethar. Her expression was composed but he could sense her delight. "Come, Belush," she said sweetly. "I have some chores for you."

Eighteen

They had stopped for a rest twice more and each time Vyk had landed to regard them in his silent, sinister manner.

Gavriel had found some wild roeberries, which he'd spread out on a makeshift bed of leaves together with the sweet nut that was abundant in this part of the realm.

"I never thought I'd be dining on crabnut," Leo said, cracking the brittle shell with his teeth and digging out the distinctive purplish flesh.

"Tastes good though, doesn't it?" Gavriel replied absently, his gaze focused on the raven.

"Anything does when you're as hungry as I am," Leo grumbled, but it was a hollow whinge with no heat. If anything Leo was calmer, more in control than ever before.

Although they were in unfamiliar territory and under threat from the marauders, Gavriel believed being on the run and out of Brighthelm was the best set of circumstances for the young king. The ingress had become oppressive, more like a prison than a haven, and he had had very little way of protecting Leo from the cruel scenes that would no doubt continue to unfold before them. "Eat plenty of the berries to help keep you refreshed," he encouraged. "My father always told us they are as good as drinking a cup of water."

"I'm done. If I eat any more I think I'll get belly cramp," Leo said, wiping the blood-red juice of the berries on his trousers. "Mother would screech if she saw me do this," he said and Gavriel heard the soft sorrow in his voice.

"I think she'd forgive you under the circumstances," he replied, pushing himself off the ground. "We need to keep going."

"I could lie down and sleep right now. We've got to have covered ten miles."

"I know. But we must gain more distance from Brighthelm. We'll stop as soon as it gets dark, which won't be long now. If we get lucky I can shoot us a rabbit."

Leo sighed and hauled himself to his feet. "Come on, Vyk," he murmured, and Gavriel grimaced.

"Don't encourage him."

"It seems to me he does exactly what he wants anyway."

As Gavriel reached for his bow, Vyk began to clack his beak, and then gave voice to what was clearly alarm. The boys turned to see Vyk lift his heavy body up into the trees, where he quietened but continued to stare at them intently.

"What was that about?" Leo wondered aloud.

"Daft bird," Gavriel muttered. He pulled his bow across him. "Come on, L—"

"And who have we got here?" a voice said.

Gavriel spun, instinctively reaching for Leo, intensely angry with himself for unbuckling his sword. He could see it on the ground just a few paces from reach, and yet it might as well have been a hundred miles away.

"Boys?" said the man. He looked behind him as a companion appeared. "Look, Jok, poachers."

"We're not poachers," Gavriel said, indignantly.

"What are you doing here, then?" the first man asked.

"Travelling," Gavriel answered, hoping he sounded more confident than he felt. "You look like Penravians, so presumably you're aware of what's happening in our own realm."

The man's gaze narrowed. "No smart lip from you, lad. And, just as an observation, that sword looks far too fine to belong to someone as scruffy as you appear."

Gavriel felt a surge of relief. At least his precaution of

roughing up their clothes and removing as much finery as possible had stood up to a cursory glance. The ruse wouldn't bear intense scrutiny but hopefully it wouldn't have to.

"That sword belonged to my father," he lied. "And he gave it to me."

"Who gave it to him, I wonder?"

Gavriel shrugged. "My father travelled a lot. I have no idea. Probably won it at darts."

"He must have been good," the man commented.

"The best," Gavriel replied.

"And does the skill run in the family?"

Gavriel nodded, unsure of where the man was going with this. "I've a good eye, if that's what you mean."

Both men laughed.

"Is this your brother?"

Gavriel gripped Leo's shoulder more tightly. "Yes, this is Lewk. My name's Gaven. And you?"

"Jok and Alfric. Al to my friends."

Gavriel tried to give a friendly nod although he felt trapped. He could hear the damn raven clacking high in the trees now.

"Where have you come from?" Alfric asked.

"The city's too dangerous. We were going there to work the leaf-fall with my uncle. He's a smith who does a lot of jobs for the palace."

"I would have thought there would be plenty of work around."

"There is but the marauders are still in a killing frame of mind. It's early days."

"Still got the smell of blood in their nostrils, eh?"

Gavriel nodded. "Still capable of much cruelty, yes. It's not a place for my brother. I promised our mother I'd keep him safe."

"Where's she?"

"Dead. Both our parents are. But I gave that promise years ago."

"So where are you headed?"

"North."

"Why?"

Gavriel was tired of being polite but knew he must not be impetuous, not now. "What does it matter?"

"I'm interested."

"Well, I don't tell everyone our business."

"Why so reluctant, boy? Something to hide?"

"No. But we're tired and hungry. I have to find a place for Lewk to sleep that's not out in the open like this. You obviously know the forest well. Wolves must know it too."

"You don't look like brothers, you know?" Jok piped up.

Gavriel deliberately showed all the exasperation he was feeling. "That's because he's adopted. Much as I'd enjoy sharing our entire life history with you both—perhaps over a mug of tea and quiet night by the fire—we need to be on our way."

Alfric laughed. "How well can you use that sword, boy?"

"Well enough," Gavriel replied, his anger rising. He knew where this was going now; had hoped to avoid it. "But I don't want to use it."

"I like your confidence."

"You don't want to do this. We have no argument with you."

"But I don't believe your story. I think you're poachers and we don't take kindly to poachers in our forest."

Gavriel looked at them, aghast, but was shocked when Leo spoke. "You don't own these lands, sir."

"The hell I don't!" Alfric said. "I don't care what's happening out there," he said, pointing back toward Penraven, "but I sure care about what goes on in the forest, especially with whippersnappers like you thinking you can join the game."

"Game?" Gavriel spat. "You should care about what's going on back there because it's going to spill into the forest soon enough. Do you honestly believe the barbarians aren't just as at home in the woods as they are on their plains? They prefer the wilderness to the city. Loethar's men will be swarming through here soon enough. I say again, we are not poachers. You carry on with whatever you do. We'll just carry on our journey north. We have no argument."

But Gavriel could see in the dull-eyed look of these men that an argument was precisely what they wanted. He'd seen it before. They were probably not yet frightened of Loethar's presence because it played into their own pleasure of anarchy. He knew these men followed the laws of Penraven about as closely as any one of the barbarians. They had obviously stayed clear of the fighting thus far, but in doing so they had become bored. Now they had two seemingly helpless youngsters on whom they could take out their boredom. He noted that they had a sword each, and both were heavy-set men—the taller, Alfric, was much plumper, perhaps not so fast on his feet.

"Ever killed anyone, boy?"

"No."

Alfric laughed. "Always a first time, eh?"

"I didn't say that. I don't want to fight you, Alfric."

"You sound scared."

"*You* should be scared," Leo hurled at the men. "Don't say we haven't warned you."

Even Jok joined in the mirth now. "Cor, I'm really shaking in my boots now, Al."

"Why are you doing this?" Gavriel asked, unembarrassed by the plea even he could hear in his voice.

"Because we don't like the look of you, because we think you're lying, because you're on our land, because I hate the refined way you speak, boy, and because your brother looks at us as though he's important. I see hate in his eyes."

"Can you blame him?" Gavriel demanded. "You're frightening him."

"I'll frighten him a lot more once I get my hands on him," Alfric said and to Gavriel's revulsion Jok actually licked his lips in a deliberately lascivious manner.

So that was it! They'd probably had no women in an age. Gavriel moved quickly, reaching for the hilt of his sword. With his movement came a rush of fury. "You'll not lay a finger on him," he snarled. "Run!" he urged Leo and in a sweeping move not only lifted his sword but instantly lunged to cut off Jok as the man moved to give chase to Leo. "Oh, no you don't!" he baited. "You deal with me first." He feinted at Jok again, who backed up a step or two.

"Oh for Lo's sake, what are you frightened of? He's half your age!" Alfric scorned as he drew his weapon. Gavriel could see it had rust spots and was not a well cared for sword. He had to hope it was not as sharp as his own.

The two men tried to encircle him but Gavriel deliberately lunged, keeping them herded together. It was easier to keep them crowded and fighting shoulder to shoulder than it would be if one got out of his line of vision.

"I thought you said you weren't any good?" Jok whinged.

"I said I used it well enough. I also told you I didn't want to use it. You've started this; now you pay the consequences."

Jok made a rush at him and Gavriel parried, getting his first taste of their skill. Though Jok was strong, he was flat-footed, and his short stature meant that he didn't have much reach. Gavriel stepped back but kept his fighting stance.

"Looks like we have a jolly one here, Jok. When this is done, we'll hang his body from this tree here so no one else gets the idea that this forest belongs to everyone."

"You're mad. I'm not your enemy. The real enemy may be yet to arrive in the woods, but he's coming, trust me. In fact I suspect he's already on his way."

"The barbarian is not interested in the forest, you fool. He's after riches that only the city can offer."

"Which makes me realize you're even more stupid than you look, Al!" Gavriel taunted, hoping to provoke the man into a move.

The big man moved fast—much faster than Gavriel had given him credit for being able to. He felt the blade swipe through the top of his arm and if he hadn't spun in that second, the wound would have gone deep to the bone. As it was, blood bloomed, soaking his shirt sleeve.

"How does that make you feel?" Alfric baited.

Gavriel was used to drills; he'd never really had to fight in a genuine situation. Never had to make the decision of kill or be killed. How did it feel? It hurt, like a flame burning on his skin. "Angry," Gavriel growled and lurched first left before rapidly launching himself to the right to avoid Jok trying to sneak around him. Within moments he was frantically engaged in a battle with both men, desperate to keep them occupied so that neither could break away and run after Leo. His non-fighting arm was bleeding profusely; the wound needed to be staunched which meant he would have to deal with these two amateurs swiftly. Still angry with himself for opening himself up to the early cut, he began backing away from where Leo had run, drawing Alfric and Jok toward him.

"You obviously want to die, boy," Alfric sneered.

"Not really. Just wanted to reassure myself that you are genuinely two fat, incapable fighters with limited sword skills," he hurled back, swiping at Jok, who yelled as his knee opened and he fell forward.

Alfric paused in surprise to glance at his felled friend. Gavriel darted into the sudden stillness, hacking away Alfric's sword and kicking away Jok's weapon. He pressed his sword into the big man's throat, a line of blood already beginning to dribble down his neck.

"Don't do it, Jok," Gavriel warned. "I know what you're thinking but Alfric here is already out of breath and it will take very little effort for me to dispatch both of you."

Jok withdrew the hand he had been reaching toward Gavriel's leg. Gavriel stepped away from both men. "Now what's it to be? Alfric, you can help your friend and flee together—without your weapons or food, of course—or I can kill you both now and save the realm your ugliness. I am impatient; you would do better to choose quickly." He looked into the distance. "Lewk!" he yelled and was relieved to see the king step out from behind a tree.

He returned his attention to the men. "Remove your belts

and sacks. Leave them on the ground and go. You'll have to pick him up, Al. Jok's not going anywhere without your shoulder to lean against."

Alfric reluctantly untied his sword belt and pulled off the rucksack on his back. Jok followed suit, pulling the small sack slung across his body over his head and casting it behind him. "Hope you choke on the food in there," he said.

"I'll think of you when I'm dining tonight," Gavriel replied. "Now lift your trouser legs, both of you," he ordered, his sword still hovering near Alfric. "Ah, there we are," he said, a note of triumph in his voice. "There's always a concealed blade, isn't there? Uh-uh, don't reach for them. I'll get them." Carefully he retrieved both daggers and hooked them into his own belt. "Now go."

"What are we supposed to eat?" Alfric bleated.

"Why am I supposed to care? I hope you starve, although I suspect the blubber you carry will sustain you. Unless the wolves get you. Now get out of my sight."

"Don't think we'll forget you, boy," Alfric snarled, hauling up a grimacing Jok.

"Well just remember this *boy* kicked your fat arses," Gavriel taunted. "Now sod off."

They moved down the slight incline awkwardly, Jok limping badly and Alfric muttering beneath his breath. Gavriel swiftly picked up all the tackle associated with their weapons.

Leo approached him. "What makes you think they won't come back?"

"They won't, they know I'm a better fighter now, although that's not such a good thing."

"Why?"

"It marks us. I wanted to travel unnoticed and now someone already knows about the two of us. We've barely been on the move for a day."

"They're idiots, Gav," Leo said, picking up the sacks of food. "I'll take these."

"Idiots or not, they're dangerous. Their tongues will wag."

"I doubt it. Do you think they're going to admit to being soundly beaten by someone more than half their age?"

"I hope you're right," Gavriel mumbled. "Come on. At least we've got food for the night and a weapon for you."

"What about your arm? That looks like it needs stitching."

Gavriel nodded. Leo was right but there was little they could do about it right now. "Hopefully we can find an abandoned crofter's cottage, or—"

"Or one of the gamekeepers' huts. There has to be one somewhere in this vicinity," Leo said, his eyes shining with his own inspiration.

"Good thought." Gavriel glanced at the sky. "The light's going so someone may light a candle or lamp soon enough. We'll see it if we're near."

"And if not?"

"Don't think about it. I promise you I'm not going to bleed to death. We'll think of some other way. For now use a belt to tie off my arm. You'll have to pull really tight. It will slow the blood down until we find a solution."

Leothar had called for Freath to meet him in the library. When the aide arrived, he was perusing the shelves.

"Sire?"

"Ah, there you are, Freath," Loethar said, turning.

Freath halted, obviously caught off guard.

"Is something wrong?" Loethar watched the aide struggle to find some composure. "I know I look a bit different but surely it's not such a shock."

"It's a remarkable change, if you don't mind my mentioning it," Freath replied and Loethar knew the aide chose his words with care.

"So my mother tells me," Loethar admitted.

"Surely she minded what could be seen as your turning your back on your heritage?"

Was that a carefully provocative but well couched question? "Not really," he said, deliberately offhand. "We always knew that if I were to rule the Set I would achieve acceptance faster if I looked less like a tribal warlord."

"Your appearance is certainly less intimidating, sire."

"You were right; the De Vis wardrobe is a good fit."

Freath nodded. "The legate had exceptional taste, if I may say so."

"So I look every inch a Set man, you think?" Loethar tested, moving slightly to show off the cut of the clothes on his frame.

"Every inch, sire," Freath agreed. Loethar sensed the man was unnerved, though he couldn't gauge why. "Forgive me," the aide continued, "I mean no offense when I say that I hadn't realized you could not only speak our language but read it also?"

"I can't. It's interesting that all of you believe we don't share the same language, though."

Freath nodded. "You are right. I don't know why I assumed you'd have a tribal language."

"Oh we do, or at least we did. Some of the old folk still know it, and we keep it going with the youngsters so it's not lost entirely. But Set is what the Steppes people have spoken for centuries. We have no need for writing or reading, though. I need someone to help interpret for me."

"Perhaps I can—"

"No, Freath, I have another job for you. Presumably there was a custodian of some sort, someone who looked after these books?"

"We had Jynes, but he died in the fighting," Freath replied.

"I see. There was no one else?"

Freath shook his head.

"This was a private Valisar library. Brennus was the only one who used it. The queen was not interested in history, nor were her sons." He glanced at Piven, who was stroking the leather bindings of some of the books on the lower shelves nearby.

"I can imagine. Other than you, who else reads?"

"Er . . . well let me see—"

"Oh, come now, there must be someone left. Even your Vested helpers . . . didn't one of them come from the Academy at Cremond?"

"Forgive me for thinking so slowly, sire. Of course, there is Master Kirin but I think you may find Father Briar to be of better assistance."

"Father Briar? I haven't met him yet."

"He helped with the cremation of the princess; he was the man who delivered the ashes to the rooftop that day."

"I can bring him to mind now. I can find him in the chapel?"

"Or the infirmary. He is a placid, very learned man. May I ask what it is you seek? If it's something specific I might be able to help."

"I want to know all the Valisar secrets hidden in these books, Freath. The dynasty, I gather, was one of the most, if not the most, pedantic hoarders of information. The family didn't pass down its secrets by word of mouth. I suspect it recorded them, and that I can find most in the pages of vellum right here."

"What sort of secrets, my lord?" Freath asked, a quizzical expression creasing his forehead.

"If I knew I wouldn't have to search," Loethar admonished. "I'm not sure, although talk of the Valisar Legacy reached even as far as the Steppes."

Freath smiled indulgently. "Yes, the story is bigger than the myth that began it."

"So you don't believe in it?"

Freath looked back at him, surprised. "Me? No, sire. No one did, not even the king. Believe me, had there been any key that unlocked the magic of coercion, I feel absolutely convinced I would have been privy to the Valisars' knowledge. I honestly can't remember King Brennus even searching for it."

"The Valisars were always a secretive lot. Perhaps you were not privy because you are not of their blood."

Freath nodded. "You could be right but I was very good at spying on the royals, my lord. I'm sure I would have picked up some snippet if such a magic existed. I'm not even sure I know what it is."

"Coercion? Exactly what it sounds like, Freath. The person with this talent can coerce another to do his bidding."

"I see. A talent anyone would wish for," Freath said, chuckling softly.

His humor seemed patronizing. "So you find me amusing, Freath?"

The aide's mirth fled instantly. "No, sire, I beg your deepest pardon. I smile only because the other realms in the Set have been jealous of the supposed power of the Valisars for centuries, when in fact I am firmly of the belief that the Valisars under Cormoron likely made up all these magics to keep their rivals on the back foot. Cormoron was extraordinarily cunning. Although he was a great warrior, he also understood that might did not necessarily equal respect. It was Cormoron, as you probably already know, who established the Set, who united all the families but gave each independence to run their own realm."

"So long as fealty was paid to Penraven."

"Not fealty so much, sire, as simply being allies. Penraven was the largest and most powerful of all the realms, with the longest coastline and plenty of natural wealth. It soon had the highest population and the best trained army. It did lead and the other, smaller realms followed, but each carved out its own style."

"Why was Droste not invited to join the Set?"

"It is my understanding that Droste refused to recognize Penraven as any sort of leader. Cormoron, all those centuries back, probably believed he'd made the greatest sacrifice in uniting the realms; undoubtedly he didn't want a rebel in the ranks. But history has shown that equality was in fact achieved. The Valisars have never had to use their might to enforce anything. The Set has been peaceful and each ruling family has run its realm in harmony for centuries. The families have bound themselves through marriages as well to ensure the links remain strong."

"Except Brennus, it seemed."

Freath looked suitably sheepish. "Well, there you have me, sire. Our own king went looking further afield. I gather his marriage to Iselda was not planned. And to all intents and purposes the linking of Galinsea and Penraven—and thus the whole Set—was a formidable and much envied bond. Iselda brought more than just beauty to her king."

"You sound impressed, Freath," Loethar said, replacing a book that he had been leafing absently through back onto its shelf.

"I hate the Valisars, my lord. But that doesn't mean I have not admired them or been impressed by their ruthlessness. Marriage is but one area King Brennus made tough decisions."

"I appreciate your candor. When exactly did you join the Valisar employ, Freath?"

"I was appointed the day Princess Iselda arrived in our realm. I am originally from Penraven, although I travelled widely in working for a number of noble families. As fate would have it the duke I was working for was visiting Barronel at the same time as the king was passing through. Brennus called in on the same noble family and he saw something in me, I suppose."

"Ambition, perhaps?"

"Perhaps. I cannot say. But I was employed to look after the young princess, to help turn her into a queen."

"You did well."

Freath simply nodded.

"So you were not aware of the plight troth made to the king and Queen of Droste for the hand of their daughter?" Loethar spoke casually, feigning interest in another book as he watched the man carefully. His barb hit the mark. Freath blanched.

"Pardon, my lord?"

"Brennus offered marriage to the Crown Princess of Droste."

Freath's mouth opened and closed. "I'm sorry. I don't know about this."

"It must have happened before your time. And it seems it was kept quite secret."

"Are you sure?"

"As sure as I stand here."

"How can you know about this?"

"Because I know the crown princess and I have no reason to doubt her. In fact you two make a fine pair, both with deep grudges against Iselda."

Freath blinked furiously, his lips thinning. Loethar could almost see the wheels turning in the man's mind. "Lady Valya?" he suddenly asked, incredulous.

"Crown Princess Valya, no less, Freath."

"You've shocked me, my lord."

"So I can see."

"Valya is a popular Set name. It never occurred to me that she could be the princess. And we had so little to do with Droste."

"And now you know why."

"Why have you told me this, sire?" Freath asked.

"Because I intend to right the Valisar wrong."

"I'm not sure I understand."

"I will marry Valya. She will be the Queen of Penraven and indeed Droste, once I make sure her father understands who exactly is in charge in this region. But most importantly she will be Empress of the Set."

He watched Freath swallow; he had to assume the man was playing for time and was convinced this was so when he uttered his next question.

"Are you certain about this, my lord?"

Loethar wasn't sure whether to be insulted or amused. He chose the latter, quirking an eyebrow and lifting one corner of his mouth.

Freath hurried with his assurances. "Forgive me, this is not my place, but I intend to be your ears and eyes as you've asked, sire, and both senses tell me that your feelings for the lady . . . er, Princess Valya, do not stretch to love."

Loethar was impressed. This man, however sneaky Negev felt he was, was endowed with acute judgment. He sighed. "In this assumption you are correct, Freath. But should you ever breathe a word of my admission I will first deny it and then kill you with my bare hands. Do you understand?"

"Implicitly, my lord."

"Good. This will be a strategic marriage. Droste comes into the Set and thus allows the Steppes people to move and trade freely."

"I see. And does the princess understand your marriage is for this reason?"

"I suspect Valya is not as dimmed by love as some might think. I believe she is a realist and I know she is a survivor. She is happy to take her advantages wherever she can find them; if she weren't, she would never have come looking for me in the first place."

"She looked for you?"

"Oh yes. She hunted me down, fearlessly entered the Steppes alone. Dirty, bedraggled, with no weapons, little food, and a half dead mare beneath her, she came to offer her hand in marriage with the promise that the Set could be taken if I worked with her."

"Princess Valya masterminded your campaign?" Freath asked, clearly unable to hide his astonishment.

"Entirely. She understands the west. Your king should never have misjudged or shamed her the way he did. She has taught me plenty. We knew when and where to strike because of her; and it was Valya who advised us to hold Penraven until last. My inclination would have been to take Penraven first, driving the rest of the realms to capitulate once their leader fell. But Valya said Brennus was so arrogant, always so sure of his mighty Valisar reign, that if we struck hard into Cremond and

Dregon, effectively cutting off any flight, other than via ship, we would have the Valisars cornered."

"She was right, sire," Freath replied with just the right amount of admiration to impress Loethar.

"My mother doesn't credit Valya with much sense, although I'm sure you've already worked that out, Freath. It seems you have the measure of all of us."

Freath nodded graciously. "My role has always been one of diplomacy, my lord. And now my role is to protect you as best I can using the same skills in diplomacy, politics and—"

"Cunning?"

Freath gave a short, mirthless smile. "I was going to say knowledge, sire, but perhaps knowledge allows one to be forewarned and therefore cunning."

Loethar mentally applauded the man. Slippery, indeed. He would be a real asset. "Anyway, I need a wedding organized. I want all the Set involved."

"Very good, sire," Freath replied, although Loethar heard understandable apprehension in the man's voice.

"But before the marriage takes place we have something far less palatable for the people to cope with."

"Really? Do you think the people of the Set have not already seen enough to turn their stomachs, sire?"

Loethar laughed at the aide's dry humor. "I want to be absolutely sure I have their attention, Freath. I actually came in here hoping to find someone who could help me with census records."

"Census? Really? Why?"

"I want to quickly assemble the names of every child born approximately a dozen years ago."

Freath frowned and blew out his cheeks but Loethar was not fooled. He knew the man was already leaping to the right conclusion. "It is very important that the people throughout the region understand that I will not tolerate any rebellion. I plan to quash it before it begins."

"My lord, fear not. I am utterly convinced the people are

still in such shock—their royals are dead, their armies decimated, their realms fully defeated. Many have fled to lands far away. Where do you suppose rebellion will spring from?"

"From the lad we allowed to slip through our fingers," Loethar growled, flinging the book he was holding across the room, startling Piven and making Freath flinch.

The aide wisely waited until Loethar's anger had cooled again. "Leonel is too young, too cowardly, and too inexperienced to even think of rebellion."

"But people will rally to him, Freath, and you know that. The boy is Valisar. The name is enough. I vowed to destroy all who come from the Valisar seed. I am sparing the halfwit because he is not of the blood but perhaps I should destroy him as well."

"No need," Freath answered calmly. "I still believe his humiliation is worth far more to you. Ask Princess Valya. It will turn everyone's stomachs to see the Valisars' act of charity paraded about on a leash."

"I do believe you're right in this."

"So you intend to round up all the boys of like age to the prince, am I right?"

"No. I intend to slaughter them."

Freath paused only a heartbeat before starting to clap. "Oh, sire, that is a plan worthy of any king," he said, his tone filled with admiration. "But surely the threat is enough. The people will yield the boy quickly."

Loethar walked over and picked up the book he'd hurled, studied the corner that he'd damaged. Making a soft sound of admonishment, he replied, "I don't think so. I think they need to see their sons' blood running through the villages to truly understand how determined I am to have Prince Leonel in my possession or dead at my feet. So take me to Father Briar now, Freath."

"I can fetch him for you, sire, if you wish to remain—"

"No, let us walk. I want to tell you what I'm going to do should the first pass of killings not deliver the prince."

Nineteen

Genrie eyed the approaching unlikely pair. One glided ahead, head held high, the other lumbered behind, head hung.

"I can't remember your name," Valya said to her, "but this is Belush. He is now my servant."

Genrie's gaze slipped from the vile woman to the hulking terror of a man who surely belonged in the barracks. "You wish him to sleep nearby?"

"The emperor would likely wish him chained to the wall but I am a merciful person. I was raised in the west and we do not chain our servants, do we?"

All sorts of responses sprang to mind but Genrie gave the answer Valya wanted to hear. "No, of course not. Can I make up the anteroom for Belush?"

"No, you may not," Valya snapped. Taking a slow breath, she continued. "Give him anything you wish him to carry and have my things brought over close to Legate De Vis's former chambers."

Genrie made the mistake of hesitating, raising her eyebrows in query.

"Now!" the woman snarled. "How dare you not curtsey and act immediately upon my words."

"Forgive me. It's just that we were given instructions by the emperor to accommodate you in the chambers we've already settled you into."

"Well, unsettle me and do as I say," Valya enunciated as

though she were talking to an imbecile. "The emperor—just for your information—has barely an hour ago proposed marriage to me. Do you think he wants to be separated from me? I need to be close for all his needs. Do you understand?"

"Yes," Genrie said, noticing the blood spattered on the woman's riding garb.

"Good. And he will do precisely as you say," she said, pointing to Belush, "or he knows his entire precious Greens will be punished on his behalf."

"I didn't ask you to spare my life," the man growled.

"And I didn't spare it for any other reason than my own amusement," she replied. "You are my slave now, Belush . . . my toy, and as I promised myself when you were doing your best to humiliate me, I am going to make you pay every waking moment of your days." She turned to Genrie. "Show him the way to my former quarters. And then have a bath drawn for me—in my new chambers. Don't fill it with that essence of goat or whatever you've palmed off onto me. I can smell the oil of miramel up here so take a look in your former queen's rooms. She has no use for it now. Make sure it's poured into my bath generously. And wipe that defiance from your gaze or I'll have you gutted. And since it's now public, from now on you call me by my true title, princess."

Genrie lowered her eyes and heard rather than saw Valya stomp away, her boot heels loud against the stone stairs. Finally she looked at Belush. She wasn't sure what possessed her to speak but her words were out before she could stop them. "We are enemies, yet we are bonded by our singular hatred for Valya, I'm sure."

He stared at her and for a few heartstopping moments she thought she'd read the warrior wrong. Finally he replied, "I shall see her dead as soon as it is politically possible and I shall dance on her bones before I scatter them to the six winds."

Genrie felt a flare of satisfaction burn brightly for just the shortest but sweetest of times. She knew that the enmity between her and Belush could not stifle their shared hatred. Perhaps here was their first ally in the enemy camp.

"Follow me, Belush," she said softly.

They found Father Briar after a long search and much to Freath's growing anxiety precisely where he'd hoped he would not be.

"Father Briar!" he called, hoping his fear did not sound as alarming in his voice as it felt inside his mind.

The priest turned from where he was buckling down a cartload of goods beneath a canopy. Upon catching sight of Loethar Briar instantly looked terrified—downright guilty, in fact—as far as Freath was concerned. The priest must have a Vested hidden somewhere under the goods.

"Emperor Loethar, this is Father Briar, no doubt about to take a load of no longer needed produce to the needy." Freath hoped his tone could urge Briar to agree, to do something other than look so very mortified, so hideously culpable.

"Father Briar," Loethar said, nodding politely. "You're a difficult man to pin down."

Briar's glance flicked conspiratorially to Freath before settling back on the emperor's calm gaze. His chins began to wobble and Freath, against his own inclinations, closed his eyes with silent despair.

When Briar remained silent, Freath pulled himself together. "Forgive him, sire. I think Father Briar is disarmed by your arrival," he tried, begging Briar with his eyes to answer for himself.

"Surely Father Briar has a tongue in his head and can speak for himself, Freath?" Loethar admonished.

Once again the priest hesitated, once again glancing Freath's way.

"Are you scared of me, Father Briar?"

The man nodded.

"Hmmm," Loethar murmured. "I suppose I shouldn't be

surprised." He looked over at the cart, moved closer to it. "What have you got under here, Father?"

Freath held his breath.

"It's stale food mainly, my lord," the priest stammered.

"Stale, eh?"

Briar mercifully found his voice. He nodded. "Mainly bread, though also some greens, fruit, old cheeses, that sort of thing. People are starving, my lord. I am trying to offer families some respite now that the fighting is done. There are children who need feeding." He glanced over to where the young Valisar, on his leash, skipped toward them. "Not all are as fortunate as Piven," he added.

"What does that mean?" Loethar said, absently lifting the corner of the canopy.

Freath felt fear race up his spine. He deliberately tripped Piven, who fell down loudly, his wail strange and mournful. "I'm so sorry for the noise, my lord," he said, reaching down to lift the youngster back to his feet.

Loethar frowned. "That's the first sound I've heard him make. I forget how silent he truly is."

"Nevertheless he is blessed by your favor," Briar said.

"That was not my intention, Father Briar."

"If you mean that it humiliates our people to see the Valisar child as nothing more than a pet dog, you are right, highness." He hesitated, then, much to Freath's astonishment, continued. "But don't ignore the effect that not killing him may have, er . . . highness."

Loethar looked at Freath, equally bemused. At least the cart was forgotten for the time being, Freath thought. But what was in Briar's head to goad the barbarian king like this?

Briar seemed to have found his voice fully. "And although you didn't mean for this effect, my lord, it cannot be a bad thing. The realms are in turmoil. The emotional state of the people is at the lowest ebb. Perhaps this small mercy of yours will give them hope. Perhaps this food should go out to the needy under your name?" Freath couldn't believe it when Father Briar actually shrugged nonchalantly. "We have no royalty to challenge you, sire. Your rule has to start somewhere and it doesn't necessarily have to continue with bloodshed. It could start with mercy." He looked up, finally raising his eyes to Loethar's.

Freath couldn't breathe.

"It could," Loethar replied softly and Freath sensed the barbarian had not entirely rejected the priest's counsel. "But first we need to impress upon these same people my terms."

"Which are?"

"No Valisars."

"But Piven—"

"Piven is not Valisar by blood, Father Briar," Freath censured. "He could not wear the crown even if he were of sound mind." His stern look warned the priest to rein in his personal thoughts.

"Who are Piven's parents, do we know?" Loethar suddenly asked.

"They were not even from Penraven, as I understand it, my lord. Isn't that right, Master Freath?"

"Indeed. They lived in Barronel."

"And how did this adoption come about?" Loethar gestured for Father Briar to hook up the mule to the cart. "Carry on."

Freath let out a silent breath of relief. "The queen was passing through Barronel on a goodwill visit to the royals of that realm. She was grieving over the loss of yet another baby—a son, this time dying at the moment of birth—and obviously every child she saw tugged at her heartstrings. But Piven won her attention because she learned his parents had drowned in an accident during a flash flood. He had no other living relatives, and was barely a day or so old. She offered to take him from the woman who was caring for him alongside eight other children."

"I didn't think any royal cared that much. There is plenty of suffering around them. To single out one peasant child seems rather extraordinary."

"I agree. I think it was hypocritical," Freath said, suddenly realizing he must have sounded too admiring. "And selfish too. Iselda was thinking purely of her own hurt when she offered Piven a home."

"If she was as uncaring as you make out, Freath, I would have thought she'd have adopted a healthy child, not this strange creature."

Freath shrugged. "Iselda was conniving. She cared very much about presenting the right image even if she didn't live up to that image in real life." He glanced over at Briar, who nodded to say he was ready. "You see, my lord, in the same way that you hope to mock the Valisars using Piven, I think they mocked their people through him. He was a symbol of their caring and yet people like me were made to suffer right under their noses." He spat, refused to even meet Father Briar's gaze. "Piven made them look every inch the generous royals. He was a showpiece of their magnanimity."

"I had no argument with our royals, sire. I have no argument with you other than the killing must stop," Briar spoke up, rather courageously, Freath thought.

"For someone who was scared of me, priest, you seem rather brave in telling me how to run my conquered realms."

Briar flinched. "You terrify me, my lord. But because you could have me killed at the mere glance to one of your henchman, I realize I have nothing more to fear from you. I might as well be true to my god and behave as he would want."

"The killing will stop when the people give me what I want. And what I want is the Valisar heir. He was here all along, did you know that?"

The priest paled. "Here? No, my lord, how could I? I thought he must have been sent away just before the palace was taken."

"So did I. But Freath saw him and one of the legate's sons running back into the palace."

Briar looked at Freath, genuinely astonished. "It's true," Freath said, his tone as uncaring as he could achieve. "If he's still here we'll find him."

"He won't be found in the palace," Loethar cut in.

"Oh? Why's that, my lord?" Freath asked, a chill spiking through him.

"He's been spotted, we think. Slinking away from Brighthelm with his friend."

Freath felt his throat tighten. *So they'd made their dash for freedom.* "Really? Who saw them?"

"Valya did, when she was out riding. I've already sent out a hunting party, but in the meantime I shall press ahead with my plan to flush him out using his own people. Father Briar?"

"My lord?"

"When you return please send word and I shall meet you in the library. I require your assistance."

"Very good, sire," Briar said. Freath was relieved he resisted glancing toward him in enquiry. "I shall make my deliveries and be back before the next bell, my lord."

The forest was cloaked by darkness. A fat new moon loomed inordinately large overhead, throwing a watery glow between the leaves. Leo had always thought of the moon as being silvery white but when it was full like this, he could swear it possessed a golden hue. He preferred it silver and far away—this yellow felt somehow sinister. He wondered if Vyk was watching them from the treetops. As the sounds of night erupted Leo was convinced the space beneath the trees became noisier than by day. Crickets sang loudly, an owl hooted mournfully and somewhere not too far away various animals were scrabbling through the undergrowth.

Gavriel pointed. "Badger," he whispered, as though dropping in on his thoughts.

Leo nodded. It could be the bleaching effect of the moonlight but he felt sure Gavriel look paler than was safe. The blood-soaked fabric at his arm looked black. "Are you all right?" he asked.

"Don't worry about me," his friend replied, pushing Leo forward.

Leo halted suddenly. Caught in a trap in front of them was

a hare, large enough to be a buck. It stared at them, glassy-eyed and frantic, and judging by the blood, it had already begun tearing at its own leg in an attempt to free itself. As it gave a low squeal of fear, Leo re-lived his father's gutting, his mother's terrible plunge, the knowledge of his baby sister's ashes being blown into the far corners of the realm, and then Piven's ever smiling face turned sorrowful. The hare reminded him of himself. Trapped, helpless, lit up in the clearing where it lay defeated and breathing hard from its exertions at escape.

"What are you doing?" Gavriel said as Leo approached the animal.

"I'm cutting him loose."

"Are you mad? That animal could feed a family."

"He's a fine beast. He shouldn't die like this."

"How should he die, then?" Gavriel asked, irritated.

"Bravely, fighting in spring for his territory, for his mate."

"Leo, you old romantic! And you've never even kissed a girl."

Leo blushed, glad of the cover of night. "Give me a blade."

Gavriel obliged. "Keep it," he said, sounding suddenly weary.

Leo tried to calm the wild animal but the hare was suspicious, angry and injured. A bit like Gavriel, he thought, smiling. "Be still, won't you," he begged it and finally was able to cut through the braided string that had held its leg so effectively. "Count yourself lucky we didn't bring beagles," he said as he watched the hare dart, not so nimbly, off into the trees and safety.

"Not even a thank you, Leo," Gavriel said.

Before Leo could reply a new voice startled them.

"You bastards! Don't even move." They both looked up in surprise to see a woman, her arrow trained on Gavriel, the bow held taut between long slim arms. Instinctively, both raised their hands.

"That was our meat!" she snarled at them.

Leo kept his hands raised but began to rise. "Miss, I'm sorry but—"

"Be quiet, boy! You. Who are you?"

Gavriel pointed at himself. "I'm Jon, this is my brother Mat. We're—" Gavriel suddenly stopped talking, slumping over in a dead faint.

"Ga—, er, help!" Leo yelled, leaning over Gavriel.

"What's wrong with him?"

"He's bleeding, can't you see?"

"Get back. I know this is a trap," she warned.

Leo looked at her, anguished. His temper, already well and truly frayed, suddenly snapped. "Oh sod off, would you! Go back wherever you came from. I'll pay you for your damn hare but just leave us!"

She lowered the bow, astonished. "How dare—"

"Listen, either help me help him or get away from us. Do we really look that dangerous? Damn him, I knew he was lying when he told me the cut wasn't so bad." Leo had already turned away from the woman. Gavriel was conscious, groaning softly.

"Well how you do think you look with all those weapons? How safe do you reckon I feel?"

"I couldn't give a hog's arse. Please either help or just leave."

"What happened to him?" she said, flicking dark hair out of her eyes.

Leo looked up at her wearily. "We ran into the wrong sort. He fought them off but he got hurt. I think he's burning with fever. Can it come on that fast?"

"Oh, get out of the way," she said, irritated, pushing Leo aside. She laid her hand on Gavriel's forehead. "Yes, big fever. Help me get him up. Neither of us can carry him alone."

Impossibly, Gavriel appeared to rouse as they hauled him to his feet.

"Where to?" Leo asked, genuinely glad of her help.

"My father's hut."

"What's your name?"

"Not until you tell me yours. I know he was lying."

"Mine's Lewk. His is Gaven. And we don't mean you any harm and I am sorry about losing you your hare."

She nodded. "I'm Lilyan . . . Lily."

"Thank you for your help, Lily."

"Neither of you deserve it," she replied, still clearly angry, but nonetheless bearing the greater burden of Gavriel's weight as they half walked, half dragged him through the forest. Almost impossibly Gavriel began to sing deliriously at the top of his weakened voice. Leo recognized one of the soldiers' favorite ballads—comparing a woman's arse to a ripe peach. He didn't know whether to grin helplessly or blush even more furiously, for Lily certainly had a delicious arse.

Finally a small hut came into view. Leo dropped Gavriel as they approached and his sudden letting go dragged Lily down with his friend. She landed on top of De Vis but Gavriel made no protest.

"I think he's unconscious," she said, alarmed.

"What's all this, Lily?" asked a tremulous voice from the doorway. Leo looked up to see a robed figure, illuminated from behind by the glow of a single candle. He was pulling on a hood, though it really wasn't that cold. His voice sounded old and fragile; perhaps he felt the cold more, Leo thought.

"It's all right, father. They're no danger."

"What's happening?" he asked, walking out toward them, suddenly sounding much stronger, much younger.

"I came across these travellers. They'd been set upon by thieves. This one's wounded. This other one's name's Lewk."

"Lewk," the man acknowledged.

Leo couldn't see his face, shrouded beneath the hood, but he held out his hand. "Lily's been very kind to help us. I'm afraid we owe her for the hare we let go."

She shook her head. "Let's not worry about that for now. Let's just get your friend inside. Here, father, you take the other arm." The father and daughter hauled Gavriel into the hut, leaving Leo to trail behind.

"Onto the bed," the man said.

Leo wondered what he meant. He saw no bed. They laid Gavriel down onto a rug beneath which was strewn some straw on a pallet. *Ah, the bed*, he thought, surprised, suddenly acutely aware of how unfamiliar he was with life beyond the palace gates.

"Get the candle, Lily," her father said, ripping Gavriel's sleeve open. "This young man's lost quite a bit of blood, I think."

Lily placed the candle on a small shelf just above Gavriel's face. The man pulled back his hood and Leo reared back, unable to stop himself. His reaction drew their gazes and though neither looked embarrassed—they were obviously used to this—he read a fleeting pain in Lily's eyes that made him feel instantly contrite.

"I'm sorry," he bleated, honesty coming before he could think of anything polite.

"We're used to it, son," the man said, "and that's why we prefer to live here in solitude. Not that it's good for my daughter, but—"

"Hush, father. That's our business and it's very old ground we've trodden too often."

The man sighed, flicked a wry glance at Leo and focused his attention on Gavriel. "This is a deep wound. It's also infected. Must have been a filthy blade that cut him."

"Can you help him?" Leo asked.

"Let's get it all cleaned out and see what we're up against," the man said kindly. "I'm Greven, by the way."

Leo nodded. He wasn't very good at aging people but Greven looked no older than his own father. His graying hair was neatly tied back and, despite the ravages of his face, his body looked lean and fit. "What can I do?"

"Help Lily to get some water boiled. She'll show you where everything is." He directed the rest of his instructions to Lily. "We'll need some willow sap, comfrey balm, and a posset with some liquor to get his strength back. Oh, and mix up some henbane for the pain."

"But we have so little left, and it's for your—"

"Oh, Lily, don't fuss. Let's do what we can for this young man, shall we? And then we'll worry about ourselves."

Leo felt another stab of guilt. To think he'd deprived these good people of that hare. It probably would have lasted them several meals.

"I'll also need some of that white lichen. We're going to have to cover the wound with that once we've done the clirren leaves."

"I wish I understood all this," Leo said, impressed. "He's going to be all right, isn't he?"

"Is he your brother?"

Leo nodded, hating to lie outright.

"Where have you come from?"

"Er, around Brighthelm," Leo said, sticking as close to the truth as he could.

"Is it true the barbarian has moved into the palace?" Lily asked, wide-eyed, as she gathered up various small pots and containers. "Here, hang this over those coals," she said, pointing to a spouted container. "It's not long since it boiled anyway," she said.

Leo did as asked. "He has," he said, turning away.

"So the king and queen are dead? The rumors are right?"

"Yes," he answered coldly.

"We heard that the queen gave birth—" Greven began.

"She did. The news from the palace is that the baby died immediately."

Lily's expression darkened. "Too much sadness for one family. Is the mad son—"

"Not mad," Leo corrected too abruptly, wishing he hadn't as both of them looked up sharply. "I have met him once or twice. Our, er, father worked at the palace. One of the royal guards," he said, thinking it up as he went along and hoping the story held enough weight. "Piven is just simple, not mad."

Lily nodded. "And the heir? Where is he? He'd be about your age, wouldn't he?"

"Bit younger I think," Leo said, amazed by how easily the lies rolled off his tongue. Gav and Corb had always said he acted well beyond his years. He prayed that characteristic would hold now for him. "I've only seen him from a distance and I don't know his fate."

"I saw the queen once," Greven mused. "A beautiful woman. She paused on her journey back into the palace to say hello to me. Can you imagine that? And me so ugly."

"You're not ugly, father."

"I'm hardly pretty, Lily."

"What . . . is it?" Leo asked hesitatingly.

The man sighed. "Leprosy, son."

"The townfolk insisted he wear this robe and although he does that much I'll be damned if I'll agree to his having to cover his mouth or make the noise with the wretched clappers to signal his approach," Lily said, and Leo could hear the anger driving her words.

"I'm sorry," he said, at a loss for further words.

"He doesn't want pity. He just wants to be left alone. So now we live here in peace."

"What about you?" Leo asked.

"Me? The leprosy doesn't touch me but that doesn't matter to them. I'm tainted by his sickness. So long as I keep my distance and don't infect them," she snarled, "they will tolerate me. They won't even accept our money because it's deemed unclean. The few things that we need are bartered."

Leo frowned. "What do you exchange?"

"Father's a herbalist, if you hadn't guessed. Your brother chose the right people to collapse in front of."

"A shaman?" Leo asked, his interest fired further in the man.

"No," Greven said brusquely. Then his voice softened. "I just understand the natural world."

"Then why can't you cure yourself?"

He shrugged. "I love a youngster's logic. I'm afraid there's no cure for me."

Leo looked at Lily, who wore a sneer she wasn't disguising very well. "Father believes this is a punishment. A divine curse for being a coward."

"Hush, child," Greven admonished. "Hurry with all that stuff."

Leo followed Lily, carrying the tray she handed him, while she carefully lifted the boiled water and carried it over to her father.

"Coward?" Leo asked.

"My mother died not long after I was born," Lily explained. "She was very sick. We used to live in Cremond and some of the local folk brought in a healer who wanted father to make an offering in blood to Lo. They believed it would save her."

"The boy doesn't need to hear any of this, Lily," her father warned as he carefully cleaned Gavriel's wound.

Lily tipped a bitter-smelling liquid into Gavriel's mouth as she spoke. "This will dull the pain," she explained. "Anyway, father knew more than them about healing and, as he says, his beloved wife was already past help. But the villagers thought he was frightened of the blood price, which had to be drawn from me as I was the cause of her sickness."

"Absolute claptrap!" her father growled as he worked.

Leo smiled in spite of the sad story.

"After she died," Lily continued, threading a needle she had heated in the candle flame, "we came here."

"And I got leprosy," her father finished.

"As his punishment," she said in the same tone, as though mocking him. Then she turned to Leo. "And I grew up alone with my grumpy old leper father and learned much about living in a forest. There's our story, Lewk. How about you?"

Leo hesitated. He wasn't ready to craft the right sort of lie.

Greven saved him. "Right, enough jawing. Start sucking on those leaves, both of you."

Lily gave Leo a look of disgust. "Now the nasty bit. Come on, you don't get out of it. He's your brother."

"What do I do?"

Greven handed him some silvery green leaves. "Chew on these, son, and then spit them into this bowl. These are amazing leaves from the clirren, powerful infection fighters. Once you've chewed them into a paste, we need to put as much into the wound as possible, which we'll also pack with the lichen. In a few hours we can stitch him and then it's up to his own defenses—and he's got plenty of them, lad."

"What about the fever?" Leo asked, after spitting out the first gob of chewed leaf. "That's awful," he added, pulling a face.

Father and daughter smiled. "The fever is just the body's way of showing infection. It will pass once his body starts to fight back. We're just going to help the fight get started," Greven explained.

"How do you know all this?" Leo asked, spitting again.

"Careful, Lewk," Lily said, flicking some of his leaf debris from her blouse.

He gave her a look of apology, reddening with embarrassment. He caught himself staring at her breasts, before quickly looking away.

"He won't tell anyone," she continued, "so don't bother pursuing it."

"It's a gift," Greven declared loftily. "That's plenty. Let me have the bowl."

Leo watched as Greven worked dexterously to push the chewed clirren into the wound. He winced at the way the flap of skin was lifted until the wound bulged with the soggy medicine. "Now, the moss," Greven said, applying the white lichen.

"Why has only one side of your face been affected by the leprosy?" Leo blurted out.

Greven sighed. "I'm not sure. I have only seen one other case and the poor man's whole face had erupted with weeping sores. His lips, nose, and cheekbones all looked as though they had been bubbled over a furnace." Leo felt ill, more than able to imagine it from Greven's description. "Mine looks different, and it doesn't weep. It's always dry and a bit warm to the touch."

"Is it anywhere else on your body?"

"Just my face for now," Greven replied, stretching. "Ah, well, we've done our best. Now we wait."

"A few hours, you said?" Leo confirmed.

"That's right. Why, are you in a hurry?"

Leo had only just begun to think about the fact that they could already be under hunt. If anyone had seen them leaving the palace—although he wasn't convinced anyone had—the barbarians would know they were in the forest. And of course Al and Jok might help spread the word.

"Are you worried about those thieves who set upon you?" Lily asked.

"Yes, I am." Leo leapt upon the easy excuse.

"We're well hidden, Lewk," she assured. "And in case you hadn't realized it, we travelled at least a mile with Gaven. You won't be easy to find."

"Trackers could find us, though."

"Trackers?" Greven queried. "Why on earth would you be considered so important? Have you done something criminal?"

"No, no, nothing like that. We were, er, just passing through the forest, minding our own business."

"Where are you headed?" Greven asked conversationally but Leo was sharp enough to note the glance between father and daughter.

"North," he said. "I don't know why. Gav said it was best."

"North, eh? Bit dangerous for a couple of youngish fellows, don't you think?" Greven said, seating himself at the tiny table. "How about some food for the boy, Lily. Must be hungry, eh, Lewk?"

Leo nodded. He was starving, to tell the truth.

"Sit down," Lily offered. "I'll get something. I've nothing warm, mind."

"I wish I could pay you for this. I lost Lily's hare," Leo explained to Greven.

"Lost it? You set it free!" she said, scowling.

"I'm sorry," he said again.

Greven smiled, contorting his face horribly on the ravaged side. "Do you know the folklore surrounding the hare, Lewk?"

He shook his head as Lily set down a cup of creamy milk. Nodding his thanks, he began to swallow it in greedy gulps. Nothing had ever tasted so good.

"Well, the hare is associated with the moon. There's even a series of stars that take their shape and name from the hare."

Lily hacked off some cheese she'd unwrapped and put it onto a brick of bread. She reached for a jar of preserves. "Chutney?" At Leo's nod, she raised her eyebrows. "Very grown up," she murmured. After dolloping some on top of the cheese, she set the delicious looking pile of food before him. "Don't waste a crumb."

He didn't intend to and began eating hungrily. "It's a full moon tonight," he said to Greven, although with his stuffed mouth it came out as more of a mumble.

The leper seemed to understand all the same. He nodded. "The harvest moon, burning brightest of all. Well, as I say, hares and moons share some folklore. Maybe it was a good thing you turned that buck free tonight, Lewk."

"I don't know what struck me. I saw it struggling and I just didn't want to see it die."

Greven looked thoughtful. "There's been enough killing in our land. Perhaps it was an omen for you. After the harvest moon comes the hunting moon."

Leo's food turned sour in his mouth. He swallowed the final chunk. "I think Gav and I should make tracks as soon as he wakes."

"Wakes?" Greven laughed. "There will be no waking for him tonight, lad. He may surface but he won't really be aware of much."

Leo couldn't even swallow the rest of the milk now. He imagined what would happen to these good people if Loethar tracked him to this hut. "As soon as he wakes we have to leave."

"What's troubling you?" Lily asked. "You can stay here tonight. We won't cast you out. The hare is forgotten; stop worrying about it."

"I can see that something's amiss here, Lewk," Greven added. "If hiding is what you're after, Lily will show you a place you can stash yourself for the night. Fret not, you won't be discovered, and we won't disturb you."

Leo looked at them both. He dared not tell the truth. "Thank you."

Lily looked perplexed. "All right. Come with me, then." She led him to the back of the hut and moved aside one of the few items of furniture, a small sideboard. Then she easily pulled up a handful of floorboards, revealing a specially excavated area. It smelled musty but looked safe. "In there is a crawlspace. Here, take this blanket. It's mild up here but cool down there, I can assure you."

"Why do you have it?" Leo asked, amazed.

"Father worries about my living out here with him. He still frets that nasty men might come looking to abuse people, men like that pair you met today." She shrugged, embarrassed. "He feels better knowing I can hide myself very quickly if need be."

"Thanks for everything, Lily."

She nodded, looking slightly skeptical. "Sleep well. Hope you're not scared of spiders." Once Leo had lowered himself, she replaced the boards and he heard her pull the small chest back. He could follow the footsteps of Lily returning to her father and then muffled voices. There was nothing he could do now except wait. And with a full belly on top of being exhausted it didn't take much to convince Leo to curl up as best he could and sleep.

Twenty

Overhead the sky had paled to a murky charcoal. Glowing slashes of light were scored across the eastern skies; dawn was close. Buffeted by winds coming off the sea, the bird, which had covered much ground during the night, searched for the marker that would prompt it to swoop and soar downward. The forests were well behind it and it was now into open country, tracing the cliffs. In the distance it spotted a tiny pile of stones and flew faster toward it, hitting its highest speed now despite its fatigue. Once over the stones, it banked skyward and then in a display of acrobatics that would have impressed anyone watching, it twisted mid-air, performing a complex series of barrels before soaring downward. At the precise moment when it seemed it was going to plunge into the sea it swooped, skimming agilely above the waves. As it reached the beach it slowed and then, spotting what it looked for, it flapped its wings once again, gliding more gently now to land on a low ledge.

Show off, the man said, lightly disgusted. *Hello, Ravan. You took your time.*

I have been occupied, the bird replied, *doing your bidding.*

Well, you're looking thin. I've trapped you some voles. I've been hoping for your return the past moon. Hungry?

Ravenous.

The man turned, smiled wryly at the jest. *I hate it when you go silent on me, you know. I miss you.*

You know I must not risk it.

He sighed. *Yes, indeed. So come on in. Tell me everything.*

The bird hopped heavily behind, following the man into the small hut that was built on the ledge but protected by cliffs that curved around in a natural crescent. Inside it was warm and dry. The dull roar of the waves crashing to shore was a comforting rhythm in the background.

Go feed, the man said, pointing to the small pit where a pile of freshly killed rodents was heaped. He shut the window against the rattling wind. *And then we can talk.*

While Ravan fed, the man busied himself warming a small pot of water over the fire. He never worried about the smoke being seen. Courtesy of the sea breezes, it seemed to disperse long before it ever reached the cliff's summit. No, he was well hidden here. Had lived here in this hut he built himself for over two decades now, although he had long ago stopped keeping track of the years, or of his age. He threw some herbs and leaves he had dried himself into the fizzing water and waited patiently while it came back to its gentle boil. After a few minutes, he took it off the flames and set the pot aside for its contents to cool and infuse. Still not looking at the bird, he reached for the honey jar from his meager supplies and stirred a generous spoon into the mug once he'd added the amber liquid.

Finally Ravan turned from his food.

Better? the man asked.

Much. How are you anyway?

The usual. Same old aches and pains.

Ravan hopped closer. *Then you'd better drink more of your healing tea. It has begun.*

I know, Ravan. I know it has. It began before Loethar conquered Penraven, before he even invaded the Set.

I have been away too long.

The plains are too far for me to expect you to visit often.

We are much closer now. I can see you regularly.

Does he suspect?

How can he, Sergius? I am simply Vyk, the sinister, silent raven.

The man nodded. *Tell me everything you have learned.*

Ravan began to recount everything he had witnessed or heard since he'd last been with his oldest friend.

In a trice, Lily leapt into bed beside Gavriel.

"I'm awake," he said, noting the sudden fear in her eyes. "I can hear them."

"You're my husband Jon," she hissed. "You got wounded chopping down some branches. You fell, and a sharp stake ripped through your arm. All right?" He nodded, helplessly held by her gaze. Her skin was creamy, soft against his own. He felt a surge of desire that betrayed him and her instant scowl told him she felt it too.

Dizzy from the pain in his arm and a different sort of ache between his legs, his head felt dull and thick. "What's your name?"

"Lily. My father is Greven. He's—"

"Who lives here?" bellowed a voice from outside.

Gavriel started, anxiously rubbing his face only to realize he suddenly had a beard.

"Don't touch it!" Lily warned. "Who is it?" she called, but before she could move to the door, it was kicked in and three huge men piled in.

"What is happening?" the old man Gavriel hadn't noticed until now quailed, his voice tremulous. His face hidden behind a hood, he stood, reaching out blindly toward the men.

"Please!" Lily screamed. "What do you want? My father's half blind, my husband is hurt."

"Out, all of you!" the leader ordered.

Lily continued a barrage of pathetic complaint. Two of the men hauled Gavriel out of bed but he managed to protect his arm. He felt light-headed and unsteady on his feet but the tatua on the men terrified him more than his discomfort and he gave not a word of complaint. "Names?" the leader said, looking first at the elderly man.

"I am Greven," he said, pushing back his hood. The three intruders stepped back, disgusted. "A leper!" one of them cried.

Greven shrugged humbly. "I live here well away from other people, with my daughter, who is also in the early stages of leprosy, and her husband, who is wounded. We're a sorry lot, I'm afraid."

"She's a leper as well?" one of the others asked, scowling.

"Early stages, very contagious. Her sores are angry today," Greven said, nodding toward Lily's bare arms, which bore raised red welts. "I would keep your distance. Me, I'm not so infectious any more." He sneezed and the men stepped to the side.

"Pity," the second admitted. "She looks tasty."

"What do you want?" Lily asked, ignoring the comment, scratching gently at her welts.

"We're your new rulers," the leader said viciously.

"So I've heard," Lily replied, her tone polite. "Can we offer you something?"

"We're searching for two people." He looked over at Gavriel. "What's your name?"

"I'm Jon Farthing, married to this man's daughter, Lily."

"How do you fuck a leper?" the second warrior muttered to the third behind their leader.

"In much the same way you'd fuck one of your women," Gavriel said, knowing it was a mistake before the words were even out of his mouth.

The leader struck fast, punching Gavriel's now stitched and bandaged wound as hard as he could. Gavriel fell to the ground, retching with pain. The barbarians laughed.

"The next smart comment that comes out of your mouth means I'll kill the whole family," the leader warned.

"No need for that, sir. Please forgive my son-in-law," Greven soothed. "He's in pain and unable to work. He's angry and he's stupid for saying what he did."

"Who are you seeking?" Lily asked.

"A tall young man travelling with a boy. The boy's about twelve."

Gavriel, still on the ground, had stopped heaving. The pain was like a white fire in his arm but he had the presence of mind to realize how intensely dangerous their situation had become. Where was Leo? Had the king shared their secret with Lily and her father?

"I saw tracks yesterday," he offered from the ground.

"Get up!" the man ordered. Lily helped Gavriel back to his feet.

"Backaways, opposite direction. We were trapping hares and it seems someone got to my beasts first—one was missing. I think whoever you seek probably took it."

"What do you want with these people?" Lily asked.

"They're on the run," the man growled. "Go check inside," he ordered his two soldiers.

"You're after a child?"

"Not an ordinary child, leper-woman. The Valisar heir!"

Lily glanced up at Gavriel, unable to hide her shock. Gavriel took her hand, squeezed it reassuringly.

"And the other?" Greven asked, not looking at Gavriel.

"Your former legate's son—one of them, anyway."

The men emerged from the hut. "There's nothing in there," one replied. "Just the stench of death. Shall we kill them?"

Gavriel's heart lurched in his chest.

"I don't want to get that close to the lepers. Leave them; they can rot out here alone," the leader said, his mouth twisted into a cruel sneer.

"Thank you," Greven said, so politely it made Gavriel's anger flare. Wisely, however, he held his tongue, enjoying seeing the barbarians flinch as the older man stepped to offer his gratitude.

"Back off, leper," one man warned.

"What does your king want with our prince?" Lily persisted.

"Your new emperor, leper-woman, wants him dead."

"But this realm is huge. How will you find him if he's on the loose?"

"We'll keep tracking," the leader said, making to leave. "And if we don't find him, the Set people will give him to us anyway, especially when the killing begins."

"What do you mean?" Gavriel asked.

"All sons of the Set aged eleven to thirteen summertides are to be beheaded, starting today. You Set people shouldn't be so eager to keep records. You've made it very easy for us."

They left the trio standing in a heavy silence that continued long after they heard the men disappear. Finally, Lily broke the awkward impasse.

"You're the legate's son?"

Gavriel nodded. "Gavriel de Vis, my lady," he said, giving a brief, awkward bow.

"And that's the crown prince hiding beneath our hut?" she asked, incredulous.

"Not crown prince, no." He saw relief briefly flicker in her eyes. "King Leonel of Penraven is his title now."

Gasping, Lily clutched her hand to her throat.

Gavriel rubbed his face, pulling off the false beard in clumps. "Thank you for this and for helping us."

"Your arm's going to need re-stitching," Greven said, approaching.

Gavriel hadn't looked at the older man fully until now and didn't want to stare. Though his disfigurement was hideous on one side of his face, in profile—on the right side—he looked perfectly whole. "I'll fetch Leo and get us well away from here. We've put you in enough danger as it is."

"I put the King of Penraven down a hole beneath my hut?" Lily repeated, dismayed.

"And saved his life," Gavriel said, still pulling at his beard. "Strike me, what is this?"

"Otter fur," she answered, glaring at him. "We had to make do with whatever we had."

"Get the boy out," Greven said. Lily headed into the hut,

the two men following behind. "Tell me what happened," Greven ordered. "How did you end up here?"

Gavriel gave Greven a shortened version of their circumstances from the moment he had seen his father's head hacked in two.

Leo emerged from the crawlspace looking defiant. "You told them?"

"I had to."

Leo looked embarrassed and surprised when Greven and Lily uttered "Your majesty," in tandem. They both bowed.

Leo cleared his throat, embarrassed. "Thank you."

"What can we do to help?" Lily asked, searching Gavriel's face. "They're going to kill him."

"You've done enough. You've already risked everything. We must leave."

"But—"

"No buts," Gavriel replied. "I would be grateful if you'd fix up my arm as best you can, and perhaps pack us some food, but we've got to be gone from here as soon as possible. They could come back."

Greven shook his head. "They won't. Lepers scare people."

"I'm sorry we lied," Leo said. "I felt badly because you've been so good but we had no choice."

"We understand," Greven said.

"Lily, your arms!" Leo suddenly gasped.

She rubbed at them self-consciously. "Nettles. They work a treat and usually fool people—another of my father's very bright ideas. I'd better find some dock leaves. Resisting the itch is not easy."

"My king," Greven began. "Tell us what we can do. I mean it. We are loyal to the Valisars. Those men alone were terrifying."

"And they were nothing compared to the leader of the Greens." Gavriel pointed to his face. "Each barbarian tribe wears different colored tatua. No, Greven, we are not leading a rebellion yet. Just now we are merely trying to survive.

I gave my word to King Brennus and my father that I would protect Leo with my life. I have to keep him alive, on the run for many years if necessary, until he's of an age to think about rallying his own forces."

"Now is not that time," Greven agreed. "Our majesty is too young, too vulnerable and the realm is presumably in tatters."

"It is," Gavriel agreed. "But not just ours. Every royal family has been slaughtered throughout the Set. Leo and his adopted brother, Piven, are all that remain of the Set royalty." He gestured at Leo. "He is precious for all the realms of the Set."

"Where will you go?" Lily asked, anxiously.

"We're trying to find a band of outlaws led by a man named Kilt Faris."

Lily nodded. "I've heard of him. They say his camp is in the far north."

"That's what we've heard too. But I haven't been able to find out exactly where his camp is."

"I suspect if he's as elusive as the rumors suggest, if he doesn't want to be found, he won't be," Greven said.

"He's our hope, though," Leo joined in. "We think that, aside from hating the barbarian invasion, he has a genuine interest in keeping the Valisar throne safe."

"So he can keep plundering taxes and exploiting the king's wealth," Gavriel explained. "We hope to make a bargain with him."

Lily shook her head with disbelief. "Good luck," she said wryly. "If the right price is offered by the barbarian king I reckon Kilt Faris would sell his very soul. Please don't tell me you're counting on Faris having any loyalty to the realm."

"No, not loyalty," Leo answered. "You don't get to be as successful as Faris without keeping a close eye on the palace and its comings and goings. My father believed Faris not only had spies but that he was never overly greedy with what he stole from the crown. Enough to be irritating, not enough to warrant an all-out price on his head. Father believed he still had some measure of respect for the crown. More, I'm sure, than he'll have for Loethar, who will not grant him quite the same grace that my father permitted."

Lily walked away, shaking her head, and busied herself packing food.

"Go with them, Lily," Greven suggested.

"Are you mad, father? Walk into an outlaw's den? One woman amongst all those desperates?"

"Travel as a leper. You know how to do it."

Lily gave a sound of disgust just as Gavriel shook his head. "Absolutely not. It's hard enough keeping the king safe without another person to protect."

"I don't remember your doing much protecting last night. I was able to sneak up on you pretty easily," Lily snapped, slamming the hunk of cheese from the previous evening into a sack.

"I didn't mean—"

"Lily, go. You know this part of the forest like the back of your hand. And you've got a good sense of how to travel the woods silently, quickly. These two are like lumbering badgers by comparison."

She smiled at her father with genuine affection. "Father, I can't leave you alone."

"You can, and you will. I'm not an invalid. I'm a leper, that's all. More than capable of looking after myself. We have to do this, don't you see? We can't stand by and meekly hand over our king to the barbarian invaders. We have to protect him. All of us, not just Gavriel de Vis."

She looked down.

Glancing from Greven to Lily, Leo began, "Listen, I appreciate—"

"I'm sorry, majesty," Greven interrupted. "But this is not your decision. You may be royal and you may be king, but you are still a child. Our job, as grown-ups, is to protect our young. And I've made my decision and unless my daughter's a coward—which I know she's not," he added as she opened her mouth defensively, "then she will pack herself some food in that sack and set out this very morning to lead you north."

Silence gripped the room.

Gavriel broke it. "It's up to you, Lily."

"Father's right. We have to protect our king."

Greven nodded. "Good. Let's see to your arm, and let's make some porridge—no one should travel on an empty belly—and let's get you on your way."

Sergius took a long breath. *Searching for an aegis, eh? Are you sure they didn't see you, don't suspect anything?*

They didn't see me. Everyone ignores me now.

Very cunning of this Freath fellow. I'm impressed.

How do you find a stranger with no name, when you don't even know what he looks like?

Sometimes they find you. Otherwise you have to know what you're looking for. Leonel's aegis will be within eight to ten anni of his own age, I'm guessing. It's not certain but it's a starting point.

Was the Vested man right in how he said it must occur?

Absolutely right. To bond the aegis, part of him must be consumed by the Valisar. That's the trammelling. It's not for the faint-hearted.

What about Brennus's aegis? Does he just die?

Well, the aegis is already dead in a way. His spirit is owned by the king and it is the king's life that sustains his aegis. So if the king dies, so does his spirit.

Ravan thought about this. *What if the king never found his aegis, never trammelled him?*

Ah, interesting question. Then the aegis lives his normal life. He is never bonded, so he dies only of natural causes.

Can anyone else trammel him?

People have tried over the centuries but no, only a true heir can trammel an aegis. Yes, Leonel could bond his father's aegis but there's only one aegis per king. So if that were to happen Leonel's own aegis would go free.

And there is an aegis born for all heirs.

Of course, Sergius said, pouring himself a fresh brew. *If one of Iselda's other sons had made it past childbirth, he would have had his own aegis.*

Speaking of Iselda's other sons . . . there's something about Piven.

What do you mean?

I'm not sure yet. There's just something about him.

Brennus assured me he is completely lost.

He is, but . . .

What? Sergius sat forward.

I could have imagined it but when Brennus died it was as though I sensed something flare within the boy. I wasn't really paying much attention to him in truth—there was a great deal happening that night. But the child was paying attention to me. He likes me, recognizes me or at least is drawn to me.

When you say "sensed," what do you mean exactly?

It's hard to describe. It was like an awakening. Piven is always stroking me or near enough to me that our bodies touch. We were touching when his father was killed and I felt something pass through the boy. As Sergius flinched, Ravan cut off his train of thought. *Don't ask me what it was, exactly, because I don't know. It was a feeling, a sensation . . . a . . . a pulse.*

Have you noticed a difference in him since then?

Well, increasingly I get the strangest notion that he's trying to actually communicate with me.

Sergius pushed away from the table and stood. He paced, frowning, arms folded, deep in thought.

What are you thinking, old man? Ravan flew to his shoulder.

I don't know what to make of it but I also don't think we should mistrust your feelings. Fly back now. Keep a close eye on the boy. Try and communicate with him, perhaps. If you notice any substantial change I must know about it.

Twenty-One

Kirin and Clovis had moved relatively freely throughout the palace thanks to the ribbon that proclaimed them Freath's servants. They had got chatting with a young barbarian, whom they found playing with a kitten he'd obviously found that had been skulking near the kitchens. His name was Barc and Clovis was sure he recognized the youngster from part of the armed guard that escorted the Vested through the Set ultimately to Penraven.

Kirin soon worked out that Barc's youth and need to boast meant his mouth was looser than other of the barbarians and had suggested to Clovis he might as well see if the kitchens could spare some food as neither had yet eaten. Clovis had taken the hint and moved off in search of the food they did not need.

"How are you feeling being so far from home, Barc?" Kirin continued.

The boy dangled a long stem of grass in front of the kitten who found the game irresistible. "I miss it. I love the horses, the open plains. Everything here smells strange. And it's so closed in."

"You speak excellent Set. All of you, in fact."

Barc nodded. "We all speak it from birth."

"I didn't know that. How did that come about?"

Barc shrugged. "Perhaps many years ago we had teachers from here."

"Prisoners, you mean, or paid teachers?"

"I don't know."

Kirin suspected it was both. As much as the Set ignored the tribes of the plains politically, at a more domestic level there was a brisk trade. Plains people bred magnificent horses and were excellent craftsmen and good farmers. There was a natural flow of Set people into the plains, and over the centuries some must have stayed. "You're awfully young to go to war, aren't you?"

The young man beat his chest and grinned. "Warriors must prove themselves as soon as they have lived past fifteen plains blows. Then we are ready to fight. I have proven myself." He pointed at the intricate pattern on his face.

"And you belong to the Reds," Kirin said, hating to state the obvious but trying to learn as much as he could.

"The tatua is very fresh. It still stings."

"Will your family come and join you now?"

Barc smiled. "Yes, now that we have been triumphant, all our families, especially the women, can join us. Our leader wants the tribes to mix with the Set people. He will form a new race, he says."

"Does that worry you?"

"Why should it?" the boy countered, frowning. He stroked the kitten. "This was the plan. And because I bear the tatua I can now take a wife, start my own family."

"Will you remain Red even if you take a Set wife?"

"I will."

"Do you think your leader would mind your talking to us?"

The youngster looked untroubled. "No. You are defeated. You have no army—your soldiers are either dead or under our control." He flexed his muscles, beating the left side of his chest as he added, "And you have no heart now that all your royals are dead. Your people have to accept the peace terms and our rule. They'll get used to it."

Kirin nodded, wondering how the Set that worshipped Lo would be expected to easily give their faith over to countless new gods from one that was responsible for fertility to another that could just as easily visit plague upon your kind. "And what of the Vested that were gathered up?"

"Vested? Ah—the people who possess magic, you mean? I was among the warriors who brought them here."

"I was one of them. How are the others?"

"You have magic?" The boy looked impressed.

Kirin shrugged. "Not really. I can predict weather patterns," he offered, "not always as accurately as some would like, but I get it right a lot of the time."

This didn't seem to interest Barc much, as Kirin had hoped. "We have people who use magic. We call them The Masked. But we use them to communicate with the gods; each family has one."

This didn't interest Kirin but he nodded as though paying close attention. Clovis returned, bearing a bowl of porridge. "I ate outside the kitchen," he said. "Couldn't wait."

Kirin began eating the porridge as he talked. "I was hoping to see some of the people I was rounded up with. Do you know where they are?"

"I have a feeling they were taken to some important religious place south of here but I don't know for sure. I was given other duties once we arrived at Brighthelm."

A bell sounded and Barc leapt to his feet. "I have to go. I'm back on duty now."

"Thanks, Barc. It's been nice talking with you," Kirin said.

"We are meant to be enemies," the boy said, "but perhaps in time we can live together easily." He hurried away.

"Not likely," Clovis said.

Kirin murmured agreement. "Do you know what he meant by the religious place south of here?"

Clovis shook his head. "No, but Freath will."

They found Freath pale and anxious, hurrying through one of the corridors with Genrie.

"We know where the Vested are being kept," Kirin said, sensing the tension and keeping it brief. "Apparently they've been taken to a religious house south of here."

"Buckden Abbey," Genrie murmured.

Freath nodded. He looked around carefully. "We shall have to head there. But you should know what Loethar has commanded in our realm. It could spill into the others. He wants all males aged eleven to thirteen summertides to be killed."

"Every boy?" Kirin queried, his mouth suddenly dry.

"And we're going to provide the census records so they are easily found. Our most recent was last Harvest Festival, so it's very accurate," Freath said, mournfully. "I don't know what to do. I can't save these children. I can't even save the boy we strive to protect. Valya thinks she saw the king and De Vis fleeing into the woods."

"Is she sure?" Clovis asked.

"No, but it must be them. They've taken their chances and gone on the run."

"So Loethar will flush him out by killing all the males of the king's age across all realms."

"Starting with Penraven. That's hundreds of innocents savagely murdered in our realm alone."

"How can we stop it?" Kirin asked.

"We can't," Freath growled. "But we will use it to find and protect Leo. We have to."

"Use it?" Clovis frowned.

"I'm going with Stracker because I can read the census. He can't. I can ensure that the killing is as merciful as possible. And you two are coming with me."

"What?" Kirin and Clovis roared.

Genrie bundled them all into a chamber. "Hush. If we are found now, all is lost. Speak, Master Freath. You two, shut up and listen."

The three men obeyed her command. Freath explained, "We cannot stop this now. Loethar is a man driven beyond all reason. He wants Leo dead. But I think I have a way to halt his madness before the headcount gets too high. In the meantime, with the freedom we'll have to travel, perhaps you will find it easier to hunt for the aegis. Either way, I could use your help, your eyes and ears."

"What about the Vested at the abbey?"

"At least we know where they are. This new development takes preference. To be honest I doubt whether the person I seek is among those who were rounded up. Anyone with potential to be an aegis would have hidden himself beneath many layers of life's disguises."

"It could be a child again," Clovis reminded him.

"How many children were with you?" Freath asked.

"Very few. I think almost all, if not all but the very young, were killed."

"Are you sure the aegis will even know what he or she is?"

"No, but the old writings suggest that each aegis is born with the inherent knowledge of who they are and what they're capable of. But these people run from their calling. They fight its pull every day; they know that once they are trapped in the net of championship, their lives are over. They will die of old age, bonded to their king—unless their bonded dies of poor health or accident first, in which case they die then, too."

"They can't be released?"

"I don't think so. But that's an irrelevant detail right now. All that matters is finding this person."

Clovis turned away. "I can't do it, I won't. Kirin can accompany you. I would rather die than bear witness to the slaughter of more children."

"We need you, Clovis," Freath urged.

"What makes you think I'm capable of it?" Kirin asked, horrified.

"You haven't lost your own child to the barbarian! You forget I saw Stracker spear my daughter with his garforsaken blade. No, I refuse."

The other three shared glances and Freath nodded. "All right, Clovis. I understand. You will remain behind. Keep your ears and eyes open and keep Genrie abreast of everything you learn. You now have more freedom than she."

Clovis nodded unhappily but said nothing.

"We'll be missed if we spend another moment here," Genrie cautioned. "Have you heard that Loethar's bringing in a new set of servants for the palace?"

Freath shook his head with exasperation. "No."

"It was the old woman's suggestion and she's supervising it. She's also planning a barbarian celebration. No one in the Set will be permitted to celebrate Harvest Festival this year. It's going to be replaced with a new event. I should also tell you there's a wedding in the air."

"I've heard," Freath said sourly. "Still, we have no control over any of this. We must remain focused on securing our king's protection."

"I must go," Genrie said. "Don't leave immediately after me. Good luck, Freath." Her gaze rested momentarily on the older man before she nodded at the other two and slipped out of the door.

It was difficult saying farewell to brave Greven, even harder watching Lily hug her father goodbye. Leo wondered if they would ever see him again. He doubted it. The leper had already said in passing that without his daughter's welfare to think about, he might not stay put. He had admitted that the hut and even the forest would seem horribly empty without her. Leo felt the guilt of more people's sacrifices settle around his shoulders. Perhaps it would be easier to simply give himself up to Loethar, to get it all over and done with.

Both Gavriel and Lily had halted, looking at him with a mixture of astonishment and anger, and Leo realized he had spoken his thoughts aloud.

"I didn't mean to say that," he said.

"I should hope not," Lily said. "I'm not doing this because it's an adventure I've been longing for."

Gavriel threw him a sympathetic look. "Leo, this is not just about you. This is about our realm, about the Set, about preserving our way of life and fighting against the oppression of the barbarian. We know he's got his own agenda and from what we saw it is not simply about claiming triumph over the Set."

"What do you mean?" Lily said.

Gavriel had already told her how they'd hidden in the ingress, even though Leo had scowled at him, preferring to keep it a secret. But he understood that Gavriel's admission was necessary; Lily would demand to know how they had seen so much or knew so much about Loethar. If they hadn't been honest with her from the beginning, she would have begun mistrusting them. And right now, Lily was their guide, their hope for reaching the den of Kilt Faris quickly. "Tell her," he said.

Gavriel made a rueful face and Leo realized he hadn't been seeking permission. "Loethar's angry. He's on a personal crusade of destruction. If he could he would wipe the Valisar name and its history from all records and everyone's memories, I think that—and only that—might appease him. But that's not possible, so instead he's settling for destroying every living Valisar. Ruling the Set as an emperor is not yet enough . . . not until Leo dies. And we know he's hardly threatened by a child, not with his marauding army. So his quest goes deeper but I don't understand it."

"I don't think you're meant to," Lily said, clambering up a new incline. "Watch it here, it's quite slippery," she said, reaching for a tree branch to haul herself up. "By the sounds of all you've said, he's obviously quite mad."

"I don't think so," Leo said, accepting her hand to pull him up and then turning to do the same for Gavriel. "He is frighteningly sane when you watch him up close."

"His half-brother is the reckless one, the brute who does his dirty work. Loethar is far more sophisticated in thought and action," Gavriel agreed.

"None of this makes sense, of course," Lily added. "My father said the Set and Steppes people have historically been on good terms with one another. We've had centuries of peace."

"Was your father really serious about leaving the forest?"

Leo asked. "Surely it's familiar, home?" Somehow the man reminded him of his father. Perhaps because he was about the same age as Brennus.

"Oh, that man!" she replied, exasperated. "He'll get himself killed. I know it appears to you as though he has hidden in the forest for his own sake but the truth is he lives within the cocoon of the woods for me. I am the one who craved its peace and solitude. I was the one who wanted him to be away from those who treated him badly. He lived the quiet life to please me but my father is a traveller at heart. He doesn't like to be still. If he could have convinced me, we would have wandered the realms as travelling herbalists, with me as the face of our service."

"They'd have still made him wear the hooded robe," Leo began.

"And sound his clappers, yes," she sighed. "But he never minded the humiliation. I did."

"I'm sorry we've taken you from him, Lily," Leo said, taking her hand, feeling a thrill at touching her. He'd already worked out that this woman was not one given to crying. But she was clearly very sad.

"We're all making sacrifices, Leo. I make mine gladly for you because I don't want to be a barbarian's woman and that's what I face if we don't make a stand."

"Then marry me now, Lily. I'll save you from the tatua oafs," Gavriel said theatrically.

Leo scowled at him. "You'll never be a barbarian's wife. I won't let it happen."

"Thank you, my king," she said and kissed his hand playfully.

She had no idea what that did to Leo. For a period after the kiss he could say nothing. He knew his cheeks were burning, and his mind was racing down pathways it shouldn't. He suddenly really minded Gavriel's easy-going manner and even easier conversation with Lily.

". . . after all, we have now shared a bed," he heard Gavriel say as he came out of his thoughts.

Leo stopped walking. "What?"

"Pay him no heed," Lily soothed. "He's delusional."

Gavriel grinned broadly. Leo suddenly became aware, perhaps for the first time, how helplessly handsome Gavriel was. Leo knew girls had always found Gavriel irresistible but that knowledge had never interrupted the fun he'd shared with the De Vis twins. Now he felt he was competing against Gavriel—and that he had absolutely no chance in the contest. "I was not delusional when I awoke to find you naked and next to me this morning, Lily," Gavriel continued, playfully.

Leo thought he was either going to be sick or he was going to punch Gavriel. He stomped ahead.

"Shut up," Lily said, grinning at Gavriel, unaware of how their fun injured him. "He jests, Leo, ignore him. I climbed into the bed only when we heard the men arrive so I could pretend we were husband and wife."

"Why?" Leo rounded on them.

Gavriel must have sensed Leo's unease, for he stopped leering at Lily. "Because they were obviously searching for two people who fitted our description. We must have been spotted somehow. And even if they hadn't found you, they might have grabbed me for simply looking like the fellow they were seeking," he explained, frowning at Leo. "Are you all right?"

Leo didn't want to feel angry with Gavriel, especially after all they had shared, but he couldn't quite resolve how he was feeling. "Yes, of course," he said, backing down. "I had no idea what you'd all gone through when I was hiding below ground." He sighed, changed the subject. "I think I'm hungry."

"No time to stop, your majesty," Lily said. "Come on, let's speed up. We've got a journey ahead of us."

"How long, do you think?" Gavriel asked.

Lily's expression turned unsure. "I don't really know. All I can do is keep heading us north."

Leo rallied. It would not do to create a difficult atmosphere between the three of them. "Please, no more calling me 'majesty.' Not even Leo if you want to protect me." They both nodded, although Gavriel had long ago given up titles. "On my father's maps the forest was roughly six miles from Brighthelm to its northen point."

"And how do you know Faris is north?" Lily asked.

"Father once showed me on the map where he thought the main outlaw hiding area was. It was almost at the northern tip of the forest."

"Then as the crow flies we've got at least another four miles of this rougher terrain to travel," she confirmed.

"Speaking of crows, you didn't happen to see a huge raven around the time that we came along, did you?" asked Gavriel.

Lily stopped walking. "What an odd thing for you to say."

"It's just that we were sure a raven was moving through the trees with us when we were making our escape."

"He's big," Leo added.

"I'm really staggered," Lily said and sounded it. "I did see a raven. He was very still but I was extremely aware of his presence. Huge black bird he was. I didn't see a mate, or a nest, either, and he wasn't acting territorially. He seemed rather tame, in fact. He certainly wasn't scared of me—he even flew down to the ground and hopped around, making lots of clicking and clacking sounds."

"Then what?" Gavriel demanded.

She shrugged. "Then nothing. I followed him a short while before I lost sight of him. Next thing I knew I had stumbled upon you two letting my trapped hare go."

Gavriel and Leo shared a glance.

"Why? What does that mean?" she asked, noticing it.

"Nothing," Gavriel replied. "Nothing important." He shrugged. "We'd convinced ourselves he was following us."

"I doubt it. Ravens are intelligent but not that cunning," Lily said airily. But Leo knew better and he suspected Gavriel felt the same way. He was sure they would agree that Vyk had not only followed them but had led Lily to them. *Why?*

Twenty-Two

Freath nodded as he poured wine into Loethar's goblet. "I do think it's the best solution, sire. I can read the census and I can also offer insightful information to your brother if he needs it."

"Half-brother," Loethar corrected. Freath acknowledged the correction with a dip of his head. "I wouldn't have thought witnessing killing was quite up your alley, though, Freath. You realize what you will have to watch?"

"I don't have to watch it though, my lord. My aim is to ensure it is carried out precisely to the letter, that we do indeed select the right sons from the census. I shall take only one of my Vested, so I shall be no burden on Warrior Stracker."

"He wishes to be known as general."

"Are you comfortable with this, my lord?"

"Every emperor needs his general, Freath. Stracker is mine." Loethar sipped his wine and nodded his approval.

Freath noted that Loethar didn't precisely answer his question but couldn't care less. He prayed one day the brothers—half or otherwise—would come to blows and fight it out for supremacy. So long as they killed each other, he'd be happy. For the time being he kept his expression composed, blank. "As you wish, my lord."

"I will need to send one of our tribe with you for your own protection. Stracker can be unpredictable."

"He's already on his way to the first town—Devden, correct?" Loethar nodded. "I will need to leave quickly."

"I shall brief a runner to accompany you."

"My lord, I hope you will not take offense at my question, but I wonder whether this mass murder is in your best interest?"

"I know what you're saying, Freath, but you seem to think that I care about diplomacy—about the way that you perhaps might ingratiate me into Set life. I don't share your vision. I don't care if people don't like me at the outset. I care only that we do integrate at some stage. For now I have but one request to keep me happy—that all Valisars be destroyed."

"Then may I make an equally simple suggestion?"

"Go ahead." He drained the goblet as he listened.

"As soon as the boy is found, stop the killing. The people from the Set will hate you for taking their sons, but I think we can achieve some measure of unspoken respect if you do halt the killing the moment you find your prey. Though General Stracker, I fear, may not approve of this plan."

Loethar studied Freath. "You have us well measured, Freath. No, he will not stop unless I insist. But your suggestion is a good one. When the child is found—and we know he can't be that far away yet—the slaughter ends."

Freath schooled his expression to look unimpressed. He didn't want Loethar to think he cared one way or the other. "Very good, my lord. What would you like me to arrange for Crown Princess Valya?"

"In what way?"

"For the wedding, my lord."

"In our culture we leave that to the women, Freath. I just turn up."

"So we'll be following a Steppes ceremony, my lord?"

Loethar looked irritated. Freath could tell he didn't enjoy administrative life. And being imprisoned in the palace must be hard on him, too. "What do you think?"

"Well, your bride is Drostean, after all. I think some western influence is important to show good faith to her family. Perhaps we run concurrent rituals."

Loethar nodded wearily. "Fine. Whatever she wants."

"Very well. Now, I've heard you wish to bring servants back into the palace. We've certainly been operating on the slightest number of staff—I know help would be appreciated, help in the kitchens and Genrie definitely needs more help in housekeeping. The gardens and orchards—"

"Freath, stop! Are you doing this deliberately?"

"What, my lord?"

"Boring me senseless with your tedium."

"In order to run the palace for you, I need your orders. Forgive me, sire. Perhaps I should discuss this with the crown princess?"

"How did Brennus operate?"

Freath gave a soft shrug. "The former king left us all mostly to our own devices. We had our duties, and we knew how to run the palace, sire. Iselda took charge of the household. Brennus worried about politics and running the realm."

"So include Valya. It will give her something to do."

"And perhaps Dara Negev also—unless that will cause disruptions between them?"

"Oh, you are certainly sharp, Freath," Loethar said, as much admiration as weariness in his voice.

"I have to ask, sire. We're bound to have problems if the two senior women in the palace are vying for position, especially if your servants don't fully understand the hierarchy. How would it work in Steppes society?"

"My mother would be in charge."

"Shall we keep it that way, then?"

"Yes, yes, whatever you think is best." He held out the goblet to be replenished.

"I'm sorry to test your patience, sire."

"Just find me the boy and all will be well."

Freath feigned a smile. "And there's one more thing, my lord. I would like to hire you a taster. I could have poisoned you just now." Freath registered the sound of the goblet clattering across the floor before he realized the barbarian had him by the throat.

"What is that supposed to mean?"

Freath couldn't answer. He gasped for air but couldn't seem to take a breath. Loethar pushed him and the older man stumbled back against the wall, banging his head. "See what happens when I'm angered, Freath? Next time I'll choke the last breath out of you."

Freath was seeing stars. He couldn't remember the last time anyone had manhandled him in this way. *It must have been back in my childhood,* he thought idiotically, his head swimming. Suddenly he felt himself being hauled to his feet, Loethar's fist at his shirtfront. "Are you all right?" the barbarian asked.

"I'm not sure, my lord. I can't focus properly."

"Take a drink."

"No, I'll just lean against the wall a moment. Er, forgive me my indiscretion. I meant only . . ." He had to think for a moment about what it was that he had intended to say. "I had meant only to warn you against assassins. If you are to bring in new servants, you may care to take some precautions with yourself, my lord."

Loethar looked contrite but Freath didn't expect him to back down or apologize. "I'll leave that to you to organize if you're so keen on looking out for my health."

"Thank you, my lord," Freath said. The man was suspicious of everyone, everything. He would have to keep working at gaining his trust. "Er, your raven is noticeably absent," he added.

"Vyk, yes. I have no idea where he has gone. But he is contrary like this."

"How did you come by him?" Freath asked, massaging his throat.

Loethar had turned away to pour himself a fresh goblet of wine. "That's an interesting tale. I found him as a baby in the very old forests in the far north where the plains end and mountains threaten. He'd fallen out of his nest and although I could hear his parents calling to him from the pines they refused to come to the ground. I raised him on the plains, and he adapted well enough, though he's never forgotten the forest. That's probably where he's flown off to now. I was a young warrior then, so Vyk has to be three hundred moons old now."

"Three decades! That's a wise old raven, my lord."

"Indeed." Loethar actually smiled. "No. He and I are more like brothers than Stracker and I could ever be. Vyk understands me." Freath was surprised that Loethar was being so candid. It was unnerving but he didn't want to stop the barbarian talking. "Of course, he agrees with everything I do," he went on, before pausing and adding, "because he never answers back." Freath wasn't sure whether he was supposed to chortle at what he presumed was a jest. He smiled benignly instead.

"The odd thing is," Loethar continued, sipping his wine and moving to the window as though expecting to see the raven in the distance approaching, "our people are suspicious of any bird associated with crows. They consider the crow a creature who straddles the worlds of the living and the dead. A shaman once warned me against him. Said he was dangerous."

"Why? He's just a bird."

"Well, shamans see more than the ordinary man, Freath. You and I are ordinary men. But the shaman never did explain his caution, if that's what you meant."

"But still you keep him."

"If Vyk is my enemy—and I have no reason to doubt him after all these years together—well, I still believe in keeping my enemies close."

"Is that why you allow your half-brother to remain next to you, sire?"

Loethar turned and Freath believed for one heartbeat that his life was forfeit, that he'd overstepped Loethar's tolerance for his sharp observances. But the barbarian simply stared at him coldly. "You are like my raven, Freath. I am unconvinced whether you are friend or foe. Though I am usually a reasonable judge of character, I cannot quite take your measure. You show incredible insight and everything you say appears to be for my benefit, but somehow I just cannot decide whether to trust you."

"Then I shall have to continue proving myself until I have earned your trust, my lord. I have told you that I have no loyalties to the Valisars. The truth is, I have no loyalty to anyone. But I might as well take my chances now with the new regime. I am your man, Emperor Loethar. As long as you continue to reward me, I will work tirelessly for your benefit alone."

"So allowing you to live is not simply enough any more?" It was a facetious comment.

"There's no point in living if you can't enjoy it, my lord. I want money, I want status, I want respect. I am prepared to earn those things, to prove my value to you."

"You've done well so far, Freath. You'll have to ignore my previous indiscretion."

They both glanced at the wine spilled on the floor. It looked like blood to Freath and he thanked Lo that his life had been spared . . . this time.

"It's already forgotten, my lord. Let me organize someone to clean up that mess. In the meantime may I suggest Genrie as your taster? I trust her and I think she'll do a fine job until you find someone more appropriate."

Loethar waved a hand. "Whatever you think best, Freath, as long as she doesn't start her haranguing again. You are dismissed to prepare for your journey. I shall see you on your return, hopefully triumphantly bringing me the head of Leonel of the Valisars."

This was their third morning and they'd fallen into a companionable silence. Food was scarce but no one had a particularly large appetite. Every step north seemed tinged with either sorrow at what they were leaving behind, or tension for what was ahead. Temperatures had cooled noticeably and although it was late summertide—nearly the onset of leaf-fall—Lily explained the drop in warmth was mainly due to the thickening canopy of dense trees, at first hawthorn, then beeches, birches, ash and oak, and finally, fir. There was no more dappled sunlight, no more joyful birdsong; suddenly the surrounds felt a lot more threatening even in the middle of the day.

"It's very silent here," Leo said.

"We must be close," Lily replied. "Except we don't really know what we're looking for, do we?"

"Why don't we just yell for him?" Gavriel suggested. "You said he's not going to just show himself to us. We have to lure him out. What have we got to lose?"

"Other than our lives, you mean?" Lily asked. "What makes you think Kilt Faris is the only one in the forest? Or even that he will welcome us with open arms?"

"I don't," Gavriel admitted. "I agree that this is an enormous risk but it's one Leo and I decided to take when we were trapped in the palace. You can't imagine what we witnessed there, Lily. I won't subject you to even hearing it repeated."

"Nor do I want to," she said quickly.

"My father would think much less of me if he knew he'd raised his heir to allow others to risk their lives—give their lives, even—while I ran away from the same challenge," Leo confirmed.

"Brave words," Gavriel said understandingly.

"No! You're getting this wrong, Leo. Listen to me," Lily demanded. "Everyone who is taking these risks and giving their lives is doing so to preserve yours. It's your responsibility to stay alive, no matter what."

"Lily, I—"

Leo never finished what he'd begun to say, as quivering arrow shafts struck the ground all around them.

Gavriel sounded surprisingly calm as he murmured, "Well, at least we know they don't want to kill us . . . not yet, anyway."

"Gavriel . . ." Lily murmured. Leo heard the fear in her voice even as he hated the fact that she turned to his friend first.

"Be calm, Lily. Leo, you all right?"

"Not dead yet," Leo said through gritted teeth.

"We're looking for Kilt Faris," Gavriel called, turning and yelling to the trees. His words were greeted with silence; there was nothing but shadows among the trees.

Gavriel tried again. "We've trekked three days from Brighthelm. The barbarian has proclaimed himself emperor, in case you didn't know, and we've escaped the palace to bring news. I'm sure Kilt Faris would want to hear what we have to tell him."

"We're not buying," boomed a voice.

"Fair enough, because we're not selling."

A single man, huge, with thick dark hair swirling about him strode down the incline.

"It's Algin," Leo breathed. Algin was the giant of Set myth. Gavriel seemed to find this funny but Leo was sure his chuckle was nervous laughter.

The large man arrived before them and, without a word, punched Gavriel so hard in the belly that he didn't have time to utter a protest. Silently, he crumpled to the ground like one of the paper lanterns Leo's mother used to make him.

"What in Lo's name was that for?" Lily shrieked, bending down to Gavriel. "You could kill him punching him like that, you oaf."

"Really?" the giant said. "Then perhaps he shouldn't laugh at strangers . . . especially when he's trespassing."

"Trespassing!" Lily hissed. "On whose land?" Below her, Gavriel groaned, then coughed.

"Mine!" the stranger said.

"These are crown lands," she hurled upward. "They belong to the Valisars."

"Sounds like they belong to the barbarian now."

Leo took immediate offense and used the trick Legate De Vis had taught all the boys in the cohort, taking a flying kick between the man's legs. Though it came without warning, at least Algin had time to yell his wrath before he joined Gavriel on the forest floor.

"Good kick, Leo," Gavriel congratulated, still wincing.

"Enough of this!" said a new voice as more shadows melted from behind the trees. The speaker was a normal-sized man who descended from the hill, followed by a number of men, presumably the archers. "Get up, Jewd."

Jewd was still groaning on the ground. "Little bastard," he growled. "When this pain stops I'm going to tear him limb from limb."

He sounded serious. Leo glanced at Lily, but she ignored his worried look. "Are you Kilt Faris?" she demanded of the new stranger.

"You've got until the count of ten until these men loose their arrows again. And this time they won't deliberately miss you."

Leo noticed how calmly and softly the stranger spoke and yet the words sounded all the more threatening because of it. He had not yet stepped fully out of the shadows so his features were not obvious but he wore a closely shaved beard and from what Leo could tell he was not nearly as intimidating as his giant friend. He was lean, as tall as Gavriel perhaps.

Both Jewd and Gavriel had dragged themselves to their feet. A worried glance at Gavriel told Leo that De Vis was injured again. His complexion looked pale and clammy. And his arm was bleeding.

"Come on, Lily," he said, tugging at her sleeve.

"Six," the man counted.

"We've come a long way," Lily persisted. "We have something of importance to tell Faris. If he's among you—"

"Seven," he continued, unmoved.

The men stepped back. They'd already retrieved their arrows and now nocked one in each bow.

"What, you really need all these bowmen to kill us?" Gavriel snarled. "You creep. She's unarmed, and that's a boy there, in case you hadn't noticed."

"Eight."

"Let's go, Gav," Leo said.

Lily was not easily deterred. "You have to listen to us. I'm begging you. Please tell us where Kilt Faris is. We have a message for him."

"Nine," the man uttered. At his word the bows trained on them were stretched taut in instant unison.

Leo looked around wildly. The man felt no sympathy for their plight, didn't even appear vaguely interested in their important message. He was also at home in his surrounds, confident of his place. This had to be Faris. He took the chance even though he knew Gavriel would be furious.

"Unless you're prepared to kill your king, I suggest you lower your weapons," he ordered, surprised by how commanding his newly broken voice sounded.

The man shifted his gaze. "My information tells me the king is dead—that the whole royal family is dead, in fact."

"King Brennus *is* dead," Gavriel replied. "As is Queen Iselda. And unless you like the idea of barbarian rule, the whole Set's only hope right now is his son, Leonel, the new king."

Their captor's attention slid once again, this time to Leo. Leo couldn't see his eyes clearly in the shadows, but he felt their weight resting heavily on him.

"You are Leonel?"

"I am," he said, as defiantly as he could.

The stranger stared at Leo a moment longer. Then he abruptly uttered a guttural command. The archers lowered their bows.

"Prove it," the man demanded.

Leo looked around, unsure. "How?"

The man shook his head. "That's your problem."

"Now wait a—"

"Be quiet, woman, or I'll have someone shut you up by force."

Lily went silent but Leo could feel her seething next to him.

"Well?" the man said, still calm.

Leo's mind raced. "Can you at least get him some help, please?" he said, trying to buy time, motioning toward Gavriel.

"He'll be fine. And if not, it's not our problem. You came here uninvited."

"I don't think so," Leo countered. "My father, King Brennus, told me to come here. He didn't say it directly but I think he hoped that you might become an ally. You are Kilt Faris, aren't you?"

The man stepped out from the dark that had been shading his face. He was younger than Leo had anticipated, although it was difficult to judge his age. Perhaps thirty anni, no more—and yet this man had been giving his father problems for many years—a decade of trouble at least.

"I am," he replied. "But you have still not convinced me of who you claim to be."

Faris wore no adornments, Leo noticed. His clothes were simple and practical, although the sword at his side looked to be of exceptional quality. In fact—Leo frowned—he was sure he recognized it.

"That's Faeroe," he blurted, pointing.

Faris studied him, his hand instinctively moving to touch the hilt of the sword.

"Gav, he's got Faeroe!" Leo exclaimed, now angry.

Gavriel looked at the sword, incredulous. "Are you sure?"

"No question of it. I love that blade. I'd know it anywhere. I think I even cried the day my father said he had given it to someone special. I'd always hoped it would be mine."

For the first time since they'd seen him, Faris looked remotely interested. "Bring them! Blindfold them first," he ordered and suddenly the three of them found their eyes covered before being bundled up the incline, still deeper into the forest.

Freath could hear the screaming in the streets. Mothers were swooning to the ground as precious sons were dragged from their arms. He could hear the pounding of his blood in his ears as his heartbeat soared with fear and his throat became parched. But the ale before him was no respite, tasting sour in his mouth.

"This can't be happening," Kirin said, his lips as bloodless as his suddenly paled complexion.

"It is happening. We must remain stoic."

"Stoic? You've nine names on that list. Nine lives. Nine sons of this town."

"I can count, Master Kirin," Freath reprimanded. "I cannot prevent this."

"But why are you helping the barbarians?" Kirin demanded. "You led them here, read out the names, assisted in the hunting down of these innocents. Are any of them the boy in question?"

Freath shook his head. "That's not the point. You and I both know this is about fear-mongering. They want word of this to spread like fire to other villages, towns, even realms. They want the king to be untouchable. Not only will no one offer protection, Loethar is counting on this brutal tactic to yield the boy sooner rather than later."

"But in the meantime hundreds must die . . . to what, make a point?"

"Sadly, yes, to make a point. So the Set understands that Emperor Loethar will not be defied."

"Well, I won't be part of it any more. I'm with Clovis. I'd rather die than soil my soul with this."

"War is ugly, Master Kirin. And, trust me, we are at war even though the cries of battle have ended and armies no longer march. You and I, Clovis, Genrie, Father Briar . . . we are all the Set has. If we don't fight—and, believe me, we are fighting in our own very tiny way—then not just *your* soul but all our souls are lost."

Kirin stared back at him angrily. "So you're just going to sit here, sip your ale, and allow that monster to behead nine boys in this town? While you do nothing."

"I didn't say I would do nothing. But I am saying to you that these first nine lives are indeed lost. You must pull yourself together. No amount of railing from you can save them." Freath squeezed Kirin's hand and although the Vested tried to snatch it away, Freath gripped it firmly. "Now calm yourself. And listen to me." He removed his hand, laid it back in his lap and took a deep breath. "I want you to travel ahead—go to the town of Berch. There are twenty-two lads eligible for death there. According to our census, one of them, a boy called Tomas Dole, belongs to a large family of ten children. He is destined for slaughter." He threw a pouch of coins onto the table. "Give this to the boy's parents."

Kirin stared at the leather pouch with dull confusion. "Why?"

"I'm compensating them for giving us their son."

"I don't get it."

"We are going to say that boy is King Leonel. The parents are going to swear to it too. You are going to drug the boy with this," Freath placed a vial with iridescent blue liquid in it on the table in front of Kirin, "and then you'll get word to me . . . so I can behead him." Freath swallowed hard, surprised he could even say it. Whether he could do it remained to be seen.

"What?" Kirin roared.

Freath looked around. They had been left well alone. The innkeeper, knowing they were with the barbarian party, had cleared his inn, poured them each an ale and left. Their isolation suited Freath's purposes. He had fully anticipated a loud argument with Kirin and he certainly didn't want bystanders.

"Stop bellowing. If Stracker or one of his men overhears this, all is lost. Listen, Kirin, this way we relinquish only up to thirty-four lives at worst. If I don't try this we'll lose scores across this realm alone. If you help me I can try and stop the killing before it goes much further. The Dole family lives on the fringe of the forest. It will sound plausible that Leonel was found there."

"But the child . . ." Kirin bleated, all the fight gone out of him.

"I know, I know," Freath soothed. "But his life is forfeit already. With his death he will save countless others—and he'll also protect our king."

"How will you convince Loethar that the boy is King Leonel?"

"Not that many people knew Leonel outside of the palace and I took the precaution of removing the only painting we had of him. Loethar might have seen the cross-stitch rendition that the queen made for her bed cushion but really all that gives Loethar—if he's seen it—is a very rough likeness. The queen used to have a pendant that had a very good likeness of Leonel painted on it but she told me she'd lost that many moons ago." He frowned, recalling her sadness at her carelessness. "Anyway, providing Tomas Dole is sandy haired, or golden haired . . . fair, in other words, we can pull this off. If he has dark hair, we don't go ahead and we try again with a new family. I have another marked as a potential just in case."

"This is so thin, Freath. It won't work."

"You're the one demanding I try to stop the killing. I am trying."

"And if we fail?"

"Then we go to our deaths knowing we did all we could to preserve the Valisar line, and that we risked all to stop the taking of innocent lives. Remember, Loethar just wants Leonel's death. He doesn't care about these boys. I'm sure he'd prefer not to be taking this action—not because he's squeamish or feels anything for these people, but because it's a nuisance. He wants to get on with ruling and to do that he needs the Set people compliant. This killing spree will set his timing back. So if we give him what he believes is the king's head, he's going to be content and the killing will stop. So will the hunt for our king. We just have to be convincing."

"Who knows of this plan?"

"Everyone who needs to. Most of the palace staff died in the initial storming of Brighthelm. Loethar has been running the palace on very few staff, as you know. The ones who matter, who come into contact with Loethar, I have on our side. They know about this plan and will support the false identity."

Kirin pushed his chair back and stood. The chair fell over in a loud clatter but Freath waited for the man of magic to reach his decision. He had pushed him hard enough. It was up to Kirin now. The Vested began to pace. The silence between them was shattered with the shrieking that they'd managed to drown out with their own talk and anxiety.

Freath glanced out the window and saw a youth's head hacked from his shoulders. The body slumped forward slowly, almost sorrowfully, as Stracker picked up the head and tossed it to a waiting Green. Freath felt the bile rise in his throat as the family's screams rose in unison. He closed his eyes to banish the image as Kirin ran from the room, obviously having witnessed the murder himself. Minutes passed as the heartbreaking wails of men, women and boys rang through the village square. Freath kept his eyes tightly shut, his mind closed to the sounds, even though he knew his ears were hearing them.

He finally heard Kirin return and then a jingle as the Vested picked up the pouch of coins. Opening his eyes, he saw the man wiping his wet lips with his sleeves. He'd been weeping too. He looked sweaty, and understandably shaken. "What will you tell Stracker?" Kirin said coldly.

Freath shrugged. "That I'm using you as a spy. He believes you have weak magical ability—I'm going to tell him we're putting your skills to good use, seeking out who lies."

"Will he believe you?"

"He is immersed in a blood lust, Master Kirin. I don't believe much is registering at all right now. Now go."

"And you?"

"I must go out there and check that only nine boys have been killed. Make this work, Master Kirin. I shall see you in Berch in two days."

* * *

The blindfolds were removed and they were suddenly squinting into daylight. They stood in a small clearing.

"Is it me or is it hard to breathe?" Gavriel wondered, clutching his arm.

"You'll have to get used to it. Some people suffer more than others at this height," Faris said.

Around them enormous trees encircled them in a natural amphitheater. In those trees Leo spotted a remarkable network of timber structures. "You live in the trees?" Leo asked, unable to hide his awe.

Faris nodded. "Gives us a view in all directions. We saw you coming—or should I say blundering—from miles away."

Lily made a sound of exasperation. "Well done," she said sarcastically.

This drew a fleeting grin from Faris. "But you're a good guide, Lily. You took a very direct path."

She folded her arms and looked away from him, pretending to take in her surrounds.

He seemed to enjoy baiting her. "Why don't you go and tend to your lover's wounds while I—"

The three companions protested in unison.

Faris held up a hand and they silenced. "Well, well, that touched a nerve. You can't blame me. You acted very concerned," he said, shrugging at Lily.

Leo's eyes narrowed when he noticed the smirk on Gavriel's mouth. "We travel together," he said, as firmly as he could. "We have no secrets."

"Are you sure about that?" Faris said, glancing across at the other two. "It's best you are attached, Lily, for my men have not seen a woman in several moons."

Leo felt his cheeks burn. He hated himself for being so young and, worse, for realizing his feelings must be obvious even to a stranger.

Lily ignored Faris's barbs. "Why don't you show your king some respect," she demanded.

"Because I'm not yet sure he is the king," Faris answered softly.

"You know he is," Gavriel pressed. "I saw it in your face when he mentioned the sword. No one other than those close to the royals would know its regal name . . . the name only the Valisars use."

Faris pointed to a huge old tree stump. Stools had been placed around it. "Welcome to my dining table," he said. "Oli, get them some food and ale, would you?" He turned back to his guests. "You all look very hungry," he admitted.

"We don't need your food, Faris. The king wants to talk with you," Lily said, scowling.

Faris leaned back and regarded Leo. "So talk."

"What do you want to know first?" Leo asked, glancing at Gavriel.

"We tell him everything. It's why we're here," Gavriel urged. "Go on, start from the beginning, Leo."

He did. He spared the outlaw no detail. He didn't care how it hurt Gavriel to hear his father's death described again, or that his own eyes glistened when he described Brennus's suicide, or that they welled when he told Faris of how his mother perished. But he did not weep—he refused the tears, as he had promised himself he would. He kept talking, his voice steady, getting angrier as his story built. ". . . and Lily agreed to guide us north," he finished.

Silence engulfed them. Lily looked shocked to hear the grisly details they'd tried to spare her. All the while he'd been talking, the outlaws had gathered, sat down quietly and listened to the torrid tale of siege, imprisonment and then audacious escape into the forest.

Faris had sat very still throughout the story, his chin resting on his linked hands, elbows on his knees. Leo knew the outlaw had been watching him very carefully, no doubt looking for signs of deceit. But he had spoken only truth. Now it was up to Faris.

"And what made you think of me?" the outlaw finally said.

Leo shook his head. "I honestly don't know why your name came to mind but it did. I'd heard my father and the legate talking about you often. You were a nuisance to them." Faris nodded, but said nothing. "Not long before we were invaded they'd begun talking about you a lot more often. I was permitted to hear these private discussions, although I did not join in, obviously. But I realize I was paying a lot more attention than I thought. And I suppose if I try and work out why you did come in to my head it's because I figured you have the most to lose by my father's—and thus perhaps my—not being on the throne."

"How so?"

Leo blew out his cheeks, slightly embarrassed. His plan had always been based on the very brave assumption that the outlaws preferred the enemy they knew rather than one they didn't. But now a fresh thought occurred to him. "I believe my father tolerated you. I seem to recall that Regor De Vis offered many times to send men to hunt you down. He always seemed frustrated by my father's reluctance to put the weight of the Penraven army against you."

"Is that so?"

Gavriel nodded. "You're right, Leo. My father used to complain that for all the king's ruthlessness he was surprisingly lenient with the famous outlaw of the north."

Leo regarded Faris, held the hazel-eyed stare. "I think my father—unbelievable though it seems—indulged you."

"But surely we were sworn enemies?" Faris offered softly.

Leo shook his head slowly. "Only publicly. I think privately my father saw you as the opposite. Possibly he even admired you."

"No, Leo," Gavriel broke in. "My father hated that this man stole so much from crown monies. And although the king was generous to all his people, I don't think he would admire any thief."

But finally the piece of the jigsaw Leo had been searching for fitted neatly into place. "You've met my father, haven't you? That's how you have Faeroe. Something was exchanged, a bargain reached. He turned as much of a blind eye to your wicked deeds as possible and in return you've given him something. What is it? What did you give my father?"

"I gave him nothing," Faris replied.

Leo rocked back. "But you admit you've met one another?"

Faris nodded. "Four moons ago."

The man called Oli arrived bearing a large cloth by its four corners which, when he undid it across the tree stump, revealed a small array of food. "No ale, Kilt," he said, "but Tern's bringing some watered wine." Faris nodded. He looked at the newcomers. "Rough fare, I'm afraid, for people used to much finer."

"Is this raw?" Lily asked, picking up a piece of dried meat.

"Cured. We light as few fires as possible," Faris explained. "You'll get used to it," he added, flashing her a tight, brief smile.

Gavriel reached for a hard biscuit instead. "We appreciate this," he said.

Leo had no appetite, even though he knew he'd been hungry not so long ago. "Why did you and my father meet?"

Faris looked over his shoulder. He muttered something to Jewd and the huge man strode away.

"I will explain. But first, tell me about Faeroe."

Leo loved the story attached to the sword and didn't hesitate to re-tell it. "Faeroe belonged to Cormoron, first king of the Valisars. It was said to have been forged by the last of the great Tiranamen weaponmakers of the Canuck Islands. It was forged out of three secret metals and the beautiful design on the hilt was crafted in silver by the smiths of Dornen. I'd love to tell you it has magical abilities, but it is simply a sword. A very beautiful one, of course, that probably claimed many lives down the ages."

"There is a spiritual element attached to it, though," Faris pressed.

"You refer to the snake on the hilt. That represents the mythical serpent-woman who is said to have appeared to Cormoron at Lackmarin on the Stone of Truth."

"Wait!" Gavriel interrupted. "We talked about this not so long ago and you claimed to know little of the ancient story."

Leo felt abashed. "I feel badly about that. It's habit, Gav." He shrugged. "My father taught me everything he knew about Cormoron, everything he'd learned from my grandfather and his father before him. It was meant to be passed privately down the generations. It surprised me that you knew even as much as you did."

"But Corb and I learned it from our father," Gavriel said, looking wounded.

Leo nodded. "I'm sorry, Gav. I didn't know. I was following a promise I'd given the king. Doesn't mean I didn't enjoy talking about it with you, though."

"But now it's all right to tell Faris, Lily, all of these men, I suppose?"

Leo could feel his friend's hurt. This must feel a bit like betrayal after all they'd been through together. He hated secrets but he had been raised in a family of them. "This is a time for sharing. And apparently I'm king now," he said, hoping to lighten the mood, "so I can choose with whom I share it."

Faris stared at them both with a look of mirth. "And?" he said, obviously trying to bring Leo's attention back to the specially wrought hilt on Faeroe. "The serpent?"

Leo had no choice but to ignore Gavriel's glare and continue. "The serpent appeared to Cormoron and accepted his blood oath. The story goes that it granted him the fabled Valisar magic, of which I've never seen any indication in my immediate family."

"But you admit magic is attached to this sword," Faris insisted.

"Only by association," Leo said, a weariness creeping into his voice. "It is a warrior's sword. It kills as it is meant to. It uses no special powers but the skills of the man who wields it. Which is why I find it strange—offensive, even—that you have it strapped to your hip. That sword belongs to me now that my father is dead."

Jewd returned to the group, placing something in Faris's hand.

Lily spoke up. "If it's just a sword, don't worry about it, your highness. You have bigger things with which to concern yourself than what this outlaw has stolen from your father."

"I did not steal the sword," Faris replied, indignation in his tone.

"Then what are you doing with it?" Gavriel demanded. "It's a relic of the Valisars. It belongs to the king and the king sits before you. Do you still refuse to believe he tells the truth?"

"No, I do believe him."

Leo breathed in, relieved.

"What—?" Gavriel said, astonished.

"Well, firstly, you," Faris said, nodding at Gavriel, "look hauntingly like Regor De Vis. There is no question that you are his son. Which of them I can't be sure but I'll take your word as an honorable man that you are the one called Gavriel."

Gavriel looked lost for words. Finally he offered sarcastically, "How generous."

The outlaw's gaze crossed to Leo. "And I know you are the crown prince, yet to be crowned King of Penraven, your majesty, because of this." He dropped a necklace with a locket attached onto the stump.

Leo looked stunned. "That belonged to my mother. She lost it. How did . . . ? Did you steal this?"

Faris shook his head. "I stole nothing but tax money from your father. King Brennus gave me this necklace."

"Why?" Leo remembered how much his mother had grieved over the necklace's loss.

"You do recall what it contains?" Faris tossed it across the stump and Lily picked it up.

"Shall I open it?" she asked Leo tentatively.

"You can," he said, "but I know what's in it. It's a miniature painting of me."

"That's right," Faris acknowledged. "Created by the great Claudeo himself, if I'm not mistaken. Although how he got a small child to sit still for long enough is beyond me."

"Bribery," Leo said. "So my father allowed my mother to believe she'd lost her precious locket but instead stole it from her grooming table to give it to you. Why?"

"Isn't it obvious?" Faris asked. "He wanted to make sure that I had a likeness of his precious Leonel, for when the boy came looking for me."

That comment provoked a fresh taut silence as the three newcomers digested the import of that information.

"He knew I'd come?" Leo finally said, his words clipped, his tone a mixture of anger and astonishment.

Faris nodded. "Though only if it became too dangerous at the palace, he told me."

Leo turned to Gavriel. It seemed unthinkable that his father had been second-guessing them long before their trauma had even begun. Four moons, Faris had said. How could the former king have possibly known what would happen or how they'd react?

"I can imagine what you're thinking," Faris said. "If it's any consolation your father said he could only hope you'd think it through and choose to flee here. He was never sure that you would."

"So Faeroe was the exchange?" Leo asked, feeling distraught. He didn't know whether to be angry with his father or grateful. "He gave you my sword in return for your help?"

"No." Faris unbuckled the belt and lifted the heavy weapon, placing it before Leo. "He gave this to me for safekeeping, and to give to you when and if you came. He believed you would need it."

Leo felt his world begin to spin. He stared blankly at Faris.

Faris continued. "Your father was a cunning man. He liked to win, was prepared to take risks, but at the same time he also took the time—the careful, planning and thinking time—to outplot his enemies. Leo—may I call you that?" When the young king did not answer he pressed on. "Your father believed that the rumors of an army amassing on the plains was just that. And when that army's tribal warlord marched them into the Set, he firmly believed that the strength of the realms would hold strong. When the first of the realms fell, he decided not to send any more reinforcements but to wager everything he had on Penraven prevailing—and prevailing peaceably. He miscalculated, Leo, and badly. The tribal warlord was never interested in a simple victory. Something very dark motivates him, Leo, something beyond dreams of empire. But your father had considered all eventualities, and took the precaution of setting up a 'pathway,' shall we call it? . . . just for your purpose. His single desire was to preserve his heir, to ensure the Valisar line lived on no matter what occurred. He counted on your seeking me out if he failed, had primed you, in fact, by ensuring you'd heard plenty about the rebel in the north who was enjoying making the crown look like a buffoon." Faris lifted an eyebrow. "No doubt he planted the seed in your mind that I would be happier being an outlaw against the devil I knew than the one I didn't?"

"Who else knew about the meeting?" Leo asked, refusing to meet Faris's eyes, his gaze instead fixed determindedly on the serpent hilt.

"No one. He came in secret. Sent De Vis on some seemingly vital errand and then came here, disguised, with these two items that I am now glad to return to their rightful owner."

Leo shook his head with bafflement. "What did he ask of you?"

"To be a caretaker of these objects. But also that I offer you the protection of anonymity until you are of an age to make a decision regarding your realm, regarding the Set. He told me that if you came to me the invaders would have taken the Set. My job, he said, was to hide you."

"And what do you get out of this, Faris?" Lily asked, clearly unable to stay silent any longer. There was an accusatory edge to her tone.

"I received ongoing amnesty," Faris replied evenly. "Brennus promised he would never punish me. Your father impressed me, Leo. He was courageous coming here, rather daring even making contact with me. I was curious. I couldn't imagine what the King of Penraven could possibly want with the likes of me. And when I learned I tried to convince myself I believed his tale even less. At that time there were only rumblings from the east, rumors that the barbarians were marching toward the Set. Nobody believed that Loethar had either the capacity or fighting knowhow to take one of the realms, let alone all. And Penraven? It was unthinkable. I remember laughing at the king, suggesting that I thought the bargain rather one-sided. Your father didn't care. He said I could keep the sword and sell the necklace should you not turn up within three moons of Brighthelm's fall . . . if it fell. And yet here you are, not so much different from the artist's miniature, just days after the barbarian claimed conquest. You followed the plan much faster than even the king anticipated."

"I'm still surprised he consorted with the enemy," Leo said. From the corner of his eye he saw a youngish man arrive breathlessly, whispering to Jewd. Jewd remained expressionless but listened carefully.

"Not really enemies, majesty," Faris continued without shifting his gaze, although Leo could tell that he too was aware of the runner's arrival. "I was simply someone who didn't follow the law. I have never killed when thieving, I always picked my targets very carefully and if you knew me better you would know that I hardly live the life of a wealthy man."

"Are you saying we should have respect for your deeds, Faris?" Lily said, incredulous.

"Not respect, no. Perhaps understanding," he said softly. "The king certainly could appreciate the benefits of treating me as an ally rather than a foe. I am no enemy to this realm."

Gavriel had clearly tired of the semantics. "So what else did he plan? Is there anything we should know?"

Faris shook his head. "It never stretched beyond the idea that we were to offer sanctuary. Oh, actually there is one more thing," he said, returning his gaze to Leo. "He did specify that I was to take you to Lackmarin. It is not too far from here. He wished you to make your oath, as all Valisar kings must, at the Stone of Truth."

"How long will it take to get there?" Leo asked.

"Two, possibly three days' walk. It depends how fast you're prepared to journey."

Leo nodded. "Good. Let's go."

"Now?" Faris asked. For a second time Leo saw the man caught off guard.

"I'd rather stay on the move. The barbarians are tracking us."

"Have no fear, they'll never find you here. We track better than anyone. Jewd, do you have news for us?"

Jewd nodded. "None of it good. The barbarian is not content to simply hunt the king. He's hoping to flush him out with tricks." Faris frowned, and Leo felt a splinter of ice move through his gut. "He's sent out an edict that every boy over the age of eleven summertides and under thirteen is to be beheaded."

"He's mad!" Lily gasped.

"We've known that since the beginning," Gavriel said, rising to his feet and pacing. "So he's doing this so that the people will have no inducement to hide Leo—are compelled, in fact, to give him up."

"That's about the size of it," Faris agreed. "He's clever, turning the people against their king. It matters not that this is a barbarian order; the people will, without really meaning to, blame the crown."

"They'll think I'm a coward if I don't give myself up," Leo said.

"And he'll kill you the second he lays sight on you if you do," Gavriel warned. "Don't even think about it."

"Surely this is an empty threat?" Lily asked hopefully.

Jewd shook his head. "Our messenger has just come from down in the valleys. The killing's apparently begun; seventeen lads already slaughtered. They're on their way toward Berch."

"I can't let this happen!" Leo said, standing, looking around wildly.

"You can't stop it, majesty," Faris said, irritatingly calm.

"But he could kill hundreds."

"He already has. This is really no different from what he's been wreaking across the entire Set these past moons."

"We're talking about boys! How can you sit there and be so rational?" Lily accused.

"Because someone has to be rational. Someone has to stop our young king making the emotional and ridiculous mistake of believing that giving himself up will appease the barbarian. Loethar will not kill every boy across the Set who fits his age group. Trust me. Something will stop him— but it will not be you," he said to Leo. "You have another path to follow. If you diverge from it, you mock everything your father risked to put it in place." He shrugged. "I watched you struggle to control your emotions when you spoke of how your father died; how that barbarian roasted him and feasted on him in front of your mother."

"Shut up, Faris!" Lily yelled.

"I watched you fight those tears again when you told me how your mother was thrown from her window by her treacherous aide. And how Loethar humiliates your family, parading your simple orphan brother on a leash. Feel the anger, majesty, let it fester. This is the time to feel rage. To walk down and meekly present yourself to Loethar now would be a grave error. Live to fight another day, and to meet Loethar as a man . . . that was your father's plan."

Leo felt the words melt into his mind. *Live to fight another day, as a man.* Faris was right. He nodded, unclenched his fists. "I'm all right, Lily. Come on, Gav, we're going to Lackmarin."

He reached for Faeroe and strapped it on, not bothered that it felt too large for his slim hips and still shortish stature. It made him feel like the king he had become. And when he looked up from buckling on the sword he saw everyone gathered—Gavriel, Lily, Faris and the rest of the outlaws—bowing low.

"Valisar!" they said as they straightened, fists over their hearts.

Gavriel read his thoughts. "It's a start, King Leonel," he murmured grimly.

Twenty-Three

Kirin stabled his horse and half-walked, half-ran toward the Dole cottage. All the way to Berch he had tried to imagine how he might start the conversation that would end in the parents handing over their son to have his head chopped off. Every time he tried to make plans he abandoned them with a mixture of fear and nausea. And still he had pressed on to Berch, knowing that however much he despised what had been asked of him, it was still the only way they might attempt to halt the slaughter of hundreds more.

It seemed news of the terror had arrived before him. The town felt jittery and the streets seemed too quiet. He imagined how many mothers must be trying to pack up families to flee, or were packing food and sending their boys off to try their luck in the forest.

He passed through the town and took the lonely small road that led up toward the forest. It was a bright late summertide's day and he could hear the hum of bees near a hive not far away, and birds chittering happily in the lower woodland. Butterflies flitted among the wildflowers that grew along the road and it felt impossible that all this beauty was about to be shattered. A cottage sat alone on the fringe of the woods, as Freath had predicted, and a woman was standing outside, seemingly waiting for him.

"I know what you're here for," she snarled. "You won't find him."

"Mistress Dole, I'm not who you think I am. But you are right about what I'm here to discuss."

"I don't care who you are. My boy is gone. So hunt him down yourself but you're wasting your time."

Kirin felt as though he carried the weight of the entire Set's despair about his shoulders. As he stood there looking at the defiant expression on the Dole woman's face, he thought of Clovis and his daughter. He knew Clovis would never be free of the horror of that loss. If he could view Leonel in the same context then yes, any pain was worth saving the life of one child. And that was the only way he could view this now because if he thought about Tomas and the lives that still must be lost to save Leonel, he might as well lie down by the side of the road and will himself to death. Freath was right; someone had to fight for Leonel. That boy represented all the innocents of the realm and freedom from Loethar's oppression. Tomas was their chance to staunch the bloodshed, minimize the death count.

He rallied, pulling out the small sack of coins. Freath had been generous—perhaps used all his own resources, although Kirin privately hoped he'd stolen the money from the crown's coffers. A family like this wouldn't see even a quarter of the amount in the sack if they toiled all their lives. And as sick as this whole bargain was making him feel, he prayed that Lo would put the right words into his mouth to allow this mother to see that her doomed son's death could count for something.

He threw the sack and it landed with a heavy chink at her feet. "I have to discuss something very important with you, Mistress Dole. May I come in?"

It was early evening but it was still light and warm. Loethar found her where she said she'd be. He'd taken the precaution of letting men know where he'd be. He looked at the seated woman and the set of her mouth told him droves. "Come on, Piven, let's take our medicine."

The boy's permanent smile did not falter. He hopped alongside him, no doubt, Loethar thought, not understanding the words, just following movement.

"Mother," he began. "I didn't know you were one for appreciating a garden."

"I'm not and you know that, Loethar. I am a woman born and bred of the plains. Look at this, will you! What is all this for?"

He knew her remark was rhetorical but he chose to answer it as though taking her comment seriously. Anything to hold off the inevitable confrontation. "Well, I think if you just consider its sheer beauty and the peace it can bring, you'll understand why the people of the west cultivate them. I—"

"Oh, stop, Loethar. I'm not here to pass the time of day with you in empty banter."

"Then why did you summon me, mother?"

"I'm surprised you came, to tell the truth. Does that ridiculous child-pet have to come with you everywhere?"

He tousled Piven's dark hair, surprising himself with the show of affection. Giving the boy a small push, he undid the leash. Piven seemed to grasp he had some freedom and Loethar watched him wander as far as the herbs. The boy sat down, chewing some fragrant leaves, quietly humming random notes. Loethar sighed, glad that the boy was using his voice, even so tunelessly. He finally turned away from Piven and sat down to face his mother. "I'm here. What is it you wish to speak with me about?"

"You've offered Valya marriage."

"I have."

"Is that wise?"

"Strategically, yes."

"I don't believe you need to do this even for strategic reasons. If you threaten her parents they'll bend over like the plains grasses in the wind."

"They gave us access into the Set."

"Bah! What does that tell you about them?" she said, rising

imperiously. "They could hardly deny you. They are weak and cowardly. At least I can respect Barronel, Dregon— they all fought with valor. You don't have to marry their daughter to have Droste compliant."

"I don't want Droste compliant. I want to make it part of the Set and I gave my word it could be achieved without bloodshed."

She turned away, seemingly disgusted.

"Why are you using a stick?" he asked, noticing only now the gnarled and yet beautifully fashioned walking aide she used.

"My hips ache, if you must know," she said turning. "I found this in the palace." She understood his silence, adding, "We all get old sometime."

"You've always seemed rather invincible to me, mother."

"That Genrie woman found this for me when she noticed me limping."

"I recognize that timber. It's very beautiful."

"I've never seen it before. I remarked on it. She called it weaven."

He nodded. "There's not much in the palace but I have some in my chamber. That was quite thoughtful of her."

"Genrie? I suppose. There's a defiance in that girl but she's efficient."

"You like her?"

"I don't care one way or the other for her. Or any other Penravian, for that matter."

"Freath says I should use her as a taster. He trusts her."

"To do what, though?" The way she loaded her comment with derision made him smile.

"Yes, she could poison me, but I don't think so. The palace staff is too scared of Stracker and the tribes. They know that I am all that stands between order and a lot more heartache for the Set. In this I am their ally. Ironic, don't you think?"

"I still don't think you should trust a westerner. Which is why Valya troubles me."

"Listen, mother, Valya needs me a lot more than I need her."

"Precisely! She's like dead wood around your neck. Marry a woman from the Greens."

He looked at her, exasperated. "We've been down this road before."

"Marrying into the tribes only makes our hold over the Set stronger."

"No, it weakens it. I know you can't see this yet, but I need to produce heirs that look western, are raised in the western way."

She nodded, a grim smile at her lips. "You certainly look the part all of a sudden."

"You always knew I would. Why else did you set me on this path?"

"You know why. This was your only path. Keeping you on the plains would have allowed him to make a mockery of me, of you, of our people. We've made him pay for his ignorance and for his cruelty."

Loethar sighed. He'd heard it all before—all his life, in fact. "Valya is western. Any sons I sire on her will look like they belong. It's my intention that if we rule well, we will be accepted in time. Who's to say a fresh era is not beginning? Gradually as I get to know the families in the other realms we will allow them some say in the running of their realms. Actually—they are to be known as provinces now. There are no more kingdoms in the Set.

"Penraven remains one," Negev contradicted.

He ignored her vindictiveness. "Not for long. The killing has begun. We shall have our Leonel very soon."

"Are you sure about that?"

"Utterly," he said, standing. "The boy is on foot with no food, no money, no weapons from what Valya could see—if indeed she saw him and I have to assume she did. That means he's still in Penraven and although I'm happily threatening all the sons of the Set, I believe he's still very close. And soon no one will want to help him. If he wants his crown, he's going to have to come and get it. Until I'm satisfied—until his head is dropped at my feet—I shall keep killing the boys of his age. Each year I'll kill more either side of his age. Trust me, the people will not stand for it. He will be given up by his own."

"I hope you're right."

"I am."

"When is the wedding ceremony?"

Loethar immediately felt disgruntled. "Valya is organizing it now. Soon. Perhaps you should help her. Try and be friendly. It's in your best interest, mother dear, if you want to see your son and your son's sons rule."

Negev opened her mouth but was interrupted by the young Red, Barc, who, breathing heavily, arrived in the gardens.

"My lord," he said, bowing.

"What is it?"

"We have news, my lord, from a town called Berch. The messenger refuses to give it to anyone but you. He carries it from General Stracker."

"Excuse me, mother. This is important."

"Go . . . go," she urged. "Perhaps your Valisar runt is already found."

He left running with the young Red trotting behind and the old woman limping in their wake.

No one remembered Piven.

"You'd better be sure about this, Freath!"

"General Stracker," the aide said, careful now to always give the man his title, "I think I know the Valisar heir when I see him. It's only been a matter of days since I was last waiting on him."

The head of Tomas Dole had been put into a separate sack in the cart, which would carry all the heads of the twenty-nine boys slaughtered in Stracker's killing spree. Upon arriving in the town of Berch, Freath had known the ruse was on when Kirin gave a grave, surreptitious nod the moment Freath had alighted from his horse on arrival. He had immediately gone to Stracker, explaining that his plan to use magic ahead of the soldiers had worked and that he believed his Vested had hunted down a potential impostor.

He had outlined to Stracker that the boy had tried to blend in with the Dole family. They'd taken him in, not knowing he was anything but a stray child who had wandered into their lives only the previous day from the forest. It had helped immeasurably that a quivering Mistress Dole had hesitantly explained this just minutes earlier, through sobs to both Freath and Stracker.

Stracker had mercifully not been interested in her or the rest of her family and she'd been pushed aside as he had stomped toward the boy in question. Fair haired, grimy-looking and scrawny, the child had been glassy-eyed.

"What's wrong with him?" Stracker had demanded.

Freath had shrugged. "I have no idea. He's terrified, I should imagine. Think about what he's been through since you took rule. Both his parents are dead and he's been living in the forest with no food."

"What about De Vis?"

Again Freath had shrugged. It was right now that the whole ruse could come crashing down around them. If he couldn't convince Stracker, there was a good chance he wouldn't even leave this town alive, let alone bring the ploy to Loethar. "That is Leonel," he had pressed.

"Why doesn't he recognize you?"

"I don't think the child can recognize anyone. Look at him. He's lost his wits."

Stracker had given orders to send a message to the palace.

"I think you should behead him now," Freath had urged. He certainly hadn't wanted Tomas Dole being taken back to the palace whole.

Stracker frowned. "Loethar should know we may have found him."

"*May* have?" Freath queried, aghast. "If you don't mind my saying so, I think you should beat the messengers back to Brighthelm in order to present that boy's head to your brother. You have succeeded far more quickly than he could have imagined. I anticipate much celebration on his part."

Stracker had advanced on him. "Why are you so eager for more blood? You're a coward most of the time, lurking behind closed doors."

Freath had forced himself to hold his nerve. "I never claimed to have the constitution of one of your warriors, general. I admit, apart from that moment of blood rage against the queen, I am weak of belly for this sort of thing. I am not so much eager for more blood as for the ending of it. We can return to Penraven triumphant. Your efforts mean your brother can sit his emperor's throne without any further threat from the Valisar line, which ends with this child."

He had watched Stracker think this through. He had carefully chosen his words in order to preen Stracker's feathers more than his brother's. Pressing, he added, "How soon before the messenger reaches the palace?"

"We use the chain," Stracker had said cryptically.

"I don't understand."

Stracker had sneered. "Do you remember my leaving my men along the way at strategic points?"

"Yes. I thought they were simply on guard."

The huge warrior had laughed, his tatua twisting on his face. "For what?"

"I have no idea. I don't understand soldiering. I am a palace aide."

"We leave these men so that messages can be delivered down the chain far more quickly than if one rider was sent to cover the entire distance. This way men are always fresh, horses never tired. Loethar will know about this before dusk if the riders go hard."

"Then let the next message say that you are bringing the head of Leonel Valisar home."

Freath had desperately needed Tomas killed first before

any of the townsfolk heard of it and could claim he was anything but a Valisar. Fortunately, fear of the barbarians had worked to his advantage. The streets had been deserted when Stracker's party had thundered into town, on Freath's advice riding straight up to the cottage.

"Maybe I don't want to stop, Freath," Stracker had said, a sinister note in his tone.

"That's up to you, general," Freath had replied nonchalantly, despite the flare of anxiety that had shot through him. "I was sent along to ensure that the right boys were selected according to the census. When this boy has been dealt with, my job will be done and I will return to the palace and let my superior know everything that I do."

"I hope you're not threatening me, Freath?"

Freath pasted an expression of dismay on his face. "I wouldn't dare. Your brother gave me orders to return once this job was done. As far as I'm concerned, it's done. I'm frightened of both of you. I don't plan to let either of you down. Shall we get this done before the women start their inevitable wailing?"

"I rather like it when they carry on. This town's a bit quiet for me."

"These people knew we were coming. I think they're in shock. Also, she's got her own brood to think of." He had made a great show of consulting his paperwork. "Nine, all younger than this one," he lied.

Stracker had become tired of the talk. "Get the boy," he had said to one of his leering men.

Freath had spoken too soon. A loud keening had issued from the cottage and he had felt his very soul darken at its sound.

Valya had stepped back with surprise as the door she had knocked at had suddenly been flung wide. "Sorry to disappoint you," she said, frowning. "Who did you think I was?"

Loethar paced. "I shouldn't have imagined it was my

half-brother. He couldn't have got back already and he doesn't know how to knock on a door anyway," he said, tightly.

"Why do you await Stracker so anxiously?" she asked, moving into the salon.

"Because, Valya, he has hunted down my prey."

She had been moving toward the tapestry cord to ring for a servant but turned rapidly. "Truly?"

"That's not something I would jest about," he replied.

"That was fast."

"Yes, much quicker than I'd anticipated. Clearly Penraven has no stomach for fighting or bloodshed. They train and parade armies with such pomp and yet cower into submission when real threat comes along."

Valya privately thought that the Set armies had actually put up a good fight. It was just that they were simply no match for the bloodlust of the barbarians, who were bred tough on the Likurian Steppes. She knew the only reason she'd survived as long as she had was because of Loethar's indulgence and the allowances he made for her. Which was probably another reason Negev hated her so much, come to think of it.

"Well, you've destroyed their armies and their leaders as well as their weapons. They have no means to fight, no line of command to lead."

"No barbarian warrior horde would let that stop them."

Valya abruptly changed the subject. "Anyway, you've had word from Stracker."

"I gather one of the Vested was put to good use in teasing out a liar in a nearby town. Once his magic had isolated them, Freath apparently noted a discrepancy in the number of children attached to one particular family and once he saw them he found it very easy to pick out Valisar."

"But so soon?"

"He couldn't have gone very far without supplies, without help, without a horse."

"Where was he found?"

"A town called Berch. He'd probably flanked the main villages and then found this place to come out of hiding—no doubt for food. He wouldn't know how to hunt or trap his own," he said with a sneer.

"And they're sure this boy is the Valisar?"

"I have to assume so, Valya. Do you really think Stracker would get my hopes up if he weren't certain?"

"No, but—"

"Freath recognized the boy instantly."

"And they've already killed him?"

"Ah, that I can't say. Stracker may decide to bring him back so I can gut him myself, but he may have been beheaded when Freath recognized him."

"You're placing a lot of faith in the Valisar aide," Valya said, brushing aside her golden hair.

"Not really."

She held her tongue. She didn't want to anger Loethar by being deliberately contrary but she didn't trust Freath an inch. In fairness, she couldn't imagine what he had to gain from killing the queen, for instance—and so callously. "I've noticed Freath and that maid are quite thick with each other."

"Is that important?"

"They're both servants of the Valisars."

"Former servants," he corrected. "Both were happy to swap loyalties."

"You said that the woman openly defied you."

"She did, but she also wants to live. Especially since Freath told me who her family is. She has been told that if she gives us any trouble, they will die. She has given me no cause for concern. Has she done anything that worries you?"

"No, but—"

"Fret not, Valya. I am suspicious enough for both of us. The servant woman is running this palace almost single-handedly and doing a good job. We need her in place until others arrive. Now what is it you wanted to see me about?"

She had been naïve to believe Loethar would suddenly lose his brusque manner with her simply because she had agreed to be his wife. "Well, I thought you might like me to share your bed tonight, my love. Also I'd hoped you might have told your mother about our betrothal."

"I have told her. She is going to offer her assistance, I'm sure. As to my bed, by all means. I aim to be celebrating the end of the Valisar line tonight."

Why did it always sound as though he was granting her a favor? Smiling graciously, she hid her anger. "I shall look forward to it, my love."

"Leave me now, Valya. I need time to myself to think."

"This must be the first time in a long time you'll be alone," she said tartly as she moved toward the door.

"Vyk will be back. He's simply getting used to his surrounds. He finds the forest irresistible."

"I wasn't referring to that bird of yours. I meant the lunatic child you're so close to."

Valya couldn't imagine what she'd said that so dismayed Loethar but suddenly he pushed past her out of the chamber and, face pinched, actually ran away from her down the corridor.

Piven had been attracted by a familiar sound. He had been chewing the sweet scented leaves of kellet. The fragrance had penetrated through to his strange world, reminding him of the woman who had lavished him with attention. She had chewed kellet and so now he copied her. It made him smile. Where were the others? They had talked, then left. He didn't care. It was warm here. He might lie down among the kellet and its companions for a while.

But a sound had nagged at him. It was the one sound he could concentrate on. Most other sounds were simply noises but this one had resonance, this one seemed to make sense in the chaos of his mind, instantly calming him. And now the sound was calling to him.

He couldn't see the voice. Standing, he instinctively moved toward the sound. Soon enough he arrived at the forest edge.

Piven was pleased by the soft sun rays leaking through the

leaves of the trees. The big black bird was perched on the low branch of the beech tree beneath which Piven stood. He smiled at the bird. The raven stopped its curious chuckling and flew down to settle on the shoulder of the man who also waited.

"And you must be Piven," the stranger said.

Piven liked the gentle voice and, more importantly, trusted the bird.

"Come, Piven. You no longer need that collar," the man said, undoing the buckle of the collar that the little boy had been wearing since Loethar had put it on him.

Piven scratched absently at the red mark that the collar had left.

"And we must find you a fresh shirt," he said, pointing to the bloodstains on the little boy's chest. The man opened his palm, offering it to Piven before taking his hand. Piven liked the way his own fitted into that huge, strange hand. Its grip around him felt warm and dry and safe. The sensation prompted another distant memory of another man. A man he had spent much time with, who seemed to love the woman who chewed kellet. That man had hugged him almost as much as she did. He couldn't even remember the man's face but he recalled it was bearded and kind. And he could hear the man's voice in his mind—gruff with most but tender with him. Where was that man now? Where was the woman? There was another one he liked a great deal but that memory was gone, the hole filled by the numbers and patterns and the pictures he saw in his mind. Everything was a distinct shape. He could remember shapes. And here was a new shape that he walked next to. He liked the rough feel of the man's robe now against his cheek and at Vyk's encouraging caw he skipped off beside the man, beneath the canopy of the beech trees, the sunlight warm and inviting, creating a halo of light guiding them toward the darkening depths of the forest.

Piven did not see the bird pick up the collar in his beak and fly in the opposite direction.

Twenty-Four

Dusk had given way to twilight by the time Stracker's men thundered beneath the gates of Brighthelm but Loethar was standing on the palace steps grimly awaiting them.

"Do you need me?" Kirin asked.

Freath shook his head. "If you see Genrie or Father Briar, let them know. But be very sure not to be seen talking to them. A simple nod will do. They know what we've been doing."

"Why do I have the feeling the worst is yet to come?"

"Because it is. Stracker is not stupid but he's single-minded, driven by more visceral needs. His half-brother's mind is far more fluid. It flows into the crevices that Stracker's never could. Be careful, Kirin."

"You too," the Vested said, drifting away from the main group.

Freath waited, deliberately making himself inconspicuous in the chaos of all the horses and men dismounting. Stracker finally found him. Catching his eye, the barbarian called, "Come on! He's like a cat with its tail on fire."

Somehow Freath was sure Stracker knew what a cat with its tail on fire looked like. He followed the huge man.

"Is it true?" Loethar said, meeting them at the bottom of the steps. He looked directly at Freath.

Freath forbade himself to swallow the lump of fear that threatened in his throat. "Yes, my lord," he said somberly, but not without satisfaction. "We have brought you back the head of Leonel of Penraven."

"How many did it take?" Loethar demanded of his half-brother.

"I wasn't counting," Stracker admitted.

"Er, twenty-nine, my lord," Freath answered. "I have the record if you—"

"No, that's fine. Twenty-nine. Not many."

Stracker shrugged. "It wouldn't have bothered me if it was twenty-nine hundred."

Loethar gave a tight, mirthless smile. "Bring them all," he answered.

"All, sire?" Freath repeated, hardly able to breathe.

"All," Loethar confirmed. "But, Freath, you carry Valisar. And follow me directly." He turned and marched away.

Stracker smiled at Freath. "He's not in a very good mood."

Freath said nothing but moved toward the cart to pick out the single bloodied sack that carried the head of Tomas Dole.

Freath found himself gathered with all of his enemies in the king's salon. He imagined, with a sour tang forming in his mouth, that Loethar was going to make something of a show of his proud achievement. He stared at the two sacks on the floor, one—the heaviest—still wet with oozing blood. It had taken two men to carry that one in. The other, which Freath had placed on the flagstones, had only a large stain of dried blood on its exterior to show for Tomas's cruel end.

He stood quietly in the shadows as Dara Negev, Princess Valya and General Stracker arrived. Finally Masters Kirin and Clovis were ushered in. He had hoped they would be spared this grisly scene but he now had to trust them to be of stout heart. He ignored their downcast looks of anxiety.

The emperor, Freath noted, was twitchy. He was definitely angry about something. Surely their ruse had not been discovered?

Loethar offered him a goblet of wine.

"No, but thank you, my lord. It's been a day that has set

my belly on edge, to tell the truth. I could not eat or drink a thing."

"Not up to the life of a barbarian warrior, eh, Freath?" Valya said, arriving by the side of her husband-to-be.

"No, Princess Valya. I'm afraid I never aspired to either barbarian or warrior. I am a dreadful coward and hideously squeamish."

"Oh, I don't know," Stracker joined in. "You've killed a queen and you seemed to cope rather well during the death of her son at Berch."

"Ah, well, the first was driven by years of rage and I was happy to get my hands dirty. And the second—well, that was one death I did want to witness," Freath said, grinning falsely. "When the Valisar head rolled, I admit I felt only elation."

"We'll make a barbarian of you yet, then, Freath," Loethar quipped. "So why don't you show me young Leonel."

"Of course, my lord," Freath said, approaching the sack once again. He hoped this was the last time he would have to look upon the sad face of Tomas Dole, who mercifully had gone quietly. The drug had worked well, keeping him vacant and oblivious. It wasn't hard to paste a look of disgust on his face as he reached into the sack and lifted out the head of the child. Surprised by its weight, he held it up by the hair for Loethar to admire.

"So this is him. My nemesis."

"This is Leonel, the former heir to the Crown of Penraven, yes, my lord," Freath said, appropriately grave though with a hint of triumph.

"Of course none of us would know if this were not the boy," Loethar said, looking at the others.

"I can assure you, my lord," Freath replied as evenly as he could as a cold trickle of fear ran down his back, "this is Leonel."

"We are to take your word alone, Freath?" Valya said.

"I've looked right around the palace. There is no painting of the child or likeness of any sort other than this," Dara

Negev added, reaching behind a chair to pick up Iselda's cushion, which she threw down at Freath's feet.

Loethar cocked his head and in a careful show went through the theatrics of studying the embroidery, then regarding the head that suddenly felt twice as heavy in Freath's hand. Finally Loethar looked around at everyone with a softly quizzical expression, although Freath believed it to be feigned. "Well, it does resemble him, I suppose."

"But that's about all we could say," Valya countered. "There is a vague likeness. We have only this former Valisar aide to confirm the match."

Dara Negev looked around in a slightly exaggerated fashion. "Surely there are other servants who can confirm who the head belongs to."

"Good idea, mother," Loethar said. "Of course, the two Vested belong to Master Freath and neither of you would know Leonel of Valisar, would you?"

Kirin and Cloris both looked dismayed to be addressed. They shook their heads as one, but then Kirin spoke up. "I was able to help only in locating what I thought was a lie, my lord. And even that almost eluded me. I'm afraid my powers are weak," he said, much to Freath's relief.

"I have never seen any of the royals," Clovis admitted, refusing to meet anyone's eyes.

"Why don't you both stand over there?" Loethar said, pointing to the end of the room.

They both obliged. Freath felt a fresh thrill of fear. Loethar was up to something.

"Good. Stracker, why don't you pick out, oh, let's say three other heads that resemble Valisar."

Freath watched, numb with escalating fear, as the half-brother grinned and went about his grisly business.

"Shall I take that head for you?" Loethar offered and Freath gladly relinquished it. "And perhaps you'll want that wine now, Master Freath?"

"Perhaps I will, my lord," Freath acknowledged, realizing

he had been dismissed. "Do you wish me to stay in the room?"

"Of course," Loethar replied. "In fact, I insist. I've asked your Vested to be here because one of them was helpful in hunting down Valisar. The other is here mainly to keep your trio complete."

Reading between the lines, Freath realized having Kirin and Clovis present was more like keeping them all together as prisoners than granting them the privilege of attending. Freath moved back to one of the windows. The evening air was a welcome blessing for suddenly the room felt unnaturally warm, his hands horribly clammy. Loethar's test would soon prove him to be the liar he was and he began to imagine what his blood would look like spilling onto the flagstones onto which his king's blood had spilled just days ago. If he looked hard enough he could still make out where the stain of it had not been fully scrubbed clean.

"Right, let's line them up, shall we?" Loethar said, the same flash of brightness to his voice that made Freath hate him all the more. He sent a wish to Lo that wherever Leonel was, Lo grant him the years to evade this barbarian and then one day kill him.

"I think we're ready," Loethar said to those assembled.

"What is this charade, son?" his mother queried.

So, Freath thought, he has told no one of his plans. Loethar was certainly an island of a man.

"Wait, mother, you'll see." He walked to the door and spoke to someone who was obviously waiting behind it. "Just a moment or two," he said to everyone. "Ah, here we are."

Genrie was led into the room by one of the warriors of the Greens. To her credit she did not search out Freath, though she looked frightened. "Yes, my lord?"

"Genrie, we meet again. You won't be so defiant this time, perhaps?"

"No, my lord." Her gaze kept flicking to the heads lined up. Unable to hold her nausea any longer, she began to dry retch.

"Calm now, Genrie. I need you to do something for me," Loethar soothed.

Freath knew they were lost. Poor Genrie. He could see on her face that she too knew their ruse was up.

Breaking the spell of the moment was a flap of wings as Vyk returned to his perch.

"At last!" Loethar admonished his pet. "There, you see, I said he'd return," he said to the group, as though everyone had been fretting over the raven's disappearance. "Now, Genrie, can you hold down your bile just a moment for us?"

She nodded, fearful. Freath noted that Valya's gaze was hard and glittering, clearly lapping up the opportunity to watch the young woman suffer and not at all perturbed by the sagging faces of the decapitated heads. A very hard and cruel heart must beat beneath that golden-haired, pale-skinned beauty, Freath thought. Turning from her, he felt his own heart go out to Genrie as she nodded in answer to Loethar's question.

"Good. It's very simple, Genrie. I want you to point out to me—touch it, in fact, so none of us are left uncertain—which is the head of Leonel, son of Brennus. They all look very similar so to avoid confusion, we're asking you to identify him. Very few people are left in the palace who know him. Master Freath has already kindly and very firmly made it clear which is the head of Leonel so if you'd oblige, it will end all doubt." He gave her a soft push. "Go ahead."

Freath felt only admiration that Genrie did not search out his face for a sign. Instead she lifted her chin, gathered her composure bravely and stepped forward. He could see her swallowing her disgust. Glancing over at Kirin and Clovis, he noted that Clovis was haggard with despair, no doubt recalling his own child's decapitation. Kirin simply looked glazed. Freath understood, looking away, down to the ground. He could no longer watch this.

"Must I touch it, my lord?" Genrie asked, her voice barely above a whisper. She seemed to be swaying slightly, as if dizzy. Freath couldn't blame her. He couldn't help her, either. He returned his gaze to the ground.

"Make it quick, Genrie, then it's over for you," Loethar said tightly and Freath heard only the true threat behind those words. Both their lives were forfeit, he realized.

He sensed rather than watched her move closer to the grisly lineup and held his breath, at the last moment deciding he owed it to Genrie to be fully with her in this terrible trial. Raising his chin, he gritted his teeth and clenched his fists to steady himself. He watched Genrie move before the heads, could see her body trembling as she raised a shaking arm. It was moving toward the second from the left. The wrong one. Of course it was wrong. They were all wrong. He felt a pit in his stomach open up as her forefinger pointed to the boy. He couldn't remember his name. Didn't want to.

Genrie staggered and shook her head. When she steadied herself, she seemed to change her mind. "This one," she said, pointing at the fourth head.

Freath was sure his heart stopped. She'd picked Tomas Dole.

"You're sure, now?" Loethar urged.

Genrie nodded. "I'm sorry, my lord, I couldn't concentrate at first. The heads . . . they—"

"We understand," Loethar said, although it was obvious no one from his party was in any way moved by the pathetic sight of the remains of the boys. "You may go."

She curtsied and fled from the room without looking at Freath.

"Well, Freath," Loethar said, "it seems you have indeed found whom we seek."

It took every ounce of Freath's willpower to keep his voice steady, his expression calm. "I never doubted it, my lord. I have known the child since he was born."

"Could he have told her somehow, Loethar?" Valya challenged quietly, cunning in her voice.

"I didn't permit him to speak or see anyone. He came here with me from the bailey."

Valya shrugged.

"Be sure, my son," Dara Negev spoke up.

Loethar nodded. "Just one more confirmation, Freath, if you don't mind." The barbarian's words were like a smothering blanket on the flames of Freath's elation. "We need to be absolutely certain, you understand?"

"Of course," Freath acknowledged graciously, as if Loethar should call for a dozen affirmations if that is what would put his mind at rest. He retreated another step, his heart pounding.

"Call in Father Briar—but first, change the order of the heads."

It was done and then a visibly shaking Father Briar was brought in. He spun away the moment he caught sight of the ghoulish parade. "Lo forgive me, I cannot. Why am I here?" he beseeched.

"This is hard for you, I understand, Father Briar, but you are one of only a few in the palace who knew the Valisar heir. We need to identify him."

Briar hadn't turned around. Freath suspected that if the warrior who'd brought him in had not been holding him upright, the man of Lo would be on his knees, sobbing. His cheeks were wet with tears. "These are children. Surely, my lord?"

Loethar looked at him in silent enquiry.

"We are conquered. Right across the Set our armies are broken. Those of us who still live must accept your rule, my lord . . . and do. The spirit of the people is shattered. It's time for peace to ease the collective heart of the Set. That is what I will preach when once again I have a congregation, my lord; I will tell them to embrace your sovereignty, to forge a new empire under your leadership."

"That gladdens my heart, Father Briar," Loethar said. Freath knew the priest was too far gone in his fear, and desire to make some impact on the barbarian, to hear the irony in Loethar's tone. "But right now I need your assistance. I want you to face the four heads behind you and I need you to pick out for me the one that belongs to Leonel of Valisar."

Father Briar began to shake even more. "Please do not ask this of me, my lord. I cannot."

"You must, Father Briar. I insist, or the killing can't stop. If you do not identify Leonel, I will kill every eleven-, twelve- and thirteen-year-old across the Set and I will lay their heads at your feet. You alone have the power to prevent this additional slaughter. Now Freath here has told me that I have the head of Leonel. I want you to affirm it by showing me which one you recognize. I know you knew the boy well."

The tension in the room had risen dramatically. Even the cool evening breeze could not temper the oppressive warmth around them all. Freath could see the old woman and Valya entranced by this theater, whereas Stracker looked ready to draw a sword and hack the babbling priest to bits.

Mercifully Father Briar did gather himself together, finding the courage to turn. He allowed a soft sob to escape when he finally laid eyes on the sad sight before him, and as if on cue, one of the propped heads toppled to the side. Father Briar flinched, a low shriek escaping him.

"We'll just right this one for you," Loethar said matter-of-factly, grabbing the hair and pulling the head straight to lean up against the sideboard on which they'd been placed.

The room went silent.

Father Briar took a shallow breath. "I feel sick, dizzy . . . I'm sorry, I—"

"Quickly, Father Briar. The sooner you do this for us, the sooner we can work out what happens next," Loethar said briskly.

Again, Freath heard the undertow of threat in the barbarian's words. His own breathing had become ragged. He wondered if his own tired heart was giving up. It felt set to burst from his chest, it was pounding so hard. Though he wanted to look away, he forced himself to fix his eyes on the priest, who had one hand on his chest and was raising the other in a shaking arc. His finger pointed but from Freath's vantage he couldn't tell which head had been chosen.

"Touch the head, Father. We must be sure," Loethar urged. "You are too far away. Hurry up; I tire of your squeamishness."

Father Briar staggered three steps and placed a hand, as though giving a blessing, on the third head—the head of Tomas Dole. "This is Leonel," he said, turning abruptly to vomit into the corner.

"Well done, Father. Let us all retire to another chamber," Loethar said. "Freath, perhaps you could have this one cleaned. Father Briar, you're free to go once you have gathered your wits. As are you, as well," he added, sweeping his gaze across the Vested. "Freath, please come and see me afterward. Thank you for your work today. I'm impressed."

Freath nodded graciously. "I'm glad to have proven myself worthy to you, my lord," he replied, resisting a desire to draw his own shaking hand across his brow.

The barbarians left hurriedly. How Freath kept his own composure he didn't know but he managed to put one step in front of the other, guiding everyone out of the stinking salon. Closing the door on their backs, he allowed himself a moment of impossible triumph combined with startling disbelief. Father Briar was trying to say prayers for the children, his words at war with his grief. Freath began to move toward the priest in an effort of consolation.

"Freath!" Clovis called, soft but urgent.

Freath turned to see Kirin collapsed on the floor.

Twenty-Five

The six of them had been walking for hours in silence. The path they'd been following was narrow, well disguised and certainly not conducive to conversation. Everyone seemed lost in thought, but no one was fatigued. Gavriel realized that he was suddenly invigorated, likely due to the fresh sense of purpose.

The tunnel-like animal track they'd been following opened up and although the single lamp that lit their way meant that they still had to walk carefully, they now had more space to spread out.

This prompted Leo to talk. "Tell me more about the meeting with my father," he said to Faris.

"What's to tell? It was a shock. But I knew he was no impostor, having seen your father many times without him realizing he was sometimes close enough to touch his most gifted thief." Faris laughed. "He was as good as his word and had come alone. We'd followed him for many miles, seen his arrival—just as we'd seen yours—for a long distance."

"How did he know where to find you?"

Faris shrugged. "Followed his nose in much the same way as Lily did hers. I know the rumor-mongering says my gang is in the north but it's a huge area. No one really knows where we are. The truth is, we found him, in the same manner that we found you."

"And he just pronounced that he had a bargain to make with you?"

"That's about right. He wasn't scared of me. But then I was hardly scared of him either, considering he had so many arrows trained on his chest. He was extremely confident. I genuinely thought he'd come to work out a deal whereby I stopped stealing taxes and he might turn a blind eye to the odd wealthy merchant being robbed on the highway. I must admit, his lack of interest regarding his own money was refreshing and his real reason for coming intriguing."

"It's incredible that he was planning for this eventuality so far ahead," Gavriel said. "Even more surprising that he kept my father at arm's length on it."

"Gavriel is now legate, by the way," Leo said. "Some day he will command the Penraven army."

"Right now, my king, there is no army to speak of. I have seen what the barbarians have done. All the Set armies are decimated; bodies still scatter your realm and the blood is yet to dry across the fields and the villages. People are still to bury stranger and foe alike before they can even mourn their own lost. The whole region is in turmoil—on its knees to Loethar, you could say. I imagine it will be years before a generation of boys grows up without memories of this bloodshed." He glanced at Gavriel. "I hate to pour water on your fire."

"Don't dash their hopes, Kilt Faris." Lily spoke up. "These two young men *are* our future. We have a king. Your men are the army that will rise from the ashes of the barbarian destruction."

Faris stopped. "Er, let me stop you there. I have nothing to do with uprising, rebellion or thoughts of re-creating the splendor of the Valisar dynasty." He took them all into his gaze and Gavriel could see he wanted none of them to get any mistaken impressions of his motivations.

"This is about money, is it?" Gavriel said.

"I am not Brennus. He had reason to preserve his line. My reasons are quite different but no more selfish than his. Let me say this. King Brennus visited me purely out of self-interest. This was not about you personally, Leo, though I hate to say it. No matter how much your father loved you, this was as much about greed for him too."

"Now wait a—"

"No, let him finish, Gav," Leo said, holding up a hand. "It's best we all understand one another."

"Thank you, majesty," Faris said. "This seems as good a place as any to rest momentarily. Jewd, check that all is safe, would you? Tern, follow suit." As the men loped off, Faris returned his attention to Leo, Gavriel and Lily. "We've made very good time. You certainly seem very committed and determined. I think it's wise we have this conversation now."

"Go ahead," Leo said. Gavriel realized that the youngster he had become nursemaid to just days previous had already aged years. *And it will need to continue if we're going to survive*, he thought grimly. Most importantly, Leo seemed ready to hear the truth . . . the secret that had been entrusted to Gavriel by Brennus. He would tell him as soon as they were alone.

"Your father had the preparedness to look into the future," Faris was saying. "He took note of the angry wind blowing from the east, and he moved to protect his most valuable possession. It was not his realm's gold, it was not his city, it was not his people, it wasn't even you, Leo . . . or your family." Gavriel watched the young king's lips thin at this. "It was something far less tangible than any of those possessions. The single most important aspect of Penraven life to your father was the name Valisar, and the fact that a Valisar had sat the throne, and was figurehead for the whole Set, for so many centuries. He was determined the dynasty would not end with him. And so, for very selfish reasons that had nothing to do with self-preservation, he came to see me. He did love you—of this there is no doubt—but he loved his heritage, his history, his whole reason for being and his sense of duty much, much more, Leo. And because he had produced an heir he was not going to relinquish the right to put the 9th king of Valisar on the throne. Brennus aimed to pass crown, sword and throne—everything that was won by Cormoron all those centuries ago—to you, Leo. You see, he was equally as selfish as you accuse me of being."

Leo regarded Faris gravely. "You want to see my father's approach as purely one of self-interest. I prefer to think of it as his desire for the realm—for the good of the people."

Faris didn't bat an eyelid at the youngster's admonishment. "Life is very much from the perspective from where you view it. However, Brennus knew the might of the barbarian's driving need to conquer, and he decided he needed time. Time for his next child to be born, time for a bargain to be struck to preserve the life of his heir, time to organize a plan. The blood of the other realms bought him that time."

Leo stood, disgusted. "This is rubbish, Faris. I won't hear another word spoken against my father like this."

"Why would I lie?" Faris replied. "Brennus admitted that the Set could not win the war unless everyone banded together. He said—and this is no lie, I give you my oath—that he had to make an ugly choice between saving the Valisar crown and saving the Set, reasoning that the chances of Leonel's survival—with the right help—were better than the Set's chances against the marauders."

"Do you honestly believe, Faris, that the king would not have aired this plan—this 'ugly decision,' as you call it—to his closest friend, companion, adviser and commander of his army?"

"I'm telling you that's exactly what he did." Gavriel glared at him as Faris continued. "I'm sorry if I'm hurting anyone's feelings here but I speak only truth. The king came here in disguise, having deliberately slipped away not only from Brighthelm but from his legate. He meant to keep his decision secret. I was the only person he shared it with."

"You know how ridiculous that sounds, don't you?" Gavriel replied, getting up and readying himself to leave. He'd had enough of this conversation and hated to think of what it might be doing to Leo's fragile state of mind. "Why would the king tell a renowned thief—an outlaw—his darkest secret?"

"Because it was safe with me. Because it meant nothing to me and he needed an ally. Don't you see? I had no reason to use it against him. Affairs of the realm are of no interest to my sort. What's more, he believed that if his plan needed to be activated it would mean that everyone who mattered, including himself, was already dead. And as you say, I'm the last person anyone would think of as an accomplice to the king." He turned around, spoke directly to Leo. "Your majesty?"

"Call me Leo," the king said.

"Do you still believe I'm making this all up?"

"I know you're not," Leo replied, surprising Gavriel. "This sounds exactly how my father's mind works. He would not have given you Faeroe, I'm sure, without reaching an agreement with you."

"Thank you," Faris said, eyeing Gavriel. "Shall we go?" At his soft whistle, his men melted out of the darkened woodland. They nodded to him. Jewd nodded to Faris, who pronounced, "All's quiet and safe. We can proceed."

"I hope that's the last of your surprises," Lily muttered as she pushed past Faris.

"Who said he told me only one secret?" Faris quipped but no one appreciated his jest and his lightheartedness was stolidly ignored.

Freath composed himself. He stood outside the oak door of one of the small halls of Brighthelm, where Genrie, on his orders and with the help of some of the barbarians, had organized a hasty fire. In late summertide, although the evenings were still mild, some of the unused chambers were cold and stale smelling.

Though his mind was ragged, he took a deep breath and knocked before entering.

"My lord," he said, bowing politely. "I'm sorry if this

chamber is not ideal. I know it hasn't been aired in a long time."

"It's fine, Freath. Genrie threw some herbs on the flames and stuck a few acorns in the kindling. No one is complaining."

Freath smiled politely, tightly. "Is there anything else I can do for you, my lord?" he offered, making a point of looking around the room at the women who had made themselves comfortable in the large chairs around the fire. Stracker was nowhere to be seen . . . probably happier in the barracks with his men. "Genrie will organize some food, which I presume you would like served in this chamber?"

"You both need some help around here, don't you?" Loethar drew Freath away from the women in a casual move that the aide nonetheless noticed.

"Brighthelm ran on a fairly modest team of thirty staff in the royal rooms, including the kitchens and infirmary. We had in addition gardeners and all manner of outdoor workers, which would have swelled that base to perhaps twice as many. I presume you plan to make Penraven your imperial seat, my lord. And if Brighthelm is to be the main palace for you and the new empress," he said, nodding politely toward Valya, "then I think adding some manpower would allow us to serve you properly and in the custom an emperor should be. After all, Brighthelm will be the standard by which all will judge you, my lord." He dropped his voice. "I mean absolutely no disrespect when I say that I presume you will want to blend into the Set quickly."

"What makes you say that?"

Freath had judged the man based on his new appearance, but he quickly came up with a more diplomatic response. "It will be easier to rule and win the Set's complicity—if not its complete trust—by changing as little as possible in the early days. I suspect, my lord, you want to be done with war and disruption now, to get on quickly with settling all the realms into a new way of life. It will be easiest to do this under an emperor who is not so very far from their previous way of life. You will give people fewer reasons to rebel."

"There will always be pockets of rebellion, Freath."

"I agree. But now that your only real threat has been dealt with, my lord, if life can quickly get back to normal—if you can establish some measure of understanding between yourself and the noble families in the other realms, for example—they will lead by example and you will find it much easier to convince the people of your intentions. War is barbaric, no matter by whom or how it is perpetrated. I'm sure King Cormoron would frighten the living daylights out of most people today. They say he smeared the blood of every person he killed, over himself."

Loethar actually laughed out loud, taking Freath by surprise. "I'm impressed with you, Freath."

Freath kept his expression unchanged. "I am here to serve, my lord. I promised you that from the outset."

"I haven't trusted you but I think tonight you've earned my favor."

A spark of triumph flared in Freath's gut but he was careful not to reflect it in his stony expression. "I'm glad, my lord."

"I want your ideas on how we must approach this blending you speak of. I do not wish the people of the Set to wrongly presume that the people of the Likurian Steppes are somehow inferior because of their more simple way of living. And although it is important, strategically, for me to make the transition for the Set as easy as possible, it is equally important that the Steppes' culture be appreciated."

"I couldn't agree more, my lord. But my counsel would be to let this happen gradually. As they say, water dripping on stone is just as powerful as a hammer . . . but it's a smoother path."

Again Loethar grinned. "Wise counsel. I will discuss this with you further, Freath. We shall arrange a meeting of all the noble families in Penraven, perhaps organize some festivals to lighten the tensions. In the meantime, I give you authority to re-staff the palace to the degree you consider appropriate."

"Very good, my lord."

"I would consider it appropriate to have some Steppes people employed too, Freath. Stracker is organizing for some of the men's women and families to enter Penraven. Perhaps you could talk about this with him. The women will want to work."

"Will they feel comfortable taking instructions from a Penravian?"

"Their empress is a westerner. They'll have to get used to it," Loethar replied, although Freath guessed he had other, more shaded reasons for infiltrating the staff of Brighthelm with barbarian women.

"Then it will be done, my lord. I shall have Genrie serve your food now, if you'll excuse me?"

Loethar nodded. "You've earned some rest, Freath. I won't be needing you any more tonight."

Freath bowed. "Your salon has been cleaned and refreshed, my lord. I trusted it was all right to leave your raven alone on the perch, er, which reminds me, I haven't seen Piven around this evening. Is he—"

Loethar's brow furrowed. "Yes. I haven't had a chance to talk to you about him this evening."

Freath noticed that the emperor looked suddenly thoughtful and worry clenched in his gut. "I do hope he hasn't upset anyone, my lord? Piven has no ability to judge anyone's feelings. We aren't even sure he experiences many of them himself. He is a gentle soul who means no one any harm and gives great affection to all."

"You seem awfully concerned for this Valisar child, Freath."

"I was fond of Piven simply because he, a commoner and one so disabled, managed to infiltrate the royals, win their hearts. But he is as happy in the company of Kings as he is with your raven, my lord. He is not discerning at all and I rather liked that," Freath lied, wondering whether his weak explanation was having any effect, for Loethar's expression remained unimpressed.

"A bit like a kindred spirit, do you mean?"

"Not exactly, although the fact that he was an orphan made him a favorite with the staff. I found it easier to like Piven simply because he was *not* Valisar."

"Should I let him join his brother in death?"

Freath shrugged, forcing down the re-emerging knot of fear. "I would not hesitate if you asked it of me, my lord," he said, answering Loethar's question, hoping it sounded convincing, praying it would never come to it.

Loethar made a gesture of indifference. "An empty question, Freath. The fact is, I have lost Piven."

Freath managed with great effort to stop his repeating Loethar's words with awed horror. So this is what had made the barbarian so angry tonight. "Er, I see. Is that a problem for you?" he asked, deliberately adopting a callous tone, as his mind scrambled for answers as to where Piven might have gone.

"Are you suggesting I should just let him go?"

"I'm trying to gauge how much he means to you, my lord, that's all."

He was surprised to see Loethar falter.

"I, I'm not sure. My raven hates people. I think he only tolerates me because I raised him from a chick. However, he has developed some affinity with Piven. I don't understand it. I don't really understand either of them but somehow I find both of them comforting . . . for their silent companionship, if nothing else."

"Then we must find him for you. Where did you last see him?" he said, holding his breath.

"I took him out with me to the herb gardens, where the sun dial is." Loethar explained.

Freath nodded. "He would have recognized it to some extent. His mother took him there often."

"I was speaking with Dara Negev and let Piven off his leash. Minutes later we received the urgent message from

Stracker and I hurried to take it directly from the messenger. My mother followed and we both forgot about the boy. Predictably he wandered off."

As Loethar explained, Freath tried to look sympathetic, when all he could really think about was the wolves and wild creatures that roamed the forest.

"He won't last long even in the nearby woodland, my lord. Piven has no ability to support himself."

"I understand. Can you organize a search party?"

"At once, my lord. Let me do that now."

"What are you both whispering about over there?" Dara Negev demanded. It was obvious the women had exhausted what little polite conversation they had.

"Nothing, mother. Do it, Freath. Keep me informed."

Freath fled. Kirin would have to wait a bit longer. Piven had to be found!

The search party, including Freath, Father Briar and an assortment of others, set out with torches. Freath organized for them to radiate from the herb garden in various directions toward the low woodland.

It wasn't long before Loethar joined the search but the barbarian's presence made little difference. After three long hours, by which they were into the dead of night, even he decided that the little boy was gone.

Freath finally said what he knew to be true. "He wouldn't necessarily answer our calls anyway. He may know his name," he said, shrugging. He knew Piven did at times recognize the sound of his name but he was contrary. "But he's less obedient than a dog to tell the truth."

"I should never have taken him off the leash!" Loethar berated himself.

"It's likely he's curled up sleeping somewhere," Father Briar offered.

"We shall have to try again as soon as dawn breaks," Freath said. Then, hoping to rub salt in the barbarian's open wound, he added, "He'll be cold, hungry, probably—"

A shout went up and Loethar spun around. A Blue warrior pounded up, holding out something in his hand.

"The collar," Loethar said, disgusted. "Where did you find it?"

The Blue pointed. "About ninety steps into the wood from where that huge forked tree is, my lord," he said.

"Is Piven capable of taking this off himself?" Loethar asked Freath. "The buckle is not easy to manipulate, especially when you can't see it."

Freath was baffled. "And especially when his small fingers don't even understand what they're supposed to do." He frowned. "I wouldn't have thought so, no." He instantly wished he hadn't aired that notion because Loethar leapt upon it.

"So someone's helped him!"

"I doubt—" Freath began, but was cut off by Loethar.

"Where is Stracker?"

A Red stepped forward. "I can fetch him. He was at the barracks, I think."

"Get him," Loethar growled. He turned back to Freath. "It's one thing to parade the disabled child of the Valisars on a leash. It's another to have him running free. People may get ideas."

"But, my lord, he is not even Valisar. I don't think you have to worry—"

"He is a symbol, Freath. And sometimes people will cling to the thinnest strands of hope. Anyone hatching plans of a fightback might clutch at the idea of Piven, now that Leonel is dead. As far as the people go he has the Valisar glow about him."

"No, my lord," Freath replied, fighting to keep his voice calm, his tone as indifferent as possible. "I don't think you should waste your time on Piven. Let him go. He'll die out in the woods sooner than you can possibly imagine—if he's not attacked by a wild animal, he'll perish from thirst or starvation. He has no defenses, no idea how to even sustain himself. Who will help him? The people of Penraven have been swamped by refugees from the other realms. Everyone has lost loved ones, people are barely functioning, the whole realm is in disarray. That's where your attention should be focused. Piven is seven, disabled to the point of not even functioning at the level of a trained dog, and he is not blood. People were fond of him, yes. But would they rally behind an orphan halfwit? No, my lord, I can assure you they would not."

His words seemed to calm Loethar. "You are probably right," the barbarian agreed. He dismissed the men.

Relief slowed Freath's hammering heart as he watched the warriors disperse, leaving him alone with Loethar, who was twirling Piven's collar loosely in his hand. "Let him die, my lord," he pressed. "It's the best solution. He will be one less concern for you."

Loethar nodded. "The saddest thing of all, Freath, is that I rather liked Piven. Unlike everyone else around me, he had no opinion, no hidden schemes. He was a void, yes, but one that was filled with warmth and affection . . . all of his attention directed toward me rather than taking from me or using me. That's something I've lacked all my life," he muttered softly, turning on his heel and striding away.

Twenty-Six

Freath found his Vested in their shared chamber, Clovis crouched over Kirin, wiping his blank face with a damp flannel.

"Whatever that was about I don't ever want to do it again," Clovis said, not even turning.

"I know it was hard for you but we saved lives this evening."

"I saw four sacrificial heads and they were probably only a smattering of the number really killed."

"Twenty-nine died to save hundreds more," Freath answered, suddenly tired of being blamed for all the ills surrounding the very people he was working so hard to protect. "I have to speak with Kirin."

"You can try," Clovis said, disdain coloring his voice. "He hasn't said a word to anyone."

"Is he conscious?" Freath asked, approaching. The man of magic looked dead.

"Yes, he's conscious, but closed, if that makes any sense. I meant what I said, Master Freath. I will not do anything like that again."

"We're all having to do things we'd rather not. You must find courage."

"I will have no part in the murder of children."

Freath considered this. He knew Clovis was predisposed to be deeply upset over any child's suffering and he couldn't blame him. Perhaps his fear could be put to use. "Then help me save a child, Clovis."

The diviner turned, looked at Freath with puzzlement. "What do you mean?"

Freath sat down on the small stool next to the bed, Kirin momentarily forgotten. He hated not being able to really think this through but time was of the essence and he had none to play with. "Do you recall Piven?"

"The imbecile?"

"The adopted simpleton son of the Valisars, yes," Freath said, wearily.

Clovis shrugged. "I've heard about him—as I suppose most have—but I've only glimpsed him a few times, running around the corridors on a leash with the barbarian."

"Well, he's slipped that leash. Piven went missing at around dusk this evening. He is nowhere to be found on the palace grounds and his collar was found on the edge of the woods."

Clovis gave a low whistle. "The last of the Valisars, eh?"

"He is not Valisar. But in terms of perception you are probably right. Losing him would be the final tragedy. I want you to find him."

"What?" Clovis said, rearing back.

"Listen to me. You have no stomach for the palace politics or Loethar's penchant for slaughter. And a child's life is in the balance."

Clovis's brow furrowed. "What do you want me to do?"

"I need you to leave tonight. He must be discovered before anyone else finds him."

"Tonight? You want me to go into the woods alone?" Clovis just stopped short of adding, "Are you mad?"

But Freath heard it beneath the awkward silence. The aide bristled. "He is alone in the dark tonight . . . in the woods."

Clovis had the grace to look admonished.

"Listen to me, he's seven. He has none of his faculties. He's just a small, confused, invalid boy. And if the wild creatures don't have a go at him, then starvation and perhaps the cold will kill him. We're fortunate the night is relatively mild but it's still cool enough. Leaf-fall is beckoning and Piven has little flesh on him as it is. He will not survive a couple of days out there alone."

"But he could be anywhere," Clovis replied, standing up and pacing.

"Yes, he could, if he were more able. He's likely still very close. I managed to stop the all-out hunt for him by the barbarians. Although it's terrifying to have Piven loose and endangered, it could play into our hands well—but only if you can find him quickly."

"And what in Lo's name am I supposed to do with him if I do find him?"

Freath shook his head. "I don't know, Clovis," he said, feeling beaten. "I'm making this up as I go along. Just get him away from here. Take him as far as you can from Loethar and this hotbed of warriors."

"What do you plan to tell our emperor?" the Vested asked, sarcasm dripping from the final word.

At this Freath's lips thinned. "I shall have to tell him you went missing. That you were deeply upset by the charade with the boys' heads and that it must have resonated too strongly with your own loss." He shrugged. "That you disappeared."

"And then he'll put a price on my head and send his warriors to hunt me down."

"I doubt it. As far as Loethar's concerned you and Kirin were deliberately presented to me because of your distinct lack of talent. He feels no threat from you. Only I know what you're capable of. Get away from here, Clovis. Put your talents to use. Go find Reuth. I know you were fond of her and if you can find Piven you can keep him safe together." He knew introducing Reuth into the conversation would likely tip the scales in his favor. Even by lamplight he had seen Clovis's flare of interest at the very mention of her name. "Perhaps Father Briar knows where she was heading. You must leave now. Wear your armband and you will not be questioned. In fact, go out with Father Briar's next cartload and once you're out of the immediate palace vicinity cut back toward the southern part of the woods. Draw an eyeline from the herb gardens. That's where Piven was last seen. He won't answer a call, but if he sees you, he will run to you."

"And what if I don't find him?"

Freath couldn't hide his despair. "Just do your best. I don't know what else to suggest."

"What if I get caught?"

"Tell whomever it is that you're acting on orders from me. I will claim that I sent you out to search because I knew that Emperor Loethar was concerned."

"But what if you've already told them I disappeared?"

"Then improvise, Clovis! Life is not neat. Take a cue from me and make something up. We are all fighting for our lives. I'll give you the whole of tomorrow until nightfall. Only then will I tell Loethar of your disappearance. I promise you, you are not important enough to him to chase. And if you haven't found Piven in that time-frame, then flee south or wherever you want to. I absolve you of all other responsibility to me, to the royals, to anyone but yourself."

"What about Kirin?"

"Kirin stays. I'll take care of him."

"What do you think happened to him?"

Freath sighed, and pushed his weary body up to stand. "I think Master Kirin is hiding a lot more than he's claiming."

In the forest smaller birds had begun heralding the dawning of a new day; the air was filled with their joyous song.

"I'd forgotten how loud the woods can be during the dawn chorus," Leo commented to Lily, whom he was walking alongside.

Kilt Faris overheard, answering, "And those of us who live within them take it for granted. We're all guilty of the same neglect of mother nature's brilliance."

"Well, I rise at the first bird's sound each morning, so I'm always listening for her," Lily admitted.

Faris nodded. "Us too, but unlike Leo here, we forget to

marvel at it, when we should be grateful another day has dawned and we are alive to welcome it."

"That sounds awfully philosophical for an outlaw," Gavriel said.

Jewd, who had been mostly silent for the entire journey, looked sideways at Gavriel. "Do you think that because we live on the edge of the law that we are unable to appreciate Lo's beauty?"

"I didn't say that," Gavriel replied. "I suppose I'm wondering whether philosophy has any place in your world, that's all."

"As much as in yours, De Vis," Faris said gently. "We steal other people's money. That's all. We don't kill. And I'm patriotic to a point. Right now I'm helping my king stay alive. I think I've earned the right to philosophize along with the best of them."

Lily glared at Gavriel and he fell silent.

"How far are we from the stone?" Leo asked, breaking into the suddenly awkward quiet.

"Just a mile ahead now. I'm impressed you've all walked through the night. We will be able to rest shortly. Jewd will go ahead and kill us a few rabbits for a meal—and not raw either. We can build a fire."

In spite of his bad mood Gavriel's spirits lifted at the thought of freshly cooked meat. He began to imagine the smell of the meat roasting over the embers and he was unnerved to find that in the few moments he'd been daydreaming about the taste of cooked rabbit, he'd not only dawdled behind the pack but that Faris had fallen back as well, and now walked at his side.

The outlaw moved closer still. Speaking quietly, he warned, "Whatever your problem is with me, De Vis, I think we should try and be civil to one another. It does not help the young king's state of mind to have his closest friend and his new conspirator at loggerheads."

Gavriel took a leaf from Corbel's book and remained silent.

It was as though Faris could hear his thoughts. "Where is

your brother, by the way? I thought you twins were very close."

"Who told you that?"

"Brennus. He said that he was placing all his faith in the two loyal and reliable De Vis boys."

"He said that?"

Faris nodded. "And that he knew in the future he was going to ask a great deal of you both. I didn't understand precisely what and he didn't enlighten me but I presume that by your presence he entrusted the safety of his heir to you."

"That's right, he did. He personally asked me to give my life to Leo, to be his protector."

"You're awfully young for that responsibility." As Gavriel bristled, Faris raised a hand. "Forgive me, that came out wrong. What I wanted to say is that it is very impressive that he chose someone so young. From what I could tell Brennus was a very sage, very cunning man. I don't for a moment imagine he made that decision lightly. If he didn't trust you and your skills implicitly he would never have handed Leo over to you. You must be good."

"In what regard?"

"Weapons, I imagine, but also in strength of mind. Anyone can fight, De Vis. There are plenty of incredibly skilled swordsmen and archers but for most that's where their minds stop working. The real champion is someone whose brain matches his speed and skill with weapons." He paused, looked wryly at Gavriel. "That was a compliment. You can smile."

Gavriel regarded Faris, searching for the outlaw's intentions. Was his praise genuine or just more of his sardonic baiting? The man's grin looked open, however, and his warm brown eyes held a hint of mischief.

"You don't need to stroke my feathers," Gavriel said, using an old saying of his father's.

"I wasn't. Nor would I," Faris answered with equal directness. "How old are you, De Vis? Sixteen, seventeen summertides?"

"Seventeen."

"Seventeen. Ho, Jewd, what were you doing at seventeen?"

The huge man scratched his beard. "Wishing I could control my huge—"

"No, Jewd," Faris cut in. "Apart from women, what were you thinking about? What were you doing?"

"I worked with my father. We helped to build ships over at Merivale; I was the lackey. I was thinking a lot about ale and women—not much else."

"So you were doing as your father told you?"

"I did what everyone told me. I was the lowest in the pecking order."

"Lily, what were you doing at seventeen? How old are you, anyway?"

"None of your business, Kilt Faris," she admonished. "But when I was seventeen my life was not much different to how my new friends found me. I was living in the forest with my father, drying herbs, making healing salves, living quietly."

Faris nodded. "Me, I was at Cremond in the Academy," he said.

"You?"

"Ah, De Vis, judgments made too soon are often wrong. Yes, the despised outlaw you see before you was once a budding scholar."

"In what?" Gavriel asked, unable to hide his disdain.

"Thaumaturgy."

"You're not empowered, surely?" Leo said, turning, obviously surprised.

"Not a skerrick of magic in my bones. But I was always fascinated by the notion of the Vested. Anyway, that was a long time ago. I attended the Academy under a false name—my parents never knew."

"Why?" Leo asked, before Gavriel could.

Faris shrugged. "I don't think I ever really wanted to be a full-time scholar. I did enjoy study but I couldn't maintain the concentration needed. The false name gave me the opportunity to get out whenever I wanted. I never quite got used to the rules and eventually I wanted freedom. But at seventeen I had no responsibilities and was knee deep in study."

"What's your point?" Gavriel asked.

"My point, De Vis, is that you are doing an extraordinary thing at seventeen. Leo has to be brave; he's king. You don't. But here you are, rushing into danger, not giving so much as a mote's concern for your own safety or future. Dare I say you're stirring rebellion against the marauding army that has destroyed the entire Set. I admire you."

Gavriel was lost for words. Praise was the last thing he had expected from Faris. Leo grinned and Lily gave him a shy, brief glance before turning away and pushing forward.

"And now I've embarrassed you, have I?" Faris continued. "My apology, I simply wanted you to understand that we are on the same side right now." He lowered his voice so only Gavriel could hear him now. "We have no argument, you and I. So don't pick one. Here, keep these on you," he said, handing Gavriel what looked like small shiny nuts.

"What are these?"

Faris grinned. "Real magic. Suck one if you're ever under genuine threat. I know better than most how difficult hiding one's identity is."

Gavriel looked at them quizzically.

The outlaw looked amused. "It's just a safeguard for you and Leo. Each one lasts a day. Don't be reckless with them—they're all I have."

He moved ahead briskly to join the others, souring Gavriel again by walking next to Lily. "Just past this next sentinel of trees and we're there," he said to everyone.

They finally arrived into a clearing surrounded by a thick overwhelming presence of oaks. The air was warmer here, and denser, since they'd been walking downhill for some time. The trees created a natural amphitheater and sitting in the middle of the "stage" was the sacred stone Gavriel had heard so much about. He found himself holding his breath as he watched Leo walk reverently toward it.

"It's not very spectacular, is it?" Lily whispered alongside him.

Gavriel shook his head to be polite but the truth was he was mesmerized by it. Its simplicity alone took his breath away. He too had anticipated a grand throne on which the Valisar Kings would seat themselves in accepting the Crown of Penraven. He had certainly not expected a hewn slab of silver branstone, resting in very uncomplicated fashion on top of two other slabs. As the sun's rays hit the branstone, its silver flecks sparkled.

He watched Leo glide his hand over the smooth, sparkling surface and he was sure they shared the same thought about how each of the great Valisar Kings had knelt at this place and sworn their lives, their duty, their blood to Penraven.

Leo looked up, his eyes immediately searching out Faris. "What should I do?"

"Nothing, yet. As I understand it from my readings at the Academy, all the Kings have taken their oaths at evening twilight—you know that twilight is considered the most magical time of the day."

"Why is that?" Lily asked, walking up to the stone.

Gavriel could see that Faris was in his element. "Because, Lily, it is considered a time that is neither day or night. It is not fully light, but neither is it fully dark. It is a sort of nether light, if you will—a nether world, even." He smiled and began to walk toward her, each word bringing him another step closer. "They say this is the time when spirits can enter our land, when magic is at its most potent, when worlds kiss." As he said the final word he leaned far too close to her for Gavriel's liking.

He slipped the seeds into his shirt pocket. "And so Leo must make his oath at this evening's twilight?" he asked, breaking whatever spell Faris was weaving over Lily. The girl, he noticed, was smiling softly and flirtatiously at the outlaw.

"Yes," Faris replied, turning to encompass everyone in the conversation. "But he must make it alone and we must respect that. There can be no witnesses."

"Why alone?" Leo had not stopped stroking the glittering stone.

Faris shrugged. "It is a private commitment you're making, a private communion with your god. And, my young king, most importantly, there may well be a private parley with Cyrena the infamous serpent." He smiled at Leo. "You must wait until the moon is fully risen, though. If Cyrena will show herself it will be during the darkness of night, lit only by her lamp in the sky. And only if you are entirely alone."

Gavriel felt exasperated. How was this man so annoyingly knowledgeable as well as infuriatingly self-possssed? And yet even though he wanted to he couldn't take offense. If anything, Faris was being helpful. But this seemed to irritate him all the more.

"Does she appear to all the Kings?" Leo asked, his eyes shining with wonder.

"I honestly don't know the answer to that. But your father confided that he didn't meet Cyrena and he wasn't sure your grandfather did either."

"Brennus confided so much in you," Gavriel remarked, working hard to keep the sarcasm he felt out of his voice.

"He and I made the same journey that we just have. He wanted to reiterate his oath to Penraven. There was plenty of time for talking," Faris said, carefully.

"Cyrena is likely just legend," Leo said to Faris.

The outlaw nodded noncommittally. "True, but we should observe tradition, do this properly. No one should ever be able to accuse you of not taking the spiritual side of your regal oath as seriously as the physical or emotional side. And I do believe in magic and if there's even a chance of Cyrena showing herself, I respect that. I will not eavesdrop, I will not guard you. No one will. We must ensure you do this in the correct manner. This is usually the last stage of the ritual of kingship."

"I know what you're going to say," Leo cut in.

"Do you?"

"I think so. I believe you were going to say that Cormoron, the first of the Valisars, took his oath before the Stone of Truth first, before any physical celebrations or crowning."

Faris smiled. "I was going to say just that. So in truth you are following tradition far more closely than your more recent ancestors did. And should Cyrena pay a visit, it might be because of that very observance of old ritual." This he said more facetiously, winning a grin from Leo.

Gavriel scowled inwardly. Though both Leo and Lily had been seduced by the outlaw, he wanted to reserve judgment.

"So we can rest, perhaps?" Lily offered into the sudden silence.

"Indeed. Now is a good time. Gavriel, I shall leave you in charge. There is no threat here; Jewd and Tern have already scouted from the trees and no one approaches. The nearest people are a trio of tribal men using a horse track that runs through this region but we're high enough not to be seen, so you are safe for me to leave. Just stay together please and take the time to rest. Jewd, myself and Tern will hunt. Here," he said, giving Gavriel a whittled whistle. "To the untrained ear this makes the sound of a bird." He grinned, annoyingly neat white teeth flashing briefly at Gavriel. "Our trained ears, however, will recognize it as your signal. Call us if you're frightened by anything."

Gavriel wondered if Faris had chosen his words to be deliberately inciting. "I don't think we're frightened by much after all we've been through."

Lily took the whistle instead. "Thanks. I'll gladly blow it if anything unnerves me." She gave Gavriel another of her stares; he scowled back.

"Right, good. Sleep, all of you. Don't leave the clearing.

You are safe here," Faris assured. He melted into the shadows beneath the oaks and was gone.

"Can you please stop," Lily demanded, rounding on Gavriel.

"What?"

"Can't you see that he's on our side?"

"Are you sure of that?"

She stared at him, her expression exasperated. "What happened to the affable, easy-going, courageous Gavriel De Vis I met just a couple of days ago?"

"Perhaps he got tired of watching you flirt with the outlaw."

She moved fast, her hand coming up to slap his face. But his reactions were honed to perfection. He was the best in the cohort; no one had more lightning reflexes than Gavriel. Instinctively, he caught her wrist before it connected.

"Let me go," she yelled at him.

Something snapped inside. Gavriel's voice was deeper, with a hollow chill through it, when he spoke again. "Don't you ever raise your hand to me again." He nodded toward the trees. "I'm no outlaw who's up for some rough fun with you, who will cast you aside as quickly as you might him. Remember who you talk to. De Vis is a proud name. We walk with kings." Though he could tell he'd frightened her initially his final jab sounded pompous even to him. As soon as it was out of his mouth he wished he'd never uttered the final sentence.

"You forget, so do I," she sneered. "Grow up, Gavriel. You're pathetic."

Her last few words stung more than the intended slap ever could have. He let her wrist go and stepped back. Glancing at Leo, Gavriel saw bitter disappointment in the king's stare. Gavriel turned on his heel and walked away.

"Gavriel!" Leo called. "We're meant to stay together."

He said nothing in reply, stomped further before the steep incline made him take up a slow trot. He didn't mean to go far but he needed to put some temporary distance between him and Leo's regret and Lily's disdain. His cheeks burned with embarrassment. He'd made a fool of himself with Faris and now he'd let himself down in front of the woman he wanted to impress. And that was the heart of it, wasn't it? He was jealous. Jealous of Faris's easy manner. He ran still further, anger fueling his legs. He'd stop in a moment and cool off before he returned. He wasn't so far away yet.

Faris was a competitor, not just for . . . Lily, but more unnervingly for Leo. He had watched Leo being seduced by the outlaw's knowledge, his devil-may-care attitude, and especially by his curious closeness to Brennus. Who could blame Leo? Faris came in precisely the right shape, size, age, looks, attitude—everything, damn him—to impress the young king. Even worse, Brennus had approved of him. Slowing down at last, Gavriel finally drew to a stop. The more dense air here helped him think clearly about the complete idiot he had been. What had he been thinking? Why had he allowed himself to become such a victim of his own insecurities? If Corb were here he'd give him one of those looks of his. *Grow up, indeed.* Lily was right. He owed them all apologies, especially Lily. And he needed to get back to Leo. Hopefully they'd both fallen asleep. He'd only been gone a short while.

He took stock of his surrounds. The trees had certainly thinned out and if he wasn't mistaken he could see right ahead the horse track that Faris had spoken of. He felt suddenly vulnerable. Turning, he took the first couple of steps back toward his friends.

It was then he heard voices and horse hooves. But there was nowhere to hide without being noticed. He froze, realizing he had no choice but to remain as still as a mouse, hoping against hope the riders—three of them, he now counted—would pass by without even glimpsing him standing in the open beneath the hawthorns. His only stroke of fortune was that he was upwind of the horses and still on the incline—if his luck held, they might pass by without even looking up, engrossed in their low conversation. He held his breath, closed his eyes and began to count. He reckoned within a count of twenty he would be behind them.

At the count of fourteen a voice yelled: "Oi, you there!"

Gavriel De Vis began running.

Twenty-Seven

Kirin stirred. His eyelids slit open and closed immediately. He groaned. He must have sensed someone nearby, for he moaned, "Clovis?" His voice cracked from a parched throat.

"It's Freath. Here, drink something."

Kirin tried but couldn't get the cup to his mouth. When Freath pushed the cup to his lips he could barely open his mouth and what little liquid passed his lips he couldn't swallow; his throat refused to obey him. After a struggle he'd managed a few drops of water only.

"How are you feeling?" Freath asked.

"I'm dizzy."

"Are you in pain?"

"Some."

"Where?"

"My head."

"Take this."

Kirin tried to look at the mug Freath held out, daring to open his eyes to slits again. "What is it?"

"Crushed peonies—a helpful painkiller. If that doesn't ease it, we'll try comfrey."

"No henbane?"

"Kirin, it seems to me that these—well, shall we call them dizzy spells of yours?—are going to happen more frequently. Perhaps we need to keep an arsenal of painkillers on hand for you. If that's going to be the case, I'd like to try to begin with the least potent so that you don't build an immunity."

Kirin sneered. "Are you adding physic to your list of talents . . . right after executioner?"

Freath bit his lip to prevent his retaliating. He had expected this attack from Clovis but had been hoping Kirin would understand. He sighed, disappointed. "Try the peony. See if it helps."

Kirin didn't move.

"Please, Kirin. You need help."

With obvious reluctance and a hefty dose of discomfort the man of magic raised himself onto his elbow and sipped the warm peony tea. "Tastes surprisingly good," he remarked, his voice bitter.

"I added some honey," Freath said. "Keep drinking. The more you get down the better, although I've made it quite strong."

Kirin sat up properly and groaned again, holding his head. "I think I'm going to hurl."

"I came prepared for that," Freath comforted, reaching for a pail. "Here, drink plenty, no matter what comes back up." He stood and moved over to the window to give Kirin a measure of privacy.

"Where's Clovis?"

"I've sent him away."

"What? Why?"

Freath explained quickly, finally adding, "He is my only hope but he has no stomach for what's happening here. He is better away from the palace and its brutality."

"What makes you think I will fare better here?" Kirin snarled.

"Because you do. Because you also believe in what we're reaching after. Clovis doesn't, or at least he is still so mired in the past and his sorrows that he cannot imagine a future. Not yet. But you can, Kirin. Or let me put it this way: You are angered enough by the present to want to change the future. And, unlike Clovis, you would not rather die than face the present hardship. Clovis's survival so far has been largely due to your encouragement and presence. But I'm afraid last night set him back; he'd become a liability—for all of us."

"Where will he go?"

"I suggested he find Reuth. I have since discovered that Father Briar got all the Vested safely away. Where they've scattered to I don't know but we did send them each with a homing pigeon. I am hoping they will use the birds to tell us where they end up."

Kirin seemed to approve. He nodded. "How will you know if he has found the child?"

"I'm not sure I will. I simply pray that he is successful. I can do no more for Piven from here without drawing suspicions."

"Are you secretly relieved, though, that Piven is no longer your responsibility?"

Why this perfectly reasonable and honest question seemed to incense Freath where far more offensive accusations had not, he did not know. But he spun angrily on Kirin, only just managing to rein in his wrath. "I'm going to forgive you for that. But I think it best I remove myself for a while. Rest. We need to talk but later."

He didn't give Kirin the chance to respond or apologize, but left the room immediately, only just managing to shut the door without banging it. As he did so he happened to catch a look of genuine surprise on the man of magic's face. Outside he forced himself to take several deep, calming breaths. This would not do. He prided himself on keeping his temper at all times. Iselda had once joked in his presence to King Brennus that she would give the scullery maid her magnificent pearl earrings if Brennus could get Freath to lose his composure just once in the ensuing hour.

Freath remembered how Brennus had smiled at his wife and said: "Iselda, my dear, I may be a gambler in some things but I'm not so naive as to take up any challenge where our

Freath is concerned. I have never seen his expression slip once in all the years he's been with our family and I can only imagine the price you'll demand when you win."

She had smiled lovingly at her husband and then given Freath a sympathetic glance. "Sorry, Freath. The new uniforms for the kitchen staff may have to wait a bit longer. Although I could always sell my pearl earrings, I suppose."

Freath now smiled sadly to himself at the memory. New uniforms had been measured and made the following moon for the entire kitchen staff through to the youngest scullery maid. Iselda had always known how to play Brennus.

He looked up to see Genrie approaching. "Master Freath," she said, curtseying, always a stickler for propriety.

"Genrie, are you all right?"

She looked at him with a cool, direct gaze. "Of course. I've just got a headache. I'm sorry about this evening."

Freath had not had a chance to discuss what had just occurred with Genrie; all he had been able to do was enquire politely how she was feeling. Genrie, in her usual no nonsense way, had muttered that she was recovered and said no more, barely giving him eye contact. And still the sight of her fired hope in him. He had loved serving Iselda. Any other woman would have suffered for his dedication to the queen and so he had never taken a wife, not even pursued a life partner. But Genrie had surprised him. Her delicious auburn waves, pale complexion and intensely green eyes aside, he adored her defiance and especially her courage. She had carried herself with dignity throughout this whole invasion, and unlike him, had convinced the barbarian that she was trustworthy without once publicly relinquishing her sympathies to the Valisars. His heart melted just a fraction more for her bravery. "You have nothing to apologize for, Genrie. You were incredibly courageous. If anyone should be sorry, it's me, for allowing you to be put through it."

She shook her head. "Neither of us have any say. I wish I could have been stronger."

He risked taking her hand, looking around furtively before pressing his lips to it. "He did not suffer, I promise you. I made sure of it." He didn't bother to mention the purse of money, for he knew no family could be compensated for the loss of a child.

She looked up at him, baffled, her eyes misty. "I don't understand what happened. I thought we were all destined for the same fate as those boys. I still can't believe—"

"I know. Coincidence, perfectly timed," he soothed, reaching now to tuck back a soft wisp of hair that had escaped her careful pinning.

"But Father Briar—was that coincidence, too?"

"Blind luck, I think. I agree, I thought we were done for."

She stared at him, confounded by his explanation. "You'd better go see Father Briar. He has a nasty headache too," she said, her eyes narrowing as she regarded him.

He cleared his throat under the scrutiny. He wasn't quite ready to admit what he believed, even if Genrie's thoughts seemed to be keeping pace with his own suspicions. "I'll do that," he said, unable to think of anything else with which to fend her off.

"And I must warn you that the Droste woman is on our path."

"What do you mean?"

"She watches me constantly. Questions me incessantly. Wants to know if I'm in liaison with you."

"Liaison? What on earth does she mean by that?" Freath felt his gut twist with horror. "Collusion?" he added.

Genrie gave him a fresh look, one that suggested he could be awfully vague for a normally sharp man. "She means a romantic liaison."

"Pardon?" He didn't like the way his voice squeaked slightly on the word.

Genrie explained wearily, "She doesn't know anything. She's simply sending out feelers in all directions."

"She's looking to make trouble, that woman," Freath said,

checking again that no one was watching them. "I so want to kiss you again but I daren't, not here."

She nodded, smiled sadly and dropped her hand. "It's more sinister than simple trouble, Freath. She's on the trail of what she believes is conspiracy. We must be very careful."

"Indeed." He already missed her touch. "I've been granted permission to personally re-staff the palace."

This caught her attention. "By whom?"

"The man himself. He is very cunning, very smart to do this. He wants to quickly return Brighthelm's life to as normal as possible."

"He'll never wash the bloodstains from it," she said, her voice bitter.

"Never let your anger show like that, Genrie, promise me. They must believe that you now work for them with diligence, if grudgingly. They must think they have cowed you through the threat to the family we've pretended you have. Each day you must show yourself to be more indispensable, more accepting of their presence, more reasonable about their needs and culture. Fake it, Genrie. If not for yourself, then for me. I could not bear to lose you." And then he bent, kissed her so fleetingly he could almost convince himself later it hadn't happened, and then he was gone, striding away, not looking back.

Neither of them saw Valya watching.

He'd run blindly, crashing through the now thinning forest's undergrowth, his only thought that he must lead them away from the Stone of Truth at Lackmarin and where King Leo hid. Stupid, stupid, stupid! He had run right into the warriors Faris had mentioned; he knew this by their horses—the stockier, more muscular breed with long manes and tails. Though Gavriel desperately wanted to head up the incline, slowing down the animals, he knew that would lead them closer to Leo and Lily.

The warriors came after him, seemingly uncaring whether their horses could handle the uneven ground. But still Gavriel ran, his arms cartwheeling to give him balance, aid his speed. His breathing was erratic, his thoughts had scattered in a dozen directions and his fear was overwhelming.

They hit him hard, his head snapping back as they leaned down from their saddles and walloped his legs out from under him; his chin hit something, he didn't know what, nor did he care. The darkness welcomed him and he moved into it willingly. His final thought was of how much he missed his brother.

Kilt Faris squinted from his perch high in one of the tall trees. He felt his gut twist at the sight of the barbarians bringing the young man down. Thank Lo he had decided to do another check on the tribal men. At least De Vis had had the presence of mind to run away from Lackmarin rather than toward it. Cursing, he called down to Jewd, "Are you going to break my fall or drop me this time?"

"Drop you," came the answer.

Faris scaled halfway down the tree and then leapt. Jewd broke his drop, cushioned the landing.

"They've got him," Faris said to his companion, scowling.

"Did you think they wouldn't?"

Faris shook his head with frustration. "To his credit he did everything right. He remained utterly still, tried his best to blend back into the forest, remained upwind of the beasts and then mercifully ran away from us."

"Not bad for a city boy."

The head of the outlaw gang regarded his giant friend ruefully. "They'll kill him, Jewd."

The big man shrugged. "He's an idiot. Idiots don't deserve to live."

Faris walked on. "I could reel off a dozen or more idiotic events from our own early years that I'm sure you don't wish to be reminded of."

"Yes, but we survived them."

"My point entirely. *We*," Faris emphasized. "De Vis has no one to look out for him. He has done a mighty job in keeping the young king safe thus far. He got him all the way here on his own, with nothing more than a sword at his hip and a bow around his chest. Come on, Jewd. De Vis is impressive and King Brennus was right to entrust the heir to him."

"I didn't say he wasn't impressive. I said he's an idiot."

"We all were at his age," Faris persisted, giving his friend a glance of admonishment. "He's just seventeen. His king is twelve. Lo's wrath, what a pair. Imagine them in another ten!"

"The new legate won't make it to that age, methinks."

Faris halted, turning on his huge partner. "He won't, unless we help him."

Jewd sighed. "Why did I know you were going to say that?"

"Because you know the promise I gave King Brennus."

"That was about the heir, not De Vis."

"When you say the name De Vis you might as well say Valisar. Brennus would expect us to include either of the twins in our ring of protection."

"Why did I know you were going to say that as well?" Jewd grumbled loudly.

"Because you know me."

"More like because I know you want to impress the woman and she'll likely kill you if you don't agree to go after him."

"Ah, you saw through my thinly veiled plot, then?"

"Rescue the boy, bed the girl, it's rather obvious, don't you think, Kilt . . . even for your simple mind to hatch?"

Faris grinned, even though he was feeling a genuine clench of fear for Gavriel. The bravado helped him remain optimistic for the youngster. "When I get him back, I'm going to kill him myself, I think."

"I'll leave you to explain that to her, then."

Faris sighed. He knew he could count on Jewd—the big man had been there for him practically since they started walking, large and strong, ever prepared to follow him right into the dangers he had always managed to find. "Right. Get

Tern to track the barbarians. You go back as far as you need to. Use arrows as soon as you can to signal the men—we'll need eight of our boys, I reckon."

"Any more people and you might as well bring instruments and play a rousing tune to herald your way in," Jewd said dryly.

Though Faris normally relished Jewd's humor, he was too annoyed about the unnecessary rescue mission to laugh. "I'll meet you back here. I've got to get the king to swear his oath this evening, no matter what's going on with De Vis."

Jewd nodded. "I'm on my way. I'll be back tomorrow."

"I hope we'll be in time."

"Kilt, you know they'll hurt him."

Faris's brow furrowed deeper. He nodded. "I just have to hope he can hold on. Go, Jewd. Hurry."

The huge man loped off, running higher into the forest, heading west. Faris turned back toward Lackmarin and the unpleasant task of telling Leo and Lily what had occurred.

He found them pacing restlessly. As soon as he emerged from the surrounding oaks, they ran up to him both telling him what he already knew: that Gavriel had disappeared.

"I know," he replied when they'd finally stopped talking at him.

"Where is he?" Leo asked, sounding relieved, scanning the trees behind Faris.

Lily quietly watched him and he could see in her eyes that she knew he brought only bad news. She said nothing, waiting for him to work out how best to deliver it.

To try and dilute the danger Gavriel was in would be to underestimate the young king—and insult him, considering the traumas he had already witnessed, survived, and buried somewhere. "He stumbled into the path of three of Loethar's warriors. He did his best to hide, and almost got away with it, but they saw him, ran him down." Leo's mouth dropped open, while Lily's face drained of color. Faris turned to Tern. "Track them," he ordered. "When you know where they camp, come back and let me know. I'll be staying here for now. Jewd's gone back." The man nodded and melted away as though he had never been among them.

Lily looked at Faris, astonished. "And you're staying here? What does that mean?"

"Someone has to watch over you two," Faris replied, sensing accusation in the words she wasn't saying.

"Was he hurt?" Leo asked.

"I can't tell. He fell heavily. He was motionless when they picked him up. They put him over a horse."

He watched Leo take a slow breath, admired the youngster all the more for his stillness. "Is he dead?"

"I doubt it. They wouldn't bother with a corpse."

"What if they know who he is? They may want to take his body back to Penraven."

"They may but again I don't think so. They stumbled upon him. They were not looking for him. These were barbarian posts, that's all. We've been aware of them for some time. They had been left there to keep guard of the low-lying areas of the forest, where it turns to the woodland that fringes the towns and villages. They're looking for people trying to move into the forest, not those running out of it. And Gavriel was certainly headed out of it."

"He's such an idiot!" Lily exclaimed.

"My thoughts exactly," Faris said, watching her carefully.

Leo rushed to his friend's defense. "He was upset. You forget Gavriel had to watch his father brutally killed. And his twin brother has disappeared without a trace. Those two were inseparable but I've never heard Gav complain. In fact all he's done is look after me. He's not an idiot, he's just . . ." Leo didn't know what to say, it seemed.

"Impulsive," Faris suggested. "The point is he's put himself into tremendous peril." He scratched his head beneath his longish dark hair.

"You are going to help him, aren't you, Kilt?" Lily said.

Hearing her say his name for the first time felt odd, but

nice. "Tern is tracking them. Jewd has already gone back to alert the men. He—"

"Back?" she quizzed, alarmed. "That will take too long."

"Not necessarily. Jewd has his ways." And as she opened her mouth to protest again, he raised a hand. "Trust me." He looked up at Leo. "Your majesty, I'm here to keep my promise to your father, to ensure that you take your oath at the stone as all your predecessors have."

Leo looked surprised. "I'd rather go after Gavriel," he said, looking between Lily and Faris. "My oath can wait."

"No, it cannot, highness," Faris assured. "I know you'd rather find your friend but we're already following him and my men will get word to me as soon as he's found. Right now he's unconscious and on horseback. These men are truly dangerous—I'm sure you know that?" Leo nodded. "It would be unwise for us to underestimate their fighting capability. For now Gavriel is a stranger to them, a lone man travelling on foot. They have no idea that we are watching them, nor will they until I make a move. And I will not run in blindly without a plan."

"So you are going after him?" Lily persisted.

"I don't intend to leave him to the barbarians, no," Faris replied. As both of them looked relieved, he added, "As for food, it's more of the same, I'm afraid. De Vis made sure there was no rabbit hunting achieved this morning."

"We'll live," Lily said, giving him a shy smile and thrilling him by laying a hand against his chest. "Thank you for helping him," she added.

Faris wanted to say something facetious but his throat was too dry. Jewd was right. He did want Lily. She intrigued him. He also realized that Lily intrigued De Vis and if his senses were serving him right, the young Valisar appeared smitten by her too. He sighed. Was pursuing her really worth the inevitable problems? He dwelled for a second longer than he meant to on her dark blue eyes before realizing he was staring. Clearing his throat, he looked away, glancing over at the king to cover his embarrassment. But Leo had not missed the lingering gaze and turned away, seemingly angry.

"I'm going to gather up some cloudberries," the king said but Faris knew he was covering his unhappiness.

"Don't go far," he replied, just as Lily said, "Stay nearby," but Leo ignored them both, stomping into the woods.

Twenty-Eight

Sergius had listened carefully to everything the bird had told him. He had remained silent, hunched over his scrubbed table through the recounting of what had been happening at Brighthelm. When Ravan finished the man sat back and took a long breath. *And they found the collar, they've fallen for your trap?*

Yes. But we must not underestimate Loethar.

Sergius nodded. *That would be a grave error,* he replied. He gave a short mirthless grin. *Loethar is clearly a man of strong emotions.*

He doesn't show them, Ravan reminded.

No, but he feels them and his decision to conquer the Set, humiliate Penraven, has been relentless and brutal.

The raven stretched his wings, shuddered slightly. *I will be missed.*

You're going?

You know I must.

What a strange and lonely life I lead, the man remarked, sighing, stretching like his friend.

How old are you, Sergius?

Too old. I've lost count of the years.

No, you haven't. I deserve to know. I do your bidding—I've never questioned it—and yet I hardly know anything about you.

You know all there is to know about me, Ravan. You've

known me since you were a hatchling. I became your mother, father, your friend.

Only in my mind and only long enough to give me to Loethar, the bird admonished. *Anyway, friends tell each other about themselves.* The raven sounded wounded.

My age, all right. Let me see. I must be more than five thousand moons.

Ravan hopped, turned his head to stare at his friend. *That's old.*

Indeed. I knew the first Valisar King, Cormoron, was present when he took his oath at the Stone of Truth, although no one witnessed it.

Ravan considered this startling news. *Sergius, would you agree that our task is the most important you've ever faced?*

Certainly. It is the only time I have been required.

Then we are living in a unique time, facing a unique situation.

We are, Sergius confirmed.

Then before I go I want to know everything.

I'm not sure I understand.

I believe you do. I believe you know much more than you have shared. And I think it's right that as your eyes and ears—as you describe me—I am privy to what our role is and why we must perform it. I have done precisely what you've asked of me since you abandoned me in the plains three decades previous. And that's another puzzle. My kind do not live this long. My kind don't talk to your kind. Who am I?

All these questions! Sergius said, disgusted, waving a hand at the raven.

They need to be answered. I want to know who we are and why we are on this path. Only then I will continue to do your bidding.

Sergius looked up, surprised. *Only then? What will you do if I refuse?* His voice was devoid of threat or challenge.

Ravan answered in the same tone. *I shall fly away and not return.*

Then I shall wear you down with constant chatter inside your head.

As you wish, old man. I shall ignore you.

I gave you life, Ravan! Sergius said, exasperated.

And I give you my life. But I must understand why and for what.

All right, all right. I shall explain. Go fly, stretch your wings, wretched bird. I must make some nettle tea before I begin.

Ravan obliged, returning not long after but by which time the old man had his steaming mug of tea on the table. He gave a soft sound of exasperation as the black bird shook its feathers and settled itself once again before him, letting Ravan know that he considered this an imposition.

Get on with it, Ravan urged with equal disdain. *Time is short.*

Sergius began, speaking aloud, knowing the bird could follow the words just as easily as if he were speaking directly into his mind. He so rarely heard his own voice these days that it felt good to stretch the long unused muscles of his throat.

"I'm not sure anyone alive today knows that Cormoron, the first of the great Valisar Kings, was a mighty sorceror—as talented with his Vested powers as he was with the sword."

Ravan hunched down.

"When he first took power the Set was divided among many different family warlords, although there were only about four of them that mattered. Cormoron did not belong to this region. He came from among the great southern land mass—a region known as Lindaran. He sailed an extraordinary voyage into unchartered waters, during which he lost only a few of his men to seasicknesses, and landed first on Medhaven. On that island he met no resistance from the goats and sheep, and the odd scattered hut with few people. He moved on to Vorgaven, where he again found little resistance for his tough fighting men, and he soon found himself on the fertile land of the vast mass that makes up the largest part of the 'hand' of today's Set. He liked what he saw. He settled. To cut this long preamble short, he made peace with the fractured family-style populations spread across the continent of the Hand. His leadership abilities were already well honed and he was a charismatic man—irresistible, really, to most. He was imposing too—as tall as he was broad with a booming voice and flowing locks of dark hair. Everything about him was strong, decisive, compelling.

"Cormoron was intelligent enough to not make war with the warlords; instead, he sat down around the parley table with them and worked out ways in which they could all live alongside one another. And in so doing he formed the Set: seven realms in the Hand, which included Medhaven. Droste was the only realm hostile to Cormoron's plan but it did not have the force necessary to attack him and, as he refused to wage any further war, he accepted Droste as a separate entity. The plains to the east—unfertile land of endless flat grasses—were seemingly uninhabited all those centuries ago."

So he became ruler of this land he called Penraven, Ravan said, pushing the old man ahead.

"Indeed," Sergius agreed, untroubled by being hurried along. "He took his oath at Lackmarin before the Stone of Truth. Now, I told you that Cormoron was a sorceror of great power. Though we know that, little is known of his abilities. He kept his powers hidden, never discussed them: indeed, rarely used them, to my knowledge."

And? Ravan pushed again.

"Well, at the time of his oath, which he saw as a momentous occasion for the region, he called down a great and ancient power from his native Lindaran. She is known as Cyrena."

The serpent, Ravan said.

"That's right."

I know this bit. She drank his blood and—

"You make it sound tedious, Ravan. There was nothing ordinary about Cyrena," Sergius admonished. "She is the most beautiful of all the ancient creatures; and furthermore, she might be the most important. She is the goddess of conscience."

Forgive me, the bird said humbly.

Sergius continued as though uninterrupted. "Cyrena made Cormoron promise that if she blessed his new realm and agreed to his supreme power over it—including ultimately the Set—he must agree never to use his magical powers against his own.

"She could not control his power but she appointed me to watch for any abuse of Valisar power—not just magical, I might add. I was once a simple healer and man of faith whom Cormoron took on his journey north. But how could I refuse her? She insisted I walk the Valisar journey from thereon. I still do not know everything there is to know and I control very little. But Cyrena did grant me certain powers too." He sighed, gave Ravan a long and meaningful stare. "She gave me you."

The raven hopped around the table, obviously fascinated by this admission. "I belong to Cyrena?"

"You are her creation, as am I," Sergius admitted, shrugging his thin shoulders.

I've lived for three decades, and known you for that time. But what did you do for all of those decades before?

"Nothing remarkable. I lived. Quietly. I have seen many Valisars come and go. I was not needed then."

But now you are needed? Ravan queried, his intrigue obvious in his tone.

Sergius gave a soft sigh and stood. "Yes, my friend, now I am needed. Pity I'm such an old fellow."

Ravan flapped his wings with obvious exasperation. *I don't understand. King Brennus is dead. The heir, Leonel, is still a boy. He has no power to abuse; he is on the run. If he can survive it will be years before he can offer any threat to Loethar.*

"I am not talking about Leonel."

Ravan cocked his head. *Piv—? No, I know that's not*

right. Sergius had already begun shaking his head. Ravan hunched down, confused. *I'm baffled.*

"Think hard. You have the intelligence to work it out," Sergius said, and smiled.

Freath had insisted Kirin take some air. They'd both had time for their tempers to cool.

"Does this help?" Freath asked.

"The fresh air is soothing. My head hurts to the point that I think I've lost some vision. Now and then the distance looks blurred around the edges of my eyesight."

"We must have a physic take a proper look at you. It's probably something transient, the result of the pain in your head."

"I think we both know that is a kind lie. I know what this is. I think the damage is permanent."

Freath didn't respond immediately, instead walking ahead, pointing to the herb garden. "Piven was lost here, apparently." He bent to pluck some leaves, which he crushed, inhaling their aroma. "This was Iselda's garden. She planted it as much for its scent as for its practicality. She loved to chew kellet; I recall its soft spicy fragrance on her breath."

"I did it, Freath. It was me," Kirin blurted as they circled the herb beds.

Freath paused before he sighed, not looking at the Vested. "I know. I worked it out." Silence stretched between them. "Did you keep that a secret from me for any reason?" he finally continued.

"I didn't know I could do that," Kirin replied, his voice laden with irritation. "I don't know what even possessed me to try—desperation, no doubt. The alternative was to watch either, or both, you and Genrie be murdered before our eyes."

Freath nodded. "Both, I would imagine. The Droste woman is highly suspicious of Genrie and Loethar has yet to fully trust me. That's why he tested me. I don't know what to say to you. Words don't seem enough. Frankly, I'm still lost in my own astonishment."

Kirin looked at him sideways. "It was my choice to attempt it."

"Did you know what you were trying?" Freath asked, allowing his awe to creep through.

"I can't remember. I think I decided in that moment in which I realized how badly wrong this was all going for you. I thought if I could just get into Genrie's mind, maybe I could force the right answer by letting her see the right boy's head in my mind. To be honest, when she chose the right one I assumed it was luck, a pure coincidence."

"So did I."

"When Loethar called in Father Briar I wasn't going to try again. I was already dizzy with nausea and I didn't want to fall over, draw attention to myself. But then I saw your face. I saw how frightened Father Briar looked and I understood how much was riding on this . . . how many lives stood in the balance. So I tried again, with no idea if what I was doing was right. I was losing consciousness before I could see which head the priest chose. Luckily Clovis caught me, kept me upright long enough for the hysteria to pass and Loethar to leave."

"Can you remember how you did what you did?"

"Not really. I don't think I ever want to try that again, though."

"Kirin, you must realize you are not only looking into people's minds but are influencing them. That is an incredibly powerful magic."

"That's prying. Now that I've had some time to consider it, I believe they both knew I was there in their minds. I suspect they're confused now but eventually they'll realize that something unusual has occurred."

"Genrie already suspects. She's waiting for my explanation, I think. They were both left dizzied, disoriented by the experience. She can put two and two together."

"What will you tell her?"

"Nothing! No one but us will ever know this. Did Clovis say anything?"

"If he did I didn't hear it."

"Well, then that's possibly three of us. Two too many! The secret remains between us."

Kirin nodded bleakly.

"I'm sorry about your eyesight, Kirin. I don't know what to—"

"It cannot be helped. I think perhaps this is what the seer on Medhaven was trying to tell me about my talent. She was right to frighten me."

"If you use this magic, it harms you—is that what you mean?"

Kirin looked away toward the forest. "I suspect that's the truth of it."

"I'm sorry."

The man of magic shook his head. "If not for you, Freath, I would be dead already. Many of us would be dead already. You have no blame in this."

"There are moments where I feel as though I am to blame for all the despair."

"I agreed to fight back. I made Clovis bury his sorrows as best he could and fight back. We have to, whatever the cost."

"Brave words," Freath murmured softly.

"They're all I have," Kirin said, equally quietly. "What now?"

"We must be very watchful. Will you be another set of eyes and ears for me?" At Kirin's nod, Freath continued. "We've managed to get this far relatively unscathed but I have no idea what lurks in Loethar's mind. He is a hard man to read and he is far, far more incisive than many may believe."

Kirin nodded. "Are we over the worst of it?"

"For now. He believes all the Valisars have now been dealt with and, apart from his genuine regret over Piven, he will be feeling relatively secure. I imagine he will turn his attention to his nuptials and to settling down the various realms. He is charismatic enough to win the nobles' support. They have seen enough bloodshed, suffered enough destruction and despair. Everyone will want peace and an end to the brutality.

If that means living under barbarian rule, they will. He understands this."

"His metamorphosis from barbarian warlord to western emperor is astonishing," Kirin commented.

"That's all part of it. He knows what he's doing. Given time I believe he will even behave fully as a Set king. He was born to lead—of that there is no doubt. It's a pity he was born into the family on the Likurian Steppes."

Kirin looked at Freath, surprised. "You can't mean that?"

"Why not?" Freath shrugged. "He isn't like Stracker. He isn't even like the mother. Stripped of the barbarian adornments and dressed in De Vis's wardrobe, he doesn't look like a man of the Steppes."

"I don't share your admiration. He's a butcher!"

"So was Cormoron all those centuries ago. We regard him as a hero in Penraven because he fought on our behalf, built this land, formed the Set. The Steppes people obviously worship Loethar with a similar loyalty."

"What about Stracker?"

"Stracker is a different person altogether. I've never seen anyone with such bloodlust. The man simply likes killing."

Kirin nodded knowingly. "All right. I'll watch and listen. I hope Clovis found Piven, and found some peace as well."

"Poor Piven. Who knows what will become of him. Clovis is our only hope; my hands are tied."

"Is it worth it?" Kirin stepped back at Feath's wounded expression. "I mean, he's so lost, really, isn't he . . . is he worth risking a life for?"

Freath's expression became even more haggard. "I gave my word to my lady queen that I would let nothing happen to her sons. I have lost both of them in a matter of days. I can offer neither of them help. I can offer neither protection. Why would she have put her faith in me?" he asked, shaking his head, turning away.

"Because she trusted you. And if you hadn't had the foresight to make it look as though you'd turned traitor, her sons wouldn't even be alive. At least King Leonel has a chance."

"That's true. And perhaps Piven, too. Thank you. I have to think that way or my grief will stop me in my tracks. Come, let's get you to a physic."

"There is no point, Freath."

"Why?"

Kirin stared at him coolly. "Because I know you plan to ask more of the same from me."

Within the palace that evening all was quiet. Loethar was somber. Although his lovemaking had been more gentle than usual, in that slower, more peaceful manner Valya sensed his distance. He was more untouchable than ever this evening and it was strange that he had taken to his bed so early. Though she didn't mind so long as she was beside him.

It was wonderful to relax in a huge, soft bed again, beneath a lush canopy and enclosed by velvet drapes. True privacy, as well as luxuriating between silk, her head cradled by pillows of down, were treats she had certainly forgotten. She had been lying in a sleepy warmth of sated lust but now she turned beneath the sheets and regarded Loethar's solemn face.

"I enjoyed that, my love. Thank you," she cooed, her voice languorous. He said nothing. She risked stroking his chest, devoid of hair, unmarked unlike his brother. "How is it that you have no tatua and yet you are the ruler of the Likurian people?" She'd never dared ask before.

He shifted his head on the pillow slightly away from her and she thought he would ignore her question but he answered, "The first tatua are made when you have marked one hundred and twenty moons against your life. It is a special time for fathers to formally welcome their sons into the tribe as warriors."

"So why not you?"

"I did not have a father to do those honors. And my mother chose not to mark me."

"That was brave."

He turned now, regarded her with an expression she

couldn't read. "What an extraordinary comment," he said, his dark eyes glittering from the lamplight overhead. "Why do you say that?"

She shrugged, her breasts quivering, though he didn't glance away from her face. "I imagine she would have been eager to mark you as soon as possible to herald your position." At his nod, she continued. "Instead she chose not to. I can only assume this was to set you apart somehow. I suspect it would have created much discussion, possibly anger, from the elders of your people."

"It did."

"Then it took courage to stand her ground."

"Indeed. That's very insightful of you, Valya. I'm impressed. It really was an incredibly brave decision on my mother's part."

"I don't only bring you beauty and a realm, Loethar," Valya said playfully, but he was having none of her coquettish behavior. He rested himself on an elbow, facing her fully, and she watched the muscles ripple on his lean frame.

"What else do you sense?"

She shook her head girlishly.

"No, I mean it. Don't play coy. There is nothing shy or reserved about you, Valya. One of the reasons we're together is because you are always so direct, so obvious in what you want and how you get it. I respect that. Tell me what else you have noticed in the short time you've lived among us."

She gave a soft sigh. "Well, you've all always kept me at arm's length so I'm not sure I can make the sort of observation you want. But I have to wonder why you are ruler when you're not the eldest male in your family. Why does Stracker allow it?"

Loethar nodded approval of her question. "Because I'm stronger."

She snorted, surprised.

"Not here," he said, pointing to his tensed arm. "Here," he said, moving his finger to his temple.

"So in your culture an heir can be overlooked?"

She saw momentary amusement in his eyes. "In our culture, Valya, there is no such thing as an heir. We fight for our right to rule."

This took her by surprise. "What? I, I thought you were royal?"

"I am."

"No, of royal blood, lineage," she explained, frowning.

"I am," he repeated.

"But you're saying that anyone could have been king."

"Yes. I fought many warriors for my right to be king."

"Wait a minute. You fought Stracker?" she asked, disbelief engulfing her.

He nodded.

"You beat all the other eligible warriors?"

"You should not be so surprised," he admonished gently. "Every male is eligible. If our king had died when I was only eleven, I could have fought then for the right to rule. I simply had to be prepared to lose my life—that's all it takes."

"I had no idea," she said. "How many did you fight?"

"Twenty-nine."

"How many died?"

"Twenty-eight."

She understood in a blink. "You spared Stracker?"

He nodded.

"I see. You spared him because he's your half-brother?"

He didn't say anything, simply stared at her, waiting for her to work it out.

"No, that didn't matter a whit to you, did it? You spared him because he was your mother's son."

"It would have been awkward," he said, smiling briefly as he said the final word.

"And that's why Stracker is so beholden to you. You spared his life and now he owes you."

"I'm not sure either of us see it that way but possibly my mother does. Certainly the various families do. Stracker knows his life was forfeit."

"And you trust him?" she asked.

"I didn't say that."

She nodded. "Good. But that doesn't answer my original question. Stracker has the tatua and he was seemingly equally capable of being king. Why were you spared the inks?"

"You'll have to ask my mother that," Loethar said, leaning back on his pillow again.

Valya knew she was highly unlikely to broach such a subject with Dara Negev. "Does no one from the tribes mind?" she pressed.

"No one minds," he echoed. "I won my title, my right through blood. That is how it is done. If I choose not to mark myself as the warrior I am, it is my loss. That's how they would see it."

"So you could still take the tatua?"

"Yes."

"But you won't."

"Not now. Not as Emperor of the Set and the Steppes."

"I don't think you would have regardless of that," she said, staring at him.

"Probably not."

"Why not?" she asked.

He didn't answer. "Changing the subject," she said, "I'm glad the Valisar boy is dead."

"You mean Leonel?"

"Of course."

"I couldn't be sure to which you referred. You never showed any warmth toward Piven."

She gave him a look of surprise. "Do you blame me?"

"I suppose not."

"Well, I suppose I'm sorry about him."

"Are you?"

She squirmed beneath his penetrating question. "I know you liked him, even though you might as well be speaking to a wall or a piece of furniture," she said, touching the smooth dark wood of the four-poster bed.

"I did like him. He turned into the very pet I thought I

could ridicule him as. I wasn't prepared to be fond of him but I was, in the end."

"You don't miss him, surely?"

"No, but I regret that he will die hungry, lost."

"That's rather sentimental of you. If it eases your mind, I doubt he'll register even that much, my love." She smiled. "How curious that you can kill people with such ruthlessness and then mourn the loss of a single halfwit child."

"I see something of myself in Piven," he admitted softly.

"Don't be ridiculous!" Valya scoffed. Then, changing the subject again, she asked, "Do you feel you can relax now that Leonel is dead?"

"I can focus on what I came here to do, which is to rule. Our wedding will herald the beginning of festivities that will bring the Set together again, start blending our peoples. I am sending for the warriors' women and I've also told Freath to hire staff for the palace—you may want to supervise that alongside him?"

"Most certainly I will," she said, making a mental note to speak with Freath the following morning.

"Bring the wedding forward. I think we should marry in leaf-fall."

This was wonderful news but it also made her nervous. "But, my love, that's just a moon away."

"Then you have plenty to do, Valya," he replied, turning his back on her.

He was asleep within minutes and Valya had never felt more lonely. It was still early enough to see through the windows. She was vaguely hungry, not tired and suddenly disgruntled. She had rung for Genrie but the girl had taken an age to arrive, then looked sullen at the request. She'd said it may take a short while because she was the only person on the staff and Dara Negev had ordered hot water be brought up. Valya had ignored what she considered whining.

"I am soon to be empress," she had reminded Genrie,

"and you'd do well to get your priorities in the right order," before she then slammed the door in the girl's face.

Overly restless, she decided not to ring for Genrie but to go down to the kitchens herself. Maybe she could find a beaker of milk, perhaps something to eat. She pulled around her shoulders a silk robe that she'd taken from Iselda's rooms, its quality attesting to the unmistakeably heavy, exquisitely embroidered fabric from Percheron. She'd found matching slippers too and those she put on as she tiptoed from the bed.

She turned to look at Loethar, who in a rare occasion was sleeping deeply. His mouth was slightly parted and she could see a neat row of teeth beneath the expressive lips that had been so well hidden once below the scraggly beard. He really was an intensely attractive man. She couldn't see his eyes but she knew that arresting dark gaze lurked beneath those closed lids and long dark lashes. Sometimes those eyes excited her. Mostly they frightened her. She wished she knew what thoughts roamed behind them, but he kept that part of him remote from everyone.

Loethar stirred, obviously aware of her scrutiny and more alert than she had given him credit for.

"What are you doing?" he murmured.

"Your piece of theater quite put me off my food this evening, my love. Now I feel hungry and can't sleep."

"Wake the girl. Genrie can fetch you something."

"No. It's too early for me to sleep, anyway. I think I'll go fetch myself a cup of warmed milk."

He murmured something.

"Pardon, my love?"

"I said, throw some liquor into it."

She smiled, hoping he was concerned for her restlessness but suspecting he simply wanted her to stop disturbing him. Still, she touched him on the shoulder gently. "Sleep well, beloved," she said softly, dropping a soft kiss to his hair.

He turned over in the bed, the sheet falling away, and she saw once again the silvery lines of long-healed wounds on his body. She could only imagine the number of blades that had attempted to take his life when he fought for the title of ruler of the Likurian Steppes. Well, now he was Emperor of the Denova Set and the entire region. She must remind him to rename the whole area in order to fully stamp his mark onto his new empire. And she would be his empress. She smiled. She couldn't wait to see her parents' faces when they learned the truth of whose arms she'd run to a year ago and to whom they must now pay fealty.

As Valya closed the door silently, her mind filled with notions of bitter triumph, she just caught sight of someone scurrying down the main flight of stairs. It was Genrie. Presumably it was early enough for the servant to still be going about her business, but Valya sensed something curious in Genrie's urgency. The servant looked behind her carefully, as if mindful of being trailed or watched. Valya had kept the deliciously clandestine nugget of information of the secret relationship between the dour Freath and the defiant Genrie to herself for now. She needed to think about how it could be used to her advantage. But perhaps the girl had more secrets Valya could explore. From the shadows high above, she decided to follow the servant.

Twenty-Nine

He felt himself reaching consciousness but had the presence of mind to remain still, keep his eyes shut while he took stock of the situation as best he could. He felt confused, disoriented. His head was on fire with pain, as was the rest of his body. It even hurt to breathe; some of his ribs must be cracked.

As he came fully to consciousness, he realized that not an inch of him didn't flare with agony. His arms were tied behind his back, his ankles tied together. He was lying on the ground. He smelled the forest but couldn't hear any birdsong, just the low voices of men and the occasional snort from a horse. His memory gave him nothing. He had no idea what he was doing here or why.

He opened his eyes, just to slits—it was all he could do, anyway—to see if he could get some bearing on his surrounds. And he realized then that his face was puffy, misshapen. His lips were not sitting right at his mouth, and, once he realized that, he noticed that his mouth was dry. No, not dry, parched. He would kill for a sip of water.

He tried to concentrate on what he could see. Right enough he was in woodland . . . but why? He turned his head but very slowly in order not to attract attention, and to protect against the pain. Three men sat around a small fire, talking in low voices. Who were they? What did they want with him? It was early evening, he knew that much. Had it rained recently? Possibly. The ground felt damp and smelled freshly earthy. In addition to the earth, he could smell the firs and smoke from the fire. The one man's face that he could see in the dimness had designs on it, some sort of dark ink. How strange. Who were these people? Why was he with them? Why was he their prisoner? Why was he hurting so much?

Time to find out.

"Hey!" He had meant to yell it in a friendly manner but it came out a low groan.

The three bulky figures moved as one, approaching him silently. They were obviously adept at stealth. The one on the far right seemed to be the leader; the other two appeared to defer to him.

"Thirsty," he explained.

The leader pulled down his trousers and unleashed hot acrid liquid all over his face. "Better?"

Coughing and spluttering, fear began edging around the horror of the man deliberately aiming for his mouth. He must know Gavriel couldn't move his head too far or too fast. He began to vomit—not from the piss but from the overwhelming nausea that engulfed as pain fully claimed him. His vision blurred as he retched and he knew his head must be injured because that's where the worst of his agony was emanating from. It was clear these men had already punished his body. But he couldn't remember it. Had they beaten him while he was unconscious?

"Why?" he managed to say.

"Because we can," another man answered. "Penraven scum. Think you can run from us, eh? Well, you won't be running any more. We've hobbled you. Perhaps you know what that means in relation to a horse?"

He did his best to nod, to be cooperative.

"Except on the plains we use ropes," the man said.

"But we're not on the plains now," the third added.

"And you're no horse," the presumed leader continued.

"So we've had to use a slightly more radical method of keeping you from moving too far."

"We broke your feet," the second one said. The three of them seemed to find this highly amusing.

Broke my feet? he repeated in his mind. Instinctively he twisted his ankles. Immediately he felt shards of white hot pain, like lightning, bolt through him until he saw stars behind his tightly shut eyelids. He began to breathe shallowly just to help him focus on the pain, riding it, hoping the concentration would make it easier to handle and then hopefully dull. Someone told him that once. He couldn't remember who.

In the shadows a figure watched, had been observing this odd quartet for a number of hours now. It was reaching twilight. Soon the wood owls would begin their mournful calls and the animals that forage in darkness would begin snuffling around the undergrowth. There were wolves in this forest. The stranger had heard them, even seen a couple, and didn't want to meet the pack that roamed this area. The eavesdropping figure did not belong here, and had not anticipated company—or such a dilemma. Good sense demanded that the quartet be left. Their prisoner had been beaten so badly that the sound of his breaking bones could be heard from this relatively distant spot. And the men had gone about their grisly task while he was out cold. How strange. Whatever their argument with the prisoner was their business, the stranger knew. But no man deserved the hiding the boy had endured and for what? The thugs were bored. Anyone could see that. And this fellow who had stupidly stumbled into their path had offered entertainment of a most base kind.

The observer looked down. A decision needed to be made.

He was half conscious again. He knew now there was no escape from these brutes. But he would give them no satisfaction. Though he suspected he would succumb quickly if they decided to finish it; they seemed to be tired of it. The call to sleep had become stronger than the call for more blood. Perhaps they'd been drinking. He was too far gone to tell. He watched them slump back down around their fire, and within minutes he heard snoring from two. The other dozed or perhaps slept silently.

He closed his eyes, hoped he might die peacefully during the night.

The arrow whizzed out from the darkness of the woodland and hit the warrior's throat so hard he didn't register his own death; his body jerked in one angry subconscious recognition of the fatal injury and then lay still. Though the other two were on their feet in a blink, the second man hardly had time to look around before another arrow came humming out of the trees, sinking into his heart. As he fell like a stone, the third man looked around wildly. An enormous stranger emerged from the trees, dressed in a simple dun garb of animal skin.

The warrior appealed to the stranger, opening his palms, the look of plea a universal expression. Dragging a huge, mean-looking blade from his scabbard, the warrior waved it, offering a far fairer way to settle whatever it was between him and the intruder.

The stranger did not hesitate, though. The bow that was trained on the barbarian tightened and then a final arrow was loosed at close range, passing through the warrior's chest and out through the other side with the greatest of ease, burying its shaft almost to the fletchings. With a groan of surprise, the leader fell to his knees, hurling some sort of insult at the stranger before crumpling to his side.

Gavriel watched this all unfold, hardly daring to believe what he was witnessing. And then he felt a fresh spike of fear as the newcomer turned and strode toward him. Was it his turn now? An arrow to the throat, perhaps? At least that would be swift.

The figure bent over him, withdrew a blade and cut his

wrists and ankles free of their bindings, then lifted his broken, pathetic frame. He moaned. He had no strength to do much else as his body gave him fresh explosions of suffering.

"Bear up," she said as he slipped back into unconsciousness.

Thirty

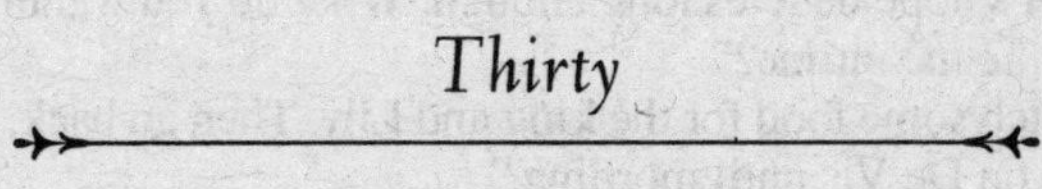

Tern had returned to brief Faris on what was occurring.

"He's unconscious?"

"You're sure?"

The man nodded. "I left them as soon as they'd finished pissing on him. They got bored, turned in for the night."

Faris looked up. "A bit early to be sleeping," he remarked.

"They'd been drinking the kern, too."

Faris nodded. Kern was a local and notorious liquor of Penraven's north. The warriors might be big and hardy but they would be no match for kern's powerful intoxication. He himself had drunk it only twice in his life, and on both occasions he had awakened the next day feeling as though he'd been kicked by a mule several times. Since then he had refused to take the fiery red liquid, distilled from the noxious aspenberries that grew with abandon on low bushes that fringed the forest.

"So he's safe for now?"

"If you can call what they've done to him keeping him safe. He's half dead, Kilt. I don't think we should leave it too long."

"We have to wait for Jewd and the others. I don't think we should go in alone."

"You and I can easily take the three of them."

"I know but I have to ensure the king takes his oath tonight. It's a full summertide moon tonight, which makes this evening all the more important. Twilight will not hold for us. And they're probably asleep already."

"So we wait until tomorrow?"

"As soon as Jewd arrives, we go in."

"Let's hope he lives long enough. What do you want me to do in the meantime?"

"Fetch some food for the king and Lily. Then go back, keep watch on De Vis until morning."

Tern left to organize the food and Faris went over to where Lily looked to be deep in thought.

"One minute we seemed to be so in control and now everything feels dangerously out of kilter," she commented as he sat down beside her.

"All will be well. Right now we must get Leo to take his oath."

"Why is that so important?" she snapped.

"I thought I'd explained. This is what Brennus asked of me. It was part of our bargain and I intend to keep it."

"Well, you'll have to make sure of that yourself. He's not paying any attention to me."

"That's because he's smitten with you."

"Don't be ridiculous."

"I'm not. Nor am I so old that I can't remember what it was like to be his age, and with a terrible crush on a much older woman." He grinned but she didn't take the bait.

"I'm worried about Gavriel."

"I understand. But I will not risk my life for him. For the king, yes, not for De Vis."

"How callous."

"Not at all. If he'd followed my instructions he would be safe among us. I can't be responsible for every petulant decision your travelling companions make while they come to terms with the fact that you find me far more engaging than either of them." Once again he'd hoped to lighten the leaden mood around her with gentle mocking but his sardonic approach did not work; in fact, it did the opposite.

Lily stood. It seemed her tinder was always dry, Faris

thought, always ready to ignite at the tiniest spark. He sighed privately, waited for the onslaught.

"How dare you, Faris! How dare you make presumptions that—"

His shrug stopped her tirade. "Sorry. I thought the hand on the chest thing was rather intimate considering you barely know me."

She slapped him. He didn't see it coming, though he realized he should have. It stung but he didn't touch his cheek. Just stared at her.

"If Gavriel dies, I'll never forgive you," she hurled at him.

He straightened his shirt. "If De Vis dies, it's your fault for not being more honest with him and your fault for leading him here into danger. I offered protection, and he flouted that protection because of a young man's perceived jealousy, even after I tried to make peace with him. You were the one who argued with him. But that's not my concern, Lily, nor is it my problem. I gave a blood promise to King Brennus and I intend to keep faith with it." He shrugged. "What you do and what De Vis does is your business."

She stared at him, her eyes glittering with fury. He felt his gut twist at the loathing in her face but he did not show his discomfort.

"Where is Tern?"

"Setting up some food, I believe, before he returns to observe De Vis."

"I'll go with him."

"Fine. It will be at your own peril, of course. Those men are dangerous."

She gave him a backward sneer, and said nothing.

Faris sighed, looked out from the highpoint of the clearing. Twilight was giving way to night. It had to happen now. He went in search of the king, and found him sitting quietly, arms around his knees not far from where he'd argued with Lily.

"I suppose you heard that?"

Leo stared at him but said nothing and Faris felt himself

suddenly become defensive. He hated that a boy who couldn't even think about growing facial hair yet managed to make him feel guilty . . . over nothing! "Why is everyone blaming me?"

"I'm not sure everyone is," Leo answered calmly.

"Lily is."

"Lily is angry over your comment. She's not blaming you for Gavriel's loss. She simply said she won't forgive you if he dies."

"That's just a different way of saying she blames me!" Faris answered, exasperated.

"Not from where I sit. Is it time?"

"Yes."

"What should I do?"

"The oath is carved into the stone. Simply read it aloud and mean it. What happens after that is left to the gods."

Leo nodded. "Will you be close by?"

"I am bound to leave you alone with Faeroe, upon whom you must swear as well."

"Thanks. Make peace with Lily . . . for me. It's bad enough losing Gavriel. I have so few people to rely on—please, Kilt."

Faris nodded. "I will at the first opportunity but I can't move from this spot here until you return. If you get into any bother, yell. Good luck."

Leo approached the Stone of Truth with trepidation. He had no idea what to expect. This was not something his father had schooled him in. The summertide moon looked huge, golden and so close he felt he could reach out and touch it. There was a thrum in the atmosphere this evening that he couldn't quite decipher, as though Faris's warnings of the potential for magic might be true.

He carefully laid Faeroe on the uneven but sparkling surface of the stone. Twilight seemed to heighten its shimmering effect and, as though they were picking up the moon's luminosity, the branstone's silver threads glittered in mesmerizing fashion. Leo found himself suddenly kneeling before the Stone of Truth. It felt right to pay it this homage. Once again he ran his fingers across the glimmering stone, over the words he must now recite.

Placing his hands on Faeroe, with great reverence he began to speak the ancient, sacred oath that the eight Valisar Kings before him had spoken.

He had no idea how far they had travelled. The swaying motion of the woman's gait as she ran, surprisingly lightly, through the forest was strangely comforting despite the pain. He was riding her back, his arms around her neck, her arms supporting his broken feet. He was sure he had blacked out several times from the waves of agony washing over him even though she was doing her best to minimize the jarring effect of their motion. The fact was, he told himself in more lucid moments, feeling that pain meant that he was alive, for which he had this curious person to thank.

Finally, she paused.

"Where are we?" he groaned.

"Far enough from where we were," she answered, cryptically, the only indication of her exertion the long, deep breaths she was taking.

"Do you know this place?"

"No. But I sense no danger. There's an old hollow up there, I think." She pointed with her chin. He could see where she meant clearly in the moonlight. "That's where we will rest this night."

He must have fainted again because when he came to she was laying him down in the cool hollow. "You're a mess," she said.

"Who are you?"

"Elka. And you?"

He frowned. "I don't know."

She regarded him with a look of skepticism.

"I promise. I have no recollection of who I am or what I

was doing there with those men. Or even what I was doing in the forest."

"You've forgotten?"

He shrugged, wincing. "I don't know. My head hurts, that's probably got something to do with it." He grimaced.

"How much pain are you in?"

"Just a smidgeon," he said sarcastically through another wince. Up close he could see that she was not just some sort of monstrosity with a woman's voice. When she smiled she was rather handsome.

"I will need to look at those ankles," she said and they both understood what that meant.

"What do you carry in that sack? Henbane, by any chance?"

She shook her head. "No, but I will make up something for you to take before we tackle it. What about the rest of you?"

It was his turn to grin mirthlessly. "What bit isn't bruised or broken?"

"I watched them beat you."

"Did you have to wait so long to protest?"

Elka smiled, embarrassed. "I couldn't make a decision about you. I know this much: you are not one of them." She nodded as he opened his mouth, and stopped his words by continuing: "I know that's obvious because you don't look or dress as they did, but I watched them bring you into that place on the back of a horse. You were unconscious so presumably they had captured you somewhere."

"But why?"

She shrugged. "I can't tell you. They said something about teaching you a lesson about running away from them."

"Where do you think I could be running from?"

"Or to?"

"Where are you from?"

"I'm of the Davarigons."

He blinked. "Should Davarigon mean something to me?"

She looked amused. "You know Lo's Teeth, the mountains that outline Droste and act as a barrier to the Great Plains?"

He shrugged. "I don't know what or where Droste is, or what the Great Plains are."

She frowned. "Well, you certainly are confused, aren't you? But you remembered henbane?"

He gave an expression to imply he was as baffled as she looked. "I don't understand, either."

"Our people have lived among those mountains for centuries."

"Are they all as . . . as . . ."

"What? Beautiful as I am?"

He grinned, amazed that he still could, his battered mouth punishing him immediately for the gesture.

"I am big in comparison to the people of these realms, that is true," she said, almost shyly.

"And strong," he added. "Elka, you picked me up like a sack of potatoes."

"Strength is in our blood, as is height." She carefully inspected his ankles, "Our people are reclusive. We have lived quietly in the mountains and our lives have not crossed those of either the Steppes or the Set. We are peaceful."

"Yes, I took note of that when you killed three men without blinking."

She laughed softly, her face brightening magnificently, crinkling her eyes. "I'm very accurate with a bow but we kill reluctantly. That's why I took so long to make my decision."

"Why did you?" he asked seriously.

She sighed. "You're young. What they did was cowardly. And wrong. If you've done something criminal, you should face your elders or whoever is in authority. It looked to me like those three were making their own judgment. There was no talk of wrongdoing, other than your running from them—as anyone might. So I decided to save your pathetic carcass."

"I'm sure if I'd done something bad, I'd feel it."

She shook her head. "I think we'd all like to think that way."

He sighed. "I owe you my life. Somehow I will repay you."

"You speak elegantly. I suspect you're from the city, perhaps even noble."

"What city?"

"Brighthelm, the palace of the Penraven Kings. Do you know what I'm talking about?"

He shook his head bleakly.

Elka let out her breath loudly. "Well, I can see I have a lot to teach you. You have a great deal to re-learn while we wait for your memory to return."

"Do you think it will?"

"You've got a huge gash on the side of your head and—" she reached behind him and he yelped—"and the most enormous lump. I imagine that is the cause of your memory loss."

He lay back, closing his eyes. "I think I'm going to be sick."

"Stay still, stay calm. I need to fetch a few things and we'll see if we can't deaden that pain for you before we set those ankles."

"You make it sound so gentle and easy."

"You'll hate me by the end of it."

"Thank you, Elka," he said, reaching for her large hand.

"You're welcome . . . What shall I call you?"

He shrugged. "How about Regor? I think I've always liked the sound of it."

"Regor it is. Good strong name. Tomorrow we'll head further toward the Dragonsback Mountains, which separate Penraven from Barronel. I'll feel more comfortable once we're in that terrain. And you'll have time and safety to get well, await your memory's return. But for now, be still."

Elka loped off and Gavriel De Vis lay back, finally allowing himself a few tears of self-pity. Somewhere deep in the recesses of his now clouded mind were flashes of thought—something about a snake and fear . . . but not for himself. He had been afraid for someone important. But when he reached for more clues, the dizziness only intensified, and he gave up. Elka was right; he needed to give it time . . . if only he didn't have the feeling that time had been his enemy in the first place.

Valya carefully followed Genrie all the way to the chapel, which surprised her. She began to believe that this was a pointless exercise, that the servant was going for a blessing from Lo or to offer up prayers. But then Genrie moved beyond the obvious door, carrying on further toward the chapel's walled garden.

She stepped back quickly as Genrie cast a worried glance around. Then Valya heard a man's voice. Recognizing it with a thrill of shock, she immediately chastised herself. She shouldn't be surprised by this. Hardly daring to breathe, she strained to hear the conversation.

"Have you got it?" Genrie said.

"Here," he replied. Valya peeped around, unable to believe what she witnessed. "Two only," he continued. "Any more and it will be recognized. It won't take any more, trust me. Are you sure?"

"This was your idea," Genrie accused. Then she shrugged. "It's too good an opportunity to miss."

"If you injure him I will declare you. I am loyal to him. Stracker will lay this realm to waste. But you need Loethar."

Valya felt a thrill of fear. Without waiting to hear the rest of the conversation, she took her chance to run away silently. When she reached Loethar's chamber he was still gently snoring in the same position she'd left him in. In contrast her heart was hammering, her breathing ragged. Even though it frightened her somewhat to do it, she woke her emperor, ignoring his angry growls, calming him so she could explain.

Freath knocked on the door of Loethar's suite. He had no idea why he'd been summoned at this hour. He shifted his shirtfront, embarrassed by how dishevelled he knew he must look, although he knew that Loethar wouldn't care.

"Come," came the voice of the barbarian. It sounded ominous.

Freath took a steadying breath and walked in. Not in his darkest thoughts could he have guessed that inside the room would he find the five people he did. His gaze was helplessly drawn to Genrie, who stood, eyes downcast, fingers opening and shutting nervously into fists at her side. Beside her stood a member of the Greens, Belush, Freath thought his name might be, and, of course, Stracker.

"My lord?" he asked, his breath shortening behind the words that flowed by instinct; those same instincts were telling him now that something exquisitely dangerous was afoot once again. His heartbeat quickened. "Is something wrong?"

"Yes, Freath, something is very wrong. I thought it appropriate that you be here for this."

Freath felt the short breath now catch in his throat. In the fleeting moment of time between Loethar's reply and his response of a short bow he was able to get a better look at Genrie: the waves of hair, presumably unpinned for the night and curling recklessly at her shoulders; the full, well-rounded breasts that sat high and proud beneath her uniform, which was unbuttoned at the throat. Just above the buttons he could see her pulse, strong and too fast, and a tiny apricot colored birthmark just at the point where her neck reached her shoulders . . . the clavicle, that's the name, he thought ridiculously, besieged now with fear. Genrie was the first woman he'd loved in . . . so long he didn't want to think about how long it had been. But now she refused to look at him.

"What seems to be the problem, my lord?" he forced out, clearing his throat.

"It seems your servant woman, Genrie, is plotting an assassination of sorts."

Freath's head rocked back. "What? No, my lord. I don't believe so." He felt confident saying this for Genrie would never try and kill Loethar, not alone and not without consulting Freath.

"I couldn't believe it either, Freath, but Princess Valya insists that Genrie is plotting death."

"My lord, I have known Genrie for some years now. She has been a hardworking servant of the royals but her real loyalties, like mine, are to her own. She has family, as you know." He shrugged. "Genrie would do nothing to injure you, my lord. In fact—"

"Not me, Freath," Loethar cut in. "Valya believes that Genrie was plotting her death."

"To kill the princess?" Freath repeated dumbly.

Loethar nodded, yawning. That casual carelessness chilled Freath all the more. The emperor would order Genrie's slaying as easily as he would swat at a fly. And now Freath could see that the ruler was tired. He'd obviously been roused from sleep and wanted to return to his bed. "So, let's just settle this once and for all, shall we?"

The pit of Freath's stomach opened up. That sort of introduction could only mean bloodshed.

"Er, my lord. May I take care of this for you?"

"Do you consider this such a petty matter that the emperor need not be involved?" Valya demanded, like a snake striking from hidden bushes. "I can't imagine you would, considering you were kissing this woman oh so tenderly not so long ago."

Freath just stopped himself from taking a step back, noticing the rueful grin on Loethar's face. No one cared. Not one of them. They were seeing this farce through to appease Valya. Stracker looked bored. The other Green seemed entirely unconcerned—and what was he doing here, anyway?

"Let's get this done with, Loethar," Stracker grumbled.

Loethar nodded. "Freath, I think we can handle this in a fairly straightforward fashion. Genrie, you've been appointed my taster by Master Freath. His romantic inclinations aside, he obviously has strong belief in you, which seems rather ironic considering what you're being accused of. So do show Princess Valya up to be the false accuser here and bear out

Freath's great faith. Drink down the milk, there's a good girl."

And now Genrie did look up. She ignored Loethar and the sneering Valya. The two Greens she seemed hardly aware of anyway. She focused all her attention on Freath.

"I tricked you, Freath, you pathetic, grasping old man. You thought you could trust me? I'm not prepared to climb into bed with these pigs, let alone you! At least this is less messy than the blade." She reached for the milk, swallowing it in four gulps. As she let the mug fall to the ground, she turned briefly to Loethar. "Never say I didn't try to help you. Kill her yourself, my lord, before she destroys you," she sneered.

Freath felt his heart lurch in his chest. It was true! His beautiful girl had attempted to poison the witch of Droste but Valya had prevailed. And now, in the face of death, another brave woman, just like the queen, was protecting his cover. He felt his heart breaking apart, shattering into dozens of pieces, as he watched Genrie begin to gasp.

She was brave to the end, refusing to show panic at her body's desperate attempts to grapple for air as it betrayed her. Freath watched numbly as the woman he loved, in heroic fashion, her body shaking from the effort of concealing her obvious suffering, lowered herself awkwardly to the floor. She lay her head back against the fireplace, the effects of the poison foaming out of her mouth, her lips already blackening, eyes glassing over.

He knew she'd held her tongue to her death and now he had to make sure that death wasn't in vain. "My lord, I have absolutely no idea what this is about," he said truthfully, unable to hide the shock in his voice.

"I know you don't, Freath, because Belush here has explained everything, particularly that it was his idea and that he was in league with the servant woman to kill the princess."

"Why?" Freath asked. Why would they be so naïve to try

such a thing? He had no delusions as to why they might want to.

Loethar waved his hand, distracted. "I can't be bothered with more of this. Stracker, you know what to do?" His half-brother nodded, glancing angrily toward the warrior at his side, who still looked unimpressed by what was unfolding. "Belush, you're an idiot. Lose your life for her?" Loethar pointed at Genrie's now frightfully swollen face.

"No, Lord Loethar. I am losing it for her," the Green spat savagely at Valya. Freath seemed to be the only one taken aback by the outburst. "This *saran*," Belush continued, loading the word with scorn, "treats your people with loathing. Forgive me, my lord, but I fear the woman who has drunk the poison is more loyal to you than the one you seek to make princess. Heed the servant's warning. I go to my death holding my head high as a Drevin. No Green bows to a Droste slut." He spat again and a gob of saliva landed on the rug glistening before them all.

Loethar nodded at Stracker but said nothing and the warrior was led away, presumably to die in some ritual or tribal manner. As far as Freath was concerned, there would now be one less barbarian to chase from Set soil.

Valya had an expression of disgust on her face. She turned to say something to Loethar but the look he gave her silenced her instantly. "I suggest you think on what has happened this night, Valya," Loethar said coldly. "For I cannot protect you for the rest of your days. Now leave."

She had the sense to turn on her heel and depart without another word, though it must have cost her to remain quiet, Freath thought. With Genrie's distorted face staring at him, he could not enjoy even a moment of cheer that Valya, who clearly saw herself as the victim in all this, had come out of it badly.

The door closed on the two men and the corpse they shared the room with.

"I think you were fond of this woman, Freath," Loethar remarked.

Freath cleared his throat, forced his gaze upon the man who had ordered Genrie to kill herself. He nodded. "She was brave," was all he could say.

"I noted. The poison she used is called strenic. It is distilled from an herb that grows wild on the Steppes. It's harmless to horses, but deadly to us." When Freath said nothing, Loethar continued. "It causes an incredibly painful death. I admired her stoicism at the end. It seems she despised Valya more than she loved her life."

It took all of Freath's courage to say what he did. "Well, my lord, at risk of sounding hilariously ironic, can I fetch you a warm drink to help return you to your slumber? I can assure you, you will find no poison in it." He tried for levity but to his ears it sounded leaden.

Loethar gave him a slow smile. "Now that I've lost my royal taster I suppose I shall have to trust you, Freath. Perhaps you could move the corpse as well?"

Freath nodded. "You go back to your chamber, my lord. I'll see to this."

It was only much later, after recruiting help to have the body carried down to the chapel, after Father Briar had recited prayers blessing Genrie's spirit, after he had finally been left alone with her, that Freath broke down and wept. Feeling old, very alone and broken, he cried for Genrie and his loss. But his tears were also for all the courageous souls who had given their lives for Valisar.

Thirty-One

King Leonel felt elemental power swirling around him, the way it feels just before a lightning storm begins to split across the sky. He felt the hair on his head begin to lift, the hair on his arms stand up and his skin begin to itch as though the very air was beginning to thicken and crackle. The forest had become utterly silent. All the noises of the birds settling down to their roosts and insects calling out to each other faded to nothing. The trees, the grass, the night . . . all blurred into a dim void.

The only thing he could see clearly, he realized, was the Stone of Truth. He could swear it was pulsing in a rhythm of its own, as though listening, responding even, to the words he recited.

He continued to speak the oath as loudly as he dared, to mean every word of what he was saying, to throw behind it all the emotion of the past few days. He wanted the very souls of his mother, father, Darros, perhaps even Cormoron to hear him make his promise as the new King of Penraven, 9th of the Valisars. He needed someone to tell him that Gavriel was going to be all right, that Corbel was safe, that he was pursuing the right path and that one day he might challenge Loethar for the crown that was rightfully his.

"Is anyone listening?" he yelled into the air that seemed to be splintering about him. Suddenly a dull rumble sounded, escalating in volume to an ear-splitting roar. He couldn't hear his own voice above the clamor and was glad his oath was spoken. "This is King Leonel of Penraven," he cried at the moon. No longer golden, it was now a glimmering silver orb that filled the space it lit with sparkles and flecks of flashing light. "I am King Leonel, the 9th," he tried again, to affirm the title to himself as much as to whomever might be listening.

And someone was listening.

Holding his breath now, Leo watched as a fissure appeared to open in the air that was rippling before him. It was as though he was straddling two worlds and into this world, where he knelt, was emerging a figure.

The Stone of Truth was blazing with blinding silver explosions of light. Though Leo had to blink and squint against it, unable to look directly at it, he could see a sinuous form stretching, unfurling from the Stone itself. He shrank back as the shape began to take a more solid form. The explosions began to recede until the figure was bathed in a constantly moving, shimmering glow.

"Do not be afraid," she said, as she finally coalesced into a curious half-woman, half-serpent beast.

"Cyrena?"

Her pale, achingly beautiful face broke into a gentle smile and all the noise quietened. "Welcome, Leonel, to the Stone of Truth," she said, reaching out to him.

"You are magnificent," he breathed, stunned by her glory. Her upper half had the proportions of the most perfectly shaped woman, with long silky hair that curled and flicked down to her elbows, but from her waist down her body became a dazzling, glittering mass of coils. Her arms were long and sinuous, shifting with the grace of a dancer.

Moving purely on instinct, Leo reached for one of those elegant hands and kissed it gently, reverently. She placed her other hand upon his head.

"Rise," she commanded.

He watched, tongue-tied, as Faeroe lifted from the stone, eased itself from its scabbard and landed effortlessly in

Cyrena's waiting hand, where it blazed with silver power. She turned the blade toward Leo and touched it to his head.

"King Leonel, I accept your oath and proclaim you ruler of Penraven, 9th of the Valisars, keeper of the Denova Set." She handed him the sword and he took it, re-sheathing it.

"Wear it with pride," she urged, and nodded, encouraging him to strap it around him, which he did. "You don't look like a Valisar but you now look like a king." Her words sounded harsh but they were said gently. "I speak the truth and answer only what you ask. Your mother was a most beautiful woman and you resemble her closely."

He nodded. "Everyone else in our family has dark hair," he admitted. Cyrena said nothing but she shimmered, the action causing her naked breasts to quiver.

"I am sorry about your parents. I imagine you come here burning with a vow to avenge them?"

"I do, Cyrena. I make that vow before you."

"Be very sure about it," she said, cryptically. "There is an old saying from the ancients—don't kill the snake and miss the scorpion." Her laugh sounded like glass chimes. "I do not refer to myself, of course."

Leo was mesmerized by her. Though he didn't understand her advice he knew he would ponder it later.

"My only intention is to bring peace back to our land and win back the crown," he emphasized, trying to make himself clear.

"I know you speak true. And the crown is rightfully yours, though the claim is a complex one."

"I don't see why. The barbarian marauder has unleashed a river of blood and despair to steal my father's throne; it cannot be rightfully his."

"Loethar seeks the magic that he believes he can attain."

"My father had no magic. I have no magic."

She shimmered silently in response.

"He *ate* my father to achieve something the king could never give him."

"Loethar is on a mission that burns so deeply, so angrily, that he will not sway from his path."

"Then he will meet me when I am a man and I will cut him down on that path which is mine," Leo vowed, his fury igniting.

She shimmered again at the passion in his voice. "The Valisars have never lacked courage."

He hung his head. "I must summon courage on behalf of all the Valisars who have died for Loethar's cause. I am the only one left."

"Are you sure?"

He stared blankly at the silver serpent woman. "My newborn sister died and—"

"Your sister did not die," she replied over his words, her form unfurling several coils so she loomed large.

Leo opened his arms in confusion, his mouth following suit. He was lost momentarily, both for words and understanding. Something in his chest tightened. "She died soon after birth. I saw her body. My mother held her dead body. She was cremated, her ashes thrown from Brighthelm's rooftops on Loethar's orders."

"You certainly saw a dead girl. Your mother certainly held a baby's corpse in her arms and a newborn was no doubt cremated, its ashes scattered as you say. But, Leo, that was not your sister."

"My mother—"

"She never knew, child. She went to her death believing her husband and daughter dead and you lost to her."

"Who knew?" he demanded, his voice breaking, remembering how his mother's heart had broken to hold the little girl she had tried so hard to win.

"Brennus."

"My father knew?"

"Your father contrived the deception."

Leo was stunned. "What did he do?"

"He made a difficult decision. He had a baby murdered to

take the place of his daughter, while your sister was sent away to grow in safety."

"She's alive?" he asked breathlessly, his mind spinning.

Cyrena nodded. "And she must return to Penraven when she is of an age."

"Where is she?"

"A place you do not know."

"Why not?" He didn't mean to sound rude; fortunately, she didn't take offense.

"It is reachable only through magic," was all she would say.

"I must find her!" Leo said.

"You must. She is important. Ah, the clouds arrive. Our time is drawing to an end."

He could sense her withdrawing. "How do I find her?"

"Corbel De Vis has the knowledge. That is all I can tell you."

"Why are there so many secrets?"

"There are always with the Valisars. Gavriel de Vis holds another." The clouds darkened over the moon. "My time here ends. The fissure closes. I must return to the world of the gods, Leonel. Be brave, be safe. Most of all, beware. Nothing is ever what it fully seems—sometimes friends are enemies and enemies are friends." She gave him a soft sad smile and the coils of her serpent form began to loop around one another, her body melting back into the stone as she began to fade.

"Cyrena, wait! Please, I have so many questions."

But she was gone. The light that had bathed him in such brilliance snapped to black. The moon was returned to its original, slightly golden orb. The birds were silent but insects sang and leaves rustled overhead.

Leo, bent over the Stone of Truth, let out a roar of despair. From the shadows Kilt Faris emerged.

"What occurred? I have barely sat down to wait."

The king raised his head. "The serpent came." He saw Faris's eyes light with interest.

"And?"

"She shared a secret."

Faris nodded. "Why is that no surprise?" He held up a hand as Leo opened his mouth. "No, my king. She shared that with you. It is not for me to hear."

Leo didn't care. He was sick of his father's secrets. "No, you need to hear this, in case anything happens to me. My sister is not dust on the winds. Her death was a ruse, orchestrated by my father much as he orchestrated my escape. He left only his adopted, disabled son to face Loethar—I see now that he gambled correctly that Piven would not be considered a threat." As Leo spoke, everything fell into place in his mind. "He planned for everything. And he has left a separate secret with each of the De Vis twins but I have no idea where Corbel is and neither does Gav. We have to find both of them."

"At the risk of sounding heartless, do you really believe your newborn sister is that important right now?"

"Faris, the Valisar line has never produced a female who has survived beyond birth. My sister's arrival must have terrified my father. I thought he was just frightened to have another child to protect. How naïve of me." He shook his head, lost in thought.

"What are you saying?" Faris prompted.

Leo looked up, his eyes slightly glassy with awe. "No female of the line has survived," he repeated. "It is said that a Valisar woman of the royal line will carry the legacy if she survives."

"Legacy?"

"The Valisar Enchantment." Leo put his hands to his head, then dropped them, shaking his head in wonder. "My tutors were obliged to teach this but my history guide never believed the tale of enchantment. He said the female strain was simply not strong enough in our line. But my father told me once that to bring forth a princess would be the greatest achievement for any Valisar king. He said the reason they were so few was that the enchantment they carried was so powerful it traditionally killed them before the babies had a chance to grow strong enough to bear it."

Faris looked stunned. "What is this enchantment?"

"The ability to coerce," Leo answered. "If she is alive, as the serpent attests, then my sister may well have the ability to force people to do things."

"She can make people obey her will, you mean?" Faris asked, astonished.

Leo nodded. "That is the magic Loethar is chasing, why he ate my father and would probably do the same to me. He doesn't know, he obviously doesn't realize that the power to coerce is carried only through females."

"Ssh!" Faris cautioned. "Keep this between us for now. It needs thinking upon."

Before any more could be said, both Tern and Lily arrived, breathless and looking anxious.

"What's happened?" Faris asked as they blundered into the clearing.

"It's De Vis," Tern said. "The three warriors who captured him are dead, arrows right through them."

"What?" Faris demanded.

Lily answered, her voice icy with repressed fury. "And Gavriel's gone."

The outlaw's gaze narrowed. "Who did this?"

Tern shrugged. "We saw nothing. It happened in the brief period of time I spoke to you and returned—barely minutes. I can't see any tracks. It was very deliberate. There was nothing accidental about the accuracy of those arrows."

"I hate you, Faris. I told you I wouldn't forgive you." Lily walked away, obviously distraught.

"That you did," he replied, frowning. "Don't go too far."

She stomped away and Faris nodded at Tern to follow. The man disappeared after Lily.

Leo's mind felt as though it were working in a blur. Too much was happening, too fast. But there was one thing he was now sure about. "Kilt. We have to rescue Gavriel."

Faris hesitated, but Leo was not to be persuaded otherwise.

"Now! He holds the key to help unlock the secret my father shared."

"Why didn't De Vis say something to you earlier?"

"I don't know but I'll never find out if we don't go after Gavriel. Whoever took him, took him for a reason. We have to find him. He is my only link to my sister."

Lily returned reluctantly with Tern. "Call your man off!" she scowled.

Faris nodded. "Tern, wait for Jewd. Tell him what has happened but keep it between him and yourself. The fewer who know about this, the better. Lily, you're staying with Tern."

"You have no right to tell me what—"

"Lily." Leo spoke up, his voice stern, suddenly commanding. "Do as he says."

Faris nodded at the king. "I have no idea what we're running toward, but I'm willing to run. Let's go, your majesty."

Epilogue

Sergius held his raven, always marvelling at its fragile network of bones and lightweight body, despite its size. He bent and kissed its head.

I will miss you.

And I you, Ravan replied.

Thank you for the news of Cyrena's appearance. Continue to see for me, look for me, hear for me.

Always.

Be safe, Ravan. We must be very careful. The Valisar Legacy is a dangerous force.

It's no longer in this world. Do not fret.

It will return. When it's ready, it will be drawn like iron to a magnet. In the wrong hands it can destroy the land.

Then we must not let it fall into the wrong hands, Sergius. You will know when it comes, will you not?

The man nodded. *I will feel it even though I cannot see it or hear it.*

Then we will be well warned. Farewell, the bird spoke into the man's mind and lifted from his arms effortlessly as Sergius flung him into the air.

Warned against what, though? Sergius wondered, frowning as he watched his raven beating its wings and gathering speed as his fear coalesced into something hard and dark in his gut.

Glossary

CHARACTERS
THE VALISAR REALM
Royalty

King Cormoron: The first Valisar king.
King Brennus the 8th: 8th king of the Valisars.
King Darros the 7th: 7th Valisar king. Father of Brennus.
Queen Iselda: Wife of Brennus. She is the daughter of a Romean prince from Romea in Galinsea. Comes from the line of King Falza.
Prince Leonel (Leo): First-born son of Brennus and Iselda.
Prince Piven: Adopted son of Brennus and Iselda.

The De Vis Family

Legate Regor De Vis: Right-hand of the king. Father to Gavriel and Corbel.
Eril De Vis: Deceased wife of Legate De Vis.
Gavriel (Gav) De Vis: First-born twin brother of Corbel. He is the champion of the Cohort.
Corbel (Corb) De Vis: Twin brother of Gavriel.

Other

Cook Faisal: Male cook of the castle.
Father Briar: The priest of Brighthelm.
Freath: Queen Iselda's aide and right-hand man.
Genrie: Household servant.
Greven: Lily's father. Is a leper.
Hana: Queen Iselda's maid.
Jynes: The castle librarian (steward).
Lilyan (Lily): Daughter of Greven.
Morkom: Prince Leo's manservant.
Physic Maser: The queen's physic.
Sarah Flarty: A girlfriend of Gavriel.
Sesaro: Famous sculptor in Penraven.
Tashi: Sesaro's daughter.
Tatie: Kitchen hand.
Tilly: Palace servant.

The Penraven Army

Brek: A soldier.
Commander Jobe: Penraven's army commander.
Captain Drate: Penraven's army captain.
Del Faren: An archer and traitor.

From outside Penraven, but still in the Set

Alys Kenric: A resident of Vorgaven.
Claudeo: A famous Set painter.
Corin: Daughter of Clovis.
Danre: Second son of the Vorgaven Royals.
Delly Bartel: Resident of Vorgaven.
Elka: From Davarigon—a giantess.
Jed Roxburgh: Wealthy land owner of Vorgaven.
Leah: Wife of Clovis.
Princess Arrania: A Dregon princess.
Tomas Dole: A boy from Berch.

The Vested

Clovis: A master diviner from Vorgaven.
Eyla: A female Healer.
Hedray: Talks to animals.
Jervyn of Medhaven: Vested.
Kes: A contortionist.
Kirin Felt: Can pry.
Perl: Reads the Runes.
Reuth Maegren: Has visions.
Tolt: Dreams future events.
Torren: Makes things grow.

The Supernatural

Algin: Giant of Set myth.
Cyrena: Goddess. The serpent denoted on the Penraven family crest.
Sergius: A minion of Cyrena.

The Highwaymen

Jewd: Friend to Kilt Faris.
Kilt Faris: Highwayman, renegade.
Tern: One of Kilt's men.

Outside the Sets

Emperor Luc: Emperor of Galinsea.
King Falza: Past king of Galinsea.
Zar Azal: Ruler of Percheron.

Loethar and his followers

Barc: A young soldier.
Belush: A Drevin soldier.
Dara Negev: Loethar's mother.

Farn: A Mear soldier.
Loethar: Tribal warlord.
(Lady) Valya of Droste: Loethar's lover.
Steppes (Plains) People: From the Likurian Steppes. Known as Barbarians.
Stracker: Loethar's right-hand man and half brother.
Vash: A soldier.
Vyk: Loethar's raven.

MAGIC

Aegis: Possesses the ability to champion with magic. Is bound to a person by the power of trammelling.
Binder or Binding: The person who binds himself to an Aegis.
Blood Diviner: A reader of blood.
Diviner: Gives impressions and foretells the future.
Dribbling: A small push of prying magic.
Prying: Entering another's mind.
Reading the Runes: Ability to foretell the future using stones.
The Valisar Enchantment: Powerful magic of coercion peculiar to the Valisar line.
Trammelling: Awakening an Aegis' power.
Trickling: Low level magic.

HEALING PRODUCTS

Willow sap, Comfrey balm (for pain)
Clirren leaves (powerful infection fighter)
Crushed peonies (for pain)
Henbane (for pain)
White lichen (used for dressing wounds)
Dock leaves (soothes itching skin)

THE DENOVA SET

The seven realms are sovereign states, self-governed with a king as head.

Barronel
Cremond
Dregon
Gormand
Medhaven
Penraven
Vorgaven

The Hand: The continent that the Denova Set sits on.

Cities/towns within the Set

Berch: close to Brighthelm. Home of the Dole family.
Brighthelm: The city stronghold (castle) and capital of Penraven.
Buckden Abbey: Religious place South of Brighthelm.
Deloran Forest: The Great Forest.
Dragonsback Mountains: They separate Penraven from Barronel.
Droste: A realm not part of the Set.
Lo's Teeth: Mountain range in Droste.
Garun Cliffs: Where chalk is mined.
Merrivale: Where shipbuilding is renowned.
Rhum Caves: Caves found in the hills outside of Brighthelm.
Skardlag: Where the famous Weaven timber comes from.
Vegero Hills: In the realm of Barronel. Famed for the marble quarried in its hills.

Places outside the Set

Galinsea: A neighboring country.
Lindaran: The great southern land mass.
Likurian Steppes (or Steppes): Treeless plains. Home to Loethar and his tribes.

Romea: Capital of Galinsea.
Percheron: A faraway country.

MONEY

Throughout the Sets: Trents

MEASUREMENTS

Span: 1,000 strides or 2,000 double steps.
Half-span: 500 strides or 1,000 double steps.

WORD GLOSSARY

Academy of Learning: At Cremond. It is the seat of learning for all of the Denova Set.
Anni: A year.
Aspenberry: Used to distil Kern liquor.
Asprey reeds: Used for support inside leather bladder balls.
Blossom: Late spring.
Blow: Winter.
Branstone: A very special silver colored stone with sparkling silver flecks.
Chest: Coffin.
Cloudberries: Forest berries.
Cohort: A group of youngsters trained to be elite sword fighters.
Crabnuts: Grow wild in the forests. They are a sweet nut, purplish in color.
Dara: Word for "king's mother" in Steppe language.
Darrasha Bushes: Planted around the castle of Brighthelm.
Faeroe: A handcrafted sword that belonged to King Cormoron.
Fan-tailed farla hen: A bright colored bird with a fan-tail.
Freeze: Late winter.
Harvest: Late autumn.
Ingress: Secret passages within the Brighthelm castle.
Kellet: A spicy fragrant herb that can be chewed.

Kern: The local and notorious fiery liquor of Penraven's North.
Lackmarin: Place where the Stone of truth lies.
Leaf-fall: Early autumn.
Leaf of the Cherrel: Chewed as a breath freshener.
Lo: Set god.
Oil of Miramel: Exotic essence.
Roeberries: Wild berries growing in forests. They are blood red.
Shaman: Spiritual healer.
Sheeca Shell: Found on the local beaches.
Shubo: In Steppes language it means second.
Stone of Truth: This truth stone is at Lackmarin. All Valisar Kings must take the oath at this stone.
Strenic: A poisonous herb growing wild on the Steppes.
Summertide: Summer.
Tatua: Tattoos on the face, shoulders and arms.
Thaw: Spring.
The Masked: Magic users of the barbarian horde.
The Vested: Magics users of the Set.
Thaumaturges: Miracle weavers.
Thaumaturgy: The study of the craft of miracle weaving.
Weaven Timber: From Skardlag. It is scarce.
Wych Elder Tree: Used for woodworking.

Fiona McIntosh's internationally bestselling

THE PERCHERON SAGA

is

"First rate."
Publishers Weekly

"[A]n exciting, magical tale of forbidden love, treachery, betrayal, and possession. Fast and furious. A great read."
Sunday Herald Sun (Melbourne, Australia)

"Nothing short of astonishing. McIntosh weaves a captivating web."
Bookreporter.com

"Riveting . . . An ages-old battle for hearts and souls."
Adelaide Advertiser

"A tale of romance and sacrifice, mystery and magic that is redolent with lavish detail. Intriguing characters and an exotic setting make this series . . . a good choice."
Library Journal

It all begins in *Odalisque*. Turn the page for a sample.

The prisoners, chained together, shuffled awkwardly into the main square of the slave market of Percheron; six men, all strangers and all captives of a trader called Varanz, who had a reputation for securing the more intriguing product for sale. And this group on offer was no exception, although most onlookers' attention was helplessly drawn to the tall man whose searing, pale-eyed stare, at odds with his long dark hair, seemed to challenge anyone brave enough to lock gazes with him.

Varanz knew it too; knew this one was special, and he sensed a good price coming for the handsome foreigner well worth the effort it had cost six of his henchmen first to bring the man down and then to rope him securely. It puzzled him why the man had been traveling across the desert, of all places—that in itself a perilous journey—but also moving alone, which meant almost certain trouble, particularly from slavers renowned in the region.

But Varanz had a policy of not inquiring into the background of his captives; perhaps to ease his conscience he didn't want to know anything about them, save what was obvious to his own eye. And this one, who refused to name himself, or indeed mutter much more than curses, was clearly in good health. That was enough for the merchant.

Trading for this cluster of slaves opened at the sound of the gong. The Master of the Market called the milling crowd of buyers to order: "Brothers, we have here Varanz Set Number Eight." His voice droned on, extolling the virtues of each on offer, but already the majority of potential buyers were in the thrall of the angry-eyed man, clearly the pick of the bunch and the only one of the six who held his head defiantly high. Sensing a lively auction, the Master of the Market decided to state more than the obvious healthy appearance, strong structure, and good teeth. "He was found emerging from the golden sands of our desert alone, not even a camel for company. Brothers, I'd hazard this one will make a fine bodyguard. If he's canny enough to travel our wasteland and remain as well as he looks, then I imagine he has excellent survival skills."

"Can he fight?" one buyer called out.

Varanz arched an eyebrow and looked toward the slave, wondering whether he'd finally get something out of the man. His instincts were right.

"I can fight," the man replied. "In fact," he challenged, "I demand to fight for my freedom."

A fresh murmuring rippled through the crowd. An oddity in Percheron's slave market was its ancient and somewhat quaint rule that a slave who was captured as a free person had one chance to buy his freedom—with a fight to the death. The Crown covered the cost of his loss, either way, to the trader. It was one of the market's oldest customs, set up by a Zar many centuries earlier who understood that such a contest from time to time would provide entertainment for the otherwise tedious business of trading in human cargo.

Such fights were rare, of course, as most prisoners took their chances with a new life as a slave. But now and then one would risk death in a bid to win back his independence.

Varanz strolled over to the man now that he knew his tongue was loosened. "You understand what you ask for?"

"I do. It was explained to us on the journey here by one of your aides. I wish to fight for my freedom. I also wish to speak with your Zar."

At this Varanz smirked. "I can't imagine he will want to speak with you."

"He might after he watches me best twelve of his strongest warriors."

Varanz was speechless at the man's arrogance. He shook his head and walked to the Master, briefly explaining in a quiet mutter what the slave was proposing. Now both of them returned to stand before the man.

"Don't try and talk me out of it. I want my freedom back. I will pay the price if I fail to win it," the slave warned them.

The Master had no intention of attempting to thwart the prospect of some sport after an already long and wearying day in the market. He could see that Varanz was unfazed, knowing that he would get a good price either way.

"What is your reserve, Varanz?" he asked.

"No less than two hundred karels for this one."

The Master nodded. "I will send a message to the palace for authorization," he said. Then, turning to the man, he insisted, "You must give us your name."

The slave knifed them with a cold gaze. "My name is Lazar."

The palace did more than give authorization. A runner returned swiftly with the news that Zar Joreb, his interest piqued, would be in attendance for the contest. "You understand how unusual it is for the Zar of Percheron to visit the slave traders," Varanz informed Lazar.

The foreigner was unmoved. "I wish to speak with him if I succeed."

Varanz nodded. "That is up to our Zar. We have told him you have offered to fight twelve of his men to the death. This is no doubt why he is coming to witness the contest."

"It is why I suggested so many."

Varanz shook his head, exasperated. "How can you best a dozen fighters, man? There's still time to change your mind and not waste your life. I will ensure a cozy position for you. A fellow like you will find himself in high demand by a rich man to escort his wives, families . . . take care of their security."

Lazar snorted. "I'm no nursery maid."

"All right." Varanz tried again. "I know I can sell you as a high-caliber bodyguard to a man who needs protection whilst he travels. I'll find you a good owner."

"I don't want to be owned," Lazar snarled. "I want my freedom."

The trader shrugged. "Well, you'll have it, my friend, but you'll be carried off in a sack."

"So be it. I slave for no one."

Their conversation was ended by the Master of the Market's hissing for silence—a troop of Percheron's guard had arrived, signifying that the Zar's karak was just moments away. Varanz nodded to one of his aides to escort the rest of the prisoners to the holding pen. Trading would resume once this piece of theater was done with.

"I wish you luck, brother," he said to Lazar, and moved away to stand with the Master, who was marshaling all the other traders into a formal line of welcome. The Zar finally arrived, flanked by several of the Percherese Guard, his karak carried by six of the red-shrouded Elim, the elite guardians of the Zar's harem who also performed bodyguard duties to royalty. The Zar's entry between the slave market's carved pillars of two griffins was heralded by the trumpeting of several of the curled Percherese horns, and everyone who was not attached to the royal retinue instantly humbled himself. No one dared raise his eyes to the Zar until given formal permission.

No one but Lazar, that is.

He was on his knees because he had been pushed down, but he brazenly watched the Zar being helped out of the karak; their gazes met and held momentarily across the dust of the slave market. Then Lazar dipped his head, just a fraction, but it was enough to tell the Zar that the brash young man had acknowledged the person who was the closest thing to the god Zarab that walked the earth.

The guard quickly set up the Zar's seat and the Elim unfurled a canopy over it. Zar Joreb settled himself. He had a wry smile as the Master of the Market made the official announcement that the prisoner, Lazar, captured by Trader Varanz, had opted to fight for his freedom against a dozen warriors from the Percherese Guard. No one watched the Master or even the Zar. All eyes were riveted on the dark foreigner, whose wrists and ankles were now unshackled and who was disrobing down to the once-white, now gray and dirty loose pants he wore. They watched his measured movements, but mostly they watched him study the twelve men taking practice swipes with their glinting swords, all bearing smirks, none prepared to take the ridiculously outnumbered contest seriously.

The gong sounded for silence and the Master outlined what was about to happen. It was a superfluous pronouncement but strict protocol was a way of life for Percheron's various markets, especially in the hallowed presence of the Zar.

". . . or to the prisoner's death," he finished somberly. He looked to Zar Joreb, who, with an almost imperceptible nod, gave the signal for combat to begin.

Those who were present at the slave market that day would talk about the fight for years to come. Lazar accepted the weapon thrown toward him and without so much as a hurried prayer to his god of choice strode out to meet the first of the warriors. To prolong the sport, the guard had decided to send out one man at a time—presumably they intended to keep wounding the arrogant prisoner until he begged for mercy and the deathblow. However, by the time the first three men were groaning and bleeding on the ground, their most senior man hurriedly sent in four at a once.

It didn't make much difference to Lazar, who appeared to the audience to be unintimidated by numbers. His face wore the grim countenance of utter focus; he made no sound, never once backed away, always threatening his enemy rather than the other way around. It was soon obvious that his sword skills could not be matched by any of the Percherese, not even fighting in tandem. His fighting arm became a blur of silver that weaved a path of wreckage through flesh, turning the dozen men, one after another, into writhing, crying heaps as they gripped torn shoulders, slashed legs, or profusely bleeding fighting arms. To their credit, the final two fought superbly, but neither could mark Lazar. He fought without fear, his speed only increasing as the battle wore on. Cutting one man down by the ankle, Lazar stomped on his sword wrist, breaking it, to ensure he did not return to the fray, and some moments later, fought the other into exhaustion until the man was on his knees. Lazar flicked the guard's sword away and gave a calculated slash across his chest. The man fell, almost grateful for the reprieve.

The slave market was uncharacteristically quiet, save for the cries of bleeding, paining men. Varanz looked around at the carnage, his nostrils flaring with the raw metallic smell of blood thick in the air, and he raised his eyebrows with surprise. No one was dead. Lazar had mercilessly and precisely disabled each of his rivals but claimed the life of none.

Throwing down his sword, Lazar stood in the circle of hurt warriors, a light sheen of perspiration on his body the only indication that he had exerted himself. His chest rose and sank steadily, calmly. He turned to the Zar and bowed long and deeply.

"Zar Joreb, will you now grant my freedom?" he said finally into the hush that had fallen.

"My men would surely rather seek death than live with the dishonor of losing this fight," was Joreb's response.

Varanz watched Lazar's curiously light eyes cloud with defiance. "They are innocent men. I will not take their lives for a piece of entertainment."

"They are soldiers! This was a fight to the death."

"Zar Joreb, this was a fight to my death, not theirs. It was made clear that I either win *my* freedom through death or through survival. I survived. No one impressed upon me the fact that anyone had to die as part of the rules of this custom."

"Arrogant pup," Joreb murmured into the silence. Then, impossibly, he laughed. "Stand before me, young man."

Lazar took two long strides and then went down on one knee, his head finally bowed.

"What is it you want, stranger?" the Zar demanded.

"I want to live in Percheron as a free man," Lazar replied, not lifting his head.

"Look at me." Lazar did so. "You've humiliated my guard. You will need to rectify that before I grant you anything."

"How can I do that, Zar Joreb?"

"By teaching them."

Lazar stared at the Zar, a quizzical look taking over his heretofore impassive face, but he said nothing.

"Become my Spur," Zar Joreb offered. "Our present Spur must retire soon. We need to inject a fresh approach. A young approach. You fight like you're chasing away demons, man. I want you to teach my army how to do that."

Lazar's gaze narrowed. His tone sounded guarded. "You're offering to pay me to live as a free man in Percheron?"

"Be my Spur," Zar Joreb urged. This time there was no humor in his voice, only passion.

The crowd collectively held its breath as Lazar paused. Finally, he nodded once, decisively. "I accept, but first you owe Varanz over there two hundred karels apparently."

Joreb laughed loudly in genuine amusement. "I like you, Lazar. Follow me back to the palace. We have much to speak of. I must say, I'm impressed by your audacity. You put your life in danger to get what you want."

"It was never in danger," Lazar replied, and the semblance of a smile twitched briefly at his mouth.

Turn the page for a sample of *Myrren's Gift*, the first installment in

Fiona McIntosh's internationally bestselling trilogy

The Quickening

"Vibrant and engaging . . . An intricately plotted tale of love and politics, set against the backdrop of a rich fantasy realm with interesting magic, and peopled with characters whom the reader grows to care about. A fast-paced and enchanting page-turner."
Kirkus Reviews (*Starred Review*)

"A just one more chapter sort of book. Don't start reading *Myrren's Gift* in the evening if you have to get up early the next morning."
Robin Hobb

"[A] winner."
Publishers Weekly

"Fiona McIntosh is a seductress. I have not moved from my sofa for three days, beguiled by her new fantasy novel, *Myrren's Gift.*"
Sydney Morning Herald (Australia)

"Fiona McIntosh scores."
The Guardian (London)

"[A] rich, satisfying confection of vivid detail, engrossing characters, and their dark doings. I was enthralled."
Lynn Flewelling, author of *The Hidden Warrior*

Gueryn looked to his left at the solemn profile of the lad who rode quietly next to him and felt another pang of concern for Wyl Thirsk, Morgravia's new General of the Legion. His father's death was as untimely as it was unexpected. Why had they all believed Fergys Thirsk would die of old age? His son was too young to take such a title and responsibility onto his shoulders. And yet he must; custom demanded it. Gueryn thanked the stars for giving the King wisdom enough to appoint a temporary commander until Wyl was of an age where men would respect him. The name of Thirsk carried much weight but no soldier would follow a near-fourteen-year-old into battle.

Hopefully, there would be no war for many years now. According to the news filtering back from the capital, Morgravia had inflicted a terrible price on Briavel's young men this time. No, Gueryn decided, there would be no fighting for a while . . . long enough for Wyl to turn into the fine young man he promised to be.

Gueryn regarded the boy, with his distinctive flame-colored hair and squat frame. He so badly needed his father's guidance, the older man thought regretfully.

Wyl had taken the news of his father's death stoically in front of the household, making Gueryn proud of the boy as he watched him comfort his younger sister. But later, behind closed doors, he had held the trembling shoulders of the lad and offered what comfort he could. The youngster had worshiped his father, and who could blame him—most of Morgravia's men had as well. It was especially sad that the boy had lost his father having not seen him in so many moons.

Ylena, at nine, was still young enough to be distracted by her loving nursemaid as well as her dolls and the new kitten Gueryn had had the foresight to grab at the local market as soon as he was delivered the news. Wyl would not be so easily diverted and Gueryn could already sense the numbing grief hardening within the boy. Wyl was a serious, complex child, and this would push him further into himself. Gueryn wondered whether being forced to the capital was such a good idea right now.

The Thirsk home in Argorn had been a happy one despite the head of the household having been absent so often. Gueryn had agreed several years back to take on what seemed the ridiculously light task of watching over the raising of the young Thirsk. But he had known from the steely gaze of the old warrior that this was a role the General considered precious and he would entrust this job only to his accomplished captain, whose mind was as sharp as the blade he wielded with such skill. Gueryn understood and with a quiet regret at leaving his beloved Legion, he had moved to live among the rolling hills of Argorn, among the lush southern counties of Morgravia.

He became Wyl's companion, military teacher, academic tutor, and close friend. As much as the boy adored his father, the General spent most of his year in the capital, and it was Gueryn who filled the gap of Fergys Thirsk's absence. It was of little wonder then that student and mentor had become so close.

"Don't watch me like that, Gueryn. I can almost smell your anxiety."

"How are you feeling about this?" the soldier asked, ignoring the boy's rebuke.

Wyl turned in his saddle to look at his friend, regarding

the handsome former captain. A flush of color to his pale, freckled face betrayed his next words. "I'm feeling fine."

"Be honest with me of all people, Wyl."

The lad looked away and they continued their steady progress toward the famed city of Pearlis. Gueryn waited, knowing his patience would win out. It had been just days since Wyl's father had died. The wound was still raw and seeping. Wyl could hide nothing from him.

"I wish I didn't have to go," Wyl finally said, and the soldier felt the tension in his body release somewhat. They could talk about it now and he could do what he could to make Wyl feel easier about his arrival in the strange, sprawling, often overwhelming capital. "But I know this was my father's dying wish," Wyl added, trying to cover his sigh.

"The King promised he would bring you to Pearlis. And he had good reason to do so. Magnus accepts that you are not ready for the role in anything but title yet but Pearlis is the only place you can learn your job and make an impression on the men you will one day command." Gueryn's tone was gentle, but the words implacable. Wyl grimaced. "You can't stamp your mark from sleepy Argorn," Gueryn added, wishing they could have had a few months—weeks even—just to get the boy used to the idea of having no parents.

Gueryn thought of the mother. Fragile and pretty, she had loved Fergys Thirsk and his gruff ways with a ferocity that belied her sweet, gentle nature. She had succumbed, seven years previous and after a determined fight, to the virulent coughing disease that had swept through Morgravia's south. If she had not been weakened from Ylena's long and painful birth she might have pulled through. The disease killed many in the household, mercifully sparing the children.

Although he rarely showed it outwardly, Wyl seemed to miss her in his own reserved way. For all his rough-and-tumble boyishness, Gueryn thought, Wyl obviously adored women. The ladies of the household loved him back, spoiling him with their affections but often whispering pitying words about his looks.

There was no escaping the fact that Wyl Thirsk was not a handsome boy. The crown of thick orange hair did nothing to help an otherwise plain, square face, and those who remembered the boy's grandfather said that Wyl resembled the old man in uncanny fashion—his ugliness was almost as legendary as his soldiering ability. The red-headed Fergys Thirsk had been no oil painting either, which is why he had lived with constant surprise that his beautiful wife had chosen to marry him. Many would understand if the betrothal had been arranged but Helyna of Ramon had loved him well and had brooked no argument to her being joined to this high-ranking, plainspoken, even plainer-looking man who walked side by side with a King.

Vicious whispers at the court, of course, accused her of choosing Thirsk for his connections but she had relentlessly proved that the colorful court of Morgravia held little interest for her. Helyna Thirsk had had no desire for political intrigues or social climbing. Her only vanity had been her love of fine clothes, which Fergys had lavished on his young wife, claiming he had nothing else to spend his money on.

Wyl interrupted his thoughts. "Gueryn, what do we know about this Celimus?"

He had been waiting for just this question. "I don't know him at all but he's a year or two older than you, and from what I hear he is fairly impressed with being the heir," he answered tactfully.

"I see," Wyl replied. "What else do you *hear* of him? Tell me honestly."

Gueryn nodded. Wyl should not be thrown into this arena without knowing as much as he could. "The King, I gather, continues to hope Celimus might be molded into the stuff Morgravia can be proud of, although I would add that Magnus has not been an exceptional father. There is little affection between them."

"Why?"

"I can tell you only what your father has shared. King Magnus married Princess Adana. It was an arranged marriage. According to Fergys, they disliked each other within days of the ceremony and it never got any easier between them. I saw her on two occasions and it is no exaggeration that Adana was a woman whose looks could take any man's breath away. But she was cold. Your father said she was not just unhappy but angry at the choice of husband and despairing of the land she had come to. She had never wanted to come to Morgravia, believing it to be filled with peasants."

The boy's eyes widened. "She said that?"

"And plenty more apparently."

"Where was she from?"

"Parrgamyn—I hope you can dredge up its location from all those geography lessons?"

Wyl made a face at Gueryn's disapproving tutorly tone. He knew exactly where Parrgamyn was situated, to the far northwest of Morgravia, in balmy waters about two hundred nautical miles west of the famed Isle of Cipres. "Exotic then?"

"Very. Hence Celimus's dark looks."

"So she would have been of Zerque faith?" he wondered aloud, and Gueryn nodded. "Go on," Wyl encouraged, glad to be thinking about something other than the pain of his father's death.

Gueryn sighed. "A long tale really, but essentially she hated the King, blamed her father for his avarice in marrying her off to what she considered an old man, and poisoned the young Celimus's mind against his father."

"She died quite young, though, didn't she?"

The soldier nodded. "Yes, but it was the how that caused the ultimate rift between father and son. Your father was with the King when the hunting accident happened and could attest to the randomness of the event. Adana lost her life with an arrow through her throat."

"The King's?" Wyl asked, shifting in his saddle. "My father never said anything about this to me."

"The arrow was fletched in the King's very own colors. There was no doubt whose quiver it had come from."

"How could it have happened?"

Gueryn shrugged. "Who knows? Fergys said the Queen was out riding where she should not have been and Magnus shot badly. Others whispered, of course, that his aim was perfect, as always." He arched a single eyebrow. It spoke plenty.

"So Celimus has never forgiven his father?"

"You could say. Celimus worshiped Adana as much as his father despised her. But in losing his mother very early there's something you and Celimus have in common and this might be helpful to you," he offered. "The lad, I'm told, is already highly accomplished in the arts of soldiering too. He has no equal in the fighting ring amongst his peers. Sword or fists, on horseback or foot, he is genuinely talented."

"Better than me?"

Gueryn grinned. "We'll see. I know of no one of your tender years who is as skilled in combat—excluding myself at your age, of course." He won a smile from the boy at this. "But, Wyl, a word of caution. It would not do to whip the backside of the young Prince. You may find it politic to play second fiddle to a king-in-waiting."

Wyl's gaze rested firmly on Gueryn. "I understand."

"Good. Your sensibility in this will protect you."

"Do I need protection?" Wyl asked, surprised.

Gueryn wished he could take back the warning. It was ill-timed but he was always honest with his charge. "I don't know yet. You are being brought to Pearlis to learn your craft and follow in your father's proud footsteps. You must consider the city your home now. You understand this? Argorn must rest in your mind as a country property you may return to from time to time. Home is Stoneheart now." He watched the sorrow as those last words took a firm hold on the boy. It was said now. Had to be aired, best out in the open and accepted. "The other reason the King is keen to have you in the capital is, I suspect, because he is concerned at his son's wayward manner."

"Oh?"

"Celimus needs someone to temper his ways. The King has been told you possess a similar countenance to your father and I gather this pleases him greatly. He has hopes that you and his son will become as close friends as he and Fergys were." Gueryn waited for Wyl to comment but the boy said nothing. "Anyway, friendship can never be forced, so let's just keep an open mind and see how it all pans out. I shall be with you the whole time."

Wyl bit his lip and nodded. "Let's not tarry then, Gueryn."

The soldier nodded in return and dug his heels into the side of his horse as the boy kicked into a gallop.